Praise for Harold Coyle

"Harold Coyle is a superbly talented storyteller . . . the Tom Clancy of ground warfare."

—W. E. B. Griffin

"Coyle is best when he's depicting soldiers facing death. . . . He knows soldiers, and he understands the brotherhood-of-arms mystique that transcends national boundaries." —*The New York Times*

"Nobody knows war like Harold Coyle, and nobody writes it better." —Stephen Coonts

"Harold Coyle has been dubbed the Tom Clancy of ground warfare, and it's easy to see why. He focuses on the grunts because no matter how fancy the weapons are, eventually the military has to send in men to take and hold new territory."

—*New York Post*

"Coyle's attention to detail, and his intimate knowledge of small-unit fighting is remarkable. On top of that, his story is told with an implied 'we'll soon be there' quality, like an ominous echo of today's headlines."

—Thomas Fleming

"Disturbingly plausible . . . [Details] the heroic patriotism of the military men and the complexities of the U.S. military situation . . . A solid read."
—*Publishers Weekly* on *They Are Soldiers*

"[A] shatteringly suspenseful tale of near-future military engagement."
—*Kirkus Reviews* on *They Are Soldiers*

"Action-filled revenge fantasy for deskbound Terminators."
—*Kirkus Reviews* on *Pandora's Legion*

ALSO BY HAROLD COYLE

HAROLD COYLE

CAT AND MOUSE

FORGE®

A TOM DOHERTY ASSOCIATES BOOK
NEW YORK

This is a work of fiction. All of the characters, organizations, and events portrayed in this novel are either products of the author's imagination or are used fictitiously.

CAT AND MOUSE

Copyright © 2007 by Harold Coyle

All rights reserved.

A Forge Book
Published by Tom Doherty Associates, LLC
175 Fifth Avenue
New York, NY 10010

www.tor-forge.com

Forge® is a registered trademark of Tom Doherty Associates, LLC.

ISBN-13: 978-0-7653-4461-8
ISBN-10: 0-7653-4461-0

First Edition: May 2007
First Mass Market Edition: November 2008

Printed in the United States of America

0 9 8 7 6 5 4 3 2 1

Whatever happens, you and I will do our duty.

Sir Arthur Wellesley, Duke of Wellington;
Remark to Lord Uxbridge on the eve of
Waterloo, June 1815

*This book is dedicated to the medics of 1st of the 12th
Cavalry and the soldiers with whom they stand,
October 2006, Iraq:*

SSG Joe Roberts	Spc. Ryan Russel
Sgt. James Currie	Spc. Joe Shenk
Sgt. Andrew Kaul	Spc. Tony Woestman
Cpl. Joel Matison	Spc. Ruben Rojas
Spc. Will Atkinson	Spc. Brian Wright
Spc. Kurt Coyle	Pfc. Kevin Harris
Spc. Dan Kershner	Pfc. Dan Nguyen
Spc. Drew Mcpeak	Pfc. Issac Warner

An enemy that commits a false step . . . is ruined, and it comes on him with an impetuosity that allows him no time to recover.

—Cuthbert Collingwood (1748–1810)

Desperate affairs require desperate remedies.

—Nelson (1758–1805)

No matter what may be the ability of the officer, if he loses the confidence of his troops disaster must sooner or later ensue.

—R. E. Lee, August 1863

CAT AND MOUSE

Prologue

BORNEO, MALAYSIAN–INDONESIAN BORDER

Fear was something that Hamdani Summirat refused to tolerate, not in the men he had handpicked and trained and especially not in himself. It was a weakness, a deadly cancer that gnawed away at a fighter's judgment and determination. Fear eroded a unit's cohesion, rending it ineffective, timid, and feeble, making it the precursor of disaster and defeat, a harbinger of death. Yet there were times when even his iron will and commanding presence were helpless in the face of the sort of panic that gripped men pursued by an unyielding and merciless foe. Even the jungle, long considered by Summirat and the men who followed him to be a place of refuge, had turned against them on this day. The dank, murky world they were fleeing through all but closed in around them. Like a heavy wool blanket it was smothering rather than comforting, hindering their every effort to seek safety, causing the exhausted insurgents to fear both the jungle as well as their pursuers. Without a shot having been fired, Summirat realized that they were already beaten.

At the moment Summirat had little choice but to flee

with his men in an effort to escape the terror that stalked the staggering column of insurgents like an unseen predator. His own labors and the tenacity of their pursuers left him with no time and even less energy to rally his men. He didn't have the breath to spare to spur them on. Their pace was just too demanding and the path he had chosen to follow too difficult for him to divert his attention away from his own exertions. It took everything he had simply to keep going, to keep moving forward as he vainly attempted to outpace the growing fear that threatened to overwhelm him with every passing minute.

Bowing his head like a condemned man, Summirat abandoned all pretenses of being a leader and focused instead on nothing more than taking his next step. Huffing and puffing like an overburdened steam locomotive, each desperate gasp for air was rewarded with a mouthful of stale, humid air. Along with the stench of rotted vegetation his efforts to take in the air his lungs demanded were more often than not rewarded with a mouthful of tiny insects that were struggling as he was to survive in the same hellish environment. Were it not for the vines he clung to as he scaled the crooked path as well as the wild jumble of tree roots underfoot that gave him some measure of purchase the sudden deluge that turned the rutted trail into a cascading sluice would have made ascending the steep ridge all but impossible. "Inconveniences" such as the torrential rains that were pelting them and rugged terrain they were traversing had been factored into Summirat's raid into Malaysia. In fact, he had counted on them to hide his movements.

As a former professional soldier he knew that a strike from such an unexpected quarter and a retreat following an uncharted route would compensate for the sluggish pace that the hostages his party had seized in neighboring Malaya would impose upon his command. His past experiences had shown how a handful of cowered captives could reduce a crack unit to a crawl even along the best of routes. So he had opted to follow one that offered him the most tactical advantages, one that would allow them to make their return trip into the interior of Borneo unhindered by local forces that seldom ventured far from established roads and trails. What he had not counted on was an aggressive pursuit by an unrelenting predator, one that he had not expected, one that was as determined and disciplined as his own fighters.

The cross-border incursion had unfolded as planned up to and including the predawn attack deep inside Malaysia. The target selected by his superiors was a rich one, a small encampment where a gaggle of American and Australian tourists were enjoying an idyllic eco-adventure in the primeval wilds of Borneo. The predawn assault was carried out flawlessly. There had been no resistance, no efforts on the part of any of the startled westerners or their local guides to save themselves or even flee. Startled by the sudden appearance of heavily armed assailants the tourists and guides had meekly allowed themselves to be herded together in the center of their well-appointed encampment like cattle. There Summirat and his deputy carefully inspected their haul before sorting them into two groups. Each hostage who found him or herself pulled out of the huddled mass by Summirat's deputy was assigned to a preselected escort whose duty it would be to care for his charge during their long trek back into the interior of Borneo. Once safely tucked away in one of Summirat's refuges, his superiors would commence negotiations with whoever was willing and able to pay for their safe return.

This pairing of hostages and his men went on until Summirat ran out of escorts. Those captives who had not been selected because of their age or an apparent weakness that Summirat's deputy judged to be too much of an impediment during his return march still had a use. They would provide Summirat with fodder for a demonstration to show the unfortunate ones who had been chosen just how precarious their plight was.

After binding the hands of all the hostages, Summirat

had those with an escort line up facing their remaining companions in parallel lines two meters apart. With pistol in hand, Summirat began to make his way between the two lines. "We are the Abu Sayyaf," he announced loudly in perfect English as he stepped before the first pair of westerners. Without taking his eyes off an American woman being held firmly from behind her, Summirat raised his pistol with a single, easy motion and fired it as soon as it had reached a height he judged sufficient to inflict a fatal wound on the middle-aged man across from her. Whether the single round he fired blindly into the unfortunate soul inflicted a fatal wound didn't really matter. What interested Summirat was the terror his unexpected act of brutality engendered in the minds of those picked to go back with him.

With one stride he moved forward, halting when he was between the next pair. "You are our hostages." Again he raised his pistol. Again he fired. And again he stepped forward paying no attention to the freshly executed corpse as it slumped down onto the ground behind him. Instead he gazed dispassionately into the eyes of each terrified hostage as he came before them. "You will obey our orders." Bang, step. "You will do exactly what you are told." Bang, step. "You will not hesitate." Bang, step. "You will not speak unless spoken to." Bang, step. "You will not resist in any way." Bang, step. "Any failure to do exactly as you are told will not be tolerated." Bang, step.

As he slowly marched down the line, pausing before each condemned hostage, Summirat enumerated a new rule while simultaneously dispatching a captive. Frozen in place by the horror that was coming their way none of the condemned were able to muster up the courage to run. A few prayed. All whom Summirat had determined could not make the return trip died like sheep being slaughtered for market, ensuring that his command would not be burdened with weaklings.

This vicious little drama was carried out quickly and without anyone other than Summirat saying a word. Having done this sort of thing before, the crack Abu Sayyaf fighters with him knew what was expected of them. If they had any feelings, any pangs of regret or unexpected sympathy for their victims they kept them to themselves, hidden behind expressionless masks. For their part the Americans and Australians, involuntarily jolted from their slumbers into the middle of a war few knew anything about were too terrified and unprepared to resist in any way. The entire raid had played out just as Summirat had planned. At least that is what Summirat had thought as he turned his back on the killing fields he had created and began to lead his band of insurgents and hostages back into the jungle. He was so sure of his techniques and tactics, so sure that they had taken the westerners by complete surprise, that he hadn't bothered to double-check the number of hostages he had taken during their initial assault against the list the head guide maintained. Nor did he bother to dispatch patrols to search the surrounding jungle for stragglers. In failing to do so Summirat missed his opportunity to scarf up Jennie Hansen and Kate Meyer, two native New Yorkers who had slipped out of camp just prior to dawn to enjoy an unscheduled excursion of their own design, one that was to prove to be Summirat's undoing.

That was not the goal that motivated this pair of twenty-something professionals to leave their camp that morning in the predawn darkness. Rather, it was an innocent quest to find a spot from which they could photograph the stunning beauty that the golden rays of the rising sun brought to the lush green jungle they had traveled so far to visit. Their search for an ideal location from which to view the daily spectacle had taken them to a sheltered ledge on the hillside overlooking their still slumbering camp. From there they were treated to a spectacle that was nothing short of breathtaking. The golden hues of the sun's first light drenching the lush jungle in a riot of colors stunned the city dwellers who labored in a world of steel and concrete where the only contrast they were treated to each day was that offered by varying degrees of gritty shades of gray. Jennie and Kate found themselves so enthralled by this exhibition of untouched beauty that they took no note of Summirat's men as they silently swept through their camp nestled in a quiet valley bellow them. While Jennie concentrated on photographing the sunrise, Kate sat at the base of the camera's tripod, describing as best she could what she was seeing to a friend who was tucked away behind a desk in a law office back on their home island of Manhattan.

It wasn't until Summirat's first shot rang out that the pair of women turned away from their whimsical pursuits to face the horror that was unfolding below them. Astonished by what they were seeing, both women found themselves wrestling with the same paralysis that had left their traveling companions so vulnerable to Summirat's assault. Realizing that there was little that she could do to help those who had been rounded up and herded into the center of the camp and without giving what she was doing any thought whatsoever, Jennie turned her camera's lens down. As dedicated to her photography as she was to her profession, she set about capturing on film an aspect of jungle life that was very different from the one she had set out to record.

Unnerved by what she was seeing, Kate Meyer, who had been chatting away with her friend on the cell phone, was gripped by a fear unlike anything she had ever known, reducing her to repeat over and over again, "Oh, my God! Oh, my God!"

A veteran of 9/11, her city-bound friend realized that something was terribly wrong. Overcoming her own growing alarm, she began to prod her friend for information. "Kate, calm down. What's happening? Are you in danger?"

With Jennie mechanically recording the slaughter that was taking place before their very eyes, Kate struggled to check her panic. The situation she found herself in was so unreal, so unimaginable, that her mind was unable to grasp and hold on to a single clear thought. Behind her she could hear her companion's camera as its autofocus zoomed in and out. From below the sound of gunfire echoed throughout the jungle valley, each shot accompanied by a desperate garbled plea or a short-lived shriek of pain. And on the phone, a voice that was so familiar to her but seemingly out of place kept calling out to her from half a world away, pleading with her to respond.

Without giving what she was saying much thought, Kate responded to her friend's desperate pleas for information with short, choppy sentences. "Armed men, terrorists. Ten, twenty, maybe more. They're attacking our camp."

"Are you safe?" her friend Carol in New York called out, doing her best to contain her own anxieties. "Are you hiding?"

"I'm safe." Then, hearing the click of the camera behind her she corrected herself. "Jennie and I are both safe. They're shooting everyone else. My God, Carol, they're shooting the rest of our group."

Unsure of what to do next, Carol did what came natural to any New Yorker. After telling her friend to stay on the line, the Manhattan lawyer yelled out to her secretary through the open door of her office. "EMMA! Dial nine-one-one and bring your phone to me."

The emergency dispatcher who took Carol's call responded with the same set reply she did to all the calls she received. While answering over her headset, she checked the phone number of the incoming call she was receiving on the computer monitor before her. It was a local call from midtown. Nothing unusual about that. Only after she heard the word "terrorist" did the dispatcher straighten up in her chair. Without hesitation she flagged her supervisor using a prearranged signal. Immediately half a dozen sets of eyes and ears around the room perked up. "Please describe the nature of the emergency."

Maintaining her poise as best she could as she listened

to her friend's desperate pleas for help over her other phone, Carol tried to explain the situation as best she could to the attentive emergency dispatchers. Prepared to unleash the vast emergency response system that New York had created for just such an event, everyone listening to Carol's call suddenly found themselves at a loss as to what to do when they discovered the event was taking place on another island on the other side of the world. It wasn't until Carol mentioned that there were Australians in the group that one of the dispatcher's supervisors decided to call the Australian consulate. Though the person who took the call was a bit puzzled as to why New York City's emergency services were calling them, he did not hesitate in the least to take the reported incident that was being relayed to him fourthhand seriously as soon as he heard the words "terrorist," "Malaysia," and "Australian citizens" all lumped together in a single sentence. "Right, please stay on the line if you will while I contact my own people."

Using a network that would have awed Alexander Graham Bell and astonished H. G. Wells, a single phone call made by a desperate woman from the heart of one of the world's most inhospitable jungles set into motion a chain of events that turned Hamdani Summirat's meticulously planned and well-executed raid into a desperate race between his hostage-burdened command and an Australian Special Air Service quick-response team that had been training in Malaysia with local forces.

It was no accident that the Australians just happened to have a special ops team training in Borneo. Like their American counterparts operating in the Sulu Archipelago to the north the Australians had adopted the practice of scheduling overlapping "training" exercises throughout the region on islands where Muslim extremists were known to be operating. While the status-of-forces agreement between Australia and the host nation spoke only of joint training, an unstated agreement existed among all the concerned parties understood what the real purpose of those exercises was. With lightning speed the SAS teams were able to transition from training exercise to execution of a real world contingency. For the members of the team the order to change over from blanks to service ammunition came as something of a relief. Like any professional they were always ready and willing to put their well-honed skills to the test, especially when those skills meant the difference between life and death for fellow citizens.

The Australians wasted little time at the desolate tourist camp. Collection of the dead was left to Malaysian forces. After extracting as much information as they could from the distraught New Yorkers who had not abandoned their secure perch until well after the Australians had arrived, the SAS team lit off after the Abu Sayyaf terrorists following a trail they had seen no need to conceal. Fresh and unburdened by hostages, the Australians sliced through the jungle with a speed and purpose that Summirat's command could not match. Unaware the day of grace that usually followed this sort of raid had been compromised by Kate Meyer's phone call, the Abu Sayyaf fighters took their time as they retraced their footsteps back into the interior of Borneo where their base camp lay comfortably nestled among tiny native villages sympathetic to their cause and appreciative of the money that found its way into the village coffers.

The first inkling Summirat had that his command was in trouble came late in the afternoon on the first day when the point element of the SAS team came across one of his men who had stopped to adjust his pack. It was a chance encounter, one that the captain leading the SAS team had been doing his best to avoid. He had hoped to close the distance between his command and the band of terrorists sometime after nightfall without making contact. Using their superior night-vision devices and battle-tested skills, the young SAS officer had planned on carrying out an extensive recon of the terrorist camp once they had stopped for the night. With the intelligence gained during it, he would be able to develop a scheme of maneuver and thoroughly brief each member of his team before deploying them in a manner that would allow them to safely secure the hostages while taking down the Abu Sayyaf fighters with the ruthless efficiency that was a hallmark of the SAS.

The unexpected confrontation between Australian and Muslim terrorist was ended by a brief exchange of fire in which the Australian bested the wayward Abu Sayyaf fighter. The real advantage, however, went to the terrorists as the unexpected chatter of small arms fire alerted Summirat that danger was near at hand. The same unexpected run-in presented the SAS captain with a terrible dilemma he had hoped to avoid. In the aftermath of the incident he guessed that he was now within easy striking distance of his quarry's main body. Just how close was unknown, but that did not matter to him at the moment. What did concern the young officer was the fact that if he pressed the terrorists too vigorously he had little doubt that they would dispose of their hostages in an effort to unburden themselves of them. On the other hand even if he didn't aggressively pursue them, there existed the very real possibility that they would still do so since that is exactly what he would have done had he been in a similar position.

To the Abu Sayyaf the hostages they seized during these raids were little more than an expendable commodity, a bargaining chip they used to secure the funds needed to wage their bloody campaign of terror against those westerners and nonbelievers who they believed threatened their way of life. Hostages were easy to come by. That morning's raid was ample proof of this. Well-trained and disciplined fighters were not. Slowly the Australian officer concluded that no matter what he did the terrorists would dispose of their hostages before escaping into the jungle. Accepting the inevitability of this, the SAS captain opted to aggressively drive forward, hoping that his tiny command could close with the terrorists before they could dispose of all of their hostages.

Up ahead the very options the SAS team commander was taking into account were being considered by his counterpart. While exhorting his men to pick up their pace with a mixture of cajoling and threats Summirat weighed the value of his hostages as opposed to the lives of his own men. The idea of dumping his hostages was inviting, one that would leave him free to disperse his command and send them off in different directions. No doubt some of his men would be hunted down and killed by their pursuers. Unlike the local forces they usually ran across, the SAS were as relentless as they were ruthless. It was said that they would hound their quarry even after their legs gave out, crawling on their hands and knees rather than admitting defeat. Once on his trail Summirat knew they would not give up until they had drawn blood. Only by scattering his command would some of them be able to evade the Australians and make their way back to their base camp from which they could continue their war against the nonbelievers on another day and place of their choosing.

Yet pride kept Summirat from making the only decision that logic and the situation he faced dictated. Just as he disdained a man who allowed fear to govern his actions, the Abu Sayyaf leader was intolerant of failure. He had no use for people who were incapable of living up to the exacting standards he demanded. He was even less forgiving to those who fell short when it came to carrying out a task he had assigned them. His ability to come through for his superiors no matter what the odds had made him a valuable commodity to an organization besieged by powerful foes from all sides. Thus, to cut and run at the first sign of trouble was something Summirat simply could not do.

His first response to the presence of an aggressive pursuer was to attempt to buy time for his slower-moving column by delaying his foe until after his own column with the hostages had crossed back into Indonesian territory. He hoped that the imaginary line drawn on the map would stop the Australians. Gathering up his most dependable fighters under the command of his deputy and turning all the explosives, grenades, and command-detonated mines his tiny band possessed to them, Summirat ordered his deputy to buy time for the rest of them. "Set out hasty booby traps, obstacles along the trail, even ambushes if you must. All you need to do is throw a bit of caution into them. Even better, if you can do so without being pinned down, draw some blood. Once burdened with casualties they will have no choice but to slow their pace."

The deputy accepted his mandate without comment, knowing that the same concern over wounded that Summirat counted on to handicap the Australians was not shared by his own commander. An Abu Sayyaf fighter who was unable to keep up was expected to martyr himself rather than become a burden to his surviving comrades.

Over the next few hours Summirat's rear guard waged a running battle with the Australians. They began by stringing trip wires attached to hand grenades across the path the Australians were following. Knowing that the enemy was at hand, the SAS commandos who made up the point element were prepared for this, disarming these nasty little gifts almost as quickly as the Abu Sayyaf could set them out.

When the Australians continued to gain on his detachment, it quickly became clear to Summirat's deputy that his unattended booby traps were doing no good. That left him little choice but to deploy the American designed M18 claymore mines, vicious little devices that scattered a shower of seven hundred deadly ten-point five-gram ball bearings about a sixty-degree arch creating a killing zone fifty meters deep. The only problem associated with this infernal machine was that it was command-detonated. Someone who had a clear view of the intended kill zone, grasping a handheld clacker attached to the mine by wire, had to lie in ambush, setting the claymore off only when the intended victims had moved into the mine's kill zone. Already cued into the presence of a foe determined to inflict harm upon them through the use of booby traps, the Australians on point had no intention of accommodating the Abu Sayyaf fighters selected to hang back, clacker in hand, waiting to set off their poorly concealed claymore mines. With a skill honed through unending exercises and training that was often more grueling than combat itself, the Australians sniffed out and took down the hapless claymore-armed terrorists one by one, leaving Summirat's deputy little choice but to gather in the last of his dwindling rear guard and set up an ambush.

The place he selected to make this stand was no accident. It was in a small valley well within the territorial boundaries of Indonesia flanked by two steep ridges and dissected by a narrow, swift-running stream. The physical attributes were important but not the only considerations the deputy took into account as he placed his exhausted men to cover the chosen ambush site. Unlike Malaysia, Indonesia did not have a standing agreement with Australia concerning military actions against the Abu Sayyaf. Each incursion into their territory had to be dealt with as a separate and unique incident that was to be debated and decided upon at the highest level. Since Indonesia was a predominantly Muslim country ruled by a government that was riddled by Abu Sayyaf sympathizers, there was little chance that the Australians would be able to secure permission to enter Indonesia. It was the political discord that would result from an unsanctioned incursion and not his tactical deployment that Summirat's deputy was relying upon to stop the Australians. Of course, if he was wrong, if these considerations failed to dissuade them the casualties he intended to inflict upon them most certainly would.

Satisfied that he had the situation well in hand, the deputy dispatched a runner to catch up with Summirat and explain his plan. This runner managed to catch the Abu

Sayyaf leader as he was in the midst of catching his breath. "We are set," the runner hastily explained, pointing down the steep trail both he and Summirat had struggled to climb. "Ali has deployed his men on this side of the stream in two groups, each set up at right angles with the other. Anyone caught in their cross fire will be dead before they know what hit them."

Laboring mightily to catch his breath, Summirat listened to the runner's report in silence. It would be nice, he thought, if that was the way things worked out. Yet in spite of his own loathing of anyone who displayed even the slightest hint of defeatism, at that moment Summirat found it all but impossible to take heart from the runner's succinct summary of the rear guard's tactical situation.

As if feeding on his negativism, the sound of small-arms fire erupted in the narrow valley below. The distinctive reports of American made M-16A2 assault rifles favored by the Australian SAS being answered by sporadically and pitifully few bursts of AK fire were all Summirat needed to hear. He had no idea how their pursuers had managed to get the drop on his deputy's small rear guard. That was no longer important. What mattered now was what they had.

With a sigh, he turned his back on the one-sided engagement that seemed to be coming to a quick and all but preordained conclusion. Tugging on the vine he had been using to assist his climb, Summirat resumed his ascent. Confused, the runner who had brought the deputy's last message hesitated, looking back and forth between the jungle below where his companions were in the throes of being slaughtered and his commander. "What do we do now?"

Summirat did not bother to look back as he answered, "What I should have done before sending those men to their death."

Still unready to surrender to the inevitable the runner stood his ground. "We can't give up the hostages. It would not be right, especially after such a terrible sacrifice."

Had he not been at the end of his own rope physically and mentally Summirat would have turned on the defiant runner, smacking him with the back of his hand. But he could not find the strength to do so. He was beaten, a proud man who had been humbled before the eyes of his followers. "There will be other days," he mumbled without much enthusiasm. "Let us put this behind us and pray that Allah will see us through."

"And the hostages?"

Summirat looked at the runner. "You know what to do."

As the runner turned to carry the order to execute the hostages, Summirat added, "Tell them to be quick about it."

Left alone, Summirat prepared to move on.

Of course, Summirat had no intention of putting this sad episode behind him. If anything, as he struggled to reach the top of the ridge he held his anger in check by making a pledge to himself, one that he had every intention of seeing through to the end regardless of the cost.

1

A Hollywood producer could not have staged a more striking scene than the one Company A, 3rd Battalion of the 75th Rangers, presented as they sallied forth from the shade provided by the hangars they had been waiting in. In single file, the Rangers trotted out into the bright sunlight that beat down upon the tarmac. Doubled over by the weight of their gear, they made for a row of waiting UH-60 Blackhawk helicopters, straining to be unleashed like a herd of Thoroughbred racehorses being held in check at the starting gate by their attentive jockeys. Not a hint of cloud corrupted the stunning azure sky above them. Only in the distance, just visible above the vibrant green jungle that surrounded the airfield did a darkening sky on the horizon serve notice to all that a line of violent storms was coming on fast.

The stage manager of this little drama was Captain Nathan Dixon, a twenty-eight-year-old graduate of the Virginia Military Institute, who looked more like someone you'd bump into on the corner of Broadway and Wall Street than the stylized image that comes to mind when one thought of the commanding officer of a Ranger company.

Nicknamed Nate by his friends and referred to as "CD" by the enlisted personnel in his company, Dixon relied upon his easygoing, confident manner to motivate his subordinates. That did not mean that he was a weak leader. When the situation required it he could conduct himself in a manner that would intimidate a great white. It was a skill he had learned from his father, a man who could bring an errant son to bay with a single, scathing glance. Fortunately, for all parties concerned, Nathan's adroitness as a leader, coupled with an innate knack for small unit tactics, tended to make the occasions when he needed to rely upon such techniques to motivate those entrusted to his command quite rare. Without exception everyone in his company was more than willing to follow him wherever he led.

Despite being of average height Nathan Dixon stood out even in the middle of soldiers similarly decked out in their full panoply of equipment and weaponry. This was an attribute that subordinates like his first sergeant found very useful at times like this. Having finished issuing instructions to the company clerk, First Sergeant William Carney headed out onto the airfield behind the last stick of Rangers who had been awaiting the word to board their assigned helicopters. When he reached the spot where Dixon was observing the embarkation of his First Platoon, Carney sidled up on his commanding officer's left. Yelling in order to be heard over the whine of the Blackhawks' turbine engines, he made his presence known. "Captain, what makes you think the Sulu Sea is going to keep our new battalion commander from finding you?"

A playful grin lit Dixon's face as he turned toward his first sergeant. "I know not what you speak of, First Sergeant. I'm just going with the boys out into the jungle for some unscheduled play time."

Word that the lieutenant colonel who had just assumed command of the 3rd of the 75th was scheduled to arrive that afternoon to conduct an unannounced inspection of Dixon's forward deployed company had been leaked to

Carney by the battalion's operations sergeant back at Fort Lewis, Washington. When Carney informed Dixon of this he changed his mind about accompanying his First Platoon on a five-day operation on the island of Jolo. It was a routine mission, one that was undertaken by one of Dixon's platoons every week or so. These forays had the dual purpose of patrolling areas where terrorists were known to be operating as well as providing the Rangers who belonged to the forward deployed company valuable training. Every now and then Dixon went along more to break the monotony, hone his own skills, and become more familiar with the areas where his company was operating than out of a need to supervise the platoon leader to whom the mission had been assigned. Up until that morning Dixon had been satisfied to sit out this particular patrol back at the company's base camp located north of Zamboanga on the island of Mindanao. Word of the surprise visit quickly convinced him to change his plans.

"You can run but you can't hide, Captain," Carney chuckled. "It won't take the colonel long to track you down and catch the next resupply hop to Jolo."

Dixon winked. "By then we'll be in the midst of the operation, circumstances that will limit the amount of time I'll have to spend with El Jefe." Pronounced hef-a, which was Spanish for "chief," the reason why the officers in the battalion had taken up calling their new battalion commander "El Jefe" even before he had arrived was a mystery. It was just one of those things that someone started and stuck. After taking a moment to inspect Carney from head to toe, noting that he was also arrayed in full battle kit and was toting his M-4 rifle as well, the smirk on Dixon's face grew. "I see you have no intention of staying behind to cover my rear."

"As they say back home," Carney quibbled, "it's not my job."

"So you're leaving the XO here to take the fire."

"It'll be good for Lieutenant Quinn, especially since he's always moaning about how company executive officers never get the face time they deserve. The way I see it, by the time he's able to arrange transportation for the colonel he'll have had his fill of one-on-one time with El Jefe."

Peter Quinn, Nathan's executive officer or XO, was a meticulous, hard charging professional, one who tended to become flustered when forced to deal with matters he considered to be trivial and nonmission essential. The image of his XO playing host to their new battalion commander caused Dixon to roar. As he did so he took note that the last man belonging to first platoon was climbing into his assigned helicopter. After composing himself, Dixon scanned the dark, ominous sky to the north. Tugging on Carney's sleeve, he pointed to the coming storm. "If we're going to make good our escape we'd best be going before that line of squalls hits the airfield." Then, he pointed to a Blackhawk farther down the line. "I think it would be a good idea if we spread the wealth. Lieutenant Grimes is on the first chopper. I'm manifested on the second. You go with Jones's squad on the number-three slick."

Carney nodded as he gave his commanding officer a quick salute and the customary "Hooah," a term that served the Rangers as a greeting, a verbal salute, an exclamation of joy, an acknowledgment at the end of a conversation, and a number of other ill-defined purposes that nevertheless always seemed to be understood and appropriate.

Satisfied that all was in order Dixon gave the line of Blackhawks straining to be cut loose one last look before tucking his head down low and making for the one he would use to whisk him away from the clutches of an ambitious new battalion commander who was headed his way like the late afternoon storm.

JOLO ISLAND, PHILIPPINES

When viewed from the helicopter's open door the jungle didn't look very threatening or dangerous. Like all of nature's wonders it had a unique beauty all its own, one that was best enjoyed from a safe distance. But Lieutenant Colonel Robert Delmont knew that appearances were deceiving, especially when Mother Nature was involved. To him the jungle was like a cat, a very large and ill-tempered one who kept her deadly claws concealed until it was too late. This analogy was all the more appropriate since his dislike for the jungle was only slightly more pronounced than his disdain for cats, creatures that possessed a streak of independence that tended to annoy the career officer.

By nature Delmont was a dog person, the sort of man who expected prompt and complete obedience. His own collection of canines included three purebred beasts. Two were Labs, a chocolate and a gold. The third was a German Shepherd, his personal darling and the offspring of champions. When not busy making the world safe for Democrats Delmont spent as much time as he could training and caring for those animals, a fact that did little to endear him or his pack to the human members of his family but won him the unflinching devotion of his four-legged charges.

Neither his wife nor his children were ever able to come to terms with the idea that the dogs they shared a house with provided the reputed head of their family with an escape from the demands that his professional and personal life placed upon him. They failed to understand that when alone with his Labs and Shepherd Delmont found himself in a perfect world, one in which he was the unquestioned master. It was a place where any and all infractions of his rules, regardless of how slight or unintentional, could be handled with little more than a stern reprimand or, if serious enough, the application of a suitable punishment. Yet no matter how severely he castigated or admonished his animals, they never showed a hint of resentment or lingering anger. Instead, even in the wake of a harsh thrashing his trio of dogs were always quick to beg his forgiveness by demonstrating an appropriate degree of contrite submission. This is not to say that Robert Delmont was a cruel or uncaring man. On the contrary. When the situation called for it he could be quite compassionate, a loving husband, and a doting father. If he had any faults it was his inability to understand that the country he was sworn to defend and the Army to which he belonged was populated with far more cats than dogs.

Without really giving it much thought Robert Delmont modeled his career after the behavior of his beloved dogs, a proclivity that endeared him to all the right people. At times his steadfast loyalty to superiors that didn't deserve it was difficult, even painful. Like all career officers he occasionally found himself the subject of undeserved verbal abuse and tirades. Yet his willingness to swallow his pride and endure this sort of treatment without a whine or whimper was not without its rewards. Rung by rung Delmont ascended the prescribed career ladder by doing exactly what he was expected to do and angling for those assignments that conventional wisdom dictated. In this he was greatly aided by a knack for aligning himself with superiors who had been pegged as rising stars by those in the Army who mattered. Eventually he became viewed as one himself, an officer worthy of being groomed for bigger and better things. Though no one told him as much, by the time the results of this year's group battalion command selection board were published, it was clear to all who understood the system that there were stars in his future, provided he continued to perform.

That is how a Special Forces officer, fresh out of an assignment in the Pentagon, managed to secure the command of a Ranger battalion. Originally Delmont had been slated to take over a 380-man-plus Special Forces battalion. From a career standpoint it was both a logical and natural progression for him, not to mention a choice assignment that many a career officer would die for. Still, it was one that would have made him little more than a manager, charged with overseeing the support and administration of his battalion's far-flung "A" teams, the twelve-man units that did all the muddy boots stuff, and the three eleven-man "Bravo" teams, each capable of supporting six "A" teams in the field. Even during a major regional contingency, more popularly known as a war Delmont would have little to do with the actual conduct of operations and no opportunity to personally participate in combat operations. Due to the nature of their work there would be times when even he would not know where many of his own troops were or what they were doing.

A Ranger battalion on the other hand provided an officer of his grade the opportunity to actually command in the field. While still part of the Army's Special Operations Command Ranger battalions were organized along conventional lines. Squads formed platoons, which belonged to companies that in turn were integral parts of a battalion headed by a lieutenant colonel selected by a Department of the Army board comprised of full colonels who had completed successful battalion commands themselves. Successful command of a battalion would boost Delmont up the next rung in the career ladder when he moved into the zone of consideration for the next higher rank.

The officers selected to sit on that board would be required to review the promotion package of every officer eligible to be considered for the grade of O-6, or full colonel. It is a simple process but a long and tedious one, one that allowed the board members something like two minutes per promotion package. Two minutes. In those two minutes each board member had to determine if the officer under consideration was worthy of promotion, if his performance in past assignments indicated that he was capable of handling greater responsibilities. Unable to read every word on every officer evaluation report, board members tended to look for indicators, little cues that stood out and marked this man as being indispensable to the future of the Army. This meant that the sort of battalion a lieutenant colonel had commanded was critical since not all battalions were viewed as being equal. While important in the overall scheme of the Army as a whole a basic training battalion did not require the same sort of leadership skills or place the same demands on its commander that an airborne infantry battalion assigned to the 82nd Airborne Division did. It goes without saying that the officer who had completed a successful command of the airborne battalion was more likely to be viewed by the colonels on the board as more deserving of promotion than the one who had been more or less a chief administrator responsible for tending to the needs of basic trainees. Even more impressive is a former commander who had led his battalion into battle, something that a basic training battalion never did.

It also didn't hurt if the officers on the promotion board understood without having to be told what the battalion did. Everyone knew what a Ranger battalion was, a fighting unit whose organization wasn't much different from an airborne or light infantry battalion. The same could not be said of a Special Forces battalion. Unless the members of the board had themselves been in the Special Forces, few fully appreciated the duties and responsibilities that commanding it carried. Hence, given the choice between selecting an officer who was fully qualified and had commanded a Ranger battalion versus one who was equally qualified and had commanded a Special Forces battalion, odds favored the former.

Robert Delmont understood the career game very well. He followed the trends, listened to the stories that made their way through the rumor mill, and analyzed the statistics that accompanied the publication of each board's results. He knew who was being promoted, who wasn't and why. For this reason he was determined to secure the command of a battalion that was not only actively engaged in counterterrorism operations but one that would afford its commanding officer numerous opportunities to play a central and aggressive role in the execution of its assigned missions. For his purposes only a Ranger battalion would do. In achieving this goal he needed a little help.

In the old Army they were known as rabbis, senior officers who took an interest in the careers of junior officers. The reason for taking on the role of champion for a subordinate officer was not always altruistic. After World War II former airborne generals were accused of creating an informal support group that became known as the Airborne Mafia. One only has to look at the pedigree of the Army's senior leadership in the late fifties and early sixties to appreciate just how effective they were in the stewardship of ambitious young paratroopers they had known during the war. Another institution within the Army is the WPPA, or West Point Protective Association. Though it's been called many things, some of which could not be uttered in polite company the WPPA's goal has always been to watch out for the well-being of the officers who graduated from the United States Military Academy, often referred to as ring knockers by those who hadn't. The standing joke in the Army was that each West Point class ring came complete with a secret transmitter that connected the newly graduated officer directly to the WPPA rep located in the Army's Personnel Office. To a lesser degree graduates from the Virginia Military Institute, the Citadel, and Texas A&M who managed to attain positions of authority responded in kind by making sure their fellow alumni didn't lose their way in a system that could be as cruel and unforgiving to its own as it was to the enemy it occasionally was dispatched to crush.

A far less attractive reason that a senior officer takes an interest in a subordinate's career is to create a pool of officers who owe their loyalty to him. As an officer collects more and more stars, his personal staff expands along with his ability to manipulate the Army's personnel system. Some senior officers like to have the best and the brightest around them, a sort of brain trust that knows how he thinks and operates and whom he can rely upon. Others prefer sycophants, people known in the corporate world as yes-men. This sort of thing has been going on since before recorded time. It's not right and it's not wrong. It's just the way things work.

The degree to which a rabbi assisted their chosen vassals varied from dispensing sound career advice on occasion to aggressively tinkering with the system on behalf of their protégé. Delmont's rabbi was the hands-on sort, one who knew how to make the system work for him and those he had taken a liking to. He knew all the right people and made sure they knew him. Through his good offices Delmont was able to secure the one assignment both he and his benefactor believed would, in time, lead him to the stars.

Of course climbing that ladder does require effort, successful completion of each assignment, and a healthy dose of luck. Upon reaching each level the career officer must not only perform if he hopes to continue on up, he must shine. Everything he does, every mission his unit is assigned, must be more than successful, it must be a brilliant success. Should there be a glitch along the way, a less than stellar performance or an outright failure, he will be held responsible even if he had nothing to do with it, since a commanding officer is ultimately held responsible for everything his unit does. Such shortfalls show up on an officer's evaluation report where a rater can ding a subordinate for a failure that was not his fault through the words he uses when writing it. Instead of using glowing terms to describe a subordinate, such as, "This officer executed all assigned duties in an exemplary manner," a rater can simply state, "This officer performed all assigned duties to standard." Members of the promotion board would see the latter comment as a clue, a hint that something had gone wrong. Perhaps the glitch that caused the rater to do this hadn't been a disaster, but one that was serious enough to put the abilities of the officer under consideration in doubt.

Like climbing a ladder, the higher one ascends the military's chain of command the more precarious one's position becomes. A larger command means there are more subordinates, individuals who are scattered throughout a much wider area of operation and responsibility. Even in the digitalized Army of the twenty-first century it is impossible for a battalion commander to have his finger on everything going on within his command twenty-four/seven. He simply cannot do everything, see everything, or make every decision. He therefore must rely on his company commanders and staff officers, each of whom has his own ideas as how best to carry out his assigned missions and run his own little fiefdom. This was especially true of his company commanders. Every one of them also has his own goals, aspirations and ambitions, a fact Delmont was well aware of. One of the greatest challenges that Robert Delmont knew he would be facing in his new assignment was imposing his will and his way of doing things upon cocky young officers who were but a few rungs below him on the same career ladder.

From his seat in the Blackhawk Delmont's mind slowly mulled over his concerns as he watched the jungle below slip away. Somewhere down there was one of those strong-willed young men. He was anxious to meet him, so anxious that he had browbeaten the senior pilot of this Blackhawk into departing on his routine resupply run a full half hour early. Part of Delmont's apprehensions regarding this particular meeting was the setting. When he had met his other company commanders back at Fort Lewis for the first time he had done so in a setting of his choice. There he had been free to employ every trick he knew to impress upon them that he was their commanding officer. During his three years at the Pentagon Delmont had become a past master at setting the stage for power meetings. Seated on a chair hiked up a couple of extra notches behind his massive desk with the national colors and the battalion standard serving as a backdrop,

Delmont had been able to lord over his subordinate officers one by one as they entered his office, took their place in a straightbacked chair placed squarely before him and listened to him wax philosophically about his philosophy on leadership and what he expected of them.

Out here things would be different. In the jungle he would not have the advantage. He would be an intruder, a most unwelcomed one at that. His interests would have to give way to the tactical concerns of his subordinate, something that Delmont was not at all comfortable with. These troubling thoughts and how he could overcome them so preoccupied him that he became oblivious to what was going on around him. It therefore came as something of a shock when the Blackhawk's pilot unexpectedly jerked his aircraft to the left.

Thrown against the stack of rations he was seated next to a stunned and wide-eyed Delmont looked around. "What the hell is going—"

Before he could finish the pilot reversed himself by throwing the Blackhawk into a violent right bank, a maneuver that flung Delmont in the opposite direction and sent the top boxes of rations crashing against him. While struggling to keep the whole stack from tumbling down upon him, Delmont caught sight of the crew chief on the right side as he charged the machine gun he was hanging on to. As soon as the jungle below came back into view he began firing away.

Confusion now gave way to alarm. Were they taking fire? He desperately wanted to call out and ask what was going on but thought better of it. Though he was the senior officer on board he was but a passenger, little different at the moment than the boxes of rations and cans of ammunition that were now sliding back and forth across the floor of the cargo bay as the pilot swerved this way then that to evade enemy ground fire. Besides, the sight of tracers out the right door racing up at them from the jungle below provided Delmont with all the answers he needed. All he could do was hang on as the pilot maneuvered his aircraft through the hail of fire directed against it by un-seen assailants and watch as the crew chief did his best to return it. Over the headphones he listened as the pilots struggled to keep them out of the enemy's line of fire while the enlisted crew chief who doubled as door gunner was doing all he could to suppress their tormentors. Everyone's words were excited but precise, crisp yet clear.

From the copilot: "More fire coming our way at my one o'clock," a declaration that was immediately followed by a quick turn to the left.

The crew chief on the right yelled out to the door gun-ner on the left; "I got him. Ned, did ya see the one at your seven o'clock?"

To this the left door gunner replied with a simple "Roger" as he brought his weapon to bear and cut loose with a long burst.

From the cockpit, the copilot's voice rang out again over a mechanical squawk. "Master alarm! We're losing power, fast."

Glancing up over their shoulders from his seat, Delmont watched as the pair of warrant officers flying the Black-hawk struggled with their stricken aircraft. Frustrated at his inability to maintain control the pilot shouted out over the intercom, "I'm losing it! Hang on!" As the aircraft be-gan to buck and the engine sputtered Delmont realized that this was more of a warning to everyone on board than an expression of anger. They were going down.

That was all the pilot had time to say before he was forced to tip the nose of his aircraft down and began a frantic search for someplace to set down.

The jungle Delmont had been watching so absentmind-edly now filled the entire windshield of the Blackhawk. Realizing that they had lost their uneven contest with their unseen tormentors the crew chief and door gunner aban-doned their weapons and settled down into a position each felt offered them the best chance of surviving the coming crash. Up front the copilot's hand shot up and pointed at something Delmont could not see. "Over there!"

Without bothering to answer, the pilot struggled to bring the nose of his aircraft around and aimed for the opening in the jungle's dense canopy his copilot had spotted. By now everyone's full attention was riveted to that clearing, the one place that offered them their only hope of landing their bird in one piece.

From his seat in the cargo bay Delmont watched in silence as the dying aircraft lurched its way toward the clearing. The sudden frenzy and wild evasive maneuvers of the engagement were replaced by a desperate lunge toward the chosen landing site. Seconds that had whizzed by like a hail of tracers slowed to a painful, nerve-racking crawl. Delmont's concerns over his future and how best to secure it were forgotten. His entire attention, the focus of his whole life, was now reduced to an open patch of ground that was a chance of nature and the next few seconds. In the twinkling of an eye an officer who was being groomed for bigger and better things had become little more than the soft squishy filling of an out-of-control projectile spinning its way back to earth.

When he judged that impact was imminent, the pilot used what little power he had left to flair his Blackhawk in an effort to soften their impact. All he managed to say, all he needed to say as he did so, was "Hang on!"

Despite having done everything he could think of to prepare himself for the coming Blackhawk's crash the impact drove Delmont down into his seat with a force that rattled him and sent a wave of pain that was all but blinding. Then, just as suddenly as the jarring blow had come, it was replaced with a sensation that caused the shaken lieutenant colonel to imagine that somehow the helicopter had lifted back up off the ground and into the air. Prying open his eyes, he saw that this was in fact the case. Had the pilot managed to regain control? Had the thumping they had just endured somehow miraculously solved their mechanical problem? He knew that the chances of either of those being true were slim. But what the hell, when death is the only other choice a mind has to ponder it will grasp on to even the most improbable alternative.

Ignoring the bittersweet taste of blood that filled his mouth Delmont stared past the back of the pilots' heads and at the open sky he could see filling the windshield between them. Then, to his horror, the nose of the aircraft leveled off before angling sharply down once more. Blue sky was replaced by the reappearance of the jungle clearing they had been aiming for. This time, however, they were right there, down among the trees. The pilot had not managed to salvage a hopeless situation. The force of their impact had simply caused the aircraft to bounce up into the air for a brief, tantalizing moment. That moment was over. Now they were going down again, this time for good. With absolutely no control over the speed or angle of their precipitous descent the pilot, like Delmont and his copilot, was now reduced to being nothing more than a spectator to a horror show they had become part of.

Due to the severe angle the Blackhawk assumed during this second plunge, though the distance back to the ground was far less than it had been before, this second impact was far more jarring than the first had been. This time there was no illusory reprieve. Instead, the aircraft slid across the broken ground, careening toward the tree line that now filled the windshield before him. Realizing that their trials were not yet at an end, Delmont prepared himself yet again for the pending collision with the wall of trees that appeared to be rushing toward them at an alarming speed. Spitting the blood that filled his mouth onto the floor, the hapless battalion commander gripped the hand straps that hung from the Blackhawk's ceiling and braced himself as discrete details of the towering trees before them became clearer, and clearer, and . . .

Following on the heels of the deafening cacophony of noise and sound that had preceded their crash, the silence that greeted Delmont's return to consciousness was stunning.

The most overwhelming sensations he immediately became aware of was the lingering taste of blood in his
mouth and the overpowering stench of aviation fuel and
warm hydraulic fluids that permeated the air. The realization that the wreck he was in could burst into a ball of
flames at any moment galvanized him to ignore the pain
that emanated from every quarter of his body. Shoving
aside a box of rations that had come to rest on his stomach, Delmont struggled to pull and push himself up off of
what he thought was the floor of the helicopter. Very
quickly he came to the realization that he was wrong.
Pausing to look up it dawned on him that he was looking
out the right door of the Blackhawk. It was lying on its
side and he, the crew chief, the door gunner and everything that had not been tied down or had been torn loose
during the dual impacts were pressed together in a heap
against the crumpled left door.

With more effort than he normally needed to do so,
Delmont lifted his head and glanced to his left toward the
front of the aircraft. Both pilots were hanging limp and
motionless against the harnesses that kept them strapped
to their seats. At the moment things did not seem as if
they could have been any worse. Only when he took a
deep breath that filled his lungs with air corrupted by the
fumes of aviation fuel that was leaking from somewhere
close by did he correct himself. Things could get a lot
worse, faster than he cared to think about.

The stirring of one of the crew chiefs sprawled against
the side of the helicopter caught Delmont's attention.
Turning, he began to dig through the tangle of loose equipment, wreckage, and cargo that all but covered him. When
he had cleared away the bulk of the debris and the crew
chief opened his eyes, Delmont paused. His first efforts
to speak failed. For some reason he couldn't seem to
make his tongue work. Pulling away from the crew chief
he had been bending over, Delmont slowly brought his
right hand up to his open mouth and touched his tongue
with the tips of his fingers. The pain was immediate and

telling. Even before he pulled his fingers away to inspect them he knew he had bitten his tongue during the crash.

Angered more by the inconvenience that this injury would cause than by the pain, Delmont turned his head before doing his best to spit as much blood from his mouth as he could. When he was finished, he renewed his efforts to speak. "Sergeant. Can you move?"

Though his words were slurred, making him sound like a cartoon character, he managed to make himself understood. Still rattled, the crew chief blinked, looking about, as he shook his head. "Don't know. Wait one." Taking his time the crew chief wiggled the fingers on his right hand, then those on his left. When he was sure they were all working he slowly lifted his arms, one at a time. A sudden pain from somewhere caused him to grimace. Pausing, he let out a low moan. When the pain had passed, he paused to catch his breath. "Damn! That smarts."

"What about your legs? Can you move them?"

As he had with his arms the crew chief moved one leg at a time. When he was finally sure that he wasn't seriously injured, he looked over at Delmont. "I'll be okay. What about Ned and the others?"

Assuming that Ned was the door gunner Delmont began to clear away the pile of stuff that was covering him. When he found Ned's face Delmont placed his fingers on the crew chief's neck and felt for the artery. "He's alive but out cold."

"The pilots?"

"Don't know. I haven't seen them move yet." Then, reminded of the precariousness of their situation by the lingering stench of aviation fuel, Delmont turned his full attention to getting up and on his feet. "We need to get out of here."

Understanding the urgency, the crew chief threw himself into the painful task of freeing himself, then his companions. When he saw that Delmont was about to toss an ammo can that he had removed from Ned's leg, the crew chief took him by the arm. "Careful, Colonel. We can't afford to make any sparks."

Nodding, Delmont carefully set the ammo can down out of the way. He was in the process of clearing off the last of the clutter from the door gunner when the sound of small arms fire off in the distance broke the eerie silence. Startled, the crew chief looked up through the right door as his right hand grasped the handle of the pistol tucked into a holster that was part of his survival vest. "Ah geez. That's all we need."

After taking a moment to listen to the gunfire in an effort to gauge how far it was from them Delmont shook his head. "That coming from M-16s and M-240s."

Cocking his head, the crew chief listened again. "Yeah, I think you're right. But how'd they find us so quickly?"

"That's not important at the moment. Getting these guys out of here is."

"Yeah, right, right. I'll check the pilots if you see what you can do for Ned."

The fact that he was being ordered around by an E-5 crew chief didn't faze Delmont. At the moment rank didn't matter. All that was important was getting clear of this derelict as quickly as they could. Ignoring the chatter of small arms fire as best they could, the two conscious survivors turned their full attention to the task at hand.

Having managed to free the unconscious door gunner, Delmont was quickly coming to the conclusion that there was nothing more he could do on his own when he was startled by a voice from above that was far too cheerful given their current situation. "Hello down there."

His efforts to spin his head about and trace the source of the voice were too fast, generating a fresh spasm of pain from his injured mouth as well as numerous other bumps and bruises that covered his body. Blinded by the bright light above, all Delmont could make out was the silhouette of a head topped off with an Army-issue boonie hat. The two peered at each other for a moment before the figure above him spoke. "Captain Dixon, commanding officer of Company A, 3rd of the 75th Rangers. If you hang on a second I'll get some of my people down there to give you a hand."

As he sat on a tree trunk applying pressure on his tongue with a square of sterile gauze the medic had given him, Robert Delmont listened to Nathan Dixon give him a quick update on their tactical situation. "We've been tracking this band of guerrillas for some time now. This morning Lieutenant Grimes's platoon picked up their trail and followed them down off the mountain into the island's central valley. We thought they were on their way to Bila'an, one of the major villages where the people cache food and supplies for them. We were hoping to catch them while they were in the midst of packing it out."

Unable to speak or ask questions at the moment all Delmont could do was listen and nod every now and then.

"This—" Nathan indicated as he pointed the muzzle of his rifle at the Blackhawk laying on its side, "—is a new wrinkle. They had four .50-caliber machine guns staggered on either side of the valley and dug in with every couple of hundred meters. We managed to take down two of them before they had the time to pack up their shit and haul ass back up the mountain. Grimes is still out there with two squads pursuing the others. His third squad came with me to secure this site."

Again all Delmont could do was nod as he sat there like a bump on a log, unable to do anything but soak up his own blood like a schoolboy who had just gotten his butt whooped in a school yard fight. He wanted to say something about Dixon's casual demeanor in the presence of a superior and comment upon verbiage that he considered less than professional. But to have done so would have been both painful and left him open to ridicule. Maybe not here or now, but Delmont knew how soldiers loved to tell tales about their commanding officers behind their backs. With his every effort to speak hampered by a tongue already swollen to twice its normal size Delmont knew it was in his best interest to remain silent and tolerate as best he could a very embarrassing situation. "The crew chief and door gunner are okay. The one they call Ned is pretty badly shaken up but otherwise intact. The same is true with the pilot. It's the copilot that the medic is worried about. Both legs and his left arm are broken in multiple places. There's also the chance that he suffered internal injuries."

The sound of small arms fire in the distance caused Nathan to stop talking and turn his back on his new battalion commander. "Ah, success. Sounds like Terry caught up with the little shits."

On the other side of the field the squad radioman stood up and called out to Dixon. "Captain, it's the LT. He wants to talk to you."

With a wave of his left hand, Nathan acknowledged the call. "I'll be right over." Then, he faced Delmont. "Excuse me, Colonel, but duty calls." Without waiting to be dismissed Nathan once more turned away from his battalion commander and trotted on over to where the radioman was waiting.

Banged up, bruised all over, and all but silenced by a bitten tongue Delmont was reduced to little more than a hapless victim with nothing better to do than sit on a log watching Nathan Dixon go about his duties, leaving him to fume at the incredible streak of bad luck that had jumped up and slapped him in the face. Being shot down was unfortunate. Being rescued by one of his own subordinates like this was deplorable. But as bad as all that was, suffering the sort of wound he had was nothing less than unbearable. It would be a long time before he lived this down. Only a flawless performance as battalion commander from here on out would eradicate this blemish from his otherwise spotless record. Either that or manage to engineer some sort of major coup. Having failed to awe and impress this particular company commander, all

Delmont could do now as he waited to be evacuated from the crash site was begin figuring out how best to achieve both of those goals. That he would eventually manage to come up with something was not in doubt. All that mattered was that he did, the quicker the better.

2

ARLINGTON, VIRGINIA

By Washington standards it was a modest affair, attended mostly by those who belonged to the second and third echelons of the nation's power elite. No one had the nerve however, to tell them that. Nor did they conduct themselves in a manner that suggested they were not as great as their respective egos imagined them to be. Throughout the adjoining rooms the smattering of senators and congressmen, reinforced by a sprinkling of officials from the current administration and a selected few from the previous one who somehow had missed the memo informing them that they were out of power, wandered about chatting, networking, and pontificating. And of course there was the military, a must at all but the most radically left-wing gatherings. Some of the uniformed attendees were enjoying themselves, mixing and mingling seamlessly with the politicians and senior federal functionaries with whom they identified. Others who found these contrived cocktail parties to be tiring and tedious, populated mainly by those wishing to promote some hidden agenda or themselves, avoided being drawn into a conversation by incessantly roaming about the room. Were it not for the fact that his wife's job required that she attend these gatherings Scott Dixon would have been at home that very minute with his nose buried in a book on military history, clad in crew socks, well-worn sweatpants, and a T-shirt sporting an irreverent saying that only a soldier could appreciate.

Jan didn't have much of a choice on these matters. As the head of the World News Network's Washington office, attending such events was all but a requirement for her. Like her husband she had next to nothing in common with the majority of the politicos, lobbyists, and sycophants who flocked to cocktail parties and receptions like moths to a lightbulb. Unfortunately, as a key member of the fourth estate Jan needed to establish and maintain as cordial a relationship as she could manage with people who wouldn't have given her the time of day were it not for the fact that she headed one of the most powerful news bureaus in one of the world's most powerful cities. So they engaged her in the artful little dance that takes place between elected officials who wish to curry a favorable opinion from the media while their journalistic partner uses every opportunity to extract newsworthy information from them. After watching her work her particular brand of magic at an event Scott once half jokingly told her that she had missed her calling. "You would have made a great spy."

Before replying to this accusation Jan maneuvered herself in front of Scott. As she lightly brushed up against him with her chin slightly tucked in, a smile danced across her lips. Slyly glancing up at him through her lashes she responded in the low, husky voice that never failed to elicit a physical response from him. "But Scott, dear, I didn't."

On this particular evening Scott occupied his usual hull-down position in a corner of the room, one that was within easy reach of the open bar. With his flank and rear thus protected he was free to watch his wife go about mixing and mingling with the grandees and ne'er-do-wells. This was the only thing he enjoyed doing at these gatherings.

Otherwise, he pretty much kept to himself, slowly sipping his drink as he avoided contact with the elected riffraff and overpaid bureaucrats. Whenever a foolish soul he didn't care to chat with took it upon themselves to keep him company or engage him in trivial chitchat, Scott dissuaded them from approaching by employing what Jan called his "piss off or I'll rip your head off" look. With close to thirty years in the Army under his belt and after raising two sons he had this expression down cold.

There were exceptions of course, particularly when the interloper was a fellow officer he knew was seeking a safe haven himself. The minute Russell Owens, a fellow lieutenant general and the deputy chief of staff for personnel set eyes on Scott he made a beeline for him. As he approached Owens smirked. "I see she managed to drag you out of your cave again."

Scott made a show of bowing in submission. "Ah, the things we must do in order to secure a little domestic tranquility."

When he was within arm's distance of Scott, Owens spun about and backed up against the wall until he was shoulder-to-shoulder with Scott. As he sipped his drink, Owens scanned the crowd. Finished, he sighed. "Anyone worth mentioning here tonight?"

"Well, the president's national security advisor is wandering about somewhere out there working the crowd. The esteemed chairman of the Senate Armed Services Committee is flitting about, hemming and hawing about the latest round of cuts he's working on. And I think the attorney general is due to make an appearance. Other than that it's about what you'd expect, the usual suspects."

Owens nodded. "What about friendly forces?"

Scott raised the hand holding his drink and pointed to the corner opposite his. "I think I saw the deputy chief of staff of the Air Force seeking cover and concealment over there behind the table with the hors d'oeuvres. Uncle Barney, our most favorite Marine general, is out there in the thick of it, griping and grinning on behalf of the Corps."

Mention of the Marine Corps commandant caused Owens to chuckle. "You gotta hand it to the Corps. They certainly know how to pick their commandants."

"You're spot on with that. Barney can be as smooth as velvet when he needs to be and as ruthless as a Hun when the situation calls for it."

"Speaking of that, Scott, how's it going between you and your new deputy?"

Scott grunted. "Oh, peachy. God's gift to the Army hasn't been my deputy two weeks and already he's bombarding me with memos promoting his pet projects."

Again Owens snickered. "We all knew that was coming. The chief of the special operations command has been lobbying the old man and the chairman for six months now to get one of his own people in a position from which he could influence operations."

Angered, Scott straightened up. "Influence! How much more influence do those prima donnas want? They're starting to get as bad as the Air Force. Christ, did you hear what they're telling the cadets at West Point these days? 'The era of conventional warfare is over. Your future lies in special ops.' I all but gag every time I hear that."

"Your son seems to have taken that message to heart."

Mollified a bit by Owens's retort, Scott reined in his indignation. "Nate's only doing what he was born to do. He's a natural when it comes to sneaking around in the dark and scaring the shit out of people, a skill his brother will gladly testify to."

"Which reminds me," Owens stated as he lifted his glass in a toast to Scott. "Congratulations on your son's latest coup."

Seeing an opportunity to twists Owens's tail, Scott regarded him a moment with a puzzled expression. "You mean Andrew, my youngest son who was just accepted as a first-year resident at the University of Colorado Hospital in Denver?"

Having forgotten the fierce pride Scott took in the

achievements of both his sons Owens did his best to hide his embarrassment at his rather presumptuous remark. "Ah, no, sorry. I was talking about Nathan. I saw a copy of the report on his company's skirmish with the Abu Sayyaf on Jolo. Nine confirmed kills together and a substantial haul of heavy weapons without a single casualty, not to mention saving his battalion commander from capture."

Scott looked down into his drink as he swirled it about, taking a moment to reflect on the affair. "That colonel of his was lucky."

Owens corrected him. "The Army was lucky. Can you imagine what would have happened if they had managed to make the commanding officer of one of our elite units a hostage? The media with their menagerie of talking heads and some of our 'dear' friends in Congress would have had a field day."

"Please, don't remind me. It would have been worse than 'seventy-eight when the Red Army Brigade kidnapped Dozer in Italy. Remember some of the jokes going around about him during that sorry affair?"

"Ah yes, the seventies," Owens mused. "A decade I dare say we'd all love to forget. Sontay, the fall of Saigon, the Mayaguez Incident, and Desert One and Jimmy Carter all sort of left a bad taste in many a mouth."

"I dare say," Scott grumbled, "those sorry chapters have haunted us ever since."

"Us, yes," Owens corrected Scott. "But not your son and his generation of officers. They're different. They've not yet tasted defeat."

This comment caused Scott to raise an eyebrow. "Ah, how quickly we forget Mogadishu."

"That was an anomaly."

Between sips Scott laughed. "What a great word for screwup. Anomaly. No doubt the staff weenie who introduced that little ditty into our arsenal of non-words earned himself a commendation."

Stepping away from the wall Owens raised the hand

holding his drink, unwrapped a finger from around the glass, and jabbed the finger into Scott's chest. "That was a successful operation. It was a bloody one, but one that achieved what they had set out to achieve. In a single stroke they cut the legs out from under Aideed and broke his back militarily. All we needed to finish the job in Somalia was political leadership who had the balls and the stomach to see the thing through."

Scott pressed himself up against the wall and threw his hands up in mock surrender. "Cease-fire. I'm on your side, amigo. I know what happened and who was at fault. Unfortunately for us Slick Willie and his willing accomplices managed to duck the blame for that and leave us looking like idiots."

Somewhat mollified, Owens took a long drink as he resumed his position against the wall next to Scott. "Sorry for getting excited like that. It's just that you know as well as I do that we're just one disaster away from having the media and a fair number of congressmen turn against us and this never-ending war we're waging against those who adhere to that most peaceful of all the world's religions. It would be a pity to give up now when we're so close to breaking their backs over there instead of here."

Scott nodded. "I know. That's why it's so damned important to keep people like Palmer and his ilk from getting out of hand. While I must admit that some of his ideas do have merit I fear they fail to understand that we can't afford even a single Pyrrhic victory like the one we scored in Somalia in ninety-three. We've got to be smart about where and how we fight."

"Not everyone agrees, Scott. There's a lot of folks who are getting tired of the manner with which we're prosecuting this war. They're wondering when it's going to end."

"Let 'em wonder. So long as I have a say in the matter we're going to fight those fights that make sense while keeping us as far off the media's radar as we can manage."

Sensing that his friend was beginning to become annoyed by this topic, Owens decided that it was time to change subjects. After a moment or two of silence, he began to look around the room. "Speaking of the media, where's your better half?"

Scott made a vague gesture with his hand. "Out there somewhere, using her charms to snare some unsuspecting schmuck into an exclusive interview on one of her shows."

"Perhaps you should go out there and save them from themselves. I've seen what her minions do to some of their guests."

Scott shook his head. "I don't think so. Most of them are grown-ups. They can fend for themselves. Besides, I think the vast majority of them enjoy the abuse."

"They must," Owens agreed. "Anyone who has to spend most of their waking hours going around begging for campaign funds from some of the loonies they have to patronize has to have a serious masochistic streak."

"Hey, that's no way to talk about our esteemed members of Congress. Their only desire is to serve."

Now it was Owens's turn to show his cynical side. "Yeah, right. And I'm just a simple soldier."

Scott looked over at him and smirked. "Yeah, I dare say you're about as simple as they come." Then noticing that the glass Owens was holding was just about empty, he stepped away from the wall and took it from his hand. "Come on, amigo. The next round is on me."

"That's real kind of you, Scott, especially considering that this is an open bar."

Bowing before heading off toward the bar, Scott smiled. "It'll be my pleasure. Now move out and follow me."

NORTH OF BANDUNG ON THE ISLAND OF JAVA, INDONESIA

The rare meeting of the polyglot council of Islamic groups and their supporters had started out tranquil enough with a representative from each of the groups belonging to an alliance that circumstances had brought together standing up, presenting the status of their organization and what it had accomplished since they had last met. All spoke of their achievements in the most glowing terms while downplaying or skipping over completely the reverses their respective organizations had suffered.

For Hamdani Summirat, still smarting from his recent run in with the Australians, listening to his brethren spin trivial events and magnify meaningless achievements proved to be all but intolerable. Sensing that this would be the case, the titular head of his group had urged Summirat beforehand to hold his tongue. "It will not do our cause any good," he pointed out, "to berate and belittle our brothers and those who support our efforts. They are no less dedicated to this struggle than we are. None of us can survive on our own. We need the money the Saudis bring to the table and the training facilities the Iranians provide us with."

Obediently Summirat did all he could to comply with the wishes of those charged with overseeing the political and financial affairs of the Abu Sayyaf, maintaining his silence as he listened to a litany that never seemed to change. This did not last long. After listening to a Palestinian describe in far greater detail than necessary the results of a spat of suicide bombings that came across as being little more than arbitrary and of no consequence whatsoever Summirat threw up his hands. "What are we doing here?" he suddenly exclaimed. Jumping to his feet, he began to pace about the well-appointed meeting room waving his right hand about in the air as he spoke. "Our friend from Hamas speaks of striking a telling blow against the Zionists. Yet neither he nor any of his compatriots can point to a single success that has contributed to the final solution which we all seek. All he's done is kill a few Jews and bring the full wrath of the Israeli state down upon their own people."

"What would you have us do?" the senior leader of Hamas shot back.

"Fight smart," Summirat bellowed without hesitation.

"Fight the sort of war that the Americans and Jews cannot possibly win."

"And just what sort of war would that be?" a Saudi prince asked in a self-assured tone that left little doubt that he was confident he did not expect a serious response.

Handed an opening like this to address the assembly that his own leadership would not have given him, Summirat ceased his pacing and angry gestures. Taking a moment, he composed himself and collected his thoughts. When he was ready he presented his ideas in a clear, well-measured manner that left little doubt that his words and the plan he laid before them were meticulously thought-out and serious.

"We are engaged in a clash of cultures, one which has spanned many centuries. It is one that cannot be won in the streets of Tel Aviv or the jungles of Mindanao. We will not succeed if all we do is target schoolchildren and rich tourists. Such attacks only serve to enflame our enemies. The victory we seek cannot be achieved by annihilating every man, woman, and child that fails to accept Allah as the one true God and the teachings of His Prophet. Rather, we will prevail only when we have broken their will to resist."

Annoyed at having been interrupted, the Hamas representative whom Summirat had interrupted huffed. "The vision our brother lays before us is nothing new to us. We are not children ignorant to the ways of this world or the mechanics of information warfare."

Summirat stared at the Palestinian. "Given the manner with which your fighters conduct themselves would lead one to believe otherwise."

Jumping to his feet the Palestinian all but lunged across the highly polished mahogany table at Summirat. While those on either side of the Palestinian did their best to restrain him, the Saudi prince chairing this gathering raised his hand, beckoning for calm. "Let us save our vitriol for those who would oppose us. Instead, we will listen patiently as our Indonesian brother enlightens us with his wisdom and insights."

Ignoring the sarcasm that permeated the Saudi's appeal, Summirat picked up where he had left off. "While laudable, many of our efforts in the past have resulted in a response that was not foreseen. One only has to look at what happened to Al Qaeda after they brought down the World Trade Center. Instead of cowering the Americans and reducing them to submission, the attacks mobilized an awful resolve. Osama bin Laden's one stunning victory unleashed a force against us all that we have been unable to stem."

Unable to remain silent the Hamas rep sneered, "And you will do better? How? Please, enlighten us."

Pretending that he did not hear this Summirat continued. "The Americans are an impatient people. They insist upon immediate results. They also have little tolerance for combat casualties. They kill over fifty thousand of their own on their highways every year without flinching. Yet the minute a handful of soldiers are killed in battle they go to pieces. Their media wail like women, pillaring their politicians in public and branding their military leaders as incompetent."

Sensing that Summirat was actually onto something, the Saudi prince leaned forward. "This is all true. Their failures in both Vietnam and Somalia as well as the internal divisions the war in Iraq has created illustrate your point quite nicely. The question I have for you, one I am sure we all share, is what do you have in mind? How do we go about exploiting these frailties?"

Doing all he could to suppress a smile, Summirat continued outlining his plan. "First, we do nothing to enflame the American public. Inaction on that front will lead to apathy and forgetfulness by the vast majority of their public. It will not take long before the shrilled warnings by those who see the danger their country faces begin to fall on deaf ears. Eventually the voices calling for vigilance and action will be drowned out by those promoting other causes, other crusades, none of which will have anything to do with us."

Sensing that this did not sit well with those who felt that they had not done enough to bring the war to the American homeland, Summirat quickly moved onto his next point. "While we are going out of our way to lull the American public into a false sense of security, we must continue to wage an aggressive campaign designed to inflict as many casualties upon American forces deployed overseas as we can. We will do this by drawing them into battles that will be fought in places and at times of our choosing. Instead of throwing the lives of our young men away in suicide attacks that do nothing to forward our cause we need to be miserly, expending their lives only when it is to our advantage to do so. In time the American people will tire of sending their sons and daughters all over the world to die in a never-ending war they no longer see as necessary."

Finished for the moment, Summirat paused in order for the gathering to take in what he had said. Even those belonging to the Hamas delegation took a moment to reflect upon this idea. Still the most vocal of their number could not help himself as he once more lashed out at Summirat. "The Japanese harbored the same illusions you do concerning the Americans. The price they paid for misjudging American resolve was total defeat and subjugation. To do what you ask is to risk the same fate. I for one do not intend to gamble the fate of our people on a shaky theory."

"So, is it your opinion," Summirat countered, "that our only recourse is to go around blowing up buses and schoolchildren at pizza parlors in the hope that the Jews will tire of burying their dead and go back to Europe? The only problem with that of course is that they have no place to go. They are far more dangerous than a cornered animal. So long as they have the full and unflinching support and empathy of the Americans, they are invulnerable."

"So, what you are advocating," the Saudi injected, "is a two-tier approach to our problems. A wearing down of American resolve through indirect action, followed by concerted effort against Israel after we have had a chance to reconstitute our respective organization and lull them into inaction. Of course, following such a course of action means embarking upon a long and protracted journey that will require many years and great patience."

"Therein lies the crux of our problem," Summirat stated succinctly. "We can choose to continue our headlong rush into oblivion or we can adopt a strategy of patience. For me, the choice is simple."

Discussion on the proposal Summirat had laid before the council took up the remainder of that day. Those who had watched the men they had carefully recruited and painstakingly trained wasted in petty attacks against meaningless targets, as Summirat had, immediately rallied behind him. One by one they stood up and voiced their support for a change in strategy that they saw as promising. Arrayed against them were others who for one reason or another found themselves unable to abandon their current programs. Between these divergent views sat those who financed their activities and provided the weapons required to carry out their war against the infidels. They listened closely to both sides as they tried to discern which path offered them the greatest return for their investment. Bit by bit they found themselves drawn toward Summirat's view. Still, they postponed a decision until such time as they could meet in private and discuss the matter among themselves.

That evening the Saudi who was chairing the council managed to find Summirat alone while he was relaxing in one of the resort's gardens as so many of the other guests did following their gourmet dinner. Polite to a fault, the Saudi asked if he could have a word with him. Sensing that his position was in the ascendancy, Summirat smiled as he came to his feet and graciously invited the Saudi to take a seat across from him.

"I would be lying," the Saudi stated frankly without preamble, "if I did not admit that your ideas have merit, not to mention a certain appeal to those of us who have had difficulty reconciling the mass murder that so many engage in."

"It pleases me to hear one as dedicated to our cause as you are to say this."

"Hyperbole, idle boasting, and exaggerated claims do nothing to advance our cause or discredit our enemies. Neither do indiscriminate attacks against civilians. Such tactics only serve to strengthen the hand of those who seek to destroy us. They also drive away those who would otherwise support us with the funds we so desperately need. On this we seem to agree."

"But?" Summirat injected when he detected the hesitancy in the Saudi's voice.

Sheepishly the Saudi looked up into Summirat's eyes. "There are some who will never agree to what you are proposing. We are already fragmented, with this group and that pulling our fragile coalition apart. Turning away from the strategy we've been following for so long to strike out in a new direction could tear it apart."

"Yet to continue to reinforce policies that have already failed," Summirat pointed out, "is to doom all our efforts to ultimate defeat. Even a blind man can see that we will never achieve anything by wasting our most faithful and courageous fighters as we have been."

"Yes, I agree. So the real question comes down to one."

"Which is?" Summirat asked, though he already knew the answer.

Sensing that this was the case, the Saudi glanced about nervously in an effort to see if anyone around them was paying attention to them. Satisfied no one was, he leaned closer to Summirat. "You understand some adjustments will need to be made if we decide to pursue the course of action you have laid out."

Settling back in his seat Summirat folded his hands and rested his chin upon them. "Yes, of course."

"These adjustments must be discreet, carried out in a manner that prevents infighting or a blood feud."

"Naturally."

"Good," the Saudi stated crisply as he stood up. "Then we understand each other."

Summirat nodded. "Completely."

3

FORT LEWIS, WASHINGTON

Standing at the door of his company arms room, Nathan Dixon watched his men file by. Every now and then he reached out and snatched a rifle out of the hands of one of his men before he was able to hand it over to the unit armorer. With well-practiced ease Nathan twilled the weapon about as he inspected it from muzzle to butt, pausing from time to time in order to take a closer look at something that caught his eye. When he was satisfied that the weapon was spotless and ready to be turned back in he handed the rifle back to the man he had taken it from. With the same swift motions that Nathan had used to take it away, the soldier snatched his weapon out of his commanding officer's hands before turning it over to the armorer to be checked in and stored.

None of the Rangers singled out by Nathan in this manner batted an eye. No one was offended or put out. They more or less expected it. In fact, had their company commander not been there checking their weapons they would have been concerned, for Nathan was doing what he and every officer who wore the Ranger tab had been instructed to do by Robert Rogers, the grandfather of the

American Rangers. The rules that he used to govern the conduct of his men in the French and Indian War were little changed from those still used by 75th Regiment. The first of these dictates stated unambiguously that an officer was to "Inspect everything." Such inspections were necessary. One simply cannot cry out during an operation, "Oh, gee, I forgot something!" and have a C-17 turn around in midair in order to return to base to pick it up. Nor is it healthy to discover in the middle of a firefight that after its last cleaning you reassembled your weapon improperly. While officers will never be able to totally eliminate every mistake a man can make, their inspections go a long way toward minimizing them, a fact most soldiers understand.

The line of Rangers waiting to shuffle past Nathan and turn their weapons in was still quite long when Nathan caught sight of his first sergeant and executive officer making their way down the corridor toward him. Returning to the doorway to take the next man's rifle, the unit armorer looked at First Sergeant Carney and First Lieutenant Quinn, then over at his company commander. "Uh, oh. Looks like trouble to me."

Glancing up from the rifle he was inspecting Nathan studied the determined expression his two most important subordinates were regarding him with. Peeking over at the armorer Nathan grunted. "No good can come of this."

The armorer chuckled. "I venture to say you're about to be double teamed, sir."

"Ah, well, you see that's why I have two bars on my collar. I can multitask."

When Carney and Quinn were within arm's reach of Nathan, Carney took up a position next to his company commander while Quinn confronted him head-on before raising up on his toes in an effort to exaggerate the considerable difference in their height. "Sir, it has been decided that you have done your duty for God and country this day and the time has come to relieve you of your post."

Maintaining a straight face Nathan glanced over at his first sergeant, then back up at his executive officer. "Is this a mutiny, mister?"

"No, sir, it is a coup."

All around them the soldiers of Company A paused what they had been doing in order to enjoy this bit of playacting.

"I see," Nathan mumbled as if pondering his next move. "And if I resist?"

Carney glared at his company commander and growled as only a first sergeant can. "Resistance is futile."

In an instant Nathan's expression changed from one of serious concern to merry placidness. "Well, if that's the case, okay."

Unable to hold back any longer both Carney and Quinn smirked. Easing back onto his heels Quinn reached out and took the rifle Nathan had been inspecting. "I'll finish up here, sir. Why don't you go home and chill out. Lord knows you've earned it."

Though he was pleased that his first sergeant and executive officer thought so highly of him that they would wish to permit him such a luxury, Nathan shook his head. "I truly do appreciate the gesture, gentlemen, but you know I can't leave till every weapon is accounted for and the last man has been dismissed."

"Oh, yes, you can," Carney countered. "And go you will." Doing his best to mimic a British sergeant major. "Now, enough of this idle chitchat, mister. Come to attention."

Snapping to a rigid position of attention Nathan let out a loud "Yes, First Sergeant!"

Up and down the corridor the men who were watching began to laugh.

Carney stepped away from Nathan to give him room to pass. "Now, at the double quick, march."

Doing his best to imitate the march of a British grenadier, Nathan began to make his way down the corridor to

Carney's cadence of "Left, right, left right," as the men lining the wall laughed.

All three—Nathan, Carney, and Quinn—understood that this sort of levity every now and then was healthy. It broke the tension and tedium associated with their profession and did wonders for morale. It also served one more, far less obvious purpose. By letting their men see them mess around like this every so often it demonstrated that each of them was completely comfortable with their assigned roles and duties. Only the most self assured and confident officers are able to let their guard down in front of their own men and allow themselves to be trifled with in this way. At the same time it served notice that the three most important people in the company, their commanding officer, his executive officer, and the first sergeant were a team, a single entity. Soldiers knew without having to be told that they could not play one against the other, that the policy or orders of one would not be countermanded or marginalized by another. Such seamless cohesion by the unit's leadership set an example and permitted every man in the company to put aside any thought of engaging in soldierly gamesmanship, leaving them little choice but to focus his full and undivided attention on what he had joined the Army to do, and that was be a Ranger. This sort of leadership is not found in a manual. Nor is it taught at Fort Benning. It is uniquely American. It's the sort of thing that makes leadership more of an art form than a skill. It is the sort of leadership that inspires, that keeps a unit together when logic and circumstances dictate otherwise. It is the sort of leadership that creates a bond that even death cannot break.

Exhaustion and weariness swept over Nathan the moment the mantle of command was lifted from his shoulder. Like a late night reviler who had enjoyed one too many he staggered home, driving extra slowly as he struggled to keep his eyes open and his full attention on the road ahead. Mechanically he staggered up the three flights of stairs of the modest apartment complex he lived in just off post, fumbling with his keys as he did so.

Step by step he made his way to his door, opened it and slithered inside, dropping his duffel bag in the small foyer before heading straight for the refrigerator where he retrieved a diet soda. Pausing there only long enough to open the can and take a sip, he wandered into the underfurnished combination living room and dining room where he plopped down in a recliner that constituted a bulk of that room's appointments. With his soda in his left hand Nathan picked up the remote with his right and clicked the on button to his TV. Without waiting to listen to what the news commentator was saying, he set aside his drink and the remote, leaned forward, and began to unlace his boots.

He was in the middle of this when something caught his attention. Startled, he sat bolt upright, his attention drawn to the small hall that led back to the apartment's single bedroom. It took his tired eyes a moment to bring the image he beheld into sharp focus.

Not waiting for him to collect his wits, Christina Dixon abandoned the provocative pose she had been holding and began to make her way to Nathan, moving her hips in a most unmilitary manner. "My, my," she mused as she slowly approached him. "The Army has certainly fallen on hard times when the likes of me, a lowly chemical corps officer, can successfully ambush a Ranger. How very slack of you."

Stunned by this unexpected apparition, Nathan simply sat there and watched as she drew near. For a brief moment he found himself wondering if his fatigued mind was simply conjuring up the image he was beholding or if by some miracle, his wife was really there, attired in nothing more than a black T-shirt with a bright yellow Ranger tab stenciled strategically across its front.

When she was but a few feet away she stopped, struck

a provocative pose, with one hand planted on her hip, and the other stretched out along her thigh as she held her head cocked to one side after giving her long auburn hair a well-practiced toss. "Well Captain Dixon, are you going to do something to show your appreciation for all the trouble I went through to get here?"

Nathan swallowed hard. "Oh, believe me when I tell you, Captain Dixon, there are parts of me that are already straining to express their approval."

This brought a smile to her face, one that lit up the room and brought new life to Nathan. Forgetting what he had been doing before he stood up, managing to take only one step toward her before tripping over his own boot lace. Lurching forward, he threw his arms out in a vain attempt to grab the only thing he could reach in an ill-advised effort to arrest his fall. Unprepared for this dazzling display of clumsiness, Christina tried to step back. Unfortunately Nathan's forward motion and grasping hands were too quick. With one single, swift motion he collided with his wife, sending her tumbling over backward. The two landed on the floor with a thud that knocked the wind out from each of them.

For a minute they could do nothing but lie there, collecting themselves and catching their breaths. Sprawled on the floor and pinned beneath her husband like a rag doll Christina looked up at him. "Are you okay?"

Though he was still rattled he lifted his head, looked into her eyes and smiled. "I dare say I could be better."

Having managed to recover from the shock of being bowled over, Christina began to relax, enjoying the feel of Nathan's weight upon her and the scent of gun oil that still permeated his hands as they slowly began to explore her body. After squirming about so as to better accommodate his efforts, she lifted her head till their lips touched. After exchanging a soft, tender kiss she eased back. "Well, Captain Dixon, shall we adjourn to the bedroom or just have at it here and now."

Grinning, Nathan reared up onto his knees before her

as shaky hands began to frantically undo stubborn buttons. "What the hell Captain Dixon. Why wait?"

The glint in his eyes and the warmth of his body against hers sent a quiver down her spine. She didn't answer, at least not verbally. Instead, she reached up and began to help him out of his uniform.

Their first bout there on the living room floor had all the finesse and subtlety of a cavalry charge. Their second go, conducted in the bedroom after one of the briefest pauses on record, was not near as frenzied, coming much closer to reflecting the true meaning of making love as opposed to simply having sex.

It was in the afterglow of this second passionate exchange that Nathan was roused from a state of near bliss by the tinny chime of the cheap apartment doorbell. Propping himself up on his elbow, he looked down at Christina. "Who the hell could that be?"

He had thought his question was rhetorical. Christina however surprised him by responding with confidence. "That must be Emmett."

Caught off guard yet again by his wife, Nathan stared at her. "Emmett? Emmett DeWitt?"

Smiling, Christina wiggled out from between her husband's arms and threw her legs over the side of the bed. "Of course, silly. How many Emmetts do you know?"

Still confused, he watched as she pulled Nathan's black Ranger T-shirt on before heading for the bedroom door. "What's going on here?"

Glancing over at the clock on the nightstand, Christina called out as she made her way out of the room. "Why, he's here to pick us up, dear."

"What?"

Ignoring her husband, Christina continued to head for the front door. Taking but a moment to give her tousled mane a quick shake, she opened the door a crack, peeked around it, and gave the tall, well-dressed African-American on the other side a smile. "Well, you are right on time."

Emmett DeWitt beamed. "I'm here to rescue you from the clutches of that heathen husband of yours."

Christina laughed. "And not a moment too soon." Then, after looking out onto the walkway, she asked De-Witt where his wife was.

"She's waiting in the car. I sort of thought you two would be ready."

"Oh, how little you know Nathan. Please, go get her. We'll need a few minutes."

"Don't take too long, Captain Dixon," DeWitt mockingly admonished her. "Our reservations are for seven-thirty and tardiness will not be tolerated."

Giving him a mock salute with her left hand, she prepared to close the door. "Yes sir, Captain, sir. Now be off, valiant knight, and fetch thy wife."

As pleased as he had been to see his wife and dumb-struck by the sudden appearance of the battalion's adjutant and his wife, Nathan enjoyed the dinner DeWitt had arranged at a quiet Italian restaurant in Tacoma. It was a perfect way to celebrate the completion of a most successful rotation to the Philippines and a long anticipated visit by his Christina. Nothing could be more perfect he thought as he looked across the table at his wife's face, softly illuminated by the glow of the single candle as she chatted with Paula DeWitt.

Catching him staring at her out of the corner of her eye, Christina paused, glanced over at him, and smiled. "Have you decided what you want for dessert yet?" she asked in a manner that left no doubt as to what she was hinting at.

Realizing that she was intentionally feeding him an opening he could not possibly allow to pass, Nathan smiled. "I'm looking at it."

Though she guessed that his answer would be something like this, Christina still found herself blushing.

Reaching over Paula DeWitt laid her hand on Christina's. "Come on, girl. Let's leave the boys here a few minutes while they settle down some."

Rising as their wives stood up, Nathan and DeWitt watched as they made their way toward the ladies' room. When they were out of sight, the two officers resumed their seats. As they did so, Nathan seized his glass of wine and raised it. "By the way, if I have neglected to do so, thanks for setting all this up."

DeWitt shook his head. "I'm not the one that deserves your thanks. Paula arranged everything and picked your wife up at the airport."

"Be that as it may, I owe the DeWitt clan a debt of gratitude, not to mention a round of applause to both my XO and first sergeant for their part in this affair." This statement was followed by a moment of silence as each settled down and enjoyed a sip of wine. Finally DeWitt broke the mellow mood by looking over at Nathan. "How much do you know about our new commanding officer?"

"You mean El Jefe?"

DeWitt chuckled. "El Jefe is out. For now you have a choice. Mumbles or Elmer Fudd."

Nathan almost choked as he guffawed. "You've got to be kidding me?"

DeWitt smiled as he shook his head. "I kid you not. Have you heard him try to speak? His tongue is still badly swollen. He's become so self-conscious of slurred speech that he's taken to hiding in his office like the captain of the USS Caine. Major Castalane has become so concerned about this that he's thinking about calling in an FBI negotiator to see if he can talk him out of there."

Nathan listened and chuckled, though he knew that his friend and the former commanding officer of the company he now commanded was trying to make a point. "You asked what I knew about Lieutenant Colonel Robert

Elliot Delmont? Nothing, other than what we all heard prior to his assumption of command and the deployment of my company to the Philippines."

Glumly, Dewitt looked down into his glass of wine that he was holding between his two hands. "Oh."

"Oh? What did you expect?"

"Well, I thought . . ."

Doing his best to hide his irritation, Nathan squirmed in his seat. "Emmett, how many times do I need to re-mind you that just because my old man happens to be the deputy chief of staff for Operations on the DA staff doesn't mean I have inside connections? On the day I took my oath to uphold and defend the Constitution of these United States he took me aside and told me I was on my own. 'Son,' Nathan stated doing his best to imitate his father's voice and manner, 'this is one minefield you're going to have to navigate on your own.' That, dear sir," Nathan stated as he reached forward to take the bottle of wine and refill his glass, "is the sum total of the career advice and insider help he's given me. Why do you ask?"

Taking a moment to mull this over DeWitt slowly swilled his drink about as he did so. "While you were out hiding in the bushes word has been trickling its way down through the grapevine that Mumbles is very well connected." Pausing, he looked up at Nathan with an ex-pression that betrayed the somberness of the subject he was being so careful to broach.

Having been around the military his entire life, Na-than had an intuitive understanding of how the Army re-ally worked. "So our fearless leader is being groomed for bigger and better things."

"Seems so," DeWitt replied as he took a sip of wine. "He's got some very powerful friends in all the right places."

Nothing more needed to be said. Nathan understood the potential hazards that this set of circumstances posed for him, his fellow officers in the battalion, and the men in his company. Delmont was here to either get his career ticket punched before being boosted up the ladder to the next rung or to prove something to someone. Either way, such ambitions could prove to be unhealthy to the people who were detailed to serve as stepping stones for the chosen. In a nutshell Emmett was warning Nathan that he would have to be careful, that he would have to keep checking his six, air force lingo for watching one's back.

In no mood to ruin what had been up to then a perfect evening, Nathan worked up a smile. "Well, gee, Emmett, I'm so glad you told me this. Care to tinkle on my other boot with some more wonderful news while you're at it?"

Walking up to the sink in the ladies' room, Christina Dixon stared into the mirror at the image being reflected back at her. The comely redhead attired in a simple, short-sleeved black cocktail dress adorned with nothing more than a simple strand of pearls didn't quite match the image of a professional officer, one she had labored to create. Yet the woman she saw was her, a woman who was as comfortable in heels and stockings as she was in the baggy battle dress uniform she wore day in and day out.

Leaning forward she grasped the edge of the counter and peered into her own eyes as if trying to see beyond the superficial, to discern some hidden truth that even she was blind to. For her this was no frivolous quest, a spur-of-the-moment self-examination triggered by an unexpected flux of hormones or circumstances. Christina had felt this conflict building for some time. If the truth be known it had always been with her, lurking below the surface but never fully addressed.

It concerned her very nature, who she was and how she expressed herself. She knew without having to give the matter any thought that she enjoyed being a woman. Despite the periodic inconveniences this entailed, she couldn't imagine being anything else. This was particularly true concerning matters of the heart. She reveled in the pleasure she derived from being with Nathan, enjoying her ability to enflame him almost as much as the passions he never failed to evoke within her while they made love.

Unfortunately for her a wicked twist of fate had saddled her with a taste for adventure and a knack for martial skills that required her to travel a path that was still viewed as unconventional by even the most enlightened and liberal societies. Everything about the Army fascinated the woman standing before the mirror wearing makeup and a dress. The challenge of pitting her abilities against an equally skilled and determined foe was exhilarating. Living in the field, being forced to give her all and then having to reach deep down inside in order to come up with more, made her feel more alive than anything else she had ever experienced. It even added a very special and most unique bond between her and the man she loved.

These two personas, roles she had worked so hard to perfect, fit her like a glove. Neither, however, was one that could stand on its own. Each provided her with a great deal of satisfaction and a sense of fulfillment that the other could not. And each required that she sacrifice certain aspects that were integral parts of the other. Herein lay the rub, the insurmountable dichotomy that was becoming harder and harder for Christina to deal with. Nathan's selection to command a Ranger company had been a cause of celebration, one that her professional side applauded, but one that meant protracted periods of separation from the man that she had given her heart to, a man she could not imagine being without.

The young chemical corps officer had hoped that over time she would be able to create an amalgam, a single entity that could move seamlessly from one role to the other without any conflict or friction, a dedicated professional soldier by day and a loving wife by night. Of course she should have known better. Other women who had traveled the road she was on had warned her that the day would come when she would have to make a choice, when she would no longer be able to balance the two. Her mother-in-law told her she could not have it all. "Just remember," Jan Fields-Dixon had warned her, "you can't cuddle up next to an outstanding résumé or an impressive job description at night. Nor can you claw your way to the top of the heap with a baby riding on your hip without leaving scars on the both of you that can never be erased. How you achieve harmony between career and family and what you decide to sacrifice to achieve that balance is up to you and you alone. Just don't wait too long before making up your mind."

That time, Christina feared as she looked at herself in the mirror, was near at hand. She felt it coming. She had experienced the tug on her heart that her need to pursue the prescribed career track she was on created when it required her to be separated from Nathan. Yet she found it all but impossible to imagine what her life would be like if she traded in army camouflage for baby comforters. Could she, she wondered really walk away from a life that took her to the edge and settled for one that consigned her to domestic bliss? Even now, as she struggled to resolve this unwelcomed conundrum she found it was the hardest choice she had ever faced in her life as well as being the most important. She would have but one chance to get it right, for once she closed the door to certain aspects of her being, she knew she would never be able to go back and revisit them.

Finished tending to her personal needs, Paula DeWitt left the stall she had been absconded in and stepped up to the mirror next to Christina. At first she didn't pay any attention to the manner in which Christina was staring into the mirror they were sharing, concentrating instead on washing her hands before arranging a bit of hair that had managed to break ranks with its neighbors. Only slowly did she begin to perceive that there was something more going on in that mirror than she could see. Pausing her grooming, Paula reached over and lightly lay her hand on Christina's forearm. "Hon, are you okay?"

Christina didn't blink as she continued to grip the countertop and gaze into her own eyes. "How do you manage?" she asked in a low, faint voice that was barely above a whisper.

Having spent her entire married life around women of all sorts to include those married to fellow officers Paula knew exactly what she was asking. Doing her best to sound cheery, she sighed. "I don't have time to manage. Why between my job, taking care of the house, raising two headstrong boys, and keeping track of Emmett I barely have time to breathe."

For the first time Christina turned away from her reflection as she looked into Paula's eyes. "Are you happy?"

The manner in which Christina asked her this question almost frightened her. It was one of those that demanded a serious, well thought out response, one that she was unable to provide. Instead, Paula smiled as she took Christina's hand. "I love my husband. And I love my children. If there's something else out there that I'm missing, I don't know what it could possibly be."

Straightening up, Christina gave Paula's hand a gentle squeeze. Then she turned toward the mirror once more and inspected the female before her to make sure that all was in order. When she was ready, she mustered up a smile and marched back out into the restaurant to where Nathan was waiting for her. As she and Paula approached the table her smile grew. "Well, have you two decided what you want for dessert?"

Without hesitation, Nathan returned her smile. "I told you. You!"

FORT LEWIS, WASHINGTON

Nathan's entry into the company orderly room was greeted with a round of knowing smiles. Those officers and senior

NCOs who had not known about the pending visit of his wife the day before had been let in on the closely guarded secret as they wandered in before their commanding officer showed up. Making his way toward the first sergeant's desk Nathan did his best to act nonchalant. The grin on his face, however, frustrated this effort. His first sergeant finished the job. Kicking back in his seat William Carney folded his hands across his midsection and beamed. "Well, I see you decided to give the missus a break."

Realizing that he had no hope of avoiding the subject Nathan opted to join in. "Now, Sergeant, you know that a gentleman never discusses such matters in public."

Springing forward, Carney slammed his hand on the surface of his desk. "Okay, you heard the captain. Clear this room." A chorus of laughter erupted.

Sensing that they had milked this little joke as much as possible, Nathan looked at the clock on the wall. "Shouldn't we be forming up the company for the morning run?"

Coming up to his side, his XO draped one of his long arms around Nathan's shoulders. "Just in case you're not up to it this morning, sir, I'm ready to take over the company."

Nathan looked up at Quinn's smug expression. "Lieutenant, the day I can't run you into the ground is the day I hang up my spurs. Now kindly remove that gangly limb of yours from me and get your bony arse out there in the company street."

While his officers and senior NCOs filed out of the orderly room, Nathan turned back to address Carney who had come to his feet. "Anything special on the schedule today?"

Carney pulled a yellow sticky note off his desk lamp's shade and handed it to Nathan. "You have a one on one meeting with the colonel at oh nine hundred this morning, sir."

Taking the note, Nathan stared at it. "Well, I guess I knew this was coming."

Carney moved out from behind his desk and came up

next to his company commander. "I don't think he's going to be too thrilled to see you again, sir."

Nathan knew better than to ask his first sergeant why he had made that statement. He already knew the answer. They had both seen Delmont just after he had been injured, which is a very vulnerable moment for anyone. To a Ranger being seen as weak or helpless is embarrassing. For a Ranger officer, it is doubly so. But for a commanding officer of Rangers, in particular one who has yet to make his mark on the unit he had just been assigned to lead, it could be catastrophic. If what DeWitt had told him the night before was even remotely true, Nathan feared that Robert Delmont would view him as a threat, an established hero within the battalion who had managed to increase his standing among his peers and the soldiers of the battalion at his expense. Just how far his new battalion commander would go to turn this sad state of affairs around to one that favored him was a question Nathan was not anxious to find out anytime soon, though he suspected that he would have a good idea by the time his nine o'clock meeting was over.

Sticking the note back on top of the stack of papers bound for his own office Nathan looked over at Carney. "Well, let's not worry about that now. We have a run to make and I'm ready to set a record."

Carney snickered. "Yeah, sure. I'll bet you are. Just be sure you hike up your sweatpants and make sure their drawstrings are secure, sir. I'd hate to see anything unsorted dragging behind you."

True to form Nathan showed up at his commanding officer's office early. It was a habit he had gotten into because of his father who ran his affairs on what he called "Vince Lombardi Time," which meant that if you were where you were supposed to be on time you were fifteen minutes late. The extra time was not wasted, being spent in Emmett DeWitt's office which was adjacent to the battalion commander's and served as an anteroom. Besides being the battalion adjutant, or S-1 charged with staff responsibility of all personnel matters within the battalion, DeWitt was expected to serve his commanding officer and the battalion executive officer as an executive secretary, maintaining their schedules, handling visitors as necessary, and screening calls coming into what was called the battalion command group. After serving as the commanding officer of a Ranger company DeWitt found this job quite tiresome, especially since Robert Delmont assumed command of the battalion. Lacking a personal aide de camp, a privilege afforded only to general officers in the United States Army, Delmont used DeWitt as if he were one.

Wandering into DeWitt's office like a cat creeping into a strange room, Nathan looked around as he advanced on the coffeepot DeWitt always kept full. After taking a paper cup off the stack and filling it, Nathan looked over at DeWitt. "What's the forecast for today?"

DeWitt looked toward the door leading to the battalion commander's office. Nathan wasn't asking about the weather outside, he was inquiring as to Delmont's mood. "Cloudy," DeWitt finally replied, "with a chance of early morning storms."

Staring out the window, Nathan slowly swirled the contents of his cup. "Great. Any particular reason?"

"Yes, you."

Turning, Nathan wandered over to the well-worn sofa that sat across from DeWitt's desk and plopped down in it. "Well, so much for making a good first impression."

"If I were you good buddy I'd keep my mouth shut and simply nod when appropriate and sound off with a hoorah every now and then."

To this sage advice, Nathan smiled. "Dear friend, what makes you think I'd do otherwise?"

DeWitt shook his head and let out a sarcastic chuckle. "Because I know you. Nate, if there's an ounce of sense anywhere in that brain housing of yours you'll check that smart mouth of yours at the door and play nice with the old man."

"Okay, okay. I'll do my best."

"Good. And don't forget, dinner at my place tonight nineteen thirty hours sharp. So do me a favor and don't show up at 7:15 with Christina. Paula doesn't appreciate that 'stand in the door' mentality of yours."

"Oh, I guess I can manage to find something to occupy those fifteen minutes," Nathan replied with a grin.

"Well, I know what you'll be doing for five of them. What will you do to occupy the other ten?"

Before he could answer, the intercom buzzed. Over the speaker Nathan heard Delmont ask DeWitt if Nathan had arrived. "Yes, sir. I'll send him right in."

Standing up, Nathan drained the coffee from the cup, dropped it in the trash can, and took a moment to straighten out his ADUs. When he was ready, he looked over at DeWitt. "Well, it's showtime."

Human nature does not permit a person to free himself from his own biases, prejudices, or preconceived notions. Everything one sees, hears, and experiences is shaded by his own beliefs and experiences. This is why two people looking at the same photo of a third whose expression is vague can express entirely different views on the emotional state of the person in the photo. One will say the photo reflects a person who is sad while the other can just as easily see a person who is thoughtful or reflective. Nor is a man, no matter how objective he endeavors to be, able to keep his personality from affecting his thoughts, his actions, or his conduct. How he responds to the world around him is governed by the sort of person he is.

When Nathan Dixon trooped into his office and presented himself in the manner prescribed by military regulations and tradition, Lieutenant Colonel Robert Delmont saw before him the scion of a military legend, a young officer who was scrambling up the same career ladder at breakneck speed as he was. Delmont prided himself on being able to spot the type. After all, he saw one whenever he had cause to look into a mirror. As best as he could tell the only difference between himself and young Dixon was that Dixon had connections that he could only dream of, not to mention an incredible run of luck when it came to the assignments that Delmont assumed Dixon's father had managed to engineer for his son.

While his own assignments up to this point were quite impressive by any measure, they all lacked something that young Dixon had in spades, combat experience. Delmont's sole brush with combat had been as a liaison officer during a brief one night raid in which he played no active role. It hadn't been all that different from his recent run in with the Abu Sayyaf. During that unfortunate affair he had also been little more than a hapless spectator, one that had been lucky to survive.

The young captain before him on the other hand had seen more combat than many professional soldiers see in a lifetime. Like the fortunate fisherman who always seemed to bring in a full net every time he cast it upon the waters, Nathan Dixon had moved from one tough assignment to the next, walking away from each with his career enhanced. Many who knew of him spoke of his luck. Those who knew him expected nothing less.

Robert Delmont did not believe in attributes that cannot be measured or quantified. Like hope, luck was not an element that a soldier is able to rely upon. In his mind there was a reason for everything, a motive behind every action, a meaning to be found in every word. To him even casual conversations were measured exchanges in which he took great care to ensure that the significance of what he was saying could not be mistaken. So as he returned Nathan's salute and motioned for him to take a seat before him Delmont was prepared to parse every word that passed between them.

"I know how busy you must be having just returned from the Philippines," Delmont stated slowly, taking great care as he did so in an effort to ensure that his still swollen tongue did not embarrass him as he spoke, "so I will not take up much of your time."

Sitting across the desk from him, Nathan found he had to employ every ounce of willpower at his command to maintain a straight face as he listened to his battalion commander's slurred words. Ignoring what Delmont was saying, he decided then and there that his vote was for Elmer Fudd, definitely Elmer Fudd.

"The task assigned to this battalion is a difficult one," Delmont continued, "one that demands a degree of dedication and professionalism that is extraordinary even for a unit of this caliber."

Nathan fought the urge to roll his eyes as a voice deep down inside him whispered, "No shit!"

"I will expect each and every man in this battalion to do more than their duty," Delmont declared. "Simply doing their job won't be good enough. Even giving the traditional one hundred and ten percent that rangers like yourself are used to won't be enough if we are going to meet the goals I have set for this battalion."

The course of Delmont's slobbering soliloquy was beginning to irritate Nathan. *You mean your goals,* he thought as he listened in silence.

"You are a company commander, the person who sets the standards and the pace for those under your command. You are also my personal representative, the man responsible for carrying out my orders, enforcing my policies, and seeing that all assigned missions are executed in a manner that reflects well upon this battalion. Anything less will not be tolerated."

As he listened to his new commanding officer do his best to overcome a swollen tongue as he articulated his view of the world and his place in it Nathan Dixon's anger gave way to one of somber reflection. From this moment forward his role would need to change. In addition to being a leader of combat soldiers charged with carrying out this man's orders he would need to become a buffer, a shock absorber to protect the men under his command from the abuses that this man's ambitions could very easily rain down upon them. It would not be easy. That sort of thing never was. But if he was to uphold his end of the unstated bargain that is struck between men who place their fates in the hands of the officer charged with leading them into battle, he would have to endure whatever came his way, no matter what price he had to pay.

When he had said all that he intended to Delmont paused as he looked into Nathan's eyes. "I hope you understand what is expected of you, captain," he stated without flinching.

Rising slowly from his seat, Nathan assumed a position of attention as he looked down on his battalion commander. "Yes, sir, I believe I do."

4

BEIRUT, LEBANON

The wisdom of going to Lebanon himself in order to clear up the differences between Abu Sayyaf and Hamas had been hotly debated between Summirat and his fellow compatriots. They went out of their way to point out that he would have no one he could really trust in the Middle East, a place populated by people who had made betrayal and duplicity something of a cottage industry. Summirat, however, would not be dissuaded. The issues that needed to be resolved were far too important to leave to others. Nor could he bring himself to trust handling the matter from Indonesia using electronic means given the ability of foreign intelligence services to monitor even the most secure system. Besides, after the abuse he had endured during the fractious meeting on Java, Summirat looked forward to coordinating some of the details himself.

At the moment there was little that he needed to do save sit back and enjoy the street-side café like any tourist would while reading his book, sipping his coffee, and waiting for his friends to show up, men who were not really his "friends" but rather the same people who had

made up the Hamas delegation that he had crossed swords
with at the Java conference. He was anxious to resolve
the differences that had arisen during the course of the
heated exchange between himself and them as quickly as
he could so that he would be free to go forward with his
program of drawing selected elements of American and
other coalition forces into sharp, bloody conflict on
ground of his choosing. "Even a cat can be taught to fear
a mouse if the mouse chooses not to behave as it should,"
he explained once it had been agreed by those that mattered that his ideas had merit. "We can never hope to kill
the cat, for in truth a single bite from even our most po-
tent fighters is easily shrugged off by the massive coalition that seeks to destroy us. But we can make them
fearful and cautious of us, unwilling to hunt us with the
same vigor and abandon that it now does. In time this
hesitation will allow us the freedom to pursue our larger
goals, to plan, prepare, and execute attacks against their
interests at home and abroad. With luck it might even
cause their own people to question the wisdom of continuing their war against us."

Despite the support, the Saudi, who had chaired the
gathering, pledged to this new initiative that there were
those who made it clear they would not abandon the
methods that they were comfortable with despite years
of effort that had yet to yield a single decisive result anywhere. This debate is what led to a rift in the already
fractious alliance that the many and diverse groups had
tried so hard to avoid. It was a desire to settle those differences that still separated Summirat's newly formed
coalition of supporters and what some were calling the
Old Guard that had left him little choice but to travel to
Lebanon.

From the corner of his eye Summirat caught sight of a
man stepping out of a doorway on the opposite side of the
street and a bit farther down from where he was sitting.
With practiced nonchalance, Summirat closed the book
before him with one hand and lifted the cup of coffee to

CAT AND MOUSE

h...
standin...
avoid draw...ing care to keep an eye on the ...
the foot traffic ...oorway who was doing his best to
who had emerged ...tention to himself. Satisfied that
to carefully studying no immediate threat, the man
He remained all but motion...rway turned his attention
ings until a trio of cars peeled ...ar traffic moving past.
and pulled up to the curb before him. ...nizing his surround-
...he flow of traffic

Then, on cue eight men surged out thr...h the same
door from which the first had appeared. They were all
Hamas. Two of them were the same men Summirat had
come to loggerheads with at the Java summit. Moving
at a brisk pace this tight little gaggle of leaders and
their bodyguards dispersed in a seemingly confused
and random manner before piling into the three cars
idling at the curb. This particular drill, which was not
impromptu at all was meant to confuse anyone who
might be interested in targeting the vehicle carrying a
specific person. When all were settled and the driver of
the lead car saw that his assigned passengers were
aboard his vehicle as well as the other two he began to
edge back into the stream of cars. Fortunately for him a
gap of some size opened between a late model
silver-gray Mercedes and a taxi when that taxi stopped
in the middle of the street to pick up a man and a
woman who had flagged it down from the sidewalk not
far from the doorway.

The small caravan of three Hamas vehicles rolled past
the small café where Summirat was enjoying the last of
his coffee. When the trail vehicle was even with him and
before the taxi following it pulled up parallel to him,
Summirat stood up, tucked the book he had been reading
under his right arm, and turned away. No one in the trio
of cars he had been watching took note of this.

The driver of the Mercedes, observing Summirat in
the driver's side mirror had. Without hesitation, he gave
the wheel of his car a quick jerk to the left while applying

76

HAROLD COYLE

the brakes, causing the rear of his vehicle ...tail around
and to the right, thus blocking ...eet. Caught off
guard the driver of the lea... vehicle slammed on
his brakes in a vain effo... a collision. In this he
failed, plowing into th... the Mercedes before him
even as the driver o... ...hicle was bailing out the passenger door opp...ercedes point of impact. Gaining his feet,
the driver of ...he ...ercedes fled the scene as fast as he
could, igno... ...he calamity that he had just caused.

Stunn... ...and rattled by the collision of their vehicle with
the Mercedes. the four men in the lead Hamas car were
slow to ...espond to this "accident." It was time that they
could ill afford.

Upon hearing the crash, Summirat turned, stepped
back behind the corner of the building, set his back against
the wall, and started to silently count backward from five.
When he reached "one" the Mercedes disappeared in an
explosion that engulfed the lead Hamas vehicle in a ball
of flame.

Not waiting to find out if any of their companions had
survived the cataclysm, the remaining Hamas tumbled
out of their respective vehicles and made for the doorway
they had emerged from but moments before. None of
them made it very far. Only a few were able to comprehend what was happening to them as the man and woman
who had flagged down the taxi stood behind the open
doors of that cab and fired their HK MP-5 submachine
guns into the surviving Hamas men. All told the entire
ambush was resolved in less than a minute, far quicker
than the debate back on Java had taken.

When they were satisfied that they had finished their
assigned tasks, the man and woman standing next to the
taxi threw their weapons into the backseat of the vehicle
and, together with their driver, fled on foot. They were
already out of sight when Summirat stepped out from
behind the corner of the building he had taken cover behind. Joining the gathering crowd of bystanders who now

came forward to gawk at the carnage left in their street, he took a moment to inspect each of the bodies as best he could without drawing undue attention to himself in an effort to make sure that the right people were well on their way to assuming room temperature. When he was positive all outstanding issues between him and the Hamas had been resolved to his satisfaction, Summirat turned away and began to make his way through the crowd. Within seconds he was gone.

ARLINGTON, VIRGINIA

Scott Dixon's sudden and brusque entry into the chief of staff's suite of offices startled General Henry Jones's entire personal staff. Dixon's expression was enough to alert Jones's aide-de-camp that the unscheduled intruder was in a foul mood. Coming to his feet, the aide did his best to rush out from behind his desk and throw himself in the path of the fast-moving general officer before he reached the door leading to Jones's office. The aide stopped short however when he caught sight of the unsheathed sword Scott was clutching at his side. Jumping back, the aide abandoned all thought of using his body to block access to his superior and instead resorted to pleading. "Sir! General Jones is on the phone at the moment with . . ."

Looking neither left nor right and showing no sign that he heard, much less cared, what the aide was saying, Dixon pressed on with undiminished fury. Even when he reached the closed door leading into Jones's personal office, Scott barely skipped a beat as he reached out, turned the knob, threw it open and passed through with a very concerned aide-de-camp following closely in his wake.

Across the room General Henry Jones, chief of staff of the Army and Scott's immediate superior sat slumped in his chair, safely absconded behind his desk holding the phone to his ear. Jones hardly flinched as Scott burst into his office with sword in hand. Clearing his throat, he cut off the person he had been listening to on the other end of the line. "Ed, something's just come up here," he stated laconically. "I'll call you back later." By the time he had reached out and returned the receiver back in its cradle Scott was standing right up against the front edge of his desk.

Without preamble or regard for the neat stack of folders and papers carefully arranged on his superior's desk, Scott tossed the old cavalry saber down. "Go ahead," he proclaimed loudly. "Cut 'em off."

Ignoring the enraged three star general before him and the ceremonial sword that normally hung on the wall behind Dixon's desk, Jones looked past Dixon at a very worried aide-de-camp standing in the open doorway. Behind him Jones could see a very anxious face belonging to a member of his security detachment. With the same calm voice that he used when dealing with even the most demanding situations, Jones waved them off. "Jerry, that will be all for now. Please close the door behind you." When they were gone Jones eased back in his seat, folded his hands together upon his stomach, and looked up at Scott. "Well," he declared while flashing a friendly smile, "what can I do for you today?"

"You might as well finish what that sneaky little bastard you saddled me with started and finish cutting my balls off."

Though he knew exactly what Scott was talking about, Jones opted to sidestep the issue until he had managed to calm Scott down a bit. "I don't think I could do that, not without consulting with Jan first. I expect she'd want first dibs on them.".

For the first time Scott held his tongue as Jones's efforts to use humor to check his anger began to have its effect. After staring into Jones's eyes for a bit longer,

Scott signaled his capitulation by looking down at the edge of the desk he was pressed up against and taking a deep breath. He took a step back at the same time he finally released it. "Oh, hell, Henry. You're right. They wouldn't look good tacked up on your wall with all your other awards and trophies anyway."

Satisfied that he had managed to disarm his long-time friend and most loyal subordinate, Jones said nothing as he allowed Scott to compose himself and collect his thoughts. Turning away, Scott folded his arms tightly across his chest and began to wander about the office as he did so. When he was back in control of his reasoning, he stopped and looked over his shoulder at Jones. "I guess it goes without saying that you had no prior knowledge of the meeting Palmer had with the Sec Def."

Losing his smile Jones's expression turned deadly earnest. "You of all people know better than that."

"Yes," Scott mumbled while shaking his head. "Still . . ."

"I know, Scott. I'm just as miffed as you are. But what are you going to do? The Sec Def is the top dog in this pound. If he happens to get it in his mind that he wants to talk to someone, he has every right to call him in and chat away with or without consulting us."

Turning to face Jones, Scott planted his fists on his hips. "Oh, please. Do you for one minute think that the secretary of defense just suddenly felt the urgent need to call Palmer to his office in order to discuss operations Palmer just happened to be promoting?"

Glancing down at his clasped hands, Jones responded in little more than a whisper. "No, I guess not."

For the first time Scott sensed that Jones really was just as miffed by this episode as he was. This did much to take the edge off his own anger. Mollified, Scott abandoned his aggressive stance before making his way over to a leather couch. With his anger spent, he plopped down on it like an unstrung puppet. After taking a minute to collect his thoughts, he looked over at Jones. "Ah hell. I'm getting too old for this."

Jones nodded as he lifted the sword lying on the desk before him and began to study it. "I think we both are, Scott. We're like this saber, a relic from the past. An outmoded piece of military hardware fit only to be hung on the wall to be admired by a new generation of warriors, soldiers who will stare at it in awe, wondering how such a crude weapon could once have been a useful instrument of war."

Unwilling to travel down the dark path that his superior's thoughts were taking them it was now Scott's turn to employ a spot of humor to steer the conversation. "Christ, Henry, you make it sound like we're a couple of old nags that are only fit for the glue factory."

After holding the sword up before his eyes for a moment longer, Jones laid it aside, sat up and turned to face Scott. "Yes, well, I suppose we both have one good charge left in each of us. I know I do."

Once more Scott sensed that Jones's mood was shifting, this time in a more meaningful direction. Looking down at the arm of the couch he was seated on, Scott stared at the back of his hand as he lightly ran the tips of his fingers along the arm's cool, smooth leather surface. "I'm game," he stated coyly.

"We've reached a critical point in this war of ours against terrorism," Jones announced calmly. "All the easy victories are behind us. All that lies ahead is a slow, unglamorous grinding away at fringe elements that have no definitive form, no true political goal to speak of and have no real geographic roots. Some don't even seem to have leadership in the conventional sense. In another day and age the people we are currently fighting would have been labeled anarchists."

"Unfortunately," Scott stated dryly, "unlike the anarchists of old who were content to toss a simple home-made bomb into the czar's carriage every so often the modern incarnation of those miscreants have access to stuff that can take out a fair portion of the population of New York City."

"Hence the need to keep after them. Unfortunately," Jones grumbled as he began to sink back down into his chair, "this war on terror is starting to resemble an effort to clear the Everglades of mosquitoes."

Letting out a cynical chuckle, Scott shifted about on the couch. "I dare say that would be far easier compared to the task we're faced with. In the swamp all one needs to do is simply stand still, let the little bloodsuckers come to you, and swat 'em before they take too much of your blood."

Raising an eyebrow, Jones regarded Scott a moment. "Strange you should make that analogy."

Settling back down, Scott looked at Jones as he waited for him to confirm what he already suspected was coming.

"A lot of people are beginning to become impatient with the way we are doing things," Jones began to explain, taking his time as he carefully selected his words. "Up until now the administration has been content to defer to our judgment concerning the overall strategy as well as to the day to day operations of this war. It has allowed us to pick those targets that we, the military in cooperation with the intelligence community, felt we were best able to deal with. Unfortunately, that attitude is in the process of changing.

"Pressure from Congress and their willing accomplices in the press are anxious to bring this war to some sort of definitive conclusion. As is their wont, those who occupy the far left use every opportunity to point out that funds we are using would be better used to expand their favorite social welfare program."

"So what's new?" Scott declared. "Even before they closed out Ground Zero in New York those folks were doing everything within their power to rein us in."

"Yes, that's true. In that regard nothing has changed. But the president's willingness to bow to calls from his political foes to bring this effort to an end has. That's what led to the appointment of our current Sec Def, a man who has made it clear that he was going to reshuffle the deck in order to bring, as he put it, 'fresh faces with fresh ideas to bear on an old problem.'"

"Hence Palmer's appointment as my deputy."

"And the meeting the Sec Def had with him this morning."

There was a pause as each man took a minute to consider the situation they now faced. Scott broke the silence. "Well, since it's clear that the new Sec Def doesn't give a hoot about the chain of command, how do we go about maintaining discipline around this place while fighting the other war out there the way it needs to be fought?"

Sitting up, Jones placed his hands on the desk before him. He stared down at them as he answered. "We do as we have always done, Scott. Our jobs. We render up our opinions on how best to do things when our superiors ask us for them and salute smartly when they issue us our marching orders. After we respectfully present the former and before the latter is set in stone we do our best to influence their decision while keeping our own people in line."

"People like Palmer."

"Yes, especially people like Palmer, a man who has aspirations and the connections to achieve them."

"Tell me about it," Scott mumbled. "I never thought the day would come when I'd find myself having to work around my own subordinates in order to do my job."

Looking up, Jones forced a smile. "Scotty my lad, I have every confidence that you will succeed."

Standing up, Scott shook his head. "When I was a spry young second lieutenant I believed that the chain of command was a real chain, a single unbroken link forged from steel that stretched from the very top all the way down to lowly little ole me. If someone had told me that the way we are doing things these days was how things really were done, I would have turned my gold bar in right then and there."

Jones smiled. "I doubt that very much." Coming to his feet, Jones once more lifted the saber before him with both hands. Slowly, the smile faded. This time when he looked up at Scott, there was a sadness in his expression that betrayed the frustration he was feeling. "Though many may see us as little more than anachronisms no different than this oversized knife of yours, we still have a place. Otherwise we wouldn't be where we are. I expect someday this sword of yours will be hanging on that wall behind me," he stated in a measured, tone. "When it is I hope you can do a better job of forging that chain than I have." With that, he offered the saber back to its owner.

Unable to find a suitable response, Scott took the ancient weapon back, nodded, and left.

FORT MEYER, ARLINGTON, VIRGINIA

Pausing only long enough to slip out of her heels, remove her coat, and hang it in the hall closet Jan Fields-Dixon set out to hunt down her husband. It didn't take long to find him. Like the creature of habit that he was, Jan found him tucked away in the room that they had set up as a combination den, home office, and personal library. He was in his usual position, slumped down in his favorite chair reading a book. Quietly she stole into the room, more due to her natural grace than from a desire to sneak up on the man she loved. Regardless of where they had lived, no matter how many times she did it, Scott always managed to act surprised when she finally reached him and planted a soft kiss on his forehead. For her part Jan was never able to figure out if she had indeed caught her beloved warrior off guard or if he was playing along with her. Not that it mattered. What was important to Jan was that it was a ritual they both delighted in, one that allowed them to enjoy a small sense of stability no matter where they lived.

After coming up behind him to plant a kiss on Scott's forehead she reached over the top of the chair with both arms, which she wrapped around her husband's neck before giving him a gentle squeeze. "Where are we tonight? In Gaul watching Romans thrash the barbarians, hiding behind a wall with the rebels plinking Redcoats, or marching through Georgia with Sherman laying waste to the Peach State?"

Taking a moment to enjoy Jan's touch and drinking in her scent Scott turned his face toward hers, which was now resting on his right shoulder. Responding to this Jan canted her head until their lips met. When they parted, he held her eyes with his a moment before he broke the spell. "I'm afraid you're wrong on all counts." Lifting the book he had been reading, he showed her the cover.

"*Hell in a Small Place* by Bernard Fall," Jan stated thoughtfully as she read.

"It's about the French defeat at Dien Bien Phu in 1954."

"Hummm, sounds more like an excellent title for a book about a cross country car trip with children."

Reaching up, Scott smiled as he took Jan's chin between his thumb and forefinger and gently shook her head from side to side. "You're being silly."

Standing up, but keeping her hands on his shoulders, Jan jokingly corrected him. "I'm being serious. I can remember one trip in particular when the boys were twelve and eight and we were headed for Fort Hood in the middle of the summer in a car with a malfunctioning air conditioner."

Scott let her chin go as he leaned his head back and chuckled. "Ah yes, I can remember it clearly. I think that's the first time Nathan had a near death experience."

"That wasn't the first time," Jan corrected him.

"And it wasn't the last either," Scott added.

The two remained stationary for a moment, each lost in their own vivid and now fond memories of that adventure. Such moments were becoming more common as these two highly successful professionals found themselves on the cusp of beginning a new adventure, one that would take them from the pinnacle of their separate careers to a life that would be even more challenging and demanding, one that would allow them to finally enjoy each other and the lifetime of memories they had accumulated.

Having finished playing out her own recollections of the trip to Fort Hood that long ago summer, Jan sighed as she gently ran her fingers lightly along the side of Scott's face. "Well, what should we do about dinner tonight? Shall we head for the kitchen and forage about in the hope of finding something edible or sally forth into the cold night and scour the surrounding environs for sustenance?"

"I took some boneless chicken breasts out of the freezer when I came in. I doubt if they're thawed, though."

"Chicken it is," Jan announced. "Next question. Do we bake it, fry it, or just eat it raw?"

To Jan's surprise, Scott did not answer her. Instead he took her hand and pulled her around until she was in front of him. While still holding her hand, he looked up at her. "What would you say if I decided to hang up my spurs after I finished this tour?"

Jan's first inclination was to respond with a witty comment. But something in her husband's expression told her that he was deadly serious. Having no idea what had brought on this sudden and totally unexpected line of thinking, Jan was wise enough to realize that this was not the time to pry into the causes behind it. Instead she simply lifted her free hand and placed it over Scott's. Doing her best to contain her own concerns, she managed to muster up a small loving smile. "Wither thou go, I go."

For a moment Jan thought she saw a hint of moisture

welling up in her husband's eyes. But before she could confirm her suspicions, Scott pulled their clasped hands toward him, bowed his head, and kissed the back of her hand.

5

FORT LEWIS, WASHINGTON STATE

Dawn was still an hour away when Nathan reluctantly slipped out of bed and made his way to the small bathroom, gathering up his clothing as he went. After carefully closing the door so as not to disturb his wife he flipped on the light and went about preparing himself for another long day.

Shuffling over to the sink, he paused before the mirror as he took a long hard look at the haggard face before him. The thrill of seeing Christina and being with her had been tempered by the stress that her presence at this time created. He was finding it almost too much for him to entertain his energetic and loving young wife after spending a harried day at the company. When he returned to his apartment each night he found Christina anxiously waiting for him, eager to cram into a single week all the things they had missed during their two months of separation, oblivious to the long and tiring day Nathan had endured.

During each and every day he faced a different set of challenges, from catching up on all the administrative matters that had languished while he had been in the field to personally overseeing the myriad inspections that were needed to sort out his men and equipment after a month of nearly round-the-clock operations in the Philippines. All of these competing demands, coupled with the physical and mental exhaustion that such a deployment extracts from a company commander, were proving to be almost too much for Nathan to handle.

Leaning forward Nathan studied the reflection of his own bloodshot eyes, wondering as he did if it had been like this for his father when he had been a young, hard-charging captain who still believed that he could take on the whole world single-handed and come out on top. Of course things had been different for him and his first mother. She had been a career wife and full-time mother. Though he couldn't remember much from those days, Nathan was able to recall how she'd go out of her way to keep him and his brother from pestering their dad after he returned from the field. "Daddy's tired," she would admonish them as she steered them away from the sofa where Scott would collapse as soon as he walked in the house after spending a long day with his company. Slowly things would return to normal as his father would regain his former energy and slip back into his old routines, around the house routines that would last until it was once more time for him to pack his kit and disappear to those mysterious places where army dads went for weeks and months on end.

The life he and Christina were sharing at the moment didn't allow him to enjoy that sort of laid-back, go-slow approach to reacquainting himself with his wife and slipping into something resembling a stable domestic routine. Like everything else in their lives the time they had to spend together was severely rationed, compelling them to seize every precious moment together that their respective careers and geographic dislocation allowed. It was this sort of frenzied urgency, one that he had to deal with even here in the stillness of his own bedroom that was proving to be more wearing than he had once imagined.

As much as he longed to say the hell with the Army, to turn out the bathroom light and crawl back into bed with Christina just this one time Nathan found he could not. He simply did not have that sort of courage. Even now, here in the calm of his own apartment, he could feel the pressure beginning to build, propelling him toward his next assigned place of duty. Straightening up, Nathan once more considered the man standing there in the mirror before him. Was that how he now saw his role in this so-called marriage of his, simply as another duty, a requirement that had to be met?

Bowing his head, he shook it from side to side as he turned away from the reflection that he could no longer face. Instead, he shuffled his way over to the shower. "It's too early for this shit," he mumbled as he cranked the shower handles to full on. Like everything else Nathan found he had only enough energy to take on each major crisis as it cropped up. At the moment the one he needed to focus on and deal with was getting his company ready to go back to the Philippines, a task he feared would be complicated by a commanding officer that he suspected was engaging in a personal campaign that had nothing to do with the battalion's stated mission.

"Downtime" is a term applied to a period during which a unit is for one reason or another allowed to slip from being fully mission ready. Downtime usually follows a major deployment such as the one Nathan's company had just completed. Yet downtime is not always synonymous with "slack time." On the contrary, more often than not it is a time of frenzied activity, a scramble by all assigned personnel to undo the wear and tear that a protracted deployment extracts upon equipment and weapons. In the case of Company A it meant that every item it relied upon to accomplish its assigned mission, from the state-of-the-art AN/PSC-5C Spitfire man-portable satellite communications set down to the very uniforms the soldiers who operated it wore, needed to be cleaned and carefully inspected to ensure that everything would meet the demands that would be placed upon it during the unit's next major operation whether it was a simple training exercise or a real-world contingency.

In the five days following the company's return to Fort Lewis the routine would not vary very much from one day to the next. There would be an early morning formation followed by physical training. Upon completion of that the unit would scatter for an hour or so while troops showered, dressed, and wolfed down some breakfast. Then there would be a few hours of maintenance on unit or personnel equipment, preparation for a formal inspection of that equipment followed by the inspection itself. Anyone failing that inspection would immediately correct the deficiencies and stand by to be reinspected at their commanding officer's leisure. To motivate his people to get it right the first time, Nathan always scheduled these reinspections after the balance of the company, those who had gotten it right the first time had been dismissed for the day.

Nothing was overlooked, nothing forgotten, as Nathan and his company's senior leadership methodically worked their way through every item that belonged to his company and his soldiers. Weapons already cleaned would be cleaned once again in preparation for a meticulous inspection during which each component of every weapon would be scrutinized and measured against established criteria to ensure that it was present, clean, and serviceable. Those parts such as barrels that were worn to the point where the weapon's accuracy was impaired or operating rod springs that no longer retained the flexibility required for proper and continuous function under all conditions were immediately replaced.

The same attention to detail was applied to mission essential nonlethal equipment such as radios, night vision devices, GPS receivers, handheld laser target designators, and countless other items that all contribute to the success of a Ranger company in battle. Either Nathan or his XO would have to inspect these critical, high-dollar items to make sure that they were fully functional and ready for use at a moment's notice. In cases where it was found during the course of an inspection that component parts or tools that belong to these items turn up missing or unserviceable, Army regulation required that an investigation be conducted to determine if the loss was unavoidable or due to carelessness or neglect on the part of the operator. Regardless of the cause, the missing or broken item had to be replaced. The crucial difference on how the matter was ultimately disposed of was determined by what the investigating officer found. If the loss was due to battle, the cost of replacing the item was absorbed by the Army much in the same way a business writes off fair wear and tear as a cost of doing business. If, however, there was human error such as neglect or simple stupidity the responsible soldier could be held liable and made to pay for some or all of the cost entailed in repairing or replacing the damaged or missing item. Since the price tag on some of the equipment Nathan's people handled on a daily basis exceeded their annual income several times over, this could be quite serious.

Unit equipment wasn't the only thing that needed to be cleaned, repaired, and replaced if missing or no longer serviceable. Each soldier had a vast array that comprised his personal kit starting with the most basic of basic items, his all-climate uniform or ACUs. This indispensable garb replaced the old battle dress uniform that came in either a woodland pattern of green, brown, and black and a desert pattern of tan and light brown. The ACUs were designed to provide the soldier with a combat uniform that could be used in any part of the world.

To protect soldiers from the extremes of weather when ACUs alone were not enough soldiers were issued a wide array of outerwear. This ranged from simple lightweight wet-weather gear designed to keep them dry for tours in the tropics across the full spectrum of climes to extreme

cold-weather gear that employed the most advanced fab-
rics known, permitting Nathan's men to survive and function in temperatures down to sixty below, though their
current cycle of deployments didn't give them much of a
need to break out the latter except when it came time to
be inspected.

On the battlefield a soldier needed to be protected
from more than the weather. This was what the body armor and ubiquitous Kevlar helmet each man was issued
furnished. Every one of Nathan's men were issued a specially designed vest known as the Ranger Armor System,
made of a Kevlar filler encased in a nylon camouflaged
printed carrier that weighed approximately eight pounds
depending on its size. An additional eight-pound ten-inch
by twelve-inch ceramic plate provided the wearer with
protection from shrapnel and small arms up to 7.62mm
rounds. Total cost of this item alone was over one thousand dollars.

To carry things those things that a soldier needed in
battle each Ranger was issued modular lightweight load-
carrying equipment, known as MOLLIE for short. The basic
component of this system was the LBV-88 load-bearing
vest that a pack/frame/pouch section was attached to. Arrayed on the outside of this vest were pockets and pouches
configured to the needs of the soldier who wore it, for the
weapon he was issued as well as common equipment
such as claymore mines or spare batteries for unit radios
that he might be assigned to carry.

Added to these major items were a number of small
but equally important items such as field dressings, canteens, a compass, sleeping bag, the helmet mount for AN/
PVS-7D night-vision goggles, and on and on and on. All
of this needed to be maintained and cared for by each
and every soldier in Nathan's company. All of it needed
to be accounted for. And on this day each and every item
needed to be laid out and spot-checked by Nathan and his
first sergeant.

The actual mechanics of those inspections were routine,

simple, and efficient. To make sure that a soldier in one platoon who might be missing an item didn't borrow it from a friend in another platoon in an effort to cover his backside, everyone was required to lay out all of their personal gear for inspection and inventory on the same day. The sequence that the platoons would be inspected was never announced in advance, though Nathan had a tendency to inspect them in order of merit, with the platoon that was currently in what was known as the "old man's doghouse" earning it the privilage to be inspected last.

Going from platoon to platoon Nathan, First Sergeant Carney, and the unit supply sergeant took their time as they conducted their inspections and inventory. Using a matrix that listed every soldier in a platoon down the left side of the page and each item a soldier had been issued as part of his personal kit printed across the top, the supply sergeant called off each item. In response every soldier then being inspected held that item up to show that he had it. They kept it aloft until Nathan and Carney checked to make sure that everyone had the item in hand and had had a chance to walk up and down the line of soldiers giving the item a quick visual inspection. If something didn't look right Nathan or Carney took the item in question in order to give it a closer, more thorough inspection. If someone did have the item the supply sergeant placed an "X" in the appropriate box. If the item proved to be unserviceable, a slash was recorded.

They were halfway through Lieutenant Edward Quintela's first platoon when someone down the hall yelled out, "COMPANY, ATTEN-TION!" Stopping in midstride both Nathan and Carney turned and looked at each other. Since Nathan was there and everyone in the company knew that the bellowed call for junior ranking soldiers to assume a position of deference meant to convey respect to a superior ranking officer could only mean that someone with more rank than he had entered the building. Knowing full well that neither the battalion XO nor the operations officer, who were both majors, was in the habit of dropping in on a company commander unannounced, that left only one possibility, the battalion commander. Anxious to head his superior off as quickly as possible and steer him away from those areas of his company he didn't want Delmont in, Nathan ordered his first sergeant to continue with the inspection while he responded to what his troops jokingly referred to as an intruder alert.

Nathan found Delmont just outside his company orderly room speaking to Peter Quinn, his executive officer. Quinn had led Company A's First Platoon when Emmett DeWitt had commanded the company, taking it into action on several occasions and earning him the nickname "Lead Bottom" as a result of a wound he had received during one of those forays. A wound, no matter how light, can effect a man in many ways. According to DeWitt it had calmed Quinn down. "He bounced back from his wound," DeWitt stated, "and came back a better officer and a damned good Ranger. If I could be sure that shooting a lieutenant in the ass would always have that sort of effect, I'd shoot every last one of them there as soon as they reported in." Quinn's subsequent performance as a platoon leader had earned him the privilege of staying with the company while most of his peers were shuffled off to assignments outside the 3rd of the 75th as soon as they had put in their time as a platoon leader. When Nathan found Quinn he was standing before Delmont at the front door of the company, taking his time briefing the battalion commander on what the company was doing at the moment while physically blocking Delmont from preceding any farther into the company without making it apparent that this was what he was doing.

Coming up next to Quinn, Nathan saluted Delmont. "Sir, how may I help you?"

Delmont thanked Quinn for briefing him, which was his way of dismissing Quinn before turning his attention on Nathan. "I assume you were inspecting one of your platoons," he stated without making any effort to greet his subordinate.

"Yes, sir, my First Platoon."

"Well then," Delmont commanded, "lead off."

Nathan had hoped that Delmont was here for another reason, but more or less suspected that his luck just wasn't that good. Delmont's pronouncement simply confirmed his worst fear. Doing his best to keep his expression from betraying him Nathan nodded. "Yes, of course, sir. If you'll follow me."

The appearance of their battalion commander startled most of First Platoon. As they had been deployed in the Philippines when Delmont had taken command few had laid eyes on him. Even at the crash site on Jolo only the unit medic, the company radioman, and a handful of soldiers charged with securing the immediate crash site had taken the time from their tactical assignments to give Delmont a second look. Seeing him right there among them was bad enough. Having him show up when all of their personnel gear was laid out ready to be inspected made more than a few of the men nervous.

By now they were all used to their company commander's way of doing things, what he was interested in checking and what he tended to ignore. While it wasn't an exact science and Nathan occasionally threw them a curveball most of the Rangers in Company A felt comfortable enough with their captain's habits that they paid less attention when caring for those things they knew he probably wouldn't check so that they could devote more to those he did. Delmont on the other hand was a total unknown. What he would do and how demanding his standards were was a question they suspected they were about to find out.

Robert Delmont didn't leave them guessing for very long. With the same sort of skill that a predator uses when singling out the weakest member of the herd he quickly made his way to where Specialist Four Anthony Park stood next to his gear. Coming to attention, Park did his best to keep his eyes front lest they betray his nervousness. Coming up behind Delmont and to his right Nathan placed himself in Park's line of sight. For the briefest of moments the two exchanged glances, but it was long enough for Nathan to sense that all was not well. Taking in a deep breath he set about preparing himself for what he feared was coming; leaning a bit to one side as he did so in an effort to peek around Delmont and see what he was doing.

Bending over, Delmont scanned the neat layout before him. Going for the quick kill he reached over and picked up one of Park's canteens. Turning it upside down he held it at arm's length, watching a trickle of water flow out and onto the rest of Park's display. This of course was a major no-no. After returning from an exercise all canteens had to be emptied and allowed to dry lest any traces of water left in them stagnate while stored between exercises. Without a word Delmont dropped the canteen and turned his attention to the camouflage cover for Park's helmet. While holding it in his right hand, Delmont slid his left hand into the opening and rummaged around inside the cover until he was able to poke a finger through a small tear he had noticed. Standing up, Delmont held the camouflage cover inches in front of Park's face. "What's this?"

"A hole, sir."

"Is it supposed to be there?"

Park shook his head. "No, sir."

Spinning about, Delmont faced Nathan while still holding the camouflage cover at eye level between the two of them. "Captain Dixon, this platoon is not even close to being ready for inspection. I dare say if I took the time to check the other platoons I'd find the same sort of inattention to detail everywhere."

Pausing, Delmont glared at Nathan almost daring him to say something, to come up with an excuse. Realizing that any answer he came up with would be the wrong one no matter how valid it was Nathan opted to hold his tongue.

When he concluded that his goading wasn't going to elicit the sort of retort he had hoped for Delmont threw Park's camouflage cover on the ground behind him while maintaining eye contact with Nathan. "If this is a sample of what the rest of your company looks like I dare say I'm disappointed."

Again there was a pause. And again Nathan chose not to fill it.

"I'm not going to waste my time finding out if this is so. Instead," he stated as he turned away from Nathan and raised his voice so everyone in the room could hear him, "I'm going to give you until nineteen hundred hours tonight to prepare for my inspection of this company."

For the first time Nathan found himself having to speak up. "Sir, I've already released one of my platoons."

Slowly rotating his head about, he looked at Nathan. When he spoke, Nathan could not help but notice the hint of a smile that lit Delmont's face as he spoke. "Well then, I guess you'll just have to recall them."

Rather than respond with the typical "Hooah" that one would expect from a Ranger, Nathan murmured a weak "Yes, sir," as he struggled to keep the seething anger welling up from within in check.

Satisfied that he had achieved what he had set out to do Delmont took one last look at all the long faces that filled the room before leaving it.

When he was gone, together with Nathan and the first sergeant following in his wake, a stunned Park looked around the room. "What in the hell just happened?"

After seeing Delmont out of the company area, Nathan, Quinn, and Carney marched into Nathan's office. Slamming the door behind him Carney glanced back and forth between the two officers. "What in the hell just happened?"

Unable to speak due to his own efforts to contain his anger, Nathan slowly made his way around his desk where he plopped down in his seat. Leaning back as far as he could, he stared up at the ceiling for a moment. Across the room Quinn shuffled over to a worn chair and took a seat, staring at his feet as he did so without saying a word. That left Carney alone, standing in the center of the room with his hands on his hips. Making no effort to hide his anger he looked at Nathan. "What did we do to deserve this?"

Lowering his eyes, Nathan looked at his first sergeant a moment without speaking. He suspected that he knew the answer to this but thought better than sharing his thoughts with his subordinates. To have done so would have been disrespectful to his superior. And while he was more than justified in doing so, Nathan knew better than to openly express his opinion of his superior in the presence of subordinates. One of the guiding leadership principles that he lived by was that respect was not automatically given, that it was earned. To achieve this a leader had to be more than tactically and technically proficient. He had to respect those who served under him and those he served. Anything else was unacceptable, regardless of circumstances.

"We have our marching orders First Sergeant," Nathan stated slowly, calmly. "Get ahold of the folks in Second Platoon who are still here and give them the bad news. I'll let everyone else know."

For a moment Carney simply stood there, looking at his company commander as if he wanted to say something. Nathan's deceptively serene expression, one Carney knew was being forced, served to warn him away from doing so. Instead, he took a deep breath. "Hooah, *sir.*"

Nathan found Christina curled up asleep on the sofa of his small apartment's combination living and dining room lit only by the flickering image thrown off by the unwatched television. After taking a moment to kick off his boots and remove his ACU shirt he made his way across the room toward her. Easing himself down onto the floor next to her, he leaned forward and lightly kissed her.

Her response was automatic and quite natural. With eyes still shut, she reacted to Nathan's gentle stimulation like a newborn kitten whose eyes had yet to open blindly seeking sustenance. Arching her neck forward ever so slightly, she pressed her lips against his while parting them ever so slightly.

Slowly Christina began to stir, reaching out to embrace Nathan as she did so. This continued until Nathan, bending over her at an awkward angle, finally found he had to break their embrace and back away. For the first time Christina opened her eyes. "Well," she sighed while stretching, "that was certainly worth the wait."

Settling back on his heels, Nathan averted his eyes as he muttered apologetically, "Things didn't go as well as I had hoped today."

When he made no effort to expand upon this simple, mournful statement Christina reached out and laid a hand on his cheek. "Want to talk about it?"

Placing his hand over hers and gently pressing it against his cheek, Nathan shook his head. "No." Then, looking into her eyes, he forced a smile. "I was hoping to make your last night here special."

Sensing that her husband was holding back, Christina returned his smile. "You don't know how much just being here, able to reach out and touch you, means to me. I love you, Nathan Dixon. I love you more than anything in this world."

Her shooting words, her soft hand upon his cheek and the sweet innocence of her expression worked their magic, allowing Nathan to set aside his cares and enjoy what little time he had left with the woman he so loved. Keeping hold of the hand she had laid on his cheek, Nathan stood up. No words passed between them as he helped her up from the sofa and led her to the bedroom. For the balance of the night the world outside Nathan's small apartment didn't exist. The cares of the world that Nathan had carried home that night like a rucksack full of rocks was, for the moment forgotten.

6

MINDANAO, PHILIPPINES

The operation was a limited one, designed by Hamdani Summirat to provide his newly reorganized military wing of the Abu Sayyaf with some practical experience and to test his theory. The laboratory for this brutal experiment was a small out-of-the-way town on the periphery of the Zamboanga del Sur region of the island, a rural community that matched Summirat's modest goal.

The population of the village was Cebuano, a distinction that is based upon the language the villagers spoke as opposed to their origin since 90 percent of all Filipinos are racially indistinct from each other. The chasm that set these rural people apart from their brethren who populated the northern and central islands of the Philippines was based almost exclusively upon their religion, for the villagers were Muslim Filipinos, a people who are collectively known as the Moros.

Throughout the modern history of the Philippines, a period one could loosely define as the period that began with the Spanish conquest of the islands in the early 1500s, the Moros population has remained outside the mainstream of national politics. In part this was due to the fierce tribal loyalties that still plague the Philippines as a whole but mostly it was their refusal to convert to Catholicism, the faith of their conquerors and of those Filipinos who eventually became the nation's ruling elite. Every effort to "Christianize" the Moros, first by the Spanish, then the Americans, and finally by well-meaning but badly misguided independent missionaries, have resulted in failures that have often been quite bloody. It was the distrust and fear that these efforts engendered in the Moros that Summirat sought to exploit on this day.

The village was the home of a small evangelical mission that included a small clinic and school. While the population was grateful for the services that the missionaries provided to them in the clinic all were suspicious of preaching that was administered by the ever cheerful Americans in tandem with the "free" medical care they dispensed. It was a price that the village Datu, or traditional Moros communal leader, found repugnant.

Equally irritating to the Datu and many of his people was the presence of an understrength company belonging to the Auxiliary Reserve Units and Citizen Armed Forces Geographic Units, or CAFGU. Ostensibly the CAFGU is the national militia of the Philippines, comprised of locals who are trained to augment the small Filipino Army in maintaining internal security against foreign and homegrown insurgents. Selected elements of the CAFGU located in those areas where this threat was particularly acute, such as Mindanao and the Sulu Archipelago, were not actually true part-time militia but full-time soldiers commanded by an officer of the regular army and led by professional NCOs who were mostly non-Muslim. This arrangement led to a split loyalty among the militiamen who were recruited from the region and lived their lives in accordance with the sharia, or sacred Islamic laws, and the norms of their community. This naturally put them at odds with their Christian officers and NCOs who owed their allegiance to the government in Manila.

Both the Christian mission run by foreigners and the presence of the CAFGU company commanded by professional soldiers who were just as alien to the locals as the Americans created a tension that made the village ripe for exploitation by a ruthless and well-financed group such as the military wing of the Abu Sayyaf, an organization that Summirat had managed to seize undisputed control of. The methods employed by Summirat to seize and secure the village had changed little from those he had previously used. The men who had served with him before and formed the core of his expanded command knew exactly what was expected of them. What had changed was the degree to which he had prepared his chosen battlefield. Previous raids had been just that, quick small-scale attacks intended to do little more than secure hostages and harass the local government. They were never part of a comprehensive strategy that had discernible and realistic goals that could be measured if one called the esoteric dream of creating an independent Islamic state centered on Mindanao and the Sulu Archipelago through disjointed and sporadic acts of terrorism against foreign civilians a strategy.

On this day Summirat would enjoy something he had never had before, the willing assistance of the local populace. Not only was the village Datu aware of what was coming and thus free to encourage his people to stay clear of the clinic, but many of those men who were supposed to defend the village against the sort of terror that Summirat's fighters were about to visit upon it managed to absent themselves from their billets either through authorized leaves or by slipping away into the night. By the time the first hint of day began to lighten the eastern sky the village was quiet and completely undefended.

Using trucks "taken" from a local plantation, three squad-size elements approached the village, two from the east and one out of the west just as night was giving way to the coming dawn. There was no advanced guard, no Abu Sayyaf fighters lingering in the shadows waiting to warn their truck-mounted brethren of trouble. The bold entrée of Summirat's fighters was made possible by information gathered surreptitiously from the villagers themselves over the course of several weeks as well as assurances from the Datu that no one would lift a finger against them. To ensure that the Datu did not experience a sudden change in heart at the last minute, a man who had served with Summirat for years and whom he trusted to carry out his orders to the letter was holding the Datu's oldest son at an undisclosed location until the operation had been completed.

The first of the two trucks coming in from the east trundled up to and through the gate of the small CAFGU compound that contained a two-story barracks building to house the enlisted militiamen, an armory constructed of concrete blocks and quarters for the NCOs assigned to the unit from the regular army. The second vehicle of this pair continued on into the center of the village where the commanding officer of the company lived in a house with his wife and three children across from the home of the village Datu. The third truck emerging from the predawn gloom didn't have far to go in order to reach the mission compound situated along the road on the edge of the village. Despite pleas from the regional military commander to the evangelical group that had established the mission to locate their facility next to the CAFGU compound, the Christians had opted to separate themselves from the military as far as they could. The missionaries wanted to do everything in their power to demonstrate to the locals that they were not associated with the government in Manila. This, of course, was wishful thinking on their part, for in the eyes of the villagers the goal of the missionaries was no different from that of the commander of the CAFGU company. To them the missionaries and the professional soldiers were uninvited strangers from a world they did not understand, foreigners who sought to separate them from their faith and their traditions, a belief that Summirat had little trouble in exploiting.

Piling out of their vehicles with their weapons at the ready the Abu Sayyaf fighters fanned out, each man making for the spot he had been assigned. No one hindered them. No one raised an alarm. The militiamen who should have been standing watch at the gates and over the village as a whole were gone, leaving no one but a few barking dogs to warn their sergeants and the missionaries of their pending doom.

On both the east and west sides of the village the sound of doors being kicked in startled those at the CAFGU compound who were still there and the missionaries. Tumbling out of their beds the startled victims came face-to-face with armed, grim-faced men hovering over them. No one spoke, no one cried out in alarm except for the CAFGU commander's wife and some of the mission's staff. Everyone knew who the intruders were and they suspected that they knew why they were there. For his part the head of the missionaries, a white-haired elderly man born and raised in Oklahoma, did his best to calm the fears of his fellow workers as they were herded together in the courtyard of their small station. The two female nurses and three young women who had left their middle-class homes in the U.S. in order to travel to the Philippines to spread the word of God huddled together in a tight knot, as much to hide the embarrassment they felt at being paraded about in their sleepwear as they were out of fear over what was about to happen to them. Making his way to them despite the protestations of the man assigned to guard him, the senior missionary did his best to calm the women's fears. "We'll be all right," he insisted. "Trust in God and do as you're told and we'll all come through this ordeal safely." Try as hard as they might, some of the women found themselves unable to find comfort in his heartfelt reassurances, encouragements that he continued to bestow upon each of them as they were led away one by one into their small chapel where the most phlegmatic member of the assault team waited to dispatch them.

On the other side of the village the officers and NCOs of the CAFGU who had been sent to this out-of-the-way village to protect it from the sort of thing that was now happening didn't have any illusions over what their fate would be. Nor did Summirat's men make any efforts to deceive them as those at the mission did. With utmost ruthlessness, the sort that hunted men are able to perfect after spending years of running and hiding from over-whelming forces arrayed against them, Summirat's fight-ers laid into the leaders of the CAFGU company where they found them. The method of execution was the sim-ple, ubiquitous machete, a tool that men who fight in the jungles learn to wield with great skill and effect. The Abu Sayyaf fighters took their time as they hacked away at the lifeless bodies long after their victims had drawn their last breath. They were under orders to make sure that those who found the mutilated remains understood the message Summirat intended to leave in the wake of this foray. The rules of the game he was playing had changed. He was through with being little more than a glorified kidnapper. Through the strength of his convic-tions and the actions of his followers he was determined to give meaning and purpose to the cause he had strug-gled so long for, regardless of the price that would have to be paid.

To a government that had managed to convince itself that they had all but won their protracted war against Moros insurgent groups such as the Abu Sayyaf, the brutal at-tack staged by Summirat's revitalized command proved to be as much an embarrassment as it was a shock. To prove that this event was little more than an anomaly, a last-gasp effort staged by a desperate band of die hard fanatics, the government in Manila demanded that the armed forces immediately seek out and destroy those re-sponsible for the atrocities. It was a mandate that the Army accepted without hesitation, especially when the details of what the terrorists had done to the professional officers and NCOs assigned to the CAFGU became known. In his instructions to the regional commander responsible for the operation, the chief of staff of the Philippines Armed Forces made his expectations clear. "Be aggressive, be decisive, be swift. Hunt the enemy day and night. Allow them no rest. Give them no quarter." These were orders that the Army was more than willing to carry out. To the chief of staff's admonishments, the regional commander added his own addendum to the units dispatched to seek out and destroy the insurgents. "Be brutal. Any commander who is even suspected of holding back will be punished."

The initial pursuit of the raiding party proved to be quite easy. The Datu and all of his people were quite forthcoming when asked about the attackers and the direction in which they had fled. No one conducting the interrogations of these "victims" bothered to ascertain who they feared most, the Abu Sayyaf who might return to punish them if they did not adhere to the detailed instructions Summirat had dictated to them or the troops themselves who took advantage of every opportunity to let it be known that they would do whatever it took to find the men who had murdered their fellow soldiers and Christians.

The lack of paved roads in the region and recent rains made tracking Summirat's fighters ridiculously simple. The distinctive tire tracks left by the trucks they had used led the troops to a spot not more than twenty miles west of the village where the raiders had abandoned the trucks and taken to foot. The only thing that caused the pursuing troops some concern was that the insurgents had made no effort to destroy or disable the trucks they had used earlier in the day. They had even left the keys in the ignition as if inviting anyone who found them to drive them away. The only person with the company assigned to hunt down the raiders who was able to supply a reasonable explanation for this was a young intelligence officer detached to that company from the division's staff. "You cannot expect to win the hearts and minds of the people you are trying to rally to your cause if you go about stealing their property and destroying it," he pointed out. "Instead," he grimly continued in an effort to caution the commander of the company he was traveling with, "you force the government troops who are already viewed as interlopers to the local populace to do that."

His words fell on deaf ears. The infantry captain in command of the unit charged with pursuing the Abu Sayyaf insurgents was in no mood to listen to such cautionary advice. He had watched while his men had collected the dismembered pieces of the CAFGU unit commander and prepared them for burial along with his wife and three children. He had listened to the pitifully lame excuses each of the CAFGU militiamen hauled before him had rendered during their interrogations as to why they had been absent from their posts or unable to prevent the butchering of their own NCOs. He had little doubt that they, as well as the Datu and his people, had been warned, a suspicion that made them as guilty of the unspeakable murders as the terrorists themselves. And while he did manage to restrain himself from dealing with the locals in a manner he believed their complicity deserved, he made no effort to mask the disdain he felt for each and every civilian who crossed his path. His unvarnished rancor set an example that every man under his command followed and amplified according to his own disposition and mood as the opportunity permitted.

Once the discovery of the trucks had been reported and the immediate area around them thoroughly searched, the captain wasted no time as he plunged headlong into the jungle at the head of his company to continue their pursuit. As they had while they had been mounted, the Abu Sayyaf fighters made no effort to cover their tracks, leaving the captain to conclude that speed was of utmost importance to them. Once more the young intelligence officer who was traveling with them stepped forward as he tried to warn the captain that all might not be as it seemed. For his pains he received a rebuke that left little doubt that the captain was in no mood to listen to anyone. "I have my orders," the captain snapped, "orders which I will gladly execute to the letter."

With no choice but to pull back and keep his own counsel, the intelligence officer made his way to the rear of the column in an effort to stay as far away from the captain as possible. He remained there throughout the balance of the day as the company pressed forward as quickly as the muddy trail and dense jungle permitted, taking as few breaks as was feasible. He was still there when the company came across a fast-running stream swollen by recent rains just as the light of day was beginning to fade. Unlike the countless streams they had previously encountered that day, this one could not be taken in stride. To effect a crossing without having men bowled over and swept away by the swift current or waste the time needed to construct a rudimentary rope bridge, the captain ordered his lead platoon to form a human chain across the stream. This technique required those designated to form the chain to sling their rifles over their backs, link arms, and plunge into the raging stream, bulling their way forward until they spanned its width. Once this platoon had managed to do so the remainder of the company would be free to make their way along the human chain from the near bank where they stood to the far bank. When everyone was across, each man who made up the chain would detach himself from it and claw his way along what was left until everyone was safely standing on the far side.

Maintaining their dispersion, the platoons farther back in the column waited until the chain was ready and they were called forward one by one to make their crossing. The progress was slow and difficult, but it was faster than any of the other alternatives available to them. The last platoon in the long serpentine column, saddled with most of the company's heavy weapons as well as the intelligence officer, was in the process of cuing up in preparation to commence their crossing when the first mortar round fell dead on in the middle of the stream, tearing the chain apart in a shower of water, churned-up mud, and dismembered human limbs. Before anyone could react the other rounds of this initial volley impacted on both banks of the river, drowning out the screams of pain and terror in a crescendo of explosions. Even the chatter of small arms fire that erupted from concealed positions and ripped through the ranks of those soldiers who were waiting to cross was all but muffled by the roar of detonating mortar shells.

Instinctively the intelligence officer flattened himself on the ground, barely escaping being cut down by the raking fire that a well-positioned machine gun somewhere off to his left marched up and down the column of waiting soldiers with deadly effectiveness. The whine of the bullets zinging just above his head and a blizzard of vegetation shredded by near misses raining down on him convinced the young officer that any effort to stand up and run or try to exercise his authority over the enlisted men who had thus far survived this withering fire would be suicidal. Besides, he kept repeating to himself as he pressed his face into the cool, wet mud of the trail they had been following all day, he was a staff officer. It wasn't his place to take charge, a point the captain who had been leading this company had made quite clear.

Any further thought of doing something heroic but short-lived was brought to an abrupt end when the body of a soldier who had reached the end of his wits and had attempted to flee toppled over on top of the forlorn intelligence officer. Knocking the wind out of him, the weight of the lifeless corpse across his back quickly became all but unbearable. As soon as he regained his senses the young officer immediately began to squirm about in the mud in an effort to free himself. In the process of doing so, he became aware that each time he moved the body lying on him jerked and quivered as if still alive. It took him a moment to realize that these spasmodic twitches were being caused by enemy bullets slamming into the body that was pinning him to the ground. As repugnant as this was to him, the intelligence officer quickly grasped that his fellow soldier was providing him a flesh and blood shield, one that he had not sought but now willingly accepted. Doing his best to relax and blend in with the dead that lay scattered all around him, the young officer decided that there was nothing more he could do. So he settled in to await his fate, praying as he did all he could to block out the sounds of battle and the cries of wounded men.

The captain and the two platoon leaders who had made their way across the human bridge before the ambush had been initiated did not have the luxury of waiting. They had to do something. It was their duty to not only do all they could to salvage some sort of control over their shattered command, but also the orders that had sent them on this headlong pursuit demanded that the captain find a way to turn the tactical situation around and go over to the attack. Fortunately for him the mortars that had been raining death down upon the human chain had ceased fire and most of the enemy's small arms fire being directed at the rear of the column seemed to be coming from well-concealed positions located on the other side of the stream. Making his way back from the head of the column where he had been when all hell had broken loose at the crossing site to a spot from which he could survey the stream and the far bank the captain quickly sized up the situation. He forced himself to ignore the lifeless corpses of his soldiers who had been caught out in the open as they drifted downstream or washed up along the banks of the stream. Instead he focused his entire attention on trying to assess the strength of the enemy he faced based on the volume of fire that they were directing against his men who had been waiting to cross over and how best to employ the men he had under his immediate control to strike back.

With one full platoon and the bulk of another at his disposal unengaged on this side of the stream the scheme of maneuver the captain came up with was as simple as it was self-evident. When he had a clear picture in his mind of the situation before him he ordered the lieutenant of the lead platoon, which had thus far escaped unscathed, to take his platoon a hundred meters or so upstream and recross it. Once they were on the other side and deployed, he was to move against the enemy positions from behind. As that maneuver was being carried out, the other platoon that had crossed would cover their assault with a base of fire from positions along the length of the stream on the banks of the stream where they currently stood. Though the captain and both his platoon leaders knew that this covering fire would be wildly inaccurate, the captain expected it would keep the enemy pinned or at least preoccupied until the maneuvering platoon was close enough to overrun the enemy positions. Once the enemy realized they were in trouble and turned to flee, the platoon deployed along the stream would join the attack by storming back across the stream and join the melee.

After issuing his orders and watching the maneuver platoon disappear into the jungle to begin their encirclement of the enemy positions, the captain turned to assist the platoon leader selected to provide covering fire. Both officers went about positioning those soldiers who remained behind along the far bank of the stream in locations where their fire would have the greatest effect on the enemy on the other side. They were in the midst of completing this redeployment when a hail of small arms fire swept through their ranks from behind. Startled, a few men managed to correctly assess the situation and spin about on their stomachs to face the new threat, one directed against them by the very foe they had been pursuing most of the day. Firing blindly into the jungle to their rear, these startled soldiers did their best to return the deadly accurate fire that was shredding their ranks. Others, totally unnerved by this stunning turn of events, either tried in vain to burrow into the ground beneath them or lost their heads completely and jumped to their feet in an effort to flee.

As with their comrades at the rear of the company column who had been raked by deadly accurate fire at the beginning of this ambush, the Filipino soldiers who their captain had taken such great care to position didn't stand a chance against this new attack that was coming from a totally unexpected quarter. With all their officers and most of the NCOs cut down by the first burst of deadly fire directed at them those who could still do so threw down their weapons and tried to surrender. To a man they failed, for it is all but impossible for soldiers locked in close combat to capitulate. A foe watching for any sign of resistance cannot take the time to determine if the man attempting to rise up off the ground across from him is trying to surrender or preparing to rush forward and attack. The chaos and pandemonium of close combat seldom allows a soldier little time to think clearly. If he hopes to live he must respond as he is trained and in a manner that affords him his best opportunity to survive. In combat it is often easier to pull a trigger and be sure than to hold back and wait, hoping that you made the right choice.

Having managed to move his platoon a fair distance before the vicious little firefight that swirled around the crossing point broke out, the young lieutenant who had been sent to recross the stream and attack the initial ambushers from the rear found himself in a most difficult position. Should he continue on as he had been ordered to in an effort to save those who had been with the rear of the column? Or would it be better if he doubled back with his platoon and did what he could to assist his captain and the men with him at the crossing site? Ordering his platoon to hold in place the young officer chose to hold off making a final decision and instead tried to raise his company commander on the radio. Quite naturally his calls went unanswered since both the captain and his radioman were already down, dead, or well on their way to being so. Not having any way of knowing this, the platoon leader repeated his efforts over and over and over.

Around him, those members of his platoon who could hear these vain attempts to contact their company commander alternated between looking at their platoon leader and then at each other. No one said a word but all entertained the same questions. What would he do, they asked themselves as the din of the vicious little battle downstream echoed through the jungle around them. What, they wondered, did the Fates have in store for them? Would their lieutenant lead them back the way they had just come and throw them into the maelstrom that was tearing apart those they left behind? Would he press on and follow orders that they all knew had been superseded by the second ambush?

In the end the young infantry officer did neither. Sensing that both of those options would do nothing more than throw his men away trying to salvage something from an engagement that he guessed was already lost, the platoon leader set about deploying his men into a loose all-round perimeter. "We will hold here until the situation clarifies itself," he halfheartedly told his squad leaders. Though none of his NCOs knew what he meant by that, they were quite content to comply. Like him they had made their own assessment of the situation and had already come to the same conclusion their platoon leader had. To go forward or back would do little more than add the names of their men under their command to a casualty list that was already far too large. Doing their best to block out the chatter of small arms that continued to lash out at their comrades on both sides of the stream the sergeants set about quietly passing on their orders and arranging their men in preparation to defend themselves.

Sensing that his fighters had achieved all that they could without paying a price he wasn't prepared to pay, Summirat ordered his scattered command to break contact and withdraw. It had been a long day and all of his men were exhausted. This was especially true of those who had attacked the village at dawn, led their pursuers to the ambush site another detachment had prepared, and then had doubled back to hit those Filipino soldiers who had crossed the river. All of his people would need time to rest, rearm, and prepare for the next act of the little bloody drama that Summirat had taken such pains to orchestrate.

That phase would be more complicated and the results would be far more problematical. But Summirat could predict some of what was about to happen with a fair degree of certainty. He had little doubt that the Manila government, aided by American intelligence assets, would now focus on Mindanao like a policeman's flashlight. They would no doubt read the tactical situation they now faced correctly and conclude that they were facing something more than a loose confederation of fanatics who were little more than bandits. Having determined this, the next troops Summirat expected they would throw against his fighters would be the best they had, members of the Filipino Army's Special Forces Regiment. To deal with this new threat he would have to employ tactics unlike anything that they had yet seen. His people would not be able to infiltrate their ranks as they had managed to when preparing to attack the CAFGU garrison. Nor would they be able to rely on the elementary tactics that had allowed Summirat to best a company of the regular army led by an impetuous young captain. When the Special Forces Regiment came after them they would do so at a time and a place of their choosing. At least Summirat would need to make sure that it seemed as if it was the case, otherwise everything he had done up to this point would be for naught.

For now he and his men would have to behave as a mouse does when danger is near. They would need to create the illusion of frantically scurrying about in panic, seeking cover wherever they could in an effort to escape the cat that had managed to catch its scent. Summirat knew this would be difficult, for the cat that would be hunting them was a crafty hunter, one who was well disciplined in the art of biding its time and pouncing only when it was ready. Timing would be everything when it did, for it would not be enough simply to scurry away and continue to hide. No, to succeed in this new war that he was opening against the traditional foes of his people the hunted would need to turn on the hunter. The mouse would have to come about while the cat was fully committed to its attack and strike a killing blow against it. They would have only one chance to do so, for a single misstep, a failure to properly choreograph their attack against the elite Special Forces Regiment that they would face would bring an end to the force that he had taken such care to recruit, arm, and train.

This was a fate Summirat had to prevent at all costs, for he was determined that his fighters would no longer slip back into their old habits and practices as they had when the government in Manila had brought the Moros to the brink before. This time they would not degenerate into pitifully small groups of bandits, becoming little more than common criminals content to sneak about on the fringes of their homeland kidnapping hostages and blowing up innocent people. From now on their struggle would have meaning. It would have realistic and discernable goals. From that point on everything they did would be directed to achieving those goals.

As he led his exhausted yet cheerful fighters through the jungle Summirat forced himself to resist celebrating their first great victory over the Filipino Army. This was

CAT AND MOUSE 117

just the beginning, he kept reminding himself, little more than the first of many bloody little battles in what he expected to be a long and bloody campaign waged first against the government in Manila and then, God willing, against the Americans to whom the Filipinos would have to turn when they found themselves incapable of dealing with a rebellion he had personally managed to resurrect. Only after he had humbled the best the Americans could throw against them by engaging them in an unending and fruitless bloodletting in the jungles of Mindanao would the American government be forced by public opinion and domestic political pressures to cut its losses and walk away from the Philippines, leaving the government in Manila no choice but to make peace with the Moros, allowing them to finally establish a truly independent Islamic republic.

That, Summirat kept telling himself as he pressed on through the darkness, was something worth fighting for. Only by achieving a noble goal such as that would he be able to justify to himself the death of so many of the men who had given him their undying loyalty and shed their blood for him. Victory alone would wash away his sins.

7

MINDANAO, PHILIPPINES

Most governments have the ability to spin one very public disaster with little trouble. Two on the same day is quite another matter, particularly when the people who engineered the calamities are the first to provide the world's ever voracious twenty-four/seven news agencies with details of their gruesome "victories" against government forces complete with video and sound bites.

The effect of this well-orchestrated media offensive was twofold. It prevented the government in Manila from stifling the story while creating the impression that the Filipino Army had been caught completely off guard by the renewed Abu Sayyaf offensive, a point that just happened to be true. Thrown into disarray, the first response by the government and military officials who were bushwhacked by roving journalists with camera crews in tow was to downplay the seriousness of the dual debacles, an effort that failed miserably. By dawn the next morning everything said by anyone connected with national security, from the president of the Philippines to the commanding general of the Southern Philippines Command, was viewed with growing skepticism. This round-the-clock drubbing at the hands of the media and the patently obvious attempts of the government to trivialize them had the effect of magnifying the humiliations the Filipino Army had sustained in the field.

Within the Filipino Army a crisis in confidence now arose. It was exacerbated by the ceaseless demand to mount an immediate response, a counterblow whose true aim was to still the harsh voices of the skeptical journalists who were branding the Army's leadership as inept while providing political opponents ample ammunition with which to undermine the island nation's current president. This was exactly the sort of response Summirat had sought to achieve, for it not only gave the counterterrorism forces of the National Army precious little time to conduct the sort of reconnaissance, planning, and preparation it needed in order to guarantee the success of their operation, but it also precluded the overt inclusion of any American forces in those operations. To have gone running to the nation's former colonial masters for assistance in this crisis would have only exacerbated the tenuous political position the government already found itself in. Such a move, in full view of the ever watchful TV cameras and covey of journalists who stalked the civilian and military decision makers as they scurried about Manila from one meeting to the next, would have been tantamount to admitting that they were impotent, unable to deal with men whom they had previously passed off as being little more than "religious fanatics" and "petty bandits." Unwilling to commit political suicide, the first decision that the president of the Philippines made was that any course of action his military chief presented to him for his approval would have to be an all Filipino operation.

That did not mean that every form of assistance the Americans had to offer was shunned, especially those that the Army's general staff was able to draw upon without their own political masters knowing. This back channel aid primarily came in the form of intelligence gleaned by sophisticated American assets that the Filipino Army could only dream of, data that could be transferred electronically or digitally via discreet and dedicated channels. This information ranged from near real-time imagery gathered by satellites and high-altitude slow-moving drones operated by the CIA to suspect cell phone conversations plucked out of the ether by the super-secret NSA from listening posts that weren't even located in the Philippines. All was requested and all was delivered through a variety of mediums that did not require person-to-person contacts. Some were even passed on by the Americans without even waiting for their Filipino counterparts to ask for them. Augmented by human intelligence sources of their own, a resource that the Filipino military did have in abundance and believed to be reliable, the general staff officers responsible for preparing a response quickly generated a plan that satisfied their government's demands for swift action. It also fulfilled the need to redeem the tarnished honor and prestige that every professional soldier felt in the wake of the embarrassing drubbing the Abu Sayyaf insurgents had handed them.

The picture that harried Filipino intelligence officers were able to pull together using these sources and hand off to the operations staff officers was as complete as time permitted. It indicated that the Abu Sayyaf insurgents responsible for the massacre of the CAFGU garrison and missionaries had taken refuge in a small tribal village tucked away in the foothills of a mountain chain that formed the spine of the Zamboanga Peninsula. Just how many fighters were there, how they were armed, and whether the village was a base camp or nothing more than a way station were impossible to determine. To confirm any of this would have required more time, a commodity that the situation on the political front did not permit. Besides, there were those in the military itself who felt that the time required to confirm much of the information would allow the insurgents to escape if it did turn out that the village was simply a convenient place they had selected to use in order to rest and regroup before pressing on. If that were true, then it was critical from a military standpoint that the Filipino Army pounce at once, while they had their foe in their sights lest their prey move on and disappear as they had on so many occasions before.

With speed and airtight operational security viewed as being the most crucial elements of the operation, the degree of risk that the major selected to lead two companies of the Special Forces Regiment was obliged to accept caused him to lodge a formal protest. The plan, he pointed out, did not permit him sufficient time to properly formulate his own scheme of maneuver, let alone run his assault through a dress rehearsal before having to take them into the action. Success would depend totally upon the training, the discipline, and the tactical flexibility of the men belonging to the two companies he would be leading. Ordinarily this would not have been a problem for he had complete confidence in the ability of his soldiers, the most highly trained in the Philippine Army, to take on anything that was thrown at them.

What concerned him was the foe they would be going against that they would soon be facing. The Abu Sayyaf's sudden change in tactics and an apparent eagerness to take on regular army units, something that they had gone out of their way to avoid in the recent past, seemed to indicate that something else was afoot, something bigger, more sinister. "This is all too easy," he pointed out to the commanding officer during the course of the mission briefing. "It is as if they are inviting us to go into that village, goading us to strike before we are ready."

The major's apprehensions were brushed aside by both his superior and the staff officer who had cobbled the plan together. "That is unlikely," the staff officer pointed out using a tone of voice that never fails to irritate field commanders when being addressed by a general staff officer. "I do not believe that the Abu Sayyaf will be able to mount anything resembling a coherent or effective response provided we hit them now, before they have an opportunity to recover from their exertions and the losses they have already sustained."

When the major attempted to point out that they did not have any evidence showing that the Abu Sayyaf fighters had suffered any casualties during either of their actions the previous day he was cut short by his colonel. "Nothing is going to keep this operation from going forward," the colonel snapped. "Nothing any of us here think or say is going to delay it. The decision to execute this mission has already been made for us. If you find that you are unable to carry out your order, I will find someone who can."

In the end, the major did as his colonel had done when he had been issued a similar fiat by his superiors; he bowed to the pressure that was being brought to bear upon them and resolved to do the best he could with what he had. Perhaps, the major told himself as he slumped down in his seat to listen to the balance of the briefing, he was wrong. Perhaps things would work out.

The village where the Filipino military intelligence and American sources had tracked the Abu Sayyaf fighters to was situated in a horseshoe formed by the two spiny ridges that jutted out from either side of a mountain. At the top or head of the horseshoe was the mountain itself. Rock-strewn and bare, its steep face formed a perfect backdrop for the drama that was about to be played out in its shadow. Reaching out like two giant arms the twin ridges curved around the village, encircling it but not quite joining before their southern tips disappeared into the jungle, creating a gap measuring just under one kilometer wide. In the center of these rugged folds was the village itself, surrounded by fields where its people managed to scratch out a modest living, safe in the embrace of their mountain and the ridges protruding from it.

The assault that shattered the early morning calm was reminiscent of another era. Skimming along at treetop level a flock of armed MD-500 helicopters, known in American special ops units as "Little Birds," swept in through the gap left by the southern tips of the two spiny ridges. Without breaking stride the lead pair lined up on their assigned targets and loosed a volley of 2.75-inch rockets at huts that were no different from any others in the village except for the people they were suspected of housing. Without waiting to see the effect that their deadly ordnance had inflicted the two MD-500s separated, each banking either to the left or right in order to keep from plowing into the mountain's face before them as they began to circle about for their next run in.

Even as the first high-explosive rockets were ripping into the targeted huts two more MD-500s roared in on their runs. Armed with 7.62mm chain guns, these helicopters unleashed a hail of lead that literally shredded two huts they had been assigned to destroy. Not every bullet they fired found its intended mark. Even some that did whistled through the flimsy huts and continued their flight until they came to rest in the ground, a hut, or an unfortunate soul who just happened to be in the wrong place. Waiting until the last possible moment to break off their attacks they executed the same steep banking maneuvers their predecessors had and split to the left and right respectively before climbing up and over the spiny ridges that flanked either side of the village.

The dazed occupants of the village had no time to recover from the shock of the sudden onslaught visited upon them by the MD-500s before a dozen single rotor transport helicopters came thundering through the gap in their wake. These vintage Bell 205 helicopters first saw battle in Vietnam where the U.S. military referred to them as UH-1D Hueys. While many of the machines

were well past their prime, each was still more than capable of carrying a squad of heavily armed soldiers
belonging to one of the two companies from the Special
Forces Regiment assigned the task of finishing off any
Abu Sayyaf insurgents who had survived the aerial assault. Everyone on board the Bell 205s, soldiers and pilots alike, were hardened veterans, men who had done
this sort of thing countless times before. None of them
needed a politician or senior officer to explain to them
why they were doing this. All these crack Filipino commandos needed to know was where and when. The rest
was more or less automatic.

With mere inches to spare these helicopters roared
over the village at speed before fanning out to deposit
their passengers in the collection of small farm plots to
the north of it. Those in the village who had not been
stunned senseless by the rocket and gun runs stopped
whatever they were doing to watch in dread as the helicopters lit upon their precious cultivated fields like gigantic dragonflies. This reaction had been anticipated by
those who had planned the attack. It allowed the next
wave of twelve Bell 205s hauling the second company of
the Special Forces Regiment to land in the fields south of
the village all but unobserved.

With practiced ease the veteran commandos of both
companies spilled out of their aircraft and deployed. In
the north the lead company spread out and took up defensive positions that roughly conformed to the same horseshoe shape created by the mountain and two ridges. Their
mission was to establish an airtight cordon on three sides
of the village to keep anyone who had survived thus far
from escaping. It would be left to the second company,
now forming up into platoon columns south of the village,
to sweep through the village and either drive the Abu
Sayyaf fighters out of their former sanctuary and into the
sights of the company waiting for them or to dig the Muslim extremists out one by one if they were hell bent on
martyrdom. Either way, everyone involved in the opera-

tion was convinced that the result would be a complete and clear-cut victory that would more than avenge the humiliation the insurgents had inflicted upon the Filipino government.

ARLINGTON, VIRGINIA

In order to document the stunning success they expected and provide all potential foes and their supporters with an object lesson on what happens when they go too far, the Filipino Army borrowed a page from the American military's manual on psychological warfare. Mixed in with the forces on the ground and aboard a helicopter dedicated specifically for this purpose were embedded three teams of reporters who were charged with the mission of furnishing the world with live television feeds and blow-by-blow narratives delivered in both English and Tagalog Filipino. This unprecedented media event was beamed through the air waves and into the homes of millions as it unfolded thanks to the good offices of an American news agency the Manila government found to be accommodating when it came to how it presented "The Facts."

One fact that was not broadcast around the globe was the price that network had paid the Minister of Information for the privilege of providing this exclusive to the world. Sidebars such as that had no relevance except to serious media wonks and those news agencies that had underbid their lucky competitor. All that mattered to the average viewer at home was that every minute of the staged raid against the suspected Abu Sayyaf sanctuary was captured by the unblinking eye of the camera manned by mixed crews of American and Filipino journalists and delivered to the viewer live and in an entertaining manner.

Half a world and twelve time zones away Jan Fields-Dixon was just pulling into the driveway of the government quarters on Fort Myer when her beeper began to chirp. For a moment she sat in her car, staring at her oversized combination purse/carryall debating whether it would be better to wait until after she was in the house to respond to its incessant squawks or simply do it right there in the privacy of her car where Scott wouldn't be able to hear her as she berated a nervous assistant producer for disturbing her with a trivial problem. Grudgingly she decided that it would be best to settle the crisis before she crossed into the sanctuary of her home. Doing her best to control her anger at being disturbed like this, Jan pulled her cell phone out of her purse and hit the speed dial for her downtown office.

The anxious voice on the other end didn't bother with preambles when he saw Jan's number pop up on the caller ID window of his phone. "Jan," he all but yelled into the receiver, "are you watching the other channel?"

"The Other Channel" was what they called their number-one news channel competitor. Already peeved at being called so soon after leaving the office and before she had even been afforded the opportunity to unwind after a long day, Jan made no effort to hide her anger. "Jerry, I'm still in my car."

The assistant producer was unfazed by her tone. "You've got to get to a TV right away. There's a live feed coming in from the Philippines like you wouldn't believe."

Already well versed on the political and military situation over there because of recent developments and her stepson's routine deployment to that troubled region, Jan had no need to ask any questions. Instead she threw open the door of her car, gathered up her belongings, and ran as fast as she could for the door of the house, keeping the cell phone glued to her ear as she did so.

Storming into the house with all the subtlety of a SWAT team conducting a forced entry Jan headed straight for the den. Scott was already there seated in his ratty old overstuffed chair, engrossed in a book on the Franco-Prussian

War. Startled by his wife's tumultuous appearance he glanced up from his book and was about to say something but stopped short as soon as he saw what he jokingly referred to as her "clear the decks for action" look.

"Scott, turn on the TV."

Sensing that something was up he lay his book on his lap without hesitation, picked up the TV's remote, and hit the power on button. In a flash the monitor came to life, displaying one of the anchormen at her own network. After dropping her purse, she pointed to the TV with her free hand. "No, no. The other channel."

Like the people in her office, Scott understood what she meant. Punching up the appropriate numbers he switched channels.

Suddenly the screen was alive with images that stood out in stark contrast to the serenity and calm of their den in Arlington, Virginia. As she watched the images of a line of soldiers in the foreground of the camera's field of vision advance on a burning village beyond, Jan backed up and settled into a Queen Anne chair that sat catty-corner to what Nathan called the Martin Crain chair. As she settled down, Jan spoke into the cell phone that was pressed against her ear. "Who do you have working up this story?" After a moment's pause, she nodded her head. "Good. Tell him not to wait for my approval. Run with whatever you have as soon as he thinks you're ready to. Then have him call me once he has a chance."

Ignoring her one-sided conversation Scott concentrated on assessing the tactical situation as best he could. The news channel covering the action on the other side of the world was doing so using a split screen. Actually, the screen was divided into quadrants. In the top left was the news anchor who was covering the story from his network's home studio. To the right were the images being provided to him from the heliborne news team hovering above the village. The bottom half of the screen displayed two different groups of soldiers already on the ground. Based upon the shadows that the figures cast,

Scott was able to determine that the Filipino Army unit already deployed in hasty defensive positions was located north of the village while the other unit, shown in the TV screen's lower right quadrant, was advancing toward it from the south. Other than that, it was difficult to judge with any certainty what was going on since TV news cameramen more often than not tended to orient on things that were spectacular while ignoring things that were of tactical significance to a trained eye.

Satisfied that the situation at her own studio was well in hand, Jan clicked off her cell phone but kept it in the palm of her hand, ready to answer as soon as the next harried news executive got around to check in with her to see if she was on top of the situation. For the first time she addressed Scott with a pitch that was approaching something resembling near normal levels. "What are they doing?"

Over the years Scott, a professional soldier through and through, and Jan, the ever voracious journalist, managed to get along by leaving their careers in their respective offices. In Scott's case this was not at all difficult since so much of the material he dealt with on a day-to-day basis was either classified or the sort of stuff that would bore a mere mortal to tears. For Jan this sometimes was a challenge, especially when she was working on an exclusive that she was all excited about. In those rare cases where her enthusiasm violated the sanctity of their home Scott did his best to listen to her attentively and without comment, using the same techniques she employed on him when she was being forced to listen to him babble on while being dragged about a vacant field that had once been a Civil War battlefield. By means of an occasional nod and a well-timed "I see," Scott was able to create the illusion that he was paying attention to her.

Every now and then there were exceptions to this policy, such as was the case this evening when the two highly trained professionals found themselves engaged in an exchange that touched upon the other's particular area of expertise. Seated in the comfort of their own home the pair watched as several hundred soldiers, aviators, and journalists methodically bore down upon a primitive village. No one seemed to be in a hurry. To Scott it appeared as if the unit making its way toward the village was deliberately taking its time as massive sheets of flames spread from hut to hut. Like the myopic eye of the helicopter-mounted camera, they watched as fire consumed the village, driving the hapless inhabitants who were little more than blurred images on the TV screen to scurry from place to place in a vain effort to find safety.

"The troops shown in the screen on the lower left," Scott explained calmly without waiting to be prodded by his wife, "seem to have taken up hasty defensive positions north of the village."

"How can you tell north from south?"

"Look at the shadows in relation to the way they are facing," Scott pointed out with a wave of his hand. "Since it's morning over there the sun is still rising in the east. The shadows cast by the soldiers who are stationary fall away to their right, which means the sun is hitting their left side. Hence, they are facing south. Over there," he continued as he shifted his hand to indicate the lower right quadrant, "the left side of the soldiers moving toward the village is in the shade, so that means they are moving north."

Taking a moment, Jan studied the screen until she was able to discern for herself what her husband was talking about. "Yes, I can see that now," she muttered as she made a mental note of this little trick.

"The unit in the north is the anvil," Scott stated as he held his open left hand up, "and those in the south are the hammer," he explained as he took his right hand, balled it up in a fist, and slammed it into the left. "Their efforts are being supported by the armed helicopter you can see zipping about over the village. They're ready to provide covering fire or take out targets of opportunity as they appear."

"I don't imagine that is going to be easy," Jan stated dryly, "not with all those civilians running around in the village."

"Provided they're civilians," Scott retorted without missing a beat.

Jan felt the need to say something more about this subject but knew better. When it came to issues such as this their respective world views diverged. To her any and all civilian deaths were tragic regardless of cause. To Scott they were collateral damage, a regrettable by-product of war that had to be ignored by professional soldiers if they hoped to keep their sanity while they were doing what needed to be done.

"It looks as if there's two companies involved," Scott continued as if he were delivering a briefing. "By the looks of the soldiers I would say they were all from the Filipino Army's Special Forces Regiment."

Jan made a mental note of this last point as well. While she had all the confidence in the world that Scott was correct, she would still need to have her people who did the fact-checking for a story confirm that particular tidbit. To Jan, having faith in one's husband was a commendable virtue. Getting every little detail of a story right before airing it was a necessity.

"It will be the task of the company pressing from the south to either drive the insurgents out into the kill zone set up by the one to the north," Scott went on. "If that doesn't work, they'll have to go in and methodically dig them out of their holes one by one."

"What happens if they don't find insurgents in the village?"

Scott chuckled. "Well, it wouldn't be the first time a military spokesman had to stand in front of a gaggle of incredulous journalists with nothing more intelligent to say than ah, hummida-hummida, and yadda-yadda-yadda."

Focused on the TV in an effort not to miss a beat as

the company advancing on the village neared the first row of huts, Jan ignored her husband's flippant remarks that he delivered with a hint of a smirk. Instead, she found herself envious of what she was watching. To secure an exclusive like this was the sort of coup that media professionals only dare to dream of. Despite the best efforts of her network to catch up, anything they came up with in their coverage would be viewed as little more than secondhand information, follow-up stories that would lack the impact this live coverage was having on all who were seeing it.

Jan was in the midst of trying to stifle the regret she was harboring over this unfortunate set of circumstances when something caught her eye. It was a distant flash on the western ridge that was caught by pure accident by the camera that was providing the feed for the lower right quadrant of the TV image. Were it not for a growing plume of white smoke that followed the sudden apparition, Jan would have discounted it as nothing more than a technical glitch, a glint of sunlight on the camera's lens or some such natural occurrence. Still, even when she concluded that it was man-made, she quickly dismissed it as little more than part of the clutter that makes a modern battle so confusing and difficult to sort out. Even when another flash, puff, and plume appeared not far from where the first had she didn't attach any great significance to what she was seeing.

If Jan didn't grasp the importance of these seemingly innocuous occurrences, Scott did. Without having to wait to see more, he saw the chance observation captured by the camera's unflinching lens for what it was. Gripping the arms of his well-worn chair with both hands he lurched forward, startling his wife in the process. Bewildered, she looked at him, then at the TV screen. "What is it?"

By now all three cameramen had caught sight of the twin smoke-spewing pinpricks of fire as they arched skyward. "SAMs," Scott muttered as he watched attentively waiting for the cameramen to pan out so that he could see what the swarm of attack helicopters that had been buzzing about over the village were doing in response to this unanticipated threat. Unschooled in the art of modern warfare, the cameramen did not know that it would have been more spectacular had they done so. Instead all three held true to form, zooming in on the lead surface-to-air missile as its flaming tail rent the pale blue sky with a strip of dirty white smoke.

Having covered a few wars in her younger days as a struggling journalist and living with a soldier, Jan didn't need Scott to explain to her what a SAM was or what its sudden appearance meant. Holding their breath the pair of dedicated professionals watched the progress of the sophisticated shoulder-fired surface-to-air missile with the same intense fixation that a spectator watched when a quarterback unleashes a Hail Mary pass as time on the game clock was expiring. This, of course, was not a game in which a desperate toss that failed to find its intended target meant little more than lost points. The events they were watching were not part of a sporting event where the players survived even the most contentious confrontation. The heat-seeking missile was a device designed to kill its foes by honing in on the heat signature of its intended target even when that target tried to dodge it. Success in this uneven contest meant sudden death.

With brutal efficiency the warhead of the lead missile detonated upon reaching a predetermined range from the MD-500 helicopter it had been aimed at, showering the aircraft with a spray of deadly fragments that peppered control surfaces and tore through the thin skin of its engine compartment. No sooner had the stricken helicopter absorbed this initial punishment than the second SAM came to the end of its flight, pelting the already doomed helicopter with a fresh burst of white-hot shards of metal.

The American journalist with the Filipino company

holding defensive positions north of the village was the first to break the stunned on-air silence. "As you just saw," he shouted out into the hand mike he gripped in his hand, "the insurgents have fired some sort of surface-to-air missiles. They've managed to shoot down one of the attack helicopters that had been supporting the ground troops. It would appear . . ."

The ground-based camera that had been following the stricken MD-500 as it plunged to earth suddenly slewed about to the left, away from the devastation wrought by the first volley of SAMs launched from the western ridge, and over toward the eastern ridge where it revealed two more pillars of smoke and flame rising up from concealed positions.

In his den, surrounded by hundreds of books that recounted the horrors and the glories of past wars Scott slumped back in his chair as he realized what was going on. "It's called a SAM-bush," he stated glumly. "The Abu Sayyaf have managed to draw the Filipinos into a trap."

Jan said nothing as she watched as a third, then a fourth pair of shoulder-fired surface-to-air missiles were loosed, lacing the sky with a crazy quilt of white smoke as they pursued the remaining helicopters that executed wild gyrations in a vain effort to escape. A second MD-500 did not make it, disappearing in a ball of fire as the world watched. She was tempted to ask her husband what this meant, but didn't need to.

Instead, she eased back in her own chair as Scott had done, squirming as she contemplated how this would affect her stepson. She knew it would, especially if the units they were watching were the best that the Filipino Army could throw against the Abu Sayyaf. In a global war that knew no boundaries, she realized that it was a simple matter of time before Nathan and other young Americans like him would be sent over there to do what the Filipinos themselves were unable to do. That her husband and Nathan's own father would have a hand in making that happen only added to the gloom that had descended upon their own little quiet corner of the world.

One by one the images of combat being beamed from the battlefield disappeared. Whether they were cut off by someone in the chain of command at the news channel providing the coverage or by a representative of the Filipino government who had the presence of mind to order the feeds to be cut didn't matter. The show was over, leaving the on-camera anchor at a momentary loss as to what to say. As he was in the process of squirming about in his seat, fumbling about in an effort to find something intelligent to say a beeper somewhere in the Dixons' den sounded. Instinctively, both Scott and Jan looked about to locate the source. "It's mine," Scott stated as soon as he caught sight of the flashing on the desk where he had left it.

Jan's summons followed within seconds of Scott's. Lifting the cell phone that was still in her hand she hit the speed dial. When a harried assistant answered and asked her if she could hold, Jan cut him off. "This is Jan. Tell Ted I should be in the office in half an hour."

Standing up, she turned and looked across the room to where Scott was standing. He had his back to her as he listened to someone at the other end of the phone he was on. Every now and then he would respond to a question by saying, "Yes, notify him," or "No, hold off on that." Despite her chosen profession she didn't want to know what he was talking about. In her heart she knew whatever Scott and those who worked with him did, it would ultimately mean that a young man who was as much a son to her as if she had conceived him herself would soon be headed back into harm's way. It did not matter to her that the military was his chosen profession. It didn't matter that if given a chance he would leap at the opportunity to lead his company into the same sort of fight that was now playing itself out half a world away. None of that was important to Jan, a woman who had dedicated much of her life to protecting and nurturing boys who Scott had brought into her life and she had let capture her heart. Perhaps, she told herself as she stood there watching her husband go about setting the wheels of America's military machine in motion, there is something to that old saying, ignorance is bliss.

8

FORT LEWIS, WASHINGTON

I f there was one thing that Robert Delmont was, it was a realist. When it came to his personality he knew he had the charisma of a dead mackerel and the charm of an abused pit bull. This dearth of affability was not viewed as being all bad by many who practiced the profession of arms. There were those who even saw it as a plus, men who felt that the "touchy-feely" school of leadership had no place in a vocation that existed for no other reason than to kill people and break things.

Others, such as Nathan Dixon, saw things differently. He believed as Erwin Rommel had. That much admired dead German general once stated that "a commander must try, above all, to establish a personal and comradely contact with his men, but without giving away an inch of his authority." This philosophy of leadership is not an easy one to follow. It requires a delicate touch and a constant balancing act. There is the ever-present danger that an officer will lose his ability to be effective in combat. Not only does it become harder for him to send men he has come to view as friends into harm's way, the loss of even one of them leaves a physiological wound that can be as crippling and painful as one caused by a bullet.

This sort of debate over leadership style was as old as warfare itself, one that every generation of soldiers has engaged in. The crux of the matter was best depicted in the classic 1949 war movie *Twelve O'Clock High,* a story that was based on the career of Major General Frank A. Armstrong during World War II. Its central theme concerned leadership style, or put another way, how a commanding officer went about motivating those under his command to do things that common sense and a human's innate sense of survival rebels against. It asked the question, just what sort of person is best suited to lead a combat unit? One who cares for his people as a doting father would to a beloved son? Or a man who stands apart from those he commands, executing his assigned duties without regard to the personal and emotional carnage that his decisions create? Most successful officers find the answer to this dilemma lies somewhere in the middle, though many belonging to the combat arms tend to gravitate toward the "Frank Savage" school of leadership. Robert Delmont was one.

Unfortunately Frank Savage was a fictional character. In the movie *Twelve O'Clock High,* this protagonist was assigned to command a bomber group that was, crudely speaking, on its ass. Its losses were high, its combat effectiveness was low, and the morale of the men assigned to it was all but nonexistent. None of these conditions existed in the unit Delmont inherited. Yet he conducted himself as if his soldiers were raw recruits who had to be whipped into shape rather than the elite, battle-hardened veterans that they were. And while it can be argued that any organization can be improved, the cost of achieving perfection is seldom worth the price that must be paid. This is particularly true when dealing with leadership and warfare, both of which are more art than science.

The results of Delmont's brusque, take-no-prisoners approach were predictable. Men who knew that they were at the top of their game resented being treated like rank amateurs. Rather than promoting greater efficiencies, Delmont's policies and style of leadership quickly fostered rebellion in the ranks, a situation that company commanders and senior NCOs found themselves dealing with more and more. Most of these leaders saw what was going on and rose to the challenge. They did their best to maintain discipline, cohesion, and morale, the key elements that make or break a unit. Others did not find it within themselves to resist the growing tide of resentment that Delmont's methods engendered. While not outwardly criticizing him, these officers and NCOs did little or nothing to rein in the crude remarks and jokes concerning Delmont the junior enlisted soldiers within their platoons, sections, and squads freely bantered about. By ignoring this behavior they tacitly endorsed open disrespect to a superior ranking officer, a practice that once started is hard to stop or restrict.

Caught in the epicenter of this crisis were the company commanders, men who were masters and servants, demigods within their own realm yet little more than executioners of the battalion commander's policies and plans. This bipolar existence in itself demanded a great deal of maturity and finesse from men who were between the ages of twenty-five and twenty-eight. When it was coupled with a leadership style akin to Delmont's and the growing dissension from below it created a situation that tested both their leadership skills and their professionalism each and every day.

Most of the five young captains responded to the challenge presented to them by their commanding officer much as Nathan did. He understood that his response to Delmont and his policies set the tone for the men in his company. To denigrate or question the judgment of his immediate superior in front of his subordinates would be akin to sanctioning such conduct, encouraging them to do the same when discussing an order or policy they did not care for regardless of who was responsible for it. Yet to say or do nothing in the face of what many saw as unwarranted abuse at the hands of their battalion commander would have been just as corrosive to Nathan's authority, for no one, especially elite fighting men such as the ones he commanded, was able to respect a weak-kneed toady and yes-man.

So Nathan and his fellow company commanders took to playing a dangerous game. While making a show of saluting smartly and going through the motions of carrying out their commanding officer's orders, each of the young company commanders continued to run their own units as they had BD, shorthand for "Before Delmont." The danger in this charade lay in what would become of their careers if Delmont caught on to what amounted to downright subversion of his authority, for the officer's evaluation reports written during his tenure as a company commander was perhaps the most important evaluations an officer received. A good one guaranteed a fully productive military career. A less than satisfactory one was a kiss of death.

In this lonely struggle the captains had no one in whom they could confide except each other, and only when they were well out of earshot of even their most trusted subordinate. Thus social gatherings that were attended only by captains became one of the few places where Nathan and his fellow company commanders could openly vent their spleen and commiserate with their fellow conspirators. "I had been hoping he was simply trying to get our attention with a little shock therapy," Nathan explained to Emmett DeWitt as they enjoyed one of Nathan's world-famous barbecue parties. "After all," he added as he waved the oversized fork around the small deck at the other captains who were gathered on it, "we can be a tough bunch to get a handle on. He's just as anxious to place his mark on the battalion as each of us was when we took over our own companies."

DeWitt, whose desk was across from the entrance to Delmont's office and who had a chance to study the man up close and personal day in and day out, didn't share Nathan's assessment. "I wish that was all there was to this," he replied as he went about wolfing down as much barbecue as he could before his wife intervened and banned him from the food table. "But I'm afeared that ain't the case. Mumbles isn't playing at being a badass son of a bitch. He is one, through and through. I've seen some hard cases before, but none of them can hold a candle to this man. I'm convinced he has but one mode of operation, and that's to kick ass twenty-four/seven."

Knowing full well that his friend was right Nathan made no effort to counter DeWitt's grim assessment. Instead, he simply bowed his head as he went about flipping ribs on the grill. "Well, I suppose you're right . . ."

"And I am," DeWitt quibbled as he tossed the gnawed bones he had been holding into the trash and reached over to snatch up a fresh rack of ribs straight off the grill. "Look, he's the battalion commander. He's going to run this battalion as he sees fit."

Nathan waited until his friend had a mouthful before continuing. "While that may be true, there is a limit to just how much abuse my people can take before the morale problems we're having to deal with begin to have serious consequences in the field. Fact is, I'm already seeing some signs that even some of my best people are getting sloppy."

"Well, you're not the only one who's been seeing that," DeWitt stated as he lifted a finger to his lips to wipe away a glob of barbecue sauce from the corner of his mouth.

He was about to lick that finger clean when Paula DeWitt, emerging through the sliding doors and onto the balcony from behind her husband, seized his hand and pulled it away from his waiting lips. "Emmett Justin DeWitt! Have you forgotten what napkins are for?"

Nathan grinned as he watched the tall muscular Ranger captain before him all but quiver in the presence of his diminutive wife. "Ah, hon. Give me a break will ya? It's not like the kids are here watching."

"And that's supposed to make all the difference?" she snapped as she looked over and saw the fresh rack of ribs in his other hand. "And how many servings does that make for you?"

Before he could answer, Nathan grinned. "Why are you bothering to ask, Paula? You know he can't count that high."

"That's what I figured." Snatching the ribs from her husband's hand despite his efforts to keep them away from her, Paula glanced over at Nathan. "I've got to call the sitter and make sure everything's okay. While I'm gone you're not to give him another thing to eat, otherwise I'll be up all night listening to him pass gas."

"Oh, yes, missy, anything you say missy," Nathan mumbled as he made a show of kowtowing to DeWitt's wife.

Grinning, Paula turned to her husband. "Now there's a man who knows how to respect authority." With that, she marched off back into Nathan's small apartment to retrieve her cell phone from her purse.

No sooner had she gone inside than DeWitt reached over and nabbed another rack of ribs. "Ooooh, you're gonna catch hell for that," Nathan mocked.

DeWitt smiled. "Not if I finish them before she gets back."

While his friend consumed his ribs as quickly as he could, Nathan considered picking up their conversation where they had left off. Then, hearing the roar of laughter from his fellow officers who were enjoying themselves all around him he decided to let it go. Everyone was having far too much fun to spoil it by discussing their commanding officer's foibles. Besides, he concluded as he went about flipping the ribs he had neatly arrayed on the grill with the same precision he used in everything he did, what was the point? DeWitt was right. Delmont was their commanding officer. As long as he was and the unit accomplished its assigned mission he could run the battalion pretty much as he wanted. The best he and the other company commanders could do was to hunker down, ride out the storm and do their best to mitigate what they saw as abuses their commanding officer seemed so intent on visiting upon them. It wasn't much of a strategy, but at the moment it was all Nathan could think of.

FORT BENNING, GEORGIA

If there was one blessing that Nathan and his cohorts could count on, it was the nature of Delmont's duties. As a commanding officer responsible for some six hundred men much of his time was consumed with dealing with administrative duties that had little to do with the actual assigned mission of the 3rd Battalion, 75th Ranger. Such noncombat and training-related chores as reviewing and commenting upon personnel actions of subordinates, ensuring that the health and welfare of the soldiers under his command were being tended to, periodically checking on the quality of life of their families, overseeing the accountability of equipment, and myriad other such obligations did much to limit his ability to meddle with how his four company commanders went about running and training their own commands. And even when he did manage to break free of these tiresome tasks and visit one of them while they were in the midst of training either in garrison or out in the field, the chances of him hitting a specific unit was one in four. It was, as Clarence Overton who commanded Company C dryly quibbled, "like playing Russian roulette. There's only one bullet and four chambers."

Never missing an opportunity to poke a hole in one of his friend's arguments, Nathan snickered. "That may be true, but when that one chamber comes around your way it's sure to ruin your day."

Besides administrative housekeeping chores Delmont also found himself spending a great deal of time dealing with higher headquarters as he participated in planning for future training exercises and overseas deployments. Having been a plans officer in the Pentagon these diversions were far more to his liking, particularly since they put him in direct contact with the people who would make or break his career. Never shy about caulking up "face time" with his superiors Delmont took every opportunity that was afforded him to go to Fort Benning, Georgia, where the regimental headquarters was located or MacDill Air Force Base, home of the Joint Special Operations Command. While there he did more than simply participate in planning sessions, tactical exercises without troops, better known as war games, and command conferences. He did everything he could to shape his own future and by default the future of the men who belonged to the 3rd Battalion, 75th Rangers.

Delmont didn't need to exert himself to make this happen. Articulate, intelligent, and well versed in all aspects of special operations, his opinion and views were not only well respected, they were aggressively solicited by senior commanders and staff officers who were not in his immediate chain of command. Among those who felt no hesitation about tapping this resource was Major General James Palmer, a man whom Delmont had served under on more than one occasion. Eager to energize and expand the Army's role in the ongoing war on terrorism, Palmer relied upon his former protégé to keep him updated with what was being said and done down "in the trenches." While doing so he also took advantage of Delmont's current position by using him as a sounding board to test ideas some of his desk-bound colleagues in Washington, D.C., were hatching. In the course of these conversations Delmont felt no qualms about putting forth his own thoughts and ideas concerning the use of his battalion. Both men realized that this sort of thing was officially frowned upon by an organization that viewed the chain of command as being something more than a symbolic term. Yet like most warriors who waged what has been dubbed unconventional warfare, they felt unrestrained by conventions and rules that did not apply to them on the battlefield or in garrison. This was how Operation Doberman made its way from the fertile imagination of a battalion commander to the desk of the deputy chief of staff for Plans and Operations, Department of the Army.

It began as all good operations should, with the originator digesting every intel summary and current assessment that dealt with the renewed threat an invigorated and resurgent Abu Sayyaf created. Once he had a handle on his foe, Delmont went to work on devising a scheme that would turn the tables on him. Quite naturally the concept of operations he generated called for the deployment of his entire battalion to the Philippines. The final product was not a bad piece of staff work. On the contrary, having drafted numerous plans for consumption by the senior members of the DA staff, Delmont knew just how to go about making his proposal all but bulletproof.

Everything he could think of was in it. In an effort to placate those who had the power to veto his plan he managed to find a role for each of the Army's sister services that would be to their liking. In addition to providing the necessary airlift capacity required to haul all the units involved in the operations from their scattered bases in the U.S. and across the Pacific to the Philippines, the Air Force would have responsibility for providing air space management over the battlefield as well as on-call, round-the-clock close air support. The Navy would add to the number of attack aircraft available by stationing a carrier battle group within easy striking distance of the area of operation. Even the Marines were afforded an opportunity to do what they do best by throwing a Marine amphibious unit ashore in order to secure a base of operation that would serve as a diversion as well as a forward operations base or FOB from which incursions into the interior of Mindanao could be launched. Those incursions of course would be carried out by a reinforced Ranger battalion. And since the 3rd Battalion, 75th Rangers was the

only one that was currently conducting active operations
in the region, there was little doubt that if his plan ever
did see the light of day his command would be the one
given the starring role.

The one thing that Delmont could not gloss over was
the hazards execution of the full plan would entail for
key elements of the ground component. From beginning
to end it was a high-risk operation, one that placed a fair
number of men in a position of risk that relied upon a
number of variables, many of which neither Delmont nor
anyone in charge of the operation would have control over.
For many career-minded soldiers risk was anathema to
them, something to be avoided at all costs lest a well-
crafted and carefully planned career disappear in a pillar
of smoke as it had for Charging Charlie Beckwith, leader
of the ill-fated Iranian hostage rescue attempt in April of
1980. So rather than present it to his immediate superior
and risk having his ideas summarily rejected Delmont
conducted an end run by going to a man whose style he
was very familiar with and who was in a position to give
his ideas wings.

Delmont's opportunity to unleash Operation Doberman on Palmer came at Fort Benning during a conference of senior infantry officers. Over drinks in Palmer's
BOQ room after a long day's worth of seminars and briefings Delmont skillfully steered the conversation from the
day's events and onto the current situation in the Philippines. When he spoke to his mentor and former superior
he did so in a manner that he would never have used before. For his part Palmer indulged this new tone of famil-
iarity. As he saw it, it was justified. While serving under
him in the Pentagon Delmont had been little more than
just another lieutenant colonel, one of hundreds who pop-
ulate the sprawling five-sided maze popularly known as
Puzzle Palace by both its occupants and those in the field
who labored under the guidance, policies, and orders
that originated from there. By becoming the commanding officer of one of only three Ranger battalions, Delmont

had managed to set himself apart from the hordes of faceless officers that Palmer passed in the halls of the Pentagon day in and day out. He was a player now.

"Up until recently," Delmont explained as the two officers lounged in overstuffed chairs that faced each other, "the Abu Sayyaf insurgents have been content with limiting their efforts to kidnapping and an occasional bombing that are rather amateurish when compared to what the Palestinians are doing these days. These new attacks, however, leave little doubt that they are part of a well-planned campaign being executed by a well-led, trained and financed foe."

Palmer swirled the ice in his glass as he spoke. "Well, they certainly have managed to get our attention. Both DIA and CIA are convinced that this is only the beginning." Turning, Palmer glanced over to his aide-de-camp, a young captain who was his latest protégé. "Doug, did you bring the file on the leader of this group?"

Palmer, of course, knew that the young officer seated off to one side had. Updating and hauling around what Palmer called his brain book was one of his duties. With the sort of efficiency that both Palmer and Delmont expected of a subordinate officer, the aide flipped to the appropriate page of the binder that had been sitting on his lap. When he was ready, he began to read. "Hamdani Summirat is by birth an Indonesian national. He graduated from the Indonesian Military Academy with honors which earned him a position in the Indonesian Army's Detachment Eighty-One, a specialized counterrevolutionary unit that was absorbed by their Special Forces in the nineties."

Delmont grunted after taking a sip of his drink. "Well, that explains a lot."

Palmer nodded in agreement. "What's the old saying? The best way to catch a thief is to use a thief? Does that info paper say what turned him, Doug?"

Taking a second to skim through the verbiage, the aide searched for an answer. "It doesn't say, sir. All it mentions is that shortly after he resigned his commission he disappeared from sight. The next mention of him comes to us via the Australian SAS. It seems they've had a few run-ins with a tough little group led by him that was originally part of the Jemaah Islamiya, an Islamic extremist group that has been known to operate throughout Southeast Asia."

"So what caused him to go over to the Dark side?" Delmont asked.

"Summirat is an ethnic Malay and Muslim as are the Moros. Like the MILA he supports the creation of a pan-Muslim republic that would incorporate Malaya, Indonesia, and the southern islands of the Philippines. The CIA believes he left the MILA and joined the Abu Sayyaf when they began to negotiate with the Manila government."

"Seems our nemesis doesn't care for diplomacy," Palmer snickered.

Ignoring his superior's snide remark, the aide went on. "A DIA report from last year that was collaborated by the Australians concludes that Summirat has become something of a freelancer who has created an elite strike force that is available to fight for any group that agrees with his political philosophy and goals."

"He's a mercenary?" Delmont asked.

"No sir, not quite. One of the reasons given here for his skipping around is because he isn't satisfied with the dedication of many of the Islamic insurgence movements in the region. It says here that during an interrogation of a member of his group captured by the SAS, the prisoner stated that Summirat was determined to rally those from various groups who were, as he put it, true believers in his vision of a pan-Islamic Southeast Asia."

"Does it say how he intends to do this?" Delmont asked.

Before his aide could answer, Palmer replied, "That's obvious. Our IMA alum intends to build an ever-conquering army around him, one that is capable of cowering the government in Manila into granting the Moros unfettered self-rule. From there I would imagine he plans to head home where he would do the same to the government in Jakarta before taking on Malaya."

This grim thought caused all three men to pause a moment as the two senior officers sipped their drinks in silence and the aide sat with binder in hand, ready to pounce upon the next inquiry either of them hurled at him.

Palmer broke the silence as he reached over, took the bottle that sat in a small side table, and poured himself another drink. "There's a reason you connived to invite yourself up here tonight, Bob, and broach this subject. Let's hear it."

"As I see it," Delmont stated in low, measured tones as he looked down at the glass he held while slowly swirling it about, "we, the U.S., have but three options when it comes to dealing with this issue. We can declare that this new effort by the Moros is an internal problem and steer clear of becoming directly involved with any direct military effort to crush Summirat and his insurgency."

"That of course doesn't really solve anything," Palmer pointed out. "It merely postpones the match."

"Yes, it does, but it is still an option some weenie in the State Department will champion." After pausing to take a sip of his drink, Delmont went back to swirling his glass as he pressed on. "The next viable course of action is to continue as we have been in the hope that our limited campaign using small-scale special ops units against the Abu Sayyaf and the MILA buys enough time for our training missions, to properly prepare the Filipino military to meet this new challenge."

"Remember what our current chief of staff is fond of saying," Palmer pointed out, "hope is not a sound basis upon which to plan."

"So that leads me to the third and by far most aggressive option, a full court press mounted by U.S. forces with the goal of wiping out Summirat and his band now, before their current effort has a chance to gain traction."

Holding his glass off to one side, Palmer smirked as he stared at his protégé. "And I suppose that you just happen to have something in mind."

Delmont looked up from his glass and smiled. "Why of course, sir. After all, wasn't it you who taught me never to ask a question unless you already have the answer for it?"

Chuckling, Palmer lifted his glass in a toast to a former subordinate whose loyalty to him and skill as a tactician promised to provide the two of them a vehicle that would propel their respective careers and reputations to new highs.

From his seat Palmer's aide watched and listened to the way Delmont went about handling a senior ranking officer, a skill every ambitious officer needed to perfect if he expected to break free of the pack and make a mark for himself in a highly competitive profession.

9

FORT LEWIS, WASHINGTON

Together with half a dozen other soldiers newly assigned to the 3rd Battalion of the 75th Rangers, Private First Class Eric White sat in the hall of the battalion headquarters waiting for someone to direct them to their next stop along the long and torturous ritual known as in-processing that all personnel reporting to a new post must endure. For White and the five who had been following him in a roundabout way for the last five months this promised to be the last stop they would need to make before they reached a goal all of them had been working on all that time. Like the accidental comrades who sat waiting with him in the hall of the battalion headquarters for someone from their newly assigned company to pick them up and lead them across the quad to their respective companies, White had opted to become a Ranger when he had joined the Army.

His reasons for doing so were just as much a mystery to him now as they had been when he had started a journey that had been long, demanding, and at times downright painful. Its origins went back to his senior year in high school when his school counselor called him to his office and asked what colleges he intended to apply to. Without having to think about it White realized that the last thing he wanted to do was to go straight off to college following graduation as his older brother and sister had. After four years and three changes in majors, his brother still wasn't quite sure what he wanted to do with his life, a point White's father carped on every time the subject came up. Besides, the thought of spending four or more years in a classroom listening to a pasty-faced assistant professor or teaching assistant babble on about something White had no interest in, while accruing a mountain of debt with no clear idea of where he was going didn't appeal to him. Nor did the thought of flipping hamburgers or working as an unskilled laborer with a crew of illegals who couldn't even speak English. Since staying at home was not something he even wanted to think about, the idea of joining the Army matured from being nothing more than a passing thought to becoming his most viable option.

If White's decision to enlist was somewhat hazy to him it came as a total shock to his parents, both of whom were college-educated, dyed-in-the-wool Democrats. Neither could phantom why one of their children would go off and do such a thing. Throughout White's senior year it became a recurring topic of discussion, one that started out reasonable enough until the date when he would have to apply for college came and went without their darling baby boy doing anything. That was when they became desperate and their demeanor strident. By graduation day they were downright frantic. "Son," White's father implored, "you can't do this to us. We've worked too hard to see you throw your life away in such a foolish manner."

Rather than knuckle under Eric White became more and more determined to go through with his decision. As an added touch, one that had not been part of his original plan, when it finally came to signing his enlistment contract with the recruiter he insisted that he be slotted for

Ranger training. In the end things became so contentious at home that his departure for Basic training at Fort Benning came as something of a relief to both White and his parents.

Signing up to become a Ranger did not a Ranger make him. To start with White had to be a three-time volunteer, which meant that in addition to joining the Army of his own free will he had to volunteer again for airborne training, and if he completed that successfully, volunteer once more for the Ranger Indoctrination Program, giving real meaning to the Ranger motto Sua Sponte, Latin for "of their own accord." But before that happened he would have to complete Basic Combat Training, an eight-week course that is often referred to as simply "Basic."

Though at times it was challenging to the young man of nineteen Basic Combat Training turned out to be the easiest of the programs he needed to endure before he became a full-fledged Ranger. Immediately following Basic came four weeks of Infantry Advanced Individual Training, or AIT, where many of the rudimentary combat skills White had picked up in Basic were honed and other more demanding tasks specific to the infantry were introduced. It was during this stretch that he noted that the attitude of the cadre responsible for training him and his fellow recruits was changing. They were becoming more exacting, less tolerant of those who did not display an all-out effort in all they did, for unlike Basic where surprisingly few who finished it would be assigned to a combat arm, everyone that went to Infantry AIT was destined for line unit. "We're here to prepare you for the ultimate Go-No Go test, combat," one drill instructor told them on their first day of instruction. "Those who get a go in battle can go home and play with Mama. Everybody else gets a toe tag and leakproof bag."

This trend redoubled at Airborne School, a three-week course where the black-hatted cadre spared no effort when it came to weeding out the weak, the lame, and the lazy. There the first sergeant of White's student company made his acquaintance with White and his fellow trainees by announcing to them in the predawn darkness of Fort Benning, "If you want a friend, get a dog. If you want to be a paratrooper, follow me." With that the gruff NCO pivoted about and led his company on a five-mile run that left White wishing he had something to throw up.

It was only after uncounted miles of running through the pine forests of Benning and five jumps from a C-17 transport that White was afforded the opportunity of volunteering one last time. On this occasion no one asked him to sign a paper or extracted an oath. Instead, prior to the graduation ceremony at which they would receive their coveted jump wings all those recruits who had previously indicated that they wanted to be Rangers were taken aside and briefed by members of the Ranger Indoctrination Program cadre. Like all the other sergeants who had been in charge of their training up to this point, these men spoke to the recruits in a tone that was blunt, explaining to the nervous, grim-faced volunteers as best they could what their lives would be like if they elected to continue along the path they had been pursuing. By the time the Ranger instructors were done, twelve of the thirty-eight men who had trooped into the room with White changed their minds. The others were greeted the next day by a bus that took them to the old jump school barracks, ancient wooden buildings from another era situated around a barren clay field known as Red Square because of the color of the Georgia clay.

The Ranger instructors wasted no time in introducing White and his comrades, now known as "rippies," to their first Ranger smoke session, jargon for tough physical training. They were taught a new way to do push-ups, for regular push-ups weren't tough enough for Rangers. From now on only elevated or Ranger push-ups were permitted, an exercise that requires the soldier to place the toes of his feet against a pole, rock, or wall as high as he can while planting his hands on the ground. When the last of them had tumbled down onto the dirt in a heap after doing as many Ranger push-ups as they could, the rippies were ordered to complete a circuit of Red Square on their stomachs under the watchful eye of Ranger instructors who used their boot to push anyone who wasn't keeping a profile that was low enough to suit the instructor down into the red clay.

The physical and verbal abuse that had been growing in intensity as he had progressed from one course to the next reached a new high, or low depending upon how you saw things. There was no viciousness behind it, no pleasure derived by those who administered it. It was not meant to be sadistic or mean-spirited. Like the extreme physical exertions that went hand in hand, its purpose was to push young Americans to their limit and beyond. None of the Ranger instructors held back, no one cut any of the rippies in their charge any slack. They always seemed to be there, ready to use a boot to press against the small of a trainee's back while he was crawling along the ground or yank him off his bunk and onto the floor if he lingered too long in it as another Ranger instructor ran through the barracks in the morning banging on a garbage can to wake them. Even in the chow line, White and his companions weren't allowed to relax. If they wanted to eat they literally had to hold their plates up to their mouths using a spoon to shovel the food down their throats without bothering to take the time to chew it.

The pressure to keep going, to endure the grueling demands that were heaped upon him every waking hour, demanded every ounce of determination and strength White could muster. Not everyone was able to preserve or tolerate the treatment that never let up, never relented. From day one to the very end a day didn't go by without someone buckling under it. To White's astonishment, a fair number of those washing out were men who he had viewed as being bigger or tougher or stronger than he. Oftentimes, when that moment came they would simply collapse right in the middle of the road or Red Square, reduced to sobbing like children when they realized that they had failed. Without ceremony these hapless souls were whisked away by the cadre. They were not afforded a second chance or permitted an opportunity to say farewells to those they had shared this man-made hell with. In the morning there was someone in the bunk on both sides of White. By evening one or both of those bunks would be empty. Like everything else, this too played upon White's mind as he soon found himself wondering not if, but when he would join them.

That day did not come. Quite suddenly it was over. Like waking up from a nightmare White and twenty-five of the sixty-three rippies he had started out with found themselves standing on Red Square with a Ranger battalion patch on their left shoulder and a distinctive tan beret covering their shaved heads. They were "batboys" now, Rangers who had met every test that had been heaped upon them and had earned the right to serve in the finest light infantry battalions in the world. And while the Ranger instructors who looked on during this final assembly knew that many days of brutal training lay ahead for these newly minted Rangers once they had reached their units, not a single man standing with White had any doubt that they could take on whatever came their way.

Still not quite recovered from the weeks of demanding training and sleep deprivation that he had endured in order to get here, White found he was unable to keep from dozing off as he sat cross-legged on the floor waiting in the hall of the 3rd Battalion's headquarters building. This was how Specialist Four Anthony Park, a rifleman in first Platoon, Company A, found him. Park had to use the tip of his crutch, tapping White's thigh several times with it before he was able to elicit a response.

Startled, the newly assigned Ranger sprang up onto his feet like a taut jack-in-the-box, almost bowling Park over in the process. The panic in White's face brought a hint of a smile to Park's face.

Still not quite over the trauma that three weeks of Ranger Indoctrination had inflicted upon his psyche, White was embarrassed and a bit rattled at being caught off guard like this. It took him several seconds to sort out that A, all that was behind him and B, he hadn't screwed up. As least he thought he hadn't screwed up.

Wide awake now White did his best to compose himself as he peered down at the Korean-American Ranger supporting himself on a pair of crutches. Park, who was a full half a head shorter than him, held his left leg cocked back. A battered cast that sported numerous handwritten mottos poked out of that ACU trouser leg. By now White and the other newly assigned Rangers who had been waiting for someone from their assigned companies to come up to battalion for them were savvy enough to know that one did not pass judgment on another man based on size alone. Instead their eyes were immediately drawn to the specialist four's left shoulder where a black and yellow Ranger tab sat proudly perched above the 3rd Battalion unit patch. That tab could only be earned by an enlisted "batboy" by attending the sixty-one-day Ranger School that White and the others had been told made all the training they had suffered through thus far pale by comparison. Even more impressive than that however was the 3rd Battalion scroll Park sported on his right shoulder. This duplicate of the unit's patch worn by everyone in the battalion on the left sleeve announced to all who saw him that he had been in combat with this unit.

Knowing that these newbies were checking him out to see if he was worthy of their respect and obedience Park paused a moment to allow the subtle meaning that his patches conveyed to sink in. Only when he was ready did Park glance down at the small three-by-five index card he held between his fingers and rattle off the names of the men he had been called to battalion to pick up. "Hupe, Gonzales, Jamison, White. You newbies are assigned to Ass-kickin' Alpha. Gather up your shit and follow me."

The four individuals Park had called out didn't hesitate

as they all but knocked each other over in their scramble to police up their gear and take off after the short, muscular Ranger who had deftly pivoted about on his crutches and begun to hobble toward the door without waiting for his charges. On their way out they passed several soldiers assigned to the battalion staff. While they were all Rangers, none of them sported a Ranger tab. Priority for filling Ranger course slots went to those enlisted men in the line companies who had been with the battalion for at least a year and were recommended by their chain of command. "Pogues," a less than affectionate moniker used to identify personnel assigned to the headquarters company, seldom were afforded that opportunity.

At the door Park paused only long enough to fish his tan beret out of a leg pocket. He took great care to smooth it down over his head, straightened up the distinctive black-bordered blue, white, red, and green flash displayed on the front of it, ensuring that it was properly situated above his right eye as he did so. With a tug he pulled the beret's outer edge down over the top of his right ear. When he was ready he took off on his crutches, bounding across the open parade ground known as the Quad as naturally as most men walk.

When they were well out of earshot of anyone else, Park began to speak. "You people are lucky to be assigned to Alpha."

Not having expected to be addressed by their crippled escort, the four newly assigned Rangers broke out of the single file they had instinctively formed behind Park and hustled up on either side of him to hear what he was saying. As before, Park didn't wait on his charges before he continued on. "The old man doesn't believe in hazing or hassling newbies. Both Captain Dixon and the First Sergeant Carney keep a tight lid on the specialist four mafia."

Foolishly Kiel Jamison asked what the specialist four mafia was.

Stopping on a dime, Park looked up at his little flock

as they reined themselves in, did a quick about-face, and gathered around him. "Me, you tabless newbie shits. Me and all the spec fours in this battalion who've earned their Ranger tabs. Here the sergeants don't have the time or the inclination to screw with your little minds like they did at Benning. So those of us who have our tabs take up the slack in an effort to make sure you don't lose your edge."

By now White had no difficulty in suppressing his urge to smirk when someone was feeding him what he took to be a line of BS. Instead, he masked his thoughts behind the deadpan expression he had used so effectively at Benning.

"Anyone else got any stupid questions?" No one said a word. Instead, the four newly assigned Rangers glanced at Parks and each other, shaking their heads as they did so. "Good! Since the whole company's out conducting a forced march and I'm the only one left all I can do is deposit you in the squad rooms the first sergeant assigned you to. You'll be living in that room with three other tabless shits like yourselves until a two-man room comes open, so feel free to make yourself at home."

White was tempted to ask Park what time the company would be back and what they should do until then but didn't, lest he incur the crippled specialist four's wrath as Jamison had. Instead, once he had been shown which room to go into White set his gear against the side of a wall locker where he thought it would be out of the way. Taking a moment, he looked about the room furnished with simple Army-issue beds, wall lockers, a couple of desks, and a few chairs. While no one would ever be able to describe it as being "cozy," his current surroundings were a damned sight better than the Early American Gulag decor he had gotten used to during his time at the RIP.

With nothing better to do at the moment and unsure which of the wall lockers would be his, White plopped down on an unmade bunk stuck off in a corner he assumed was unassigned. With his back propped up in the corner, he pulled the Clive Cussler paperback he had been reading during his long and tedious in-processing and opened it to where he had left off. Despite the intriguing story line and the gusty pace of the novel within five minutes he was sound asleep.

As before, his blissful slumber was brought to an abrupt and painful end. One moment he was peacefully dead to the world, the next he found himself crumpled up in a heap on the floor looking up into the enraged face of a fellow Ranger fully decked out in his field kit towering above him. Making no effort to check his anger, the enraged specialist four all but spit as he yelled at White. "Who the hell gave you permission to squat your ass on my bunk?"

Stunned and not a little befuddled, White struggled to untangle himself from the twisted heap he found himself in, mumbling a weak apology as he did so. "Sorry, I thought it wasn't being used by anyone."

"You thought?" White's tormentor barked. "Who gave you permission to think?"

Before he could come up with a suitable answer a voice from across the room boomed out. "Put a sock in it, Andy." In a flash the demeanor of the man who had been verbally assailing him changed as he stepped back and to one side. In his place a new figure appeared. Standing above White with his hands on his hips, the sergeant glanced down at him. "On your feet, Ranger."

Doing his best to comply as quickly as he could, White scrambled to his feet. Seeing the room was full of other sweating, steely-eyed Rangers in full field gear with the exception of their helmets, White instinctively pressed his back against the wall. Though he could clearly see his crisp, new name tab the sergeant before him began by asking him to identify himself.

"Private First Class Eric White. I was told to wait here until you returned."

"Well," the sergeant stated without a hint of a smile,

"we're back." For several seconds the two looked at each other, the sergeant standing with his hands on his hips staring at White while he stood at attention.

During this awkward standoff several other Rangers White assumed belonged to the squad began to gather around, giving the new man a once-over. One man, an African-American PFC who had jerked the bed out from under White while he had been asleep, smirked. "He doesn't look done to me. I say we ship his ass back to Benning."

Another man who stood just behind the sergeant's left shoulder shook his head. "Na! That would be a waste of taxpayers' money. We'll just march him till he drops like the last rippie they sent us and roll his worthless body into the nearest ditch."

Doing his best to keep his growing anger in check, White said nothing as one man after another let his opinion be known. The last man in the room was about to add his two cents when a voice from somewhere out in the hall caused everyone in the room to step away from White and scatter. "Okay, people, playtime is over. Weapons inspection in thirty minutes."

By the time Sergeant First Class Frederick Smart entered the room everyone but White had turned away from him and began to break down their assigned weapon as they prepared to clean them. "You, new man," Smart beckoned. "Report to the first sergeant pronto. Bring a copy of your orders with you."

Thrilled to be afforded the opportunity to escape from the room full of overbearing strangers, White shouted out the best "hooah," he could muster, picked up a manila folder that he had laid on top of his gear, and took off after Smart who had already left the room. But before White made it through the door the sergeant E-5 who had been staring him down shouted out, "Hey you, newbie. Take the rest of your shit with you."

Confused, White stopped short, pivoted about, and

looked around at everyone in the room, trying to figure if the sergeant was serious.

"You heard me. You've got five seconds to get it out of my squad room."

Deciding that he had best do so White scrambled back, gathered up his belongings one more time, and made a quick exit.

Once in the hall, White called out to Smart, "Excuse me, Sergeant."

Pausing, Smart turned around and watched as the newly assigned Ranger dragging everything he owned and had been issued since arriving on post drew near. "Specialist Four Park, the charge of quarters who greeted us at battalion told me I was going to be assigned to the first squad."

"You are," Smart responded. "But that room you were in belongs to third squad. Your squad room is farther down the hall."

White found the other three newly assigned Rangers who had accompanied him to Alpha Company were already in the orderly room filling out more forms. Depositing his gear off to one side he went over to where the first sergeant sat at an angle behind his desk, leaning back in a chair that was precariously balanced on its back legs. The company's top sergeant paid White no heed as White presented him a set of his orders. "Private First Class White reporting."

Carney, as dirty and tired as everyone else in the company from the grueling twenty-five-mile forced march they had just completed, simply glanced up from the pistol barrel he had been cleaning. "You certainly took your time reporting to me. That's not a good way to start out."

Rather than try to explain White just mumbled, "Yes, Sergeant," and waited, orders in hand to be told what to do next.

"Give those to my clerk over there," Carney stated flatly as he nodded his head toward a specialist four who was half hidden behind a desk piled high with reams of paper stuffed in bulging manila folders and a computer monitor. "He'll trade you for some more forms you need to fill out."

Up to now White had meekly done exactly what he had been told to do, asking no questions or wondering why he was being pushed, pulled, and prodded through a never-ending gauntlet. At Fort Benning he understood the logic of their methods and had accepted the harsh regime that was designed to weed out the unfit and model those who survived the ordeal into elite soldiers. He was even able to tolerate the indifference that had greeted him at both the post's central in-processing center and battalion headquarters. All through that long and grueling process he somehow was able to keep his spirits up knowing that once he reached his company things would change. He didn't quite know how they would change, but he was confident that they would.

Now that illusion, that hope that his days of trials and tribulations were over, had been crushed by the vicious little prank the specialist who had picked them up at battalion had played on him and the nonchalance with which his first sergeant was now dismissing him. Only the realization that to say something now in front of everyone would make things worse kept White from speaking up. Instead, he meekly did as he had become accustomed to doing. He swallowed hard, turned away, and shuffled on over to the desk where the company clerk was fumbling with the forward guard assembly of his rifle. There the specialist four, another tabbed Ranger like Park took White's orders and handed him a fistful of forms without even looking up at him.

White was in the midst of filling out what he thought to be the umpteen-thousandth form he had been required to complete in the past few days when an officer strolled into the orderly room. Quickly the four newly assigned men glanced at each other, wondering if they should come to attention. Throughout all their training at Benning, from Basic to RIP, being in the room with an officer was a truly rare thing. On those occasions when one graced them with his presence everyone popped to attention. Only after White and his companions saw that the presence of the captain wasn't causing a stir among the other Rangers in the room did they turn once more to look at each other, this time exchanging sheepish smirks over their unfounded nervousness before going back to filling in blank forms.

Making his way over to the first sergeant's desk, the captain paused as he waited until the company's senior NCO was finished running a cleaning rod down the barrel of his pistol. "Hey, Top, you have any clean patches?"

Looking up from the barrel he was working on, First Sergeant Carney searched his desktop before answering. "I'm afraid I'm down to my last few."

From across the room, the company clerk popped his head up over the improvised barricade of paperwork. "I've got a fresh pack you can have, sir."

Turning, the captain cupped his hands in front of him. "Great, give 'em here."

Cocking his arm back, the specialist four yelled out in a loud voice "Shot, over," and tossed the pack of cleaning patches. After catching them the captain held them up and smiled. "Splash, out. Mucho gracias, Sanchez." He was about to leave when he took a moment to look over the four privates scattered about the orderly room who had ceased filling in their forms in order to watch his every move. In turn the captain scrutinized each of them with a dispassionate eye. "This all we're getting?" he asked.

Carney paused what he was doing and turned his attention to the newly assigned Rangers. "Park tells me there were only six and we got the pick of the litter."

The captain thought about that for a moment before grunting. "Well, I guess they'll have to do." Turning away from the four enlisted men and looking back toward Carney, the captain sighed. "Top, I'm not in the mood to give them a rousing welcome speech at the moment. Have them report to me tomorrow morning."

"Roger that, sir."

Without another word the captain wandered out of the orderly room, stoop-shouldered and perplexed, as if he was preoccupied with a matter of great importance.

When each of the other Rangers who had accompanied White to Company A had completed their forms, they went up to the specialist four who was responsible for the paperwork and handed it back to him. In turn he told them to head back to their respective squads and report to their squad leaders. Being the last in, White was the only one left when it came his turn to do so. He was about to approach the specialist four seated in the corner of the room when that man stood up, raised his arms above his head, and yawned. "I'm done, Top. If you'd like I'll take your pistol down to the arms room."

Enmeshed in sorting through the contents of his in-box, the first sergeant simply nodded. "By all means, be my guest."

Passing White as if he were nothing more than a lamppost on a street corner that had to be avoided, the company clerk took Carney's pistol and left the room, leaving White standing in the middle of the room with the first sergeant and a fistful of filled-in forms. Not sure what to do, White made his way back to Carney's desk where he waited several seconds to be acknowledged, even if it were nothing more than a simple "put 'em there," or some similar remark. When it became clear that he was going to be ignored, White found he was no longer able to hold his tongue. "I know I'm out of line, and I'm gonna catch hell for what I'm about to say, but I can't not say it."

Taken aback by this unexpected outburst, Carney stopped what he was doing and looked up at White. The situation was akin to the moment in the play when little

Oliver stood before the headmaster asking for another helping of soup.

"I've been here for one whole day," White rattled on now that he had finally mustered up the necessary courage to say something. "I know that's not much but I would have thought that at some point during the day someone would have taken the time to look me in the eye and say something like welcome, or glad to see you, or how the hell are you. I mean I know this is a combat unit and I know it has the proud reputation of being the home of the baddest hombres in the whole United States Army. But is this the way it's going to be for us new guys? Are we going to be treated like contemptible little shits forever?"

Slowly, carefully, Carney eased back into his seat, looking up at White as he did so. The first sergeant had spent his entire adult life in the Army, serving in numerous units in times of peace and war. He had seen good times and bad times, enduring every sort of trial and tribulation that a professional soldier had to deal with as his youth slowly seeped away in the service of a people that often scorned the very men charged with defending their freedoms and rights. That service had cost him a wife and earned him two purple hearts. And while the enemies that he and his fellow NCOs trained their men to meet during those long and trying years changed with maddening regularity, the nature of the young men he was expected to lead never did. The names were all different as were their faces, but not their character. Some were always a bit shaky in the beginning, unsure of themselves and their chosen profession. Others were so damned self-assured that they tended to be insufferably cocky. A few, like the soldier standing before him showed spirit from the get-go, an attitude that attested to a confidence and fortitude that could not be bent or broken.

When confronted by a young soldier like this Carney found through experience that it was best to be both direct and open. A man with the sand to take on his company first sergeant on his first day in the unit needed to be carefully nurtured and guided so that his latent leadership potential could mature into a constructive and positive force rather than a loose cannon that could prove to be more deadly to its own squad mates than the enemy.

Slowly, a hint of a smile crept across Carney's face. "I imagine that after everything you've been through in order to get here your first day in Company A has turned out to be something of a real bust."

Sensing that he was free to respond, up to a point, White nodded. "I'm not looking for a bunch of glad-handing and painted on smiley faces, First Sergeant. They told us time and time again that doing time in a Ranger battalion was serious business. But I mean . . ." Pausing, White found that he needed to think about what he meant.

Sensing that the young man was perplexed, Carney stood up, came out from behind his desk, and put his hand on White's shoulder. "Grab your gear, Ranger, and follow me. I'll take you upstairs and get you settled in."

Carney's appearance with White in tow sent a powerful message to anyone else who was of a mind to screw with the new man. And should someone still not understand it, Carney made it a point to announce in a loud voice as he handed White off to his platoon sergeant, "Fred, take care to see that this Ranger is settled in. He's had a hell of a time getting here and is eager to get down to business."

Having already sorted out what Park had done to the new man before being sent down to the orderly room by him, Frederick Smart gave Carney a wink and a nod. "Not to worry, Top. I'll personally see that everything is taken care of."

"You do that."

On his way back to the orderly room Carney found himself having second thoughts about blowing the matter off as little more than another case of "old-timers" screwing with a newbie. By the time he reached his office he had pretty much decided to ignore the stack of paperwork he had left on his desk and instead he turned toward his C.O.'s office for a much-needed heart-to-heart chat that he had been putting off for far too long. Sticking his head into Nathan's office, Carney cleared his throat. "Sir, you have a moment?"

Despite his preoccupation with other issues, Nathan leaned back in his chair and motioned to his first sergeant to take a seat. Closing the door behind him Carney made his way to one of the worn Army-issue chairs that lined the walls of Nathan's small office, doing his best to avoid looking over at his commanding officer as he did so.

Just as White had done when addressing his concern with him, Carney gingerly sidled up to the issue he wished to broach with Dixon. "I know we've been over this ground before, and dwelling on it isn't going to make much of a difference one way or the other. But . . ."

Although he had suspected that he already knew what Carney was going to discuss before he had taken his seat, his first sergeant's tone of voice and his uncharacteristic hesitancy to look up at him as he spoke confirmed Nathan's suspicions. "Don't tell me," Nathan stated wearily. "Morale sucks and the natives are restless."

Sitting on the edge of his seat with his legs spread apart, elbows resting on his knees and fingers tightly laced before him, Carney looked up at his commanding officer. "Yeah, something like that."

"And you feel we need to do something about it."

Carney nodded. "Something like that."

Settling down in his own chair, Nathan folded his hands over his stomach as he rested his elbows on the worn arms of his chair while he playfully twisted his swivel seat this way and that using his feet. "Soooo, what do we do? How do we get highly trained soldiers, men who are rumored to be the best of the best, to stop acting like a whimpering pack of beaten dogs and get on with the serious business of being Rangers?"

Carney winced every time he heard his commanding officer describe the conduct of their people like this. It was Nathan's way of trying to put things in perspective, of trivializing an issue that was, when all other things were considered, anything but trivial.

Seeing that he had managed to achieve the desired effect he had been hoping for, Nathan sat bolt upright and folded his hands on his desktop before him in a single, swift motion. "Look, First Sergeant, I've been over this issue in my head again and again and again. A morning doesn't go by when I wake up thinking to myself what are we doing wrong? What can I do to make things better for our company? And no matter how I break it down, no matter how I examine every aspect of our operation inside and out, I keep coming up with the same inescapable conclusions."

Having regained his balance, Carney also straightened up in his seat. "And they are?"

"As much as you and I might dislike the colonel's style and methods, we both know that he hasn't done anything that is wrong or in violation of regulations. Everything he's done, every policy he has put forth, every reprimand and criticism he has leveled against this company as a whole or at an individual soldier belonging to it, has been correct and in the main deserved. We may not like the manner with which he points out our deficiencies or the frequency with which he does so, but that, First Sergeant, just happens to be the way he operates. Colonel Delmont just isn't a warm fuzzy sort of guy. A prick, yes. An asshole, without doubt. A dyed-in-the-wool grade-A government-certified bastard, granted. But a good-time Charlie, no. So long as he follows the book and doesn't order us to do something that is dumb or dangerous there isn't diddly squat you or I can do other than salute smartly and sound off with a rousing hooah whenever he barks."

"But that's just it, sir. This isn't a 'by the book' sort of unit. Though some may look at our organization and see a conventional battalion, we're not. This unit, and every man in it, is something special."

Maintaining a calm, even tone Nathan stared at Carney. It was a hard, uncompromising stare, the sort a father uses when he is laying down the law. "That's right, First Sergeant. They are special. They're better than this. They're hard men doing a hard job."

Having gone this far Carney wasn't about to give up, not until he had made his point. "But they are men, Captain Dixon," he stated firmly. "They're good men, each and every one of them. They're perhaps the best soldiers I have ever had the privilege of serving with. But they are just that, men, some of whom have yet to celebrate their twentieth birthday. Even you know that you can't maintain the pace we've been saddled with since we've returned from the Philippines on nothing but the steady ration of shit. I know you don't like to go about bragging and you discourage it among the rest of the company. But damn it, sir, hands down we're the best company in this battalion, if not the entire regiment."

Sensing that they were fast approaching a point that neither dare go, Nathan abruptly cut his first sergeant off. "Exactly my point! As such they should know just how pathetic it is for men of their quality to go moping about like a gaggle of cherry recruits fresh off the bus at Basic who have just been reprimanded by their drill sergeant for the first time." Squirming about in his seat, Nathan stared into Carney's eyes. "I know you're concerned about the state of the company. I know I am. And if you're like me at the moment you're frustrated as hell because you haven't got the faintest idea of what we can do to snap our people out of this funk they've managed to work themselves into."

Taking in a deep breath, Carney found he had to agree with everything his commanding officer, a man who was more than twelve years his junior had said. "You're right, Captain. Right down the line you're spot on. But," he added as he stood up, "being right about the colonel doesn't mean squat to the men in this company. While they don't expect to be praised for every little thing they do, they damn well don't deserve to be dumped upon twenty-four/seven for every hair that's out of place and button that's unbuttoned."

Nathan said nothing as he looked up at Carney. What could he say? His first sergeant was right. Sensing that he couldn't simply leave things as they stood, that he needed to put some sort of period on this tense little session and smooth things over a bit, Nathan also stood up, looking down at scribbled notes that he had been working on before Carney had interrupted as he did so. "Be that as it may," he mumbled. "At the moment we seem to have a few more immediate concerns that need to be dealt with. While they may not be as critical to the overall well-being of the company as the topic we were discussing, they are nonetheless pressing and rather time sensitive."

Resigning himself to the fact that his commanding officer was as stymied as he was when it came to finding a way of effectively dealing with the fractious effect their battalion commander's style of leadership was having on the company, Carney shrugged. "So, Captain, what's the crisis du jour?"

"We need to put out the word that there's a change in training schedule for tomorrow before the company scatters to the four winds. Instead of moving out at oh nine hundred as is currently posted we're to assemble in the battalion classroom at that hour for a block of instruction on field fortifications and defense of a strongpoint."

Caught off guard by this, Carney made a face as he shook his head. "Defense of a strongpoint? As in 'remember the Alamo'? Who dreamed this one up?"

"Well, I have my suspicions," Nathan replied quietly, "as I am sure you do. But it was Major Perry who called the change into me just before you came in."

"Who's teaching the class?"

"Lieutenant Laski has the honor of enlightening us on

the art and science of digging holes and filling sand-bags."

Carney thought for a moment. "Does he know he's been tagged for this?"

For the first time since his first sergeant had entered the room Nathan chuckled. "As a matter of fact no. But I am about to correct that minor deficiency."

Moving out from behind his desk, Nathan stepped up next to Carney. "How about the two of us sally forth and go throughout the company like Revere and Dawes, spreading the word and raising the alarm as we go."

Glad at being offered a graceful way out of the subject he'd brought up Carney forced himself to smile. "Roger that, sir." Seizing the doorknob, he opened the door and waved Nathan on. "After you, *mon capitan.*"

10

ARLINGTON, VIRGINIA

One of the first lessons anyone assigned to the Pentagon quickly learns is that the normal rules governing how things are done elsewhere in the Army do not necessarily apply within the walls of the squat five-sided maze located on the banks of the Potomac. Principles that govern how soldiers conduct themselves when executing their assigned duties that are critical to the success of operations in the field are all too often set aside by staff officers who place self-interest or the promotion of a project near and dear to their heart above the overall good of the service they represent. This results in behavior that is more comparable to the cutthroat culture of corporate America than the high-minded ideology that eager young cadets at West Point are taught to aspire to. The second lesson is closely related to the first. One only needs to attempt to make a stand against this erosion of ethics to discover that it is not only a waste of time, but from a career standpoint it can be downright dangerous. One good man, no matter how noble his cause or stout his heart, may be no match for a bureaucracy that would bring Saint George to his knees.

Being an astute tactician, Scott Dixon prided himself on his ability to quickly assess situations he often found himself facing and develop techniques that allowed him to mitigate the majority of the Machiavellian maneuvers some of his more headstrong and ambitious subordinates used to outflank him. Still, no matter how vigilant he was, Scott was not able to keep everyone from slipping under the wire in an effort to catch the ear of the Secretary of Defense without his knowing about it first. More than once Henry Jones, Scott's immediate superior, called Scott into his office to ask about an operational plan that had somehow seeped out of the bowels of Scott's section and onto the Sec Def's desk without either man knowing anything about it. On those occasions the only thing Scott could do was shrug his shoulders, tell Jones he'd get back to him as soon as he had managed to get up to speed on the issue, and make tracks back to his own office, opining as he went for the good old days when Army regulations allowed an officer to have errant subordinates flogged.

Every now and then the Fates would intervene, allowing Scott to stumble upon a hereto unknown project that he was not supposed to know about. One such slipup occurred during a routine update that Scott's executive officer, Lieutenant Colonel Frank Bellus, delivered to him each morning. While enumerating the current operational plans that were being worked on by the plans section, Bellus made mention of one that Scott had never heard of. With a wave of his hand Scott signed Bellus to pause. "Excuse me, but my mind was wandering a bit. Would you go over the status of that last OPLAN?"

Having worked with his general long enough to know that Scott's statement was simply a ploy to cover the fact that he had been caught off guard, Bellus backed up. "Operation Doberman will be ready to be briefed to the Sec Def by the end of the week."

Knowing of Palmer's affinity for canines with an

attitude, Scott didn't need to hear anything more than the name to know that this was something Palmer had dreamed up and was trying to slip by him. Leaning back in his chair, Scott looked up at the ceiling. "I see. Well, when we're done here be so kind as to have whoever is working on it bring his draft briefing and all supporting documents to me. I need to bone up on it some before we go forward with it."

Scott's response and tone warned Bellus that something was amiss. Making a note, Bellus nodded. "Yes, sir. I'll see to that personally."

Out of the corner of his eye, Scott watched his executive officer in an effort to see how Bellus was behaving, wondering if he was part of this little caper. When he caught himself doing so, Scott shook his head. Good God, he thought, I've been here way too long.

Without warning Scott lurched forward, sitting upright in his seat. This sudden response caught Bellus off guard, startling him. Embarrassed, he stared at Scott as if expecting his general to leap up out of his seat. Amused by his executive officer's expression, Scott smiled. "Sorry, Frank. I didn't mean to wake you."

Regaining his composure, Bellus sheepishly tried to brush aside his momentary lapse. "Sorry, sir. My mind was on something else."

"Hmmm. Seems to be a lot of that going around this morning."

Joining in the humor, Bellus chuckled. "Yes, sir. Seems to be. Now," he stated crisply after clearing his throat, "other OPLANs still in the mill are as follows . . ."

Just as his executive officer had briefed, Operation Doberman was all but ready to go forward. Only a few odds and ends were missing, omissions that were mostly related to the designation of the Air Force and naval units that would be tasked to support the operation. When the project officer did not have a firm commitment from his sister service counterpart he left a blank on the troop list where the identification of all elements slated to participate in Doberman were enumerated. There were no such blanks in the section delineating Army units that would be involved. Every element, down to the smallest detachment, was identified. Topping this list was the unit that would bear the brunt of the combat operations described in the OPLAN: the 3rd Battalion, 75th Rangers.

Having carefully read the entire OPLAN Scott took a moment to go over the troop list in detail, doing all sorts of mental calculations as he war-gamed the concept of the operation in his mind in an effort to see if he could discover some flaw that would invalidate the whole package. When he could not detect any obvious pitfalls or errors he took a moment to review the troop list of Army units one last time before slowly closing the cover marked "Top Secret."

With his right hand resting on the folder, Scott eased back in his seat and closed his eyes. It was moments like this that made him regret the fact that his oldest son had followed him through VMI and into the Army. All the selfish pride those seemingly innocent acts had brought him were forgotten when he realized that his current duty, in the place that generated the plans that could very well set in motion a train of events that could result in Nathan's death. How, he wondered, would he be able to live with himself if such a thing ever happened? Would he be able to look at his son's wife and tell her with a straight face how sorry he was? Would he be able to enjoy his own personal guilty pleasures again, many of which he and Nathan had once shared, knowing that Nathan would never enjoy them with him again?

Scott hated moments like this, moments when his professional duties collided with personal interests. The OPLAN before him was no different than dozens that he reviewed day in, day out. Throughout a career that stretched across thirty years he had literally written hundreds of operational plans. Were it not for the fact that his son's unit was listed as one of many elements, this plan would have been no different than any of the others.

But it was different, different because Scott could put a face to one of the thousands of men and women who would be involved in the operation. It was a very special face, one that was almost a mirror image of a younger, more carefree Scott Dixon. Opening his eyes, he looked down at the OPLAN before him. It was a good plan. A bit high risk to say the least, but a solid piece of work nonetheless, one that he could not hold up or turn back based on purely technical reasons. Were he to try to keep it from going forth he would be accused by his detractors that he was doing so for personal reasons. They would have been right, of course.

All his life Scott had soldiered on in war and peace, gladly accepting all the hardships that came his way in the hope that by doing so his sons would be able to live in a better world, one in which they would never be called upon to endure the horrors and suffering that he had been witness to. That this turned out to be a false hope pained Scott. That he would have a hand in sending one of his own sons into harm's way pained him, leading him to the terrible conclusion that in many ways his life had been a failure.

Finding himself teetering on the edge of a dark abyss that he knew he dare not look into, Scott stood up. Picking up the folder, he slowly made his way to Henry Jones's office, the next stop for Operation Doberman.

MINDANAO, PHILIPPINES

A reputation can be a powerful force, one that has the ability to win battles before the first shot is ever fired. The Mongolians understood this when they swept across the Steppes of Russia and into Eastern Europe in the thirteenth century, reaping such havoc and mayhem as they went that the mere arrival of a handful of Mongol scouts at the gates of a city was often enough to compel its inhabitants to capitulate lest they incur the invader's wrath. Hamdani Summirat also appreciated the value of a fearsome reputation, leading him to carefully nurture one that would have made a Mongol warlord proud.

It had only taken three sharp engagements to rock the Filipino military back on its heels, creating so much trepidation among the rank and file of the Army that its senior leadership had little choice but to acknowledge that it had lost its ability to conduct offensive operations against the Abu Sayyaf. Had they possessed the means to do so they would have gone after the tiny band of rebels Summirat led until they had run every last insurgent to ground. On paper they had at their command units and personnel in sufficient numbers needed for this sort of campaign. Young staff officers absconded in air-conditioned offices in Manila had even drafted plans for the employment of those masses.

Unfortunately for them and the senior officers whom they worked for, numbers meant little in the sort of war Summirat was waging. As Robert McNamara had discovered in the sixties, one could not measure the power of an army merely by counting its bayonets and those wielded by its foes. It is the will to use them and the determination required to press on until victory is achieved regardless of the hardships and losses that matter in battle. It was the lack of this will that led the generals in Manila and on Mindanao to abdicate virtual sovereignty over western Mindanao to Summirat. As difficult as it was for the proud generals who had been entrusted with defending the government in Manila and its people to accept this sad state of affairs, each man who had a say in the matter knew it would be worse than foolish to send troops who had neither the will nor the training into the jungle after Summirat. To have done so would have been criminal.

Those ignorant of this military reality failed to understand this. After counting the number of troops available to Manila and comparing it to the estimated size of the insurgents facing them they wondered aloud why the Filipino Army simply didn't march into the jungle and crush Summirat's burgeoning reign of terror. Throughout the world media pundits and the military experts they relied on excoriated the Filipino generals for not committing more manpower to Mindanao, leaving them to wonder from the safety of their plush television studios and editorial offices on the other side of the world if the Philippines possessed any soldiers with the daring, courage, and willpower needed to go eye to eye with their resurgent foe.

Of course the Filipino Army did have such men. Most every army worthy of that title possessed a core of skilled and dedicated professional soldiers. What distinguished the Army of the Philippines from the insurgents they faced was focus, law, and tradition. Summirat did not have to concern himself with defending a vast archipelago consisting of 7,100 islands with a total landmass of 296,000 square miles. He did not have to dissipate his command by allocating sizable portions of it to civil-military operations, internal security, and even ceremonial guards as the Filipino generals did. The small force Summirat led did not rely on the sort of massive logistical infrastructure that even a third-rate army such as that possessed by the Philippines relies on in order to maintain its forces in the field. Known as the "Tooth to Tail ratio," manning, maintaining, and securing this supply chain or line of communications was a task that could require as many as ten men for every single soldier on the firing line. Even in the area of recruitment modern insurgents such as Summirat had an advantage over the national armies they often faced. He was not restricted on where and how he recruited his fighters. Summirat was free to pick his followers, conferring upon him the luxury of surrounding himself with like-minded men who share his vision as well as his determination to see that vision to fruition regardless of cost or technique.

Being outside the law, Summirat and the men devoted to the cause he championed were unhindered by the sort of rules and regulations that governed the conduct of the conventional forces arrayed against them. The Abu Sayyaf fighters did not have to answer to politicians who in turn had to answer to the people who elected them and the media who kept watch on how they managed the affairs of the nation. Results, and not the methods they used to achieve them, were all that mattered to Summirat and his men. Maintaining the rule of law as put forth by their national constitution and ensuring they could be re-elected when their current terms of office expired trumped all other considerations for the men who made up the government in Manila. Being far removed from the firing line those politicians could justify their priorities by convincing themselves and their supporters that it was critical they stay in office in order to ensure continuity of the polices they had initiated to deal with the current crisis.

Not everything could be blamed on the politicians. Standing armies, armies commanded by and composed of long-serving career soldiers in the service of legitimate governments, are not only constrained by the laws they are sworn to defend and policed by a free media but by the conventions and practices that their own profession and their fellow officers impose upon them. Neither the laws of their government or the traditions of their own service could be ignored, for traditions do more than bind and unify. They tend to restrict and limit, denying the professional soldier the sort of freedom of action that an insurgent force enjoys. A victory on the battlefield by government forces achieved by devastating the homes, farms, and livelihood of the very people it is supposed to be protecting is no victory at all. If anything, such Pyrrhic victories tend to turn its own people against them, creating fertile ground from which an astute insurgent such as Summirat is able to harvest fresh recruits, not to mention bountiful propaganda.

For these reasons and many more, both the leadership of the Filipino military and Summirat had reached something of an impasse. Summirat's initial effort had run its course and the government's efforts to check it had been stymied. Both needed a respite in order to regroup, absorb the lessons they had learned thus far, observe their opponent and ruminate on what to do next.

In Manila and on the island of Mindanao itself the generals turned their attention to developing plans that would entice their foe into a fight under favorable conditions, ever conscious of the fact that even if they managed to muster up the gumption to risk all in an effort to achieve some sort of battlefield success, the odds at the moment did not favor them, for they had lost faith in the ability of their own men to come to grips with a foe that was beginning to take on something of an aura of invincibility. Already a number of former members of the Bangsa Moros Army who had been integrated in the Filipino Army under previous peace accords had undergone a change of heart and loyalties, leaving the ranks of the Filipino Army and flocking to Summirat. Faced with declining morale, growing desertions, and the decimation of the best counterinsurgence unit in the entire Filipino Army, the Army's senior leadership found no choice but to temporarily suspend its offensive against the Abu Sayyaf. Instead of going forward they chose to pull back, regroup and concentrate on containing the insurgents, watching and waiting as they did so for a chance to strike a telling blow if and when an opportunity to do so did present itself.

Hamdani Summirat had no intention of permitting the government forces arrayed against him to sort themselves out. Having secured an area of operations that provided him with a safe haven as well as a rich recruiting ground, he turned his attention to preparing his ever-expanding forces for the next phase of a deliberate campaign that was as high risk and unconventional as the plan that was being staffed throughout the Pentagon that had been crafted to counter it.

Having demonstrated that the splinter group he now led was able to take on anything that the Manila government could throw at it on ground of his choosing, Summirat now had to demonstrate to those who still doubted that his force was a credible threat, that his people possessed the ability to strike a telling blow anywhere he wished throughout the southern Philippines with impunity.

This made the next phase of his campaign critical. Its goal was to eradicate whatever authority the Manila government still retained with its own people and its allies, particularly the United States, while winning over the full support of the Islamic community throughout the Philippines. "We've managed to take a nip or two at the cat when it foolishly thrust its paw into our lair," Summirat leisurely explained to his subordinates as they sat about a fire one evening enjoying the last of a feast that had been provided to them by a local chief who sensed that appeasing these men and their messianic leader was in his best interest. "We've drawn blood, but we have yet to demonstrate our ability to inflict mortal harm. So long as the government forces are free to pull back from those remote areas we have come to dominate and protect the commercial and populated heartland of Mindanao they will be able to marginalize us."

Seated across the fire from him was his deputy, a man who not only assisted him by tending to the administrative details that any organization must contend with, but also served as a foil to Summirat. As was his habit Muzzafar Fadyl indicated that he had something to say by shifting his weight from one side to the other, twisting about where he sat as if trying to find a more comfortable position. "We've already demonstrated that we can kill their soldiers," he stated in a low voice that was barely more than a whisper. "Slaughtering a few hundred more in the jungle will prove nothing and do little to advance our cause."

Summirat continued as he cocked his head back and smiled. "As always, my old friend, you understand the problem we are facing. The enemy has removed everything of value, which includes his own soldiers, beyond what he believes to be within our reach. For the moment he is content to abdicate control over those portions of this island that are of little value to him or his economy. By doing so the generals in Manila hope they can buy themselves time to regroup, retrain, and reequip their shaken commands while at the same time creating the impression that the crisis has passed."

"If we do not do something," Fadyl countered, "the crisis will pass. You know better than I that a victory on the battlefield is wasted if the victor does not pursue his beaten foe, running them to ground and finishing the task of destroying them while they are still disorganized and demoralized. I have no doubt that if we had the men to do so," he continued after pausing a moment to let his previous statement sink in, "you would have ordered such an effort. Unfortunately we do not. While spectacular, our successes to date have shown to all who care to study what is happening here that we are incapable of delivering a coup de grace, a killing blow that will fatally cripple the government in Manila. In time the wounds we have opened will heal. Once the Army has absorbed our blows, they will return as they always have to chip away at us bit by bit."

"This is true, very true," Summirat replied as he made it appear that he was actually considering what Fadyl was saying. "Despite our best efforts thus far we have done nothing that is any different from those who have preceded us. As I said, we've only nibbled on the paw they were foolish enough to precipitously thrust into our lair, a mistake they will not repeat. That is why our next target is not the Army," he stated with a rising voice, "but rather the idea that the Army can contain us. We must demonstrate that the Army is incapable of protecting the people of the Philippines and the international interests upon which the government depends. Our next strike is not to be aimed at the body, but at their psyche."

The men gathered about the fire remained transfixed as Summirat spoke. It was not the words themselves that sent a collective chill down their spines. Rather it was the tone with which they were delivered and his distant, almost detached expression, eerily exaggerated by the flickering flames of the fire before him. "You must steel the hearts of your men for what we must do. There can be no turning back when we go forward from this time and place, for our actions will set in motion a chain of events that we will not control."

Pausing, Summirat slowly scanned the faces of his faithful lieutenants to see how they were responding to his statement, for he knew his announcement that he was prepared to embark upon a deliberate campaign over which he had little control over how it played out was out of character. Only when he was satisfied that they were prepared to place their faith in whatever he laid out before them did he continue. "A soldier's duty is to fight, and if necessary die defending his fellow countrymen and his government. All know it is a very real possibility. Yet in truth none are truly willing to make that ultimate sacrifice if there is an acceptable alternative. To die for one's country, as one American military historian once pointed out, is not career-enhancing."

Though he meant it to be a serious statement of fact, several of the men could not help but laugh at this unintended bit of humor. Even Summirat found himself unable to suppress a snicker. When the brief flicker of levity had passed, he continued. "To the general public the loss of a soldier here and there is not only acceptable, it is expected.

It is their lot, the cost that a nation must pay for its security. Even the death of civilians by terrorist attacks are now being shrugged off by the general public as barely newsworthy. These days the average man and woman take such incidents in stride with the same casual manner as they do upon hearing of deaths caused by a traffic accident. It seems the only time anyone takes note of such attacks anymore is when those attacks are aimed at symbols or segments of society thought to be immune to such dangers."

"Political assassination?" Fadyl mused.

"No. Politicians are like soldiers. They understand that upon assumption of their office they place themselves in the crosshairs of those who would stop at nothing to bring about their demise. Besides, in order to achieve our ultimate goal we must leave the government in Manila unscratched, for we will need to negotiate with them and ultimately it will be them who will see to it that our demands are met. In the twinkling of an eye a signature on a piece of paper drafted by a legitimate government will confer upon our movement the same sort of legitimacy that the Helsinki Accords did upon Yasser Arafat and the PLO. We will achieve our aspirations, justify our actions and create a legitimate state from which we will build a pan-Islamic republic encompassing all of our brethren."

The scope of Summirat's vision and the wisdom of his words stunned some of those gathered about their messianic leader. Others, such as Fadyl, were not easily awed by mere words, for they had heard such talk time and time again. Shifting about Fadyl made it known to his leader that he was not at all impressed by his quixotic declaration. "The journey that will take us from this place to the pinnacle of success will be a long one I am sure, one that will require much from those who have pledged their eternal loyalty to you, men who are at this very moment awaiting your orders."

As if awakened from a dream, Summirat looked over at his most trusted and loyal lieutenant. With a nod, he acknowledged Fadyl's less than subtle prodding and returned to discussing the issues at hand.

"As I said, the target of our operations now is not to be the government itself. We must have someone with whom to negotiate, a body that has legitimacy in the eyes of the people of this country and foreign powers. Nor would it do us any good at this point to continue to strike at the Army. We have demonstrated that we have the ability to beat it. Though we will have to fight them as we go, their defeat in the field cannot of itself be decisive. Any further attacks against it would be a waste of our time and limited resources. Instead," Summirat stated as he gathered himself up, "we will now turn our attention on those who will help us achieve our ends. We will strike at the business interests and social elite of this country, in particular the foreign business community. We will hammer away at them until they see that they have no alternative but to pressure the government they rely upon to protect them and their interests to accommodate us. In the end it will be their clamor for peace that will prove to be more irresistible than all of our feats of arms on the battlefield combined."

"And how are we to do this?" a heavyset man sitting across the fire from Summirat intoned, making no effort to hide the disgust in his voice. "Are we to resort once more to stealing the children of the rich and frightening foreign tourists? I had hoped we had moved beyond such petty theatricals, that we had become true warriors and not simply common criminals kidnapping Americans and Australians for pieces of gold."

"My dear Assam, it is through such theatrics that nations are born," Summirat replied as his mouth curled up into a smile that had no warmth. "They galvanize those who are but awaiting a sign. They panic the opposition into responding before they are ready and in ways that erode their own authority. They feed a voracious world media ever hungry for that which is spectacular and startling."

"And they invite foreign intervention," another voice from somewhere off to Summirat's right called out.

Snapping his head to face his latest critic, Summirat responded to the challenge without hesitation. "Yes, a situation that we already find ourselves facing. It is a problem that we would need to deal with regardless of what we did. So it is one that is best confronted as soon as possible and on terms that are as favorable to us as conditions will permit."

"We are talking about the Americans," Fadyl stated in a calm voice in an effort to cool the heated exchange, "a nation of warriors that has taken upon itself the task of eradicating movements such as ours. In the past few years they have become quite good at doing so."

"In doing so they have become badly overextended," Summirat countered. "And the popular support that had once cheered their soldiers on has disappeared. The political will to see their worldwide crusade against terrorism through to the end is withering in the face of opposition from within."

"But they will come," Fadyl stated defiantly.

Summirat did not respond to this challenge, at least not at once. Instead he reached behind and seized a log off a stack of wood from which they had been feeding the fire. With a casualness that belied the tenseness that had settled over the gathering he tossed the log onto the burning embers, sending a shower of bright, burning sparks high into the night sky. In silence his eyes followed them until they flickered, died and disappeared. Without looking back at his lieutenants, Summirat spoke in near reverent terms, "Yes, they will come, for we will summon them."

Slowly, he lowered his chin and once more gazed at the worried faces gathered about him. "You see, my friends, by besting the Americans in a game which they believe they have mastered we will crush all hope. By mauling the cat the government in Manila has invited in to hunt us we will leave the masters of this house little choice but to come to terms with us."

11

SAMAL ISLAND, PHILIPPINES

Relaxation was not something that came easily to Erik Hanson, one of the few who managed to dodge the dotcom bust and parlay the earnings he made off his Silicon Valley investments into a tight little fortune and a thriving business. In a world where the business cycle was measured in nanoseconds and a single wrong decision could wipe away fortunes in the twinkling of an eye, Hanson needed to keep on his toes, literally and figuratively, lest he fall by the wayside as so many of his contemporaries had. Part of the personal regime he had fashioned for himself to maintain a competitive edge was jogging at dawn. The routine served to clear his mind and prepare him for the long day ahead.

Even in the midst of a long overdue vacation he found it impossible to break from this daily routine. Long before dawn made its appearance Hanson was up, dressed, and making his way to the "T" Wharf where a small boat awaited to take him over to the main island and the well-manicured jogging trails. Behind he left his second wife, a corporate lawyer who was determined to take advantage of the private villa she and Hanson were occupying on a small island separated from the rest of the resort.

None of the resort staff took note of Hanson. Like drunken sailors roused from their bunks and sent forth to man the rigging, cooks, chambermaids, waiters, and recreational staff who were needed to tend to the early-morning needs of their foreign guests shuffled about with stooped shoulders and bowed heads as they went about their mundane chores. Each focused intently on his or her specific job, exchanging slurred greetings only when such niceties required them to do so. Even the private security guards who patrolled the thirty-acre resort restricted their activities to a set routine designed to keep the troubles of the world away from guests and staff alike. The appearance of the solitary figure of Erik Hanson slowly making his way from the main wharf to the jogging trail was barely noticed by the resort staff. Those who did bother to give the American businessman a second thought only did so in wonderment as to why someone who had paid so much to come to this place insisted on rising before the sun.

It was this inattention to everything save their own duties and reliance on an established routine that created a vulnerability Hamdani Summirat was counting on. Located in the Davao Gulf, a mere seven-hundred meters from the city of Davao, Samal Island was forty-four square miles, making it twice the size of Manhattan. There the comparisons stopped, for Samal was a garden spot that had few equals on earth, a place that sported dozens of high-class beach resorts frequented by both foreigners and Filipinos alike who fled there to enjoy its unspoiled white sandy beaches, swaying coconut trees, coral reefs, tiny native fishing villages, and mangroves. It was a sanctuary where the problems that plagued Mindanao and the rest of the day-to-day world were kept at arm's distance by the serene waters that surrounded the island. Everyone who visited the place was seduced by the ambience of this tropical retreat, even the staff and security personnel charged with making the troubles of the world disappear for those who could afford it.

The lack of serious opposition that was expected made no difference to Summirat. The assault on Samal was planned and rehearsed with the same meticulous care and attention to detail that characterized all of his previous operations. To ensure that those selected to carry out the operation saw things as he did, Summirat personally visited each of the half-dozen secluded assembly areas himself. Over and over again he admonished his men to show no mercy. "When you leave here be swift, be thorough, be brutal. Close your ears to all pleas for mercy and your heart to charity." With these words still ringing in their ears, the assault parties pushed off into the darkness to bring hell to paradise.

Within minutes Erik Hanson managed to lose himself among the tall palm trees that lined the jogging trail. Only the rhythm of his own labored breath and pounding of his running shoes on the packed surface of the jogging trail disturbed the silence as the darkness grudgingly gave way to a new day. The few members of the staff who he passed along the way didn't even bother to look up from their chores. They had no time to pay heed to the queer habits of a man who was foolish enough to leave his bed long before he needed to. There were many other, far more sensible guests who would soon require their services.

It was into this silent, sleepy world of pampered foreigners and underpaid cooks, waiters, maids, and groundskeepers that the small bands of Abu Sayyaf fighters crept. The first team to disembark from the small fishing boats they were using was the security element. This detachment was by far the heaviest-armed group, toting machine guns and a number of shoulder-fired antitank rocket launchers in addition to individual small arms. Their mission was to silence the security post that stood at the

entry gate of the resort and establish a blocking position
to keep any outside help from getting in while those with
the main body carried out their assigned tasks. Out in the
Gulf of Davao the other assault groups waited aboard
fishing boats indistinguishable from those that routinely
plied the waters around the picturesque island. Only after
the resort had been sealed off from the outside world
would these boats make their run into shore and unleash
a man-made storm none of the unsuspecting guests were
prepared for.

The main assault was carried out by six teams armed
with small arms, grenades, and machetes. Each was assigned to secure a specific portion of the resort. Three of
these teams made for the beachfront suites and houses
located on either side of the main wharf. South of it one
team was sufficient to deal with the occupants of the six
huts nestled together there. That was not the case along
the north shore. There Summirat determined two teams
were needed to clear the twenty huts and houses that
graced the smooth, sandy white beaches. Starting at either
ends of this large swath of luxury huts, the two teams
methodically worked their way in toward the center until
all occupants had been dealt with.

While this was going on two more teams landed at the
base of the wharf in the center of the resort. From there
they split off from each other. One made for the registra-
tion office, administrative building, and restaurant located between the two clusters of guest huts on the shore
while the other rushed the recreational facilities farther
inland on a small hill that dominated the entire resort.
There would only be staff at both these locations, local
people who were not the main target of Summirat's efforts. But since they had access to phones and alarms,
they needed to be rounded up and silenced lest they alert
their charges to the coming danger or summon help from
outside.

The last of the assault teams came ashore on the small
island that sat just offshore. It was on this island where

the most luxurious accommodations were located, one of which belonged to Erik Hanson. His wife was just beginning to awaken when she heard the pounding of feet on the highly polished floors just outside her bedroom. Propping herself up on her elbow she called out to her husband. "Erik? Is there something wrong?"

The response to her innocent, honey-sweet inquiry was immediate and stunning. Upon hearing the woman's voice an Abu Sayyaf fighter known as Haji kicked the door in and rushed through it. Startled, Hanson's wife recoiled as best she could, instinctively pulling the silky sheet draped about her up to her chin as she screamed in sheer terror.

Neither her efforts to retreat or her shrilled pleas stayed Haji's hand. Without hesitation he advanced to within arm's distance, raising the machete he clutched over his head as he did so. His first downward stroke was a killing blow, striking at an angle where her long, slender neck merged smoothly with her soft, bare shoulder. Heeding Summirat's instructions Haji continued flailing away. Like a crazed predator whipped up into a frenzy by the scent of fresh blood, he continued to hack away at the lifeless corpse strewn across the bloodstained sheets of the bed before him. Only repeated cries from his companion brought an end to this momentary madness.

Stunned by the rage that had possessed him, Haji stepped back as he took a moment to catch his breath. His wide eyes darted back and forth between his handiwork and the machete he slowly lifted till it was level with his eyes. Upon it rivulets of fresh blood trickled down the blade, over the hand guard and across his knuckles. Why the half-naked woman before him had to die was not his concern. Such things were not for him to judge. All that was required of him was to carry out the orders of those he had chosen to follow. Judgment as to whether those actions were right or wrong was the sole purview of Allah. Only He could see into a man's soul and determine if his deeds were worthy of praise or deserving of condemnation.

Until his day of judgment came, Haji told himself, all he could do was follow his conscience, the teachings of those wiser than he, and his orders no matter how incomprehensible or confusing they sometimes were.

What astonished the young Abu Sayyaf fighter was the fact that he had been able to muster up both the courage and the will to do such a thing. Now that it was over, now that his first freshly butchered victim lay before him, Haji found himself reflecting on just how easy it had all been. This had been easier than killing soldiers in ambush. There he had found it necessary to be patient, to take his time and assume a good firing position, take careful aim and concentrate on what he was doing as he held his breath and fired. This had been nothing more than a blind frenzy, a mindless act. He would need to take more time and greater care next time, he thought to himself. Deliberate violence, not madness was what Summirat wanted.

From somewhere outside the fighter heard his name being called over and over. "Haji! Haji! Keep moving. We must move on."

Shaken from his own macabre reflections and without giving the butchered corpse before him another thought, Haji pivoted about and hastened out of the room to join his companions who were already headed for the next hut in line where fresh targets awaited them.

Timing and opportunity were something that Erik Hanson understood perfectly well. In business they often meant the difference between failure and success, provided, of course, one knew how to optimize the advantage they conferred. On this morning the same good luck and innate intuitiveness that had allowed him to dodge the dotcom bust saved his life.

As he neared the turnaround point on the jogging trail located near the front gate Hanson noticed that there was no one in sight. On previous days his approach always caused at least one of the uniformed security men to turn to see who was approaching their post, waving at him when they were satisfied that he was one of the guests. Whether their smiles were genuine or simply part of their job as members of the resort's staff didn't matter to Hanson. The idea that there was always someone there, alert and attentively tending to his security, was enough to give him the sort of peace of mind that allowed him to enjoy this long overdue vacation.

Slowing his pace, Hanson took a moment to look about, raising up on his toes and craning his neck in order to get a better look over the top of the hedges that separated the jogging trail from the road that led to the center of the resort. When this casual inspection still failed to detect anyone, Hanson felt the hairs on the back of his neck begin to tingle. Leaving the trail he sidled up behind a palm tree that offered him an unobstructed view of the front gate and came to a complete halt. Bracing himself with his hands flat against the tree trunk, he leaned over in order to peek around the trunk and see if he could discover what the security guards were up to. That he could very well be endangering himself by doing this only slowly began to dawn upon him as he systematically searched the area. The guards, wherever they were, could misinterpret his caution, an error that could very well cause them to turn the menacing automatic rifles they carried on him.

Still, the same little voice inside his head that had served Hanson so well in the past whispered a warning that all was not well. After lingering behind the tree longer than he felt comfortable waiting for the absent guards to make an appearance, Hanson slowly backed away from the deserted gate. The failure of the Abu Sayyaf fighters securing that area to take note of Hanson's arrival or departure was not due to their inattentiveness. On the contrary, every man assigned to that detail was wide awake, ready to spring into action at the slightest hint of trouble. It was their strict adherence to their orders that proved to be the only thing that saved Hanson that day, for they had been instructed by Summirat himself to focus their full attention on fending off any police or military units that might stumble upon the raiders. "We will be depending on you to protect us from any unexpected guests," he told them in a manner that made it clear to every man on the security team that any failure on their part would not be tolerated. "So keep your eyes on the road and your weapons at the ready." To this end their full attention was oriented on the access road leading up to the resort and not behind them.

Unaware of just how near he had been to mortal danger and unsure what to make of what he observed at the gate, Hanson took his time as he walked back along the trail. Along the way he tried to come up with a reasonable explanation for what he had seen, taking care to make as little noise as he could, pausing to listen whenever he heard a suspicious noise. When he reached the starting point of the trail located on the hilltop to the rear of the recreation center, the same little voice that had given him pause at the gatehouse steered Hanson off the trail and into the bushes. And instead of moving in a straight line he zigzagged from one well-manicured bush to the next, crouching over as he did so. In the midst of his advance the vacationing American executive began to feel a bit silly, acting more like a kid playing double-oh-seven than a hard-charging businessman.

He was just beginning to wonder how he would ever be able to explain his strange behavior to someone if they caught him sneaking around when his eyes caught sight of a body sprawled upon the broad wooden stairs leading up to the recreational center. Stunned, Hanson's first response was an effort to convince himself that his eyes were deceiving him, that he really wasn't looking at a corpse. For several seconds he did his best to conjure up some sort of rational explanation that would explain how the slightly overweight woman dressed in a white bloodstained dress came to be there. Yet as much as he wished it were otherwise, it became clear that she was not the victim of a simple accident. Even at this distance and in the faint early morning light the numerous slash marks that had rent both cloth and flesh were hideously obvious.

Having come to the inescapable conclusion that something terrible had occurred while he had been out running, Erik Hanson now found that he was at a loss as to what he should do about it. Instinctively he looked about in an effort to see if there was something near at hand that he could use as a weapon. Of course there was absolutely nothing that even came close to filling that need. This was after all a recreational resort that was engineered to resemble a Caucasian's idea of a tropical paradise. All around him were manicured lawns and neatly trimmed bushes selected for their aesthetics and not lethality. And even if he did find something that would suffice as a weapon, Hanson quickly reasoned that it would only create a false sense of security for it was clear from the speed, silence, and efficiency with which the invisible assailants had struck that he wouldn't stand a chance in a face-to-face confrontation. Concealment, he concluded was the only thing that would shield him from meeting the same fate as the woman on the stairs.

Sensing that his current position was untenable, Erik Hanson slowly began to back away from the recreation center without any idea of where he was going. It was clear that the pruned bushes offered him next to no protection from detection. Only the jungle that lay just beyond the perimeter of the resort could provide him a haven. He kept telling himself he would be safe there, as he scurried from brush to bush. So long as he kept his wits about him and didn't do anything overly brave or foolish he would survive. To a pragmatic businessman who frowned on taking a risk, the words "brave" and "foolish" were synonymous.

It was not until he was safely hidden among the trees and dense undergrowth of the jungle that his thoughts turned to the fate of his wife. Sheepishly, he paused a moment to look back in the direction of the resort. She'd be safe, he told himself. After all, what possible gain could anyone derive from killing someone like her? She would be much more valuable as a hostage, Hanson concluded.

Being a very practical businessman through and through, Erik Hanson took great pride in being able to coolly measure his world and everything in it as either an asset or a debit, a gain or a loss, an opportunity or a pitfall. In his mind murdering his wife would be a foolish waste. It simply didn't make sense to him that someone would take the time to plan, stage, and execute an operation against so high-profile a target as this resort simply to butcher people that they could use as bargaining chips. Killing the staff, yes, he could understand that. No one would pay a ransom for them. But to slaughter the well-to-do Americans, Australians, and Europeans such as himself?

That he was actually living in a world where the bottom line was not written in ink but in blood never occured upon him. Not even horrific events such as 9/11 were able to shake the illusory world view people like Erik Hanson created for themselves to live in. It wasn't until he left his place of hiding upon hearing the beating blades of Filipino Army helicopters above that reality finally caught up to him, that he actually lived in a world where predators like Hamdani Summirat and not well-paid lawyers and slick politicians made the rules.

The attack on the Samal Island resort accomplished everything that Summirat had expected. Long before the sun had set a panic gripped the entire population of Davao and every foreign visitor within one hundred miles. Using whatever means of transportation that they could procure, everyone who could do so fled the island of Samal and dozens of other resorts scattered throughout Mindanao. Some didn't even bother to pack.

To the police and security personnel, it seemed as if every tourist on the island headed straight for the international airport. It did not matter to the stampeding tourists that there would be insufficient flights to handle a surge of this magnitude. Such logic didn't matter to the thousands of frightened people as they joined long lines that snaked back and forth throughout the departure terminal and outside onto the street clogged with taxis, buses, and rented cars. All that mattered to the Americans, Europeans, and Australians who had come to the Philippines in search of relaxation and fun was escape, flight from a terror all had thought they had left behind.

The resulting crush of anxious and excited people converging on Davao's airport was overwhelming but surprisingly did not result in the sort of riots or crazed panics that Hollywood movies are so fond of depicting. That's not to say that all was going smoothly. Everywhere one turned, provided they could find the room in which to do so, there were heated arguments going on between harried ticket counter agents and people employing every trick they could think of to secure a seat on a flight out. Swept up in this throng of excited people were police and security personnel who were doing their best to maintain order using procedures not designed for these circumstances. Unable to effectively assert their authority the police found that they were reduced to little more than helpless spectators, unable to do anything but watch the chaos that was engulfing them grow. It was a state of affairs that Hamdani Summirat had anticipated, one that created the stage for what would be his main effort of the day.

Like the endless queues of people that meandered this way and that everywhere one looked, the glut of traffic just outside the departure terminal crept along at a snail's pace. Nervous foreign tourists eager to make good their escape did little to help the effort of the besieged police

who were doing everything they could think of to keep
the deluge of vehicles moving. Cooped up in small taxis
and minibuses the anxious foreigners exhorted, cursed,
bribed, and pleaded with their frustrated Filipino drivers
to ignore the handful of police struggling to maintain
some semblance of order. Calls by them for reinforcements went unanswered by officials who were being
pressed from all sides to protect other, more sensitive areas using the limited pool of police and military units
available to them. The best the head of security at the
airport could secure from his superiors was the promise
that as soon as reinforcements from other regions became available, he would receive his fair share.

Summirat had no intention of waiting for this to occur.
Relying on the same impeccable sense of timing that had
permitted him to humble the Filipino Army, he now set
in motion a chain of events that would dwarf everything
he had done to embarrass the Manila government up to
this point.

From a perch that allowed him a safe and unobstructed
view of the chaotic departure terminal, Summirat studied the rhythm and pace of the traffic moving past it.
When he had a good sense of its pace and determined
that things down there had reached something of a cli-
max he issued a series of prearranged coded messages
that sent three vehicles in to join the host of cars, taxis,
vans, and buses that were already there.

One of these was a taxi containing one of his fighters
posing as a passenger and driven by a legally licensed
hack who was sympathetic to Summirat's cause. Like all
the other nondescript taxis that were making their way
toward the terminal building, this one crept along until it
reached the point where passengers were being left off.
Dutifully the man in the backseat paid the driver, grabbed
his bag, and disappeared into the teeming crush of people
pushing their way into the terminal. Inside, the "passenger" would set his bag down against a solid wall and
walk away from it. Meanwhile, outside, the taxi driver

went through the motion of pulling away from the curb as soon as he had dropped off his passenger. He didn't get far, stopping when the front of his taxi was jutting halfway into the next lane over. Leaning forward he made as if he were trying to restart his stalled vehicle. What he was actually doing was tugging at several wires that disabled it and armed an explosive device. Having set in motion a chain of events he no longer controlled, the driver climbed out. Ignoring the riot of honking horns and shrilled oaths he made his way around to the front of his vehicle where he popped the hood as if he were going to work on the engine before turning his back on the taxi and walking away.

Mixed in with dozens of other vehicles waiting to make their way to the departure terminal was a white Mercedes limousine complete with heavily tinted windows sitting in the far right-hand lane. When its driver saw the hood of the taxi go up he brought his massive vehicle to a halt. After dropping down behind his wheel he slid across the seat and slipped over the front seat into the passenger area. Once there he collected himself, threw open the rear door on the right side of the vehicle, grabbed a suitcase, and leaped out as if he were an impatient passenger who was abandoning his ride in an effort to get to the terminal faster. No one behind the Mercedes thought anything of this, not even a nearby policeman whose full attention was being drawn toward the chorus of blaring horns emanating from the spot where the abandoned taxi sat.

At the other end of this long line of vehicles a van that had already made its way past the terminal and was in the process of exiting the area pulled over to the side of the road and stopped. Unlike the taxi it only blocked one lane of traffic. But that was enough to bring every vehicle behind it to a stop, creating additional chaos as they did their best to pass it by merging into the next lane over. Ignoring the curses and universal hand gestures used by all enraged motorists to express their displeasure, the driver of the van simply got out of the passenger side door and wandered off, away from the terminal.

When Summirat saw that the last of these vehicles was in place, he hit the start button of a stopwatch he had been holding. The countdown initiated by him was intended to afford all of the drivers and the faux passenger from the taxi an opportunity to get well clear of their deserted vehicles. Unlike his Arab brethren, Summirat did not believe in throwing away the lives of good men he had taken great pains to recruit and train just to make a point. Because of this little kindness his followers were both grateful and reassured. It engendered in them a sense of trust that bound them to him and allowed him to ask them to do things many of his counterparts leading other insurgent movements would never think of.

As he waited Summirat turned to Richardo Salim, a young man he had picked to assist him with controlling this attack. His selection for this chore was based in part upon Salim's proven reliability in the past. At seventeen the youth had already been with Summirat for over two years, serving him as a courier when he wasn't tending to other more menial tasks such as carrying Summirat's bags, cleaning his personal weapons, or making sure his master had a comfortable, dry place to sleep that night. This day's task, listening to a handheld radio and responding to calls from lookouts posted throughout the area, was to Summirat just as trivial as were the other chores he assigned Salim. But to the youth, being picked to join Summirat on such an important mission was a dream come true.

Glancing down at the stopwatch, Summirat took note of the time before turning to Salim. "Anything?"

The youth shook his head. "No, sir. Nothing."

Summirat took a moment to look up at the clear blue sky. It was a perfect day, perfect in every way. After taking in a deep breath, he murmured almost as if to himself, "It is time." Looking back at Salim, he grinned. "Give Fadyl the word."

Giddy with excitement, Salim lifted the cell phone with

a walkie-talkie feature to his mouth, pressed the talk button, and recited a quote from the Koran that was the signal to initiate the attack. The use of Salim to relay his orders in this manner was more than a mechanism that Summirat employed to reward the labors of the aspiring young fighter. It was a way of keeping both domestic and foreign intelligence agencies who routinely monitored the air waves from keying in on his voice or recording it for analysis and future use.

Salim's message was picked up by Muzzafar Fadyl. Without hesitation Fadyl remotely triggered the first explosive, a comparatively small charge concealed within the suitcase that had been abandoned by the taxi's passenger. Despite its size this device created a blast that was both deafening and quite lethal to those around it thanks mainly to the concrete wall it was leaning against.

The bomb's shock wave was like the ripples created by a stone tossed into a pond. At the center its violence was tightly concentrated and quite lethal. Within ten meters it brought instant death to those whom the Fates had placed there. At twenty meters the blast lessened, as did the severity of the injuries it inflicted. While some within this band were killed outright and others would eventually join them the bomb's blast was pretty much spent, absorbed by the bodies surrounding it and the dissipation that naturally occurs as the distance from the source of the explosion increases. Still, some debris and shrapnel did manage to ride the invisible shock wave and generate wounds among the throng of unsuspecting tourists farther out. Though most of these wounds were survivable, the panic they set in motion created a different sort of damage, for past this point the injuries were not caused by the bomb itself but rather by the frantic efforts of terror-stricken people who instinctively pushed, shoved, and literally clawed their way past, through, and over their fellow travelers in an effort to escape the horrors of a device that had already spent itself.

It was the ever-expanding bands of panicked people

struggling to get away from a danger that could no longer harm them that Summirat was waiting for. Tumbling out of the terminal through every portal and door they could squeeze through, the press of people poured onto the sidewalks and out onto the roadway adjoining the departure terminal. Frantic to make good their escape they climbed over cars, taxis, and vans that could no longer move because of the stampede that engulfed them. Only when he judged that the entire area outside the terminal had reached its maximum saturation point of people did Summirat give Salim an almost casual nod, the signal to broadcast the second coded message to Fadyl.

In the twinkling of an eye the riot of foreign tourists, harried police, and stalled vehicles were consumed by three gigantic fireballs emanating from the taxi, the limousine, and the van his people had abandoned. By themselves each of the explosive-laden vehicles would have been devastating. Initiated simultaneously, the effect was catastrophic. Those who were on the outer fringes of the blast were fortunate. They at least had a chance as they were tossed about and thrown down by the shock wave emanating from the van and limousine. Anyone who was stuck anywhere in between these vehicles and the taxi or still was in the terminal didn't have a prayer. All three blasts behaved as one would expect until the fireballs and shock waves collided before rebounding off of each other and rolling over the dead and the dying once more. Those caught between them were literally crushed by the converging shock waves or shredded as razor sharp shrapnel whirled through the air like scythes and sickles wielded by the invisible force of the explosions.

In quick successsion a series of sympathetic detonations erupted as the fuel tanks of stalled vehicles throughout the area ruptured, adding to the devastation. Not even the terminal building itself was immune to the force of the three explosions. Already shaken by the first suitcase bomb, the car bombs pushed the supports and façade of the building in and set in motion a progressive collapse that brought it down on top of those who were still inside.

From beginning to end the entire event took less than two minutes. From his vantage point Summirat watched as an unnatural calm inexplicably settled over the devastation he had set in motion. For the longest time there was a painful, eerie silence that was punctuated only by low-yield explosions as the fuel tanks continued to randomly cook off. When he was satisfied that he had accomplished everything he had set out to do that day, Summirat turned toward Salim. "Well, I guess there's nothing more for us to do here," he stated in a nonchalant manner that struck Salim as being out of place given what they had just witnessed. "It's time to leave."

Mesmerized by the carnage that he had helped create, the young man found himself unable to follow Summirat when he turned to walk away. Salim had known for weeks what they would be doing. He had been allowed to sit in on the meetings when the entire plan had been laid out and each of its details was discussed. Yet nothing in his past, nothing he had heard in any of those meetings or their preparations for this day, prepared him for what he was now seeing. It was fantastic, Salim found himself thinking, utterly incredible.

When Summirat noticed that his young assistant wasn't following him down from small hillock he had been using as an observation post, he stopped and looked back over his shoulder at the young man. He knew what he was feeling, what he was thinking. Glancing down at the terminal now totally engulfed in flames, he took a moment to study the column of thick black smoke that marked the massive funeral pyre he had created. "Come," Summirat finally called out. "You've seen enough. There'll be more days like this, many more. After all, this is just the beginning."

Without a word Salim reluctantly followed his master. As he did so he found himself wondering how a man, even one like his master could possibly conceive of something like this and then simply walk away. Shaking his head the only word that came to Salim's mind was fantastic. This whole campaign conceived by Summirat, the violence and death that it had unleashed in the jungles in southwestern Mindanao and here in Davao, was fantastic. And to think that this was little more than the beginning was perhaps the most fantastic aspect of the entire affair.

12

FORT LEWIS, WASHINGTON STATE

The horrific events playing themselves out some seven thousand miles away on the island of Mindanao were of no concern to Private First Class Eric White. At the moment only two things mattered to him: staying awake and staying dry. On both accounts he was failing miserably.

With his rifle propped up on the front parapet of the shallow fighting position pointed in the general direction of his assigned sector of responsibility, White sat huddled with his back braced up against the rear wall in an upright fetal position. To preserve what little heat his body was giving off, he wrapped his arms about his knees and held them tightly up against his chest as he struggled to stay awake and alert. Throughout this ordeal the weight of his Kevlar helmet and the night vision goggles hanging from it combined with his physical exhaustion causing his head to loll about from side to side like a bobble-head toy. Were it not for the incessant rain that beat upon his helmet and filled the hole he and Spec Four Bryan Pulaski had dug, White would have drifted off to sleep hours ago.

This questionable blessing was accompanied by a very serious downside. Besides flooding the fighting position with water, the driving rain proved to be more than a match for White's high-tech wet-weather gear. In Georgia he'd been able to tolerate being soaked to the skin. At times the rain had even been something of a welcomed break from the oppressive heat and stifling humidity that made Fort Benning a garden spot and one of the Army's most sought-after recreational facilities. The Northwest, however, was an entirely different matter. Here wet equaled cold, the numbing sort of raw cold that cuts through to the bone. And unlike Georgia where rain showers tended to be short, violent downpours followed by a rapid clearing and sunny clear blue skies, once you got wet here you stayed wet, for the sun was a commodity that was strictly rationed at Fort Lewis.

An earlier effort by Pulaski to use White's poncho as overhead cover for their fighting position had been for naught, for a gusting wind ripped the poncho free of its moorings within minutes of being set up and sent it sailing off into the darkness. Claiming that he was too exhausted to try again using his poncho, Pulaski opted instead to wrap himself in it before curling up on the bottom of the muddy hole he and White shared. With the words "Wake me in an hour," Pulaski promptly fell asleep. Left to stand watch in the pounding rain that swept over Company A's base camp at maddeningly regular intervals, White flipped his night-vision goggles down, switched them on and settled in to weather the night as best he could.

Shivering from head to toe White never caught onto the fact that the same oversized raindrops filling his fighting position and drumming out a steady cadence upon his helmet severely diminished his ability to hear. Relying solely on his blurred eyesight which was limited by the vegetation that surrounded Company A's perimeter, and the field of vision of his night vision devices, White scanned his assigned sector as best he could. Unfortunately for the novice Ranger his best did not even come close to being good enough.

As often proves to be the case in combat, bad things happen when chance and simple bad luck collide. For White three totally unrelated factors that were mostly beyond his control came together in time and space to add misfortune to his physical discomfort. One element of this terrible trilogy was provided by Staff Sergeant Ted Robinson, a squad leader from second Platoon who was leading a patrol that had been sent out by Nathan hours before. For the most part Robinson followed the patrol plan he had been briefed on to the letter. He hit all the points that he had been ordered to visit in the designated sequence, taking care to scour the area for any sign of the OPFOR, or opposing force activity.

Of course he found none. Neither he nor his platoon leader, who had issued him his orders, had expected him to, for they already knew in the way that soldiers know such things that no one from the battalion or any other unit at Fort Lewis was out there playing OPFOR. Robinson's foray through the damp, moonless night was little more than part of an endless series of field exercises that Company A had been run through since their return from the Philippines. Like all the others, it was meant to hone the basic skills such as patrolling. That the grinding repetition was having just the opposite effect on Nathan's people was a fact that was not lost on anyone in the battalion except the man who had ordered them, Lieutenant Colonel Delmont. Instead of improving the overall efficiency of Company A, the repetitive exercises were having the opposite effect. From top to bottom, everyone was becoming jaded, bored, and at times a bit lazy.

Veteran Rangers like Robinson were not immune to this. He took great pride in his skills and expertise, experience that he had demonstrated countless times in Afghanistan, Iraq, and the Philippines against armed foes who were hell bent on killing him and his fellow Rangers while doing all they could to arrange a one-on-one with

Allah. So it should have come as no surprise that Robinson found it difficult to whip up a great deal of enthusiasm for a training exercise he saw as being no different than the one they had run the previous week, or the week before that doing the exact same thing over the exact same ground.

Unable to muster up the sort of zeal a leader needs to motivate his subordinates under these circumstances, Robinson found it just as difficult to keep the members of his squad focused on their mission as it was for White to stay alert. Throughout the night they had failed to move along with the sort of alacrity that he had come to expect and his platoon leader was counting on. But instead of doing all he could to shake off his own malaise and get his squad moving with a purpose, Robinson chose to ignore their slothfulness, choosing to cut corners whenever he thought he could do so in order to make up for lost time. Being an experienced professional, he put a great deal of faith in his ability to judge when he needed to come down hard in order to get his people to perform and when he could let things slide by, playing fast and loose. On this night in order to make up for lost time he opted to deviate from the patrol plan that he had been briefed on by approaching and reentering the company's base camp from a direction other than the one that had been planned for. It was a calculated risk that Robinson deemed to be acceptable. So long as his squad approached the perimeter slowly and halted when challenged by his fellow Rangers manning that perimeter all would go well and no one, meaning his platoon leader and the company commander, would be any wiser. And even if one of them did discover this minor deviation from the patrol plan, Robinson was confident that he could find refuge in the universal understanding that all operational plans are flexible and subject to change based upon the tactical situation. It wouldn't be the first time he'd resorted to a little fast talking to baffle a blurry-eyed lieutenant.

The second factor that contributed to the incident was

the rain. From time to time even the best-trained soldiers in the world find that their finely honed skills are no match for Mother Nature. The same steady drumbeat of rain on White's K-pot that rendered his sense of hearing all but useless also muffled the footfalls of Robinson's approaching patrol. This meant that the first inkling White had that his position was being approached was when the returning patrol was virtually on top of him, a discovery that he did not make for some time simply because he was looking over to his extreme left when the patrol broke cover off to his right. By the time White completed scanning his sector back toward his right two members of Robinson's patrol were within ten meters of his position and fully exposed. Startled by the unexpected apparitions looming before him White momentarily forgot everything he had been taught. Instead of calling out for the pair of intruders to halt and challenge them as he should have, he simply raised his rifle, flipped the safety off, and opened fire.

The response to this sudden eruption of small arms fire was predictable. Without waiting for orders or to assess the situation for themselves, Rangers to the left and right of White assumed they were under attack and joined in, laying down a base of fire along their respective sectors of responsibility. Like falling dominoes, all along the perimeter every man who had been teetering on the verge of falling asleep lunged for their weapons and began blazing away with blanks at targets to their front, real and imagined.

In the center of the perimeter where he shared a shallow foxhole with his first sergeant and RTO, Nathan sprang into action. In an instant he was on the radio calling for situation reports from his platoon leaders. Within their own little water-filled foxholes those officers or their platoon sergeants were demanding the same from their squad leaders. Like the outbreak of small-arms fire, the excited chatter on the company command and platoon radio nets was spontaneous and initially confusing. Only the men in Robinson's squad responded in anything resembling an intelligent and coherent manner. Despite the fact that everyone was using blank ammo, those who had been in the open instinctively threw themselves onto the ground before scurrying back to cover on all fours as quickly as they could. The remainder of the squad also flattened out upon the wet, soggy ground as their squad leader broke radio silence in an effort to inform his platoon leader, First Lieutenant Jeff Sullivan, of the error.

Upon hearing Robinson's report Sullivan took a moment to utter a rousing string of colorful expletives before contacting Nathan on the company command net to inform him of the mistake. For his part Nathan listened to Sullivan's explanation in silence, knowing full well that the other platoon leaders were monitoring everything that was being said and would order their subordinates to cease fire without having to be told. In the darkness First Sergeant Carney sat across from Nathan watching his commanding officer, taking everything in as he prepared himself for his commanding officer's response.

As a stunned silence descended all along the nervous perimeter, Nathan took a moment to collect his thoughts. When he was ready, he stretched his aching body. Following suit, Carney slowly roused himself out of the mud as well. The creaking of joints and sharp stabbing pains that this generated reminded Carney that his ability to handle the dampness and cold wasn't what it used to be. Unable to hold back, Carney let slip a low, mournful groan.

Trying to find something to take his mind off of the screwup that he was about to sort out, Nathan turned to where his first sergeant was shaking off the effects of cramped and sore muscles. "What's the problem, Top? Having trouble deploying your limbs?"

Glad to see his commanding officer could find something to joke about at a time like this Carney chuckled. "Captain, you'd best enjoy playing Ricky Ranger while you're young, 'cause it doesn't get any easier with age."

"You disappoint me, First Sergeant. I always took you to be the stoic, 'old soldiers never die, they just fade away' type."

"Well," Carney grumbled as he continued to shake out the kinks, "at the moment this old soldier is fading pretty fast."

Somewhere in the darkness and within the company's perimeter both Nathan and Carney became aware of movement. "I suspect that would be Lieutenant Sullivan headed over to marry up with Lieutenant Laski to sort out his latest guffaw," Carney stated dryly.

"Guffaw?"

"Yes, sir, guffaw. It sounds so much classier than screwup," Carney explained.

"True, but a screwup by any other name still smells like . . ."

"Yes, sir, I get the picture," Carney stated as he stepped up out of the fighting position, turned and offered his hand to help Nathan up. After collecting himself and putting on what he called his "company commander" face, Nathan grasped his first sergeant's hand, pulled himself up, and made his way to White's position.

When he had finished sorting out the particulars of the incident and gleaning whatever lessons learned he could from it with his platoon leaders Nathan took his time making his way back to his own fighting position alone so that he could give the issues that faced him and his company some thought.

It hadn't taken Nathan long to sort out what had happened, who had erred and who deserved some serious talking to. It took him even less time to figure out the reason as to why the incident had occurred. The fact was he already knew the answer to that before Robinson had come up with his less-than-brilliant idea of deviating from the patrol plan or that White had fired his first shot.

It had nothing to do with a squad leader making a bad call, a sleep-deprived newbie getting rattled, or weather that was as foul as his mood. It was all a question of morale, or more correctly the lack thereof.

In the weeks since his company had rotated back to the States after their last tour of duty in the Philippines, Nathan had watched as the spirit and the pride of his men slowly ebbed away under an avalanche of silly policies and the implementation of a mindless and repetitive training program that made no sense to his Rangers. While the other companies were running exercises designed to improve their ability to launch quick, lightning-fast platoon- and company-sized raids and assaults, Company A did nothing but occupy a base camp, dig in, and run dismounted squad patrols against a phantom foe. Other than the mind-numbing training, there was no single incident involving Delmont, no one policy of his, that Nathan could point to as the cause for the sea change that was transforming his company from a smooth-running military machine into a stumbling collection of disgruntled soldiers who were starting to act more like rank recruits than the tough professionals they were.

Perhaps, Nathan found himself thinking as he had often done in the past few weeks, his men were doing nothing more than reflecting back to him his own attitude. Enlisted men, especially the sergeants such as Robinson, had a way of knowing what their officers were thinking, sometimes even before the officers knew themselves. They had the ability to divine the truth without the need to have it explained to them and despite an officer's best efforts to hide it. This sort of intuitiveness on the part of his NCOs, their unerring sixth sense when it came to such things, was what made commanding a company of Rangers so much fun when things were going well, and something of a challenge when they were not. It created a true dilemma for Nathan.

As an officer it was his duty to obey and carry out the

orders of his superior, implementing his commander's policies and directives as if they were his own. He had the right, and some officers with a bit of backbone would claim the duty, to question those orders and policies when they seemed to be flawed or inappropriate, but only in private. Open discord and disagreement between a superior ranking officer and one who was subordinate to him in front of enlisted men could not be tolerated. While the subordinate might score some points in the eyes of his own men when he stood up for them or common sense in this manner, in the end it was a practice that undermined the entire chain of command, for a junior enlisted man who saw his lieutenant arguing with his captain would have no compunction to do the same with that lieutenant or any other officer. In order to maintain the stringent discipline that a fighting unit such as a Ranger battalion required, every link in the chain of command had to be solid and hold firm no matter how difficult or distasteful that might be.

Thus Nathan found himself in a true bind, one that demanded some sort of solution, one that did not violate his obligation to carry out Delmont's training program no matter how much Nathan disagreed with it, while at the same time shoring up the sagging discipline and pride of his company. It was a tall order, made all the more difficult since he had to do so without letting on to his ever watchful NCOs and platoon leaders just how much he hated and despised Robert Delmont, a man he saw as an opportunist, a careerist who was using the battalion as nothing more than a stepping stone to the stars.

Of all the things that irked Nathan, it was this last point that bothered him the most. He knew the type, the golden fair-haired ones like Delmont who had been singled out when they were mere captains, tagged by those with the power to do so to be groomed for senior leadership positions in the Army. As a child Nathan had often heard his father talk among his friends during social events, when the beer was running freely and they were at liberty to discuss topics they didn't dare bring up while in uniform, things like how their own contemporaries were doing in the race for the stars.

Sometimes they spoke of their peers with admiration and pride, throwing in an occasional "Yeah, I went to school with him. He was always way ahead of the pack." Or "I was lucky enough to serve with him in Iraq." Other times their tone would be decidedly incredulous, sometimes even downright nasty, when in their opinion the person they were discussing didn't warrant being fast-tracked for promotion. As Nathan grew and entered the military, he inevitably came across some of the very people his father and his friends had mentioned. Whenever this happened he found himself making mental notes of his own in an effort to discern how best to judge which of these fast movers really did have the right stuff and who had nothing more going for him than a propensity for being in the right place at the right time. By the time he and Robert Delmont crossed paths Nathan had this down to an art. Without having to compare notes with any of his own contemporaries or sound out his father, Nathan knew instinctively that Delmont not only had stars in his eyes, he had a rabbi somewhere who was taking good care of him, a combination that was fortunate for the officer who was so blessed but also dangerous in that it tended to make the chosen one cocky, giving him a false sense of invulnerability.

Perhaps, Nathan thought as he neared the pathetic hole in the ground that was serving as his company command post, that was why he was incapable of seeing what he was doing to the line companies. Either his mind was somewhere else, plotting his next career move, or his career was so secure that it didn't make any difference what he did while serving as the battalion's commander. Regardless of the reason, the only bright spot Nathan could take comfort in was that officers such as Delmont were moved about from one choice assignment to the next as quickly as possible in an effort to make sure that his professional ticket was punched by all the right people.

Plodding along in the darkness, Nathan made out the form of his first sergeant, standing off to one side of the fighting position. "Well, sir," Carney stated glumly as Nathan approached him, "it seems like the lads are getting a wee bit sloppy."

Nathan grunted as he came up to Carney. "I dare say that was a bit of an understatement." Pausing, he reached into a pocket and fished around until his fingertips lit upon a foil pack of crackers he had saved from the MRE pack that had been his evening meal. Ripping it he took out a cracker and broke off a corner of it as he spoke. "We've got us a real challenge here, First Sergeant."

Carney chuckled as Nathan popped the chunk of cracker into his mouth and began to chew. "You've already got something in mind, I take it."

Without waiting to swallow the cracker, Nathan explained as best he could while chewing on his cracker. "The men are bored and confused. They think we're being punished for some imagined crime."

Half jokingly, Carney countered, "You mean we're not?"

"The colonel is up to something," Nathan explained, doing his best to defend a man whom he had come to detest. "There's a purpose behind all of this, one which I haven't been able to figure out or get the battalion S-3 to articulate."

"Well, sir, don't feel like the Lone Ranger there. I can speak for the majority of the NCOs when I say that there isn't a man in the company who hasn't wondered out loud more than once as to why we keep coming out here, digging holes and sitting on our duffs while the rest of the battalion is off elsewhere doing the sort of thing we've been trained to do."

"Well," Nathan grumbled, "until a serious case of sanity breaks out in this battalion I'm afraid we're going to continue to march about the woods, digging those holes and sending out patrols, until we're the best damned hole diggers and patrollers in the regiment."

Carney shook his head. "The lads won't be thrilled to hear that. Oh, don't get me wrong" he quickly added, "I'll make damned sure every squad leader in the company knows that the sort of shit Robinson pulled tonight won't fly. But . . ."

Carney didn't finish his statement. He didn't need to. Nathan knew what he was driving at. "You're right, First Sergeant. Simply jacking the men up every time they screw up isn't going to shake them out of the funk that this company is wallowing in. Besides, we can't be everywhere watching everything every squad leader and their people do. They're Rangers, professionals who are supposed to do it right the first time, every time without having an officer looking over their shoulders, ready to give him a boot in the arse every time he slacks off or screws up. Which is why we're going to spice things up starting tomorrow night."

Thrilled that his company commander was finally going to do something to break the death spiral that the company's morale had been in Carney's ears perked up. "What do ya have in mind there, oh, Captain, my Captain?"

"I want you to pick six men," Nathan explained in a low, conspiratorial manner as he leaned closer to Carney. "These men have to be more than just good Rangers. They also have to be the wildest, most unconventional, crazy gung-ho sons-of-bitches we have in this company, the sort that won't let anything stand in their way of getting the job done."

Folding his arms across his chest and stroking his chin with his right hand Carney smiled. "I think I see where you're going with this."

Now Nathan smiled. "Oh, not me, First Sergeant. You. Starting tomorrow night I want you to take this dirty half dozen, set up your own little base camp a few clicks away from wherever we settle in for the evening, then raise as much hell with the rest of the company as you care to."

"Any restrictions?"

Nathan thought about it for a moment before he shook his head. "Well, so long as I have the same number of healthy, breathing people in the morning that I started out with the day before, no, there's no restrictions."

For the first time since their return from the Philippines Carney felt a twinge of excitement. "I know just the men I'll need for this."

Nathan didn't need to see Carney's face to realize that he just might have hit upon the right solution for one of his problems. A bit of freewheeling, no-holds-barred force-on-force intramural action would do wonders to shake up the men in his company and put a little bit of "fun" back into these otherwise tedious exercises they had been subjected to. Now that he had hit upon the idea and given his first sergeant his marching orders, the only thing that troubled Nathan about this whole matter was why it had taken him so long to hit upon such a simple and obvious fix to the problem.

He didn't need to ponder that question for very long. He'd been too absorbed with the way he felt about his battalion commander to think straight. Rather than separating his personal feelings on that matter from his duties as the commanding officer of a Ranger company, Nathan had allowed the two issues to overlap and become entwined. Only when he forced himself to set aside his personal, petty concerns and focus on the problems his company was facing was he able to think straight and come up with a partial solution.

Unfortunately his tactical solution would do nothing to change how he viewed Delmont. Nor would it alter the manner in which that man dealt with his company. At least, Nathan concluded as he and Carney settled in to wait out the remainder of the night in their muddy hole, while he was out here in the field he could set those grim concerns aside and do the sorts of things he enjoyed doing, which were to train, maintain, and have fun in a manner only a Ranger could enjoy.

WASHINGTON, D.C.

Not long after Nathan had settled into his muddy hole on a nameless hilltop on the other side of the country, Jan was preparing to do battle in her own unique way in a modern building that was but four blocks from Capitol Hill. Like her stepson, some of the fiercest dragons she would have to deal with this day in order to do her job came from within the ranks of her own organization. In her case she had something of an edge since she was decidedly senior to everyone working at the D.C. bureau of the World News Network. Still, that didn't necessarily make things any easier, especially since her chief detractor was a man who was supposed to be her number two, a real up-and-comer who everyone who followed the in-house politics of the network was convinced would one day eclipse old hands like Jan who had done so much to make WNN the number-one cable news network.

Chet Lyell was everything that Jan was not. He was the ultimate suit, an organization man who learned everything he knew about running a news network from within the confines of the front office. To him news was a product, something that needed to be processed, packaged, and sold to the American public just like toothpaste and toilet paper. Though he was only in his early thirties, he had the technique down pat, perhaps too pat for purists like Jan who saw news in a much different vein. It was because they each held such differing views and came from such diverse backgrounds that the management of the network had brought the two together to run the Washington bureau, much to Jan's distress. Anxious to make his mark Lyell took every opportunity afforded to him to show that he could run a major news bureau on his own. For her part, Jan had to be careful how she went about keeping her energetic subordinate in check, especially on days like this.

No matter what sort of news day it was, Jan went out of her way to conduct her early-morning meeting with all her department heads using the same calm, no-nonsense manner with which she strove to run her bureau. She did so in order to make sure that all the news stories of the day pouring in from every corner of the globe were given a fair and impartial consideration lest the excitement of the moment cause her people to overlook a significant event, one that might not be as "sexy" as the crisis du jour but was still important. Doing so was seldom easy, especially when the event was as massave as the terrorist attacks on Mindanao, one that she instinctively felt was already being overhyped by her network's competitors. The pressure to match their coverage as well as finding a new angle to a story that was being covered wall-to-wall by every cable news channel was difficult to resist. Yet through it all Jan managed to maintain a semblance of order and a wider perspective of the day's events that amazed her peers and befuddled her detractors.

Once everyone was seated at the long conference table cluttered with all sorts of scripts, notepads, half-filled coffee mugs, and other odds and ends people dragged into meetings, Jan rose from her seat at the head of the table. "All right, now that everyone is finally here," she announced in a calm voice while looking straight at a producer who had been the last to arrive, "let's see what we have out there other than the Philippines story."

From the far end of the table Lyell looked about before throwing up his hands and hunching his shoulders. "What other story is there at the moment?"

Jan glared at Lyell. "Chet, there are over seven billion people living in over 170 different countries on seven different continents. Somehow I don't think they all called in sick today just to watch us report on what's happening on Mindanao."

An assistant producer midway down the table between

Jan and Lyell whistled. "Damn! Could you imagine the rating bonanza we'd get if they did?"

A chorus of nervous laughter rippled throughout the room, causing Jan to plant her hands on her hips and smile. "Very funny, Carl. Now, if you all don't mind let's get down to business here and find out what those seven billion other people have been up to." While taking her seat, she looked over at the assistant producer who was still laughing at his own joke. "Carl, since you seem to be on the ball we'll start with you. What's going on up on Capitol Hill that's of note?"

In this manner Jan went through her staff one by one, soliciting from them whatever information, ideas, tips, and leads they might have concerning an ongoing story they had been covering or a potential one that lay within their particular realm of responsibility. When they had all had their say, Jan turned to a number of news items and topics she had gleaned from the laundry list of stories being covered by the various news agencies and wire services that Jan's bureau tapped into. If there seemed to be a consensus that the item she hit upon needed to be covered by them in this particular news cycle, or if one of their regular Washington sources might add something to it during the course of the day, Jan would assign a priority to that item and alert her production staff to plan on using the material if it did pan out. Only when she had finished running through her list did Jan pause, look about the table, and turn to the subject they were all eager to pile onto. "All right," she stated with a feigned tone of indifference, "let's go over how we're going to handle this Philippines thing."

Though they knew better, everyone about the table started talking at once. For the next twenty minutes she listened to the thoughts, ideas, and suggestions on how the people in that room could best cover the story from the nation's capital. Once she had restored a semblance of order Jan listened to each person in turn, nodding her approval if they were on the right track, or wrinkling her nose and casually suggesting a different approach if she didn't care for their initial concept. When she needed to reorient someone who was threatening to wander too far off the reservation she had no qualms about telling them they had and asking the misguided soul to rethink his or her idea and see her later if they came up with something else. In quick order everyone knew what they needed to do. All this was done without the sort of long-winded debate or petty squabbling that Jan detested. Only when it came to decide upon which talking heads they would invite into the studio to discuss the situation in the Philippines did Jan run into something of a speed bump.

From his end of the table Chet Lyell rattled off the names of people he thought they should tap, few of whom Jan favored since Lyell's personal political sentiments were diametrically opposed to those she held. Lyell was the product of the Harvard School of Journalism and all that it stood for. Jan got her degree in journalism in what Scott referred to as the school of hard knocks. Whereas Lyell had never covered a story in the field, Jan had been to many of the places that were in the headlines day after day and knew or had met more than a fair number of the people who were making those headlines. Yet her expertise and long years of experience didn't intimidate Lyell, a man who was very much a part of what some had come to call the elite media, a fact that he was quite proud of.

The pivotal debate this morning concerned which of their military experts they would call upon to come in and render an opinion on the crisis. Jan had a particular favorite she had stumbled upon thanks to a bit of help from Scott. Though this particular expert had been only a colonel when he retired Scott made it a point to read every book the man wrote on military history and evolving military theory. For Jan this was more than enough of an endorsement as to the man's credentials and credibility. Lyell on the other hand tended to use a former general who Jan knew personally and could not stand.

Even before he mentioned the general's name as a possibility, Lyell braced himself for the confrontation. "I know you're going to say no, but hear me out."

Leaning forward, Jan looked down the length of the table straight at Lyell. "If you know I'm going to say no why are you even wasting my time with this?"

"Because, Jan, the man is a general and was supreme commander of NATO."

"Correction, Chet, he was a general."

"And the yokel you always parade out was only a colonel."

Jan was unmoved and unimpressed with Lyell's argument, doing her best to show it. "Colonel Stills is one of the foremost authorities on modern warfare, a man who regularly lectures on the subject at the Army and Navy war colleges as well as serving as a consultant to the National Security Council on the subject of asymmetric warfare. General Lanes is a has-been, a blowhard who's fond of telling war stories about his career and hasn't had an original idea in decades."

"General Lanes is highly regarded in many influential circles," Lyell countered.

The influential circles that Lyell was referring to were all left-leaning newspapers that used every opportunity they could to undermine and defame the current administration's foreign and military policy, a practice that Lanes was only too happy to participate in since it had been the current president who had brought Lanes's career to an end. "Chet," Jan finally stated as she began to gather her notepad and other odds and ends, "I'm not going to argue with you. As soon as this meeting is over I want you to personally contact Colonel Stills and get him down here as quickly as you can. If he's not in town make whatever arrangements you need to with an affiliated television station to get him into their studio and ready to go on the air when we need him." Pausing, she looked up at Lyell, who by now had slumped down in his seat like a schoolchild that had just been scolded by a mean teacher. "You do have Stills's number, don't you?"

Throwing his pen down, Lyell nodded. "Yeah, I've got it."

Standing up, Jan looked about the table one more time. "Good. Then we're done. Now, let's get out there and get busy."

While everyone else was gathering up their pads, PDAs, and coffee mugs Lyell called out to Jan above the clatter and racket. "You know, Jan, it would be a big help if you could clue us in on how the military is going to respond to this crisis."

Within the space of a heartbeat the room went silent. Everyone, especially Lyell, knew better than to bring up the subject of Jan's husband. While many of her competitors and detractors openly hinted that Jan was the ultimate insider when it came to getting information from the Department of Defense, everyone who worked with her didn't even hint at this. By doing so Lyell was just trying to irritate her, something that he was quite good at.

Taking a moment to compose herself lest she say something that she would later regret, Jan forced a feigned smile. "My inside source informs me that the Department of the Army met this crisis head-on this morning by enjoying an English muffin with butter and jam, a bowl of cantaloupe and sliced banana, washed down with a glass of orange juice. Outside of that, I'm as clueless as you are, which is why we need to get Colonel Stills in here as soon as possible."

Seeing that he wasn't going to get under her skin this morning no matter how hard he tried, Lyell threw in the towel taking comfort in the fact as he watched her leave the room that there would be other days.

ARLINGTON, VIRGINIA

A few miles away, on the other side of the Potomac, the man who had consumed the breakfast Jan had described was preparing for a meeting unlike the one Jan had just wrapped up. It would be a one-sided affair, one in which Scott would not be asked for his opinion or thoughts. He knew this from the phone call Henry Jones had made to him upon his return from another meeting with the Sec Def and the other members of the Joint Chiefs.

Henry Jones wasn't in the habit of calling people he needed to meet with. He had a sizable staff of aides, assistants, and secretaries that did that for him. So when Scott was informed by his secretary that Jones wanted to talk to him on the phone about the meeting, Scott knew that something he wasn't going to care for was in the works.

"Scott," Jones stated crisply in a casual tone of voice that was very unconvincing, "the Sec Def has a meeting in two hours with the president about the situation in the Philippines. He wants to have a full-blown, ready-to-go Army option in hand he can throw on the table if the president asks for that."

Though he suspected he already knew where he was headed, Scott decided to cut through the chaff. "Which OPLANs do you want me to bring?"

"Only one, Scott. Doberman."

"You do appreciate," Scott was careful to explain, "that Doberman would require the deployment and stationing of U.S. forces in the Philippines, something that the constitution of that nation forbids."

"I know that. In fact, I'm sort of counting on the Filipino government to gag on the idea of asking their former colonial masters to station troops on their islands. The last thing we, the U.S. Army, needs at this moment is to open up another rat hole we'll be forced to throw troops into. Lord knows, we've crammed our heads into enough gaping rat holes as it is."

Scott took no comfort in Jones's effort at humor. Instead he continued to press for information. "And what if the president and the State Department folks over in Foggy Bottom convince Manila to turn a blind eye to their distaste for American troops on their soil?"

Jones hesitated a moment. When he spoke again there

was a noticeable change in his tone, a somber one Scott could not miss. "Well, we'll do what young company commanders like your Nathan do when they're told to hop to. We'll salute smartly and ask how high."

Scott sighed. "Even if it's into one of those rat holes?"

"Especially if it's one of those rat holes," Jones responded. "All we can do is hope that we won't be told to jump. But if it does come to that I want to be ready to execute as soon as possible. Maybe, just maybe, if we move fast and strike hard we can nip this thing in the bud before the government in Manila goes under and that Abu Sayyaf leader who's been running things on Mindanao becomes too well established. Otherwise, it'll be 1900 all over again."

The mention of the American pacification of the Philippines at the turn of the twentieth century, when every regiment of America's small regular army had to spend time in the Philippines putting down Moros rebels was enough to send a chill down Scott's spine. "I'll get on it right away. Anything else?"

"No, Scott, I dare say that'll be more than enough." Though Jones didn't say it, Scott could guess what he was thinking, for he was thinking the same thing. He was hoping that Doberman would be enough. He was hoping that one good plan, one well-executed operation would prove more than enough to crush the Abu Sayyaf because if it didn't, Doberman would only open up a new front in the nation's war on terror that had already stretched the Army's resources to the limit.

After a few halfhearted pleasantries, Scott hung up the phone and leaned back in his seat. In many ways his decision to leave the Army when his current tour of duty was over upset him. The idea of passing a mess like the Philippines on to another officer to sort out was repugnant. He had always made it a matter of honor to wrap up all the loose ends of an assignment he was being rotated out of before handing it off to his successor. If Doberman was implemented and it did not achieve its objective, then he'd be giving the man who would soon occupy the very seat he was sitting in a real can of worms, one that had the potential of matching the length and intensity of Vietnam. This sorry fact was matched and surpassed only by the realization that if that sad state of affairs did come to pass his oldest son would be right there, right in the middle of a messy little war that he had put into motion but had been powerless to stop, much less finish.

Too old, Scott concluded. He was getting too old and cranky for this job. Feeling the need for a little boost in his morale he picked up the phone and called Jan to see if she could break free for lunch later. After the forthcoming meeting Scott suspected he'd need to see a friendly smile, a commodity the woman he loved never seemed to be short of. Of all his achievements, Scott concluded that getting that woman to marry him was his greatest coup. Next to her all the stars in the heaven were meaningless. To him she'd become life itself.

13

A special ops unit like Nathan's Ranger company is used to receiving no-notice orders to pack up and move out to any trouble spot in the world within hours. They train for it and expect it. Some even experience something close to disappointment when a major crisis erupts and no one bothers to call upon them to go over there and sort things out. In the case of the bombings in and around Davao City on Mindanao, Nathan's overeager Rangers went through such a period of disappointment as Operation Doberman, renamed Operation Pacific Shield, went through the torturous process all plans must undergo as they are staffed through the upper echelons of the military and are transformed from being little more than a draft OPLAN into action.

Unlike the majority of the forces tagged to participate in Pacific Shield, the political and diplomatic process needed to put those units into motion were not nearly as responsive. Long before anyone even dared think of alerting the combat and combat service support units that would participate in the operation it was necessary to do a lot of behind-the-scenes political and diplomatic legwork.

This aspect of military operations was something young officers like Nathan never gave a second thought to, for it was up to the old sweats like his father and Henry Jones to navigate the byzantine world of domestic and international politics and diplomacy that any operation such as Pacific Shield must first endure.

Before Pacific Shield saw the light of day all agencies that had anything to do with national security, such as the nation's intelligence community, the State Department, the Department of Justice, and even the Department of Homeland Security needed to be briefed on it. Each was given an opportunity to determine if Pacific Shield interfered with any operation they themselves were conducting or planning and if it was, in their view viable and advisable.

Once a consensus was reached among these decision makers, the staffs of those agencies then had to determine how they could get in on the action, both to support Pacific Shield itself as well as justify their existence since the budget and staffing of all federal agencies is based upon its activities and not its effectiveness. Once the executive branch had its house in order, trusted congressional leaders were briefed in an effort to find out just what sort of support or resistance there would be for the operation from the members of that branch of the federal government. The inclusion of Congress was an important element for they not only approved all funding required to run the federal government, their collective assent to Pacific Shield would allow the administration to share the blame if things did not work out as well as Major General James Palmer and his stable of energetic young colonels projected.

Of all the steps that were required to translate a military operation such as Pacific Shield into national policy, dealing with Congress was perhaps most maddening to members of the armed forces. With few exceptions military men are dedicated to one purpose and one purpose only, defending the United States. Politicians on the other hand are not restrained by codes of conduct or ethics. Rather than principles and ideals, they find themselves beholden only to the people who elect them to office, the well-heeled individuals or special interest groups who finance their political campaigns, and fellow politicians within their own party whose support is necessary to promote and enact each other's pet projects. To satisfy all the various interests they are bound to and maintain his or her seat in Congress a politician must engage in a number of pretenses and compromises, posturing and bombast, habits and practices that are anathema to anyone in uniform. It is this system that the men and women of the armed forces are pledged to defend. They are required to obey without question the decisions and dictates of politicians who have never stood a watch or shouldered a rifle. It is not a perfect system, but it is the best that four thousand years of human civilization has come up with. And it was the system that Henry Jones, Scott Dixon, James Palmer, Robert Delmont, Nathan Dixon, and even young Eric White were dedicated to defending, with their lives if necessary.

With the same care and precision that they used when preparing for battle, Scott and his staff put together a slick briefing designed to sell Pacific Shield to the politicians in both the administration and Congress. Having grown leery of issuing blank checks to the executive branch when it came to foreign military adventures the members of Congress who would be needed to support Pacific Shield were particularly demanding when it came to covering every conceivable contingency that American forces would or could encounter while deployed in the Philippines. By far the most crucial aspect of the operation from the standpoint of the distinguished members of Congress was the exit strategy, a term that has become synonymous in some circles to bugging out when the going gets tough. To use the traditional measure of success that the military relied upon to define victory, which is the destruction of the enemy, would not do when trying to convince people who actually believed that war could be waged without suffering friendly casualties and that 750-pound bombs were precision instruments that could be used to surgically eliminate the bad guys.

Despite the tribulations Scott and his fellow officers experienced as they picked their way through the political labyrinth of their own system with the same care and trepidation they used when crossing a minefield paled in comparison to what the diplomats faced when it came time to deal with the government in Manila. The waging of that battle not only had to overcome the obvious obstacles of language and national interests, but also cultural differences and history had to be factored in, for unlike Americans, the Filipino people do not forget their past, in particular anything connected to the fifty-odd years when the Philippines was an American colony. To protect themselves from foreign domination and their own weak-willed politicians, the Filipino legislature amended their constitution after the last of the American forces withdrew from their country in the early nineties in such a way as to make it all but impossible to station foreign troops in the Philippines. Of all the obstacles that needed to be overcome, this was the most perplexing that the American military and the State Department had to face.

In order to succeed, Pacific Shield required the establishment of a secure base of operations in the portions of Mindanao where the Abu Sayyaf was operating. This base was needed so that units, ranging from small four-man recon teams dispatched to locate the Abu Sayyaf all the way up to battalion-sized task forces tailored to smash them had a place to stage before going out on operations and rest and refit when they were finished. The concept of using a forward operating base or FOB was older than the American Army itself. Under Pacific Shield a series of FOBs would be secured on Mindanao to provide the men of the 3rd Battalion of the 75th Rangers this sort of sanctuary. When Robert Rogers, the great-great-grandfather of the American Rangers led his Rangers out to hunt their illusive foes during the French and Indian Wars he did so from Fort Edward, the 1750s version of an FOB located between the headwaters of the Hudson River and Lake George. While the weaponry and means of getting about the area of operations may have changed, the concept hadn't. Nathan and his fellow company commanders would lead their people out of the modern version of Fort Edwards into the wilderness of Mindanao to find, fix, and destroy the enemy.

The problem that threatened to keep this from happening was the form that these FOBs would take. What would the Filipino government be able to tolerate without violating its own constitution or handing its political opponents a dagger with which to rip out its own heart? If the president of the Philippines and his cabinet had their druthers they would have preferred to limit U.S. assistance in this time of need to material aid and advisers as well as an occasional "training" exercise such as the one Nathan's company had been participating in when Robert Delmont's chopper had been shot down. Unfortunately, in the opinion of the American Joint Chiefs, the nature of the threat and the proven inability of Filipino forces to counter it made this option a nonstarter. A sizable commitment of American forces would be required for extended periods of time, otherwise the Abu Sayyaf would simply go to ground while the Americans were there and then, when the Americans went home go back to slaughtering their fellow countrymen in the name of Allah and an independent Moros republic.

Thus the sticking point for all parties centered upon the issue of how big a footprint American forces could make on Mindanao and the islands of the Sulu Archipelago without upsetting the political balance in Manila while, at the same time waging an effective counterguerrilla war against the Abu Sayyaf. In order for the current government in Manila to remain in power it had to follow the letter of the law as laid out in its own constitution, which meant that American forces could not be permitted to establish anything remotely resembling a permanent presence. To have done otherwise would have been akin to handing Summirat a gift-wrapped propaganda victory while simultaneously ensuring that its political opponents would unseat them during the next round of elections, provided its own military didn't stage a coup before then.

The solution that Major General James Palmer hit upon not only solved this problem, it silenced potential critics within the American department of Defense by giving all the services a key role. Unlike Fort Edward, the FOB envisioned in Pacific Shield would not be a fixed installation. Rather than establishing one massive forward operating base and anchoring themselves in one place, the joint service task force assigned to participate in Pacific Shield would use the insular nature of the Philippines and American supremacy at sea to their advantage while allowing the government in Manila to maintain the pretense that it was adhering to the letter of the law.

At the heart of this joint task force, dubbed JTF Sierra was a naval task force consisting of a carrier battle group, a Marine amphibious unit and ships hauling everything needed to sustain their operations while under way at sea and when ashore. Once American and Filipino intelligence located a hotbed of Abu Sayyaf activity the Marines would go in first, as was their wont. Their mission was to secure an FOB from which Army aviation units, the Rangers, and Army combat service support units could operate. While the Marines provided local security for this lodgment as well as conducting their own combat patrols, a company of the 3rd of the 75th Rangers would be moved farther inland by helicopter to establish a series of patrol bases much like the ones Nathan and his company had been perfecting during their training at Fort Lewis. If and when Nathan's squad-sized patrols thrown out from this forward deployed patrol base found the enemy, the rest of the battalion, supported by Air Force units that rotated between forward operating airfields on Mindanao and permanent bases in Guam, would pile on.

In the event the company operating from the patrol base failed to make any meaningful contact in one area it would be lifted back to the FOB where it would have a chance to rest, refit, and rearm before being sent out again. This would continue until it was determined that a district had been secured or more lucrative opportunities presented themselves elsewhere. When that happened the Army units would be withdrawn, the Air Force would wing their way home, the Marines would re-embark and the entire task force would sail away to green pastures where the whole process would be repeated. To ensure that the Abu Sayyaf did not return, Filipino Army units that had undergone retraining in counterguerrilla warfare provided by Green Beret "A" teams would occupy the area recently vacated by JTF Sierra. "Like a skilled surgical team," Palmer explained straight-faced whenever he was winding up a brief of his plan, "JTF Sierra will go in and remove the tumor, leaving the long-term care and recovery to the nursing staff."

Step by step everyone signed on to Pacific Shield. The transient nature of the American FOBs provided the Filipino government sufficient cover to justify its support and allowed it to tell its people that there would be no permanent presence of foreigners on their soil. The inclusion of all services ensured that there would be no infighting between the various branches of the armed forces, eager to protect their turf while justifying their existence. And the relatively small footprint, one that kept moving around and presented terrorists a moving target coupled with the concept of deploying Filipino troops to follow up each American insertion, went a long way to calm nervous American politicians who feared another protracted quagmire. Only when all the loose ends had been gathered up and tied together into one neat little package did warning orders go out to those ships, ground units, air wings, and combat service support elements that would be part of JTF Sierra. Only then did Pacific Shield finish its long and arduous journey from

Robert Delmont's fertile mind, over to James Palmer who cobbled it into a draft operational plan, into the hands of Scott Dixon and his stable of high-caliber plans officers who roughed out the final plan and staffed it, and through the chambers of the National Security council, the halls of Congress, and across to Manila. Only when all of that was finished was Nathan Dixon and Company A, 3rd of the 75th Rangers, made aware that their days of training were about to end, that once more they were being called upon to place themselves in harm's way.

FORT LEWIS, WASHINGTON

Unlike the treacherous Machiavellian machinations that his father and his peers were forced to employ in their efforts to translate Pacific Shield into action, the path to war of Company A, 3rd Battalion 75th Rangers was well defined and quite routine. Units such as Nathan's command did this sort of thing all the time, for the procedures required to prepare his people for deployment to the Philippines was no different from those they used when going out to local training areas for an exercise. Well, they were almost the same. There were a few differences, some subtle, some quite sobering.

On the road to war every soldier is required to participate in a quaint Army tradition called a POM, short for preparation for overseas movement. It was an event that required members of a unit tagged for overseas deployment to line up and parade through a number of stations set up in a gym or auditorium to review all of their personal affairs in order to make sure that everything was correct and current. One of the stops was a check of dog tags, newfangled ones with an imbedded computer chip that bore little resemblance to the stamped aluminum sort that soldiers who had fought in World War II, Korea, and Vietnam wore. At another station each man was asked to review his serviceman's group life insurance data to make sure that everything was in order and up-to-date, in particular the name and address of his next of kin.

And then there was the most beloved station of all, medical records and shots. Every man knew before they reached that station that regardless of how up-to-date they were on their shots, a medic there would always find a reason to inject them with some sort of vaccine, especially when the unit was headed for a country that was as rich in natural and exotic diseases, plagues, pestilence, and bacteria as the Philippines was. There was even a station where a rep from the Army Community Service handed out pamphlets describing all the services that the military and various support groups could provide to the spouses of soldiers who would be left behind.

These proceedings gave the members of Company A ample opportunity to talk about what each of them was going to do during the block leave that the entire battalion was being granted. Since no one had any idea how long Pacific Shield would last and a unit engaged in an active theater of operations cannot allow more than 5, at the most 10, percent of its people to go home on leave or R & R at any one time, everyone is granted leave at the same time before the unit ships out. This concept allows critical members of the unit such as the battalion commander, the operations officer, company commanders, and company clerks, the people who really keep a company's day-to-day affairs in order an opportunity to take leave and enjoy it since everyone's gone and on leave.

PFC Eric White was minding his own business, not thinking about anything in particular, when Anthony Park, who was ahead of him in line turned toward him. "Hey, newbie, where are you gonna go during your leave?"

White was initially taken aback by Park's question. Up till now he and the other members of the squad, in particular those who belonged to the spec four mafia, hadn't bothered with him except in the line of duty or to mess with him.

Annoyed that White was taking so long to answer,

Park made a face. "It's not a hard question. Where you gonna go? Back home to see Mama and Papa?"

Not having given the subject much thought White shook his head. "No, I don't think so. I saw them after I finished up at Benning and before heading out here. But if it's a choice between staying here and doing nothing, I suppose . . ." ·

"Are you broke?" Park asked without hesitation. "I mean, do you have a few hundred bucks you could afford to invest in a venture that's far more interesting than a trip back to, where was it you said you were from?"

"Tennessee, eastern Tennessee. Not far from Knox-ville."

"Yeah, whatever. Have you ever been to Vegas?"

"Las Vegas? In Nevada?"

"The one and only." ·

"No, I've never been there. Why?"

Park broke out into a broad smile, one that reminded White of the sort a used-car salesman wears. "Well, my friend, today's your lucky day, for today you will be af-forded the opportunity to join me and a few of our dear-est squad mates on an adventure of a lifetime." Reeling White in like a fisherman hauling in a prize catch Park wrapped his arm around his newfound friend and ex-plained their concept of operation.

Farther ahead in the line Nathan was keeping to him-self. The idea behind the procedures employed during POM was something that soldiers accepted without com-plaint. To have done so would have been a waste, for even a rookie like White appreciated that this sort of thing was the most efficient and effective way of processing a large collection of people in the shortest possible time. Some, like Kim even saw this as something of a break from their strenuous training schedule. While Nathan would never have admitted anything like that, even to himself, he was more than prepared to disengage his mind and meekly follow the man in line before him, responding succinctly to each question thrown at him and tending to whatever paperwork he was presented with in order to keep his personal affairs in order.

His mind was off wandering about someplace far from the crowded gym where the POM was taking place when he came to the table being manned by an excessively cheery Army Community Service volunteer. Assuming that she was the center of Nathan's full and undivided attention, she launched into her prescribed spiel. "Are you married, Captain?"

It took a moment for Nathan to redirect his meandering train of thought from where it had been rambling about aimlessly and back to the here and now. "Excuse me?"

Speaking slower, as if that would help the befuddled officer understand her better, the perky young ACS volunteer repeated her question. "Are—you—married?"

"Oh, yes. Yes I am."

Satisfied that she had managed to penetrate the invisible shield that had initially deflected her questions, the volunteer moved on to the next question in the decision tree that dictated the manner in which she interrogated each and every Ranger as they paraded before her. "Will she be remaining here in the Fort Lewis area or will she be staying with other family members while you are deployed?"

Processing the question on its face value, Nathan gave her what he deemed to be the most direct and accurate answer. "No."

Unprepared for this response the volunteer blinked. "Excuse me?"

Thinking that she had not understood him, Nathan rephrased his reply. "She will be doing neither."

Having been thrown off her script, the ACS volunteer proceeded with caution. "Well," she stated slowly as her brain raced at high speed in order to sort this messy situation out. "Where will she be staying?"

Now it was Nathan's turn to be confused. For a moment

he simply looked at the woman as if she were simple-minded. "In her apartment, of course."

"And that apartment is located where?"

Even more befuddled, Nathan came to the conclusion that this poor girl really was a beer short of a six-pack. "Just outside of Fort Benning, of course."

Believing that she now understood the question, the ACS volunteer's smile returned. "Oh, I see. She hasn't been able to join you here yet."

Again, Nathan responded in the same short, direct manner that he always did. "No, we haven't been able to make the necessary arrangements."

"Well, is your wife planning on staying in North Carolina, move to the Fort Lewis area while you're overseas, or go home to stay with her parents?"

Suddenly it dawned upon Nathan why the woman before him was having such a hard time understanding his responses. Having been bored silly by the POM up to this point Nathan decided to have a little fun with the volunteer. "I think the Army would prefer that she stayed where she was for a while."

His answer only served to add to her confusion, causing her to shake her head as her smile disappeared. "Why is that? Is she in trouble with the Army?"

"Well, the last time I spoke to her she wasn't. But given how she treats all those hard-charging infantry types, that tends to change on a daily basis."

Realizing that she was out of her depths, a look of concern darkened the volunteer's face. Thinking the worst and somewhat unsure if she wanted to hear the answer she was cautious as she pressed on. "Well, what does she do?"

"She's a captain in the Army. That's where she is assigned."

It finally dawned upon the volunteer that Nathan had been messing with her mind. "Oh. I see." There was a protracted pause during which she looked down at the stack of forms and pamphlets neatly stacked on her table in an effort to avert her eyes. "I guess there's nothing I can help you with then, is there?"

"Why not?"

"Well," the volunteer replied as she glanced up at him "the information we have here is only for a normal family."

Taken aback by her answer, Nathan wanted to ask her to define what she meant by that but decided not to waste his time, her time, as well as that of the men who were stacking up behind him. With a shrug, he turned away and began to make his way to the next table.

As he did so, her words resonated in his mind. "A normal family," he muttered. He had never thought of his marriage to Chris as anything but normal. In many ways it was quite normal for a man and a woman of their age and generation to be actively pursuing careers that required them to live apart as they did. In the eyes of the Army however his marriage was far from the norm. Of course there were a number of families headed by two people who were in the service. It was officially sanctioned and official policy required that the Army do its best to make sure that the husband and wife be assigned together whenever it was feasible. But normal? Not in the eyes of one of the nation's last bastions of traditional family values. Though no senior officer would ever dare say so, if they had their druthers all such marriages would be against regulations. This included his own father who never said anything to Nathan, but made his feelings known on the subject in the way that only a father could. So, since the generals charged with running the Army were required to hold their collective nose and adhere to the politically correct norms of the society they are charged with defending, a marriage such as Nathan's and Chris's had to be tolerated, more or less.

With the words "normal family" rolling about in his head Nathan continued on through the line, responding to whatever inquiries were thrown at him with answers that were crisp to the point of being abrupt. When he was finished, he made his way back to his office, ignoring his company clerk who was hell-bent on handing him a message. With a wave of his hand Nathan told the animated clerk to give it to the first sergeant before closing the door behind him.

Absentmindedly Nathan slumped down in the well-worn Army-issue sofa that sat against one of the walls of his office. For a brief moment the stillness of the room was shattered by the sound of air rushing out of the sofa's plastic covered foam rubber cushions. In the silence that followed Nathan pondered what sort of family the ACS volunteer and her pamphlets envisioned. A husband and wife with a prescribed number of children? A domestic arrangement in which the male labored away at an off-site location all day while the female toiled away maintaining the home between trips to deposit the by-products of the adult relationship at school, soccer games, and such? What, Nathan wondered was a normal family?

The question made him sorry that he hadn't picked up one of the brochures the ACS volunteer was eagerly handing out to everyone who claimed to be part of a normal family. His father was a three-star general, an important man doing an important job at an important time in his nation's history. Of course, as far back as Nathan could remember his father had always been doing an important job. He had to be. He always seemed to be gone, either on gunnery ranges, or in the field engaged in training exercises, or deployed overseas on unaccompanied tours. His stepmother did her best to fill in during his absences, but she also had an important job to do, one that took her away from their home almost as much.

What was a family, Nathan found himself thinking. What was a home? He was keenly familiar with the sort of family that the Army liked its officers to establish, the sort that all his friends on base had, cluttered, lively places where he and his brother spent a great deal of time when duty called his father away and the pressing needs of his mother's job kept her at the office late. The structure he called home had been a place where his father stored his gear when he wasn't out making the world safe for democracy, a place that was comfortable, always clean, and well furnished. But it had the soul of a room display in a furniture store: proper, tasteful, but lifeless.

Uneasy with his thoughts yet unable to brush them aside Nathan folded his arms, dropped his chin till it almost rested upon his chest and squirmed, causing the seat cushions to squeak. Had things always been like that? he wondered. Had it been that way before his father remarried? Nathan liked his stepmom. His father loved her dearly. She had always been kind to him and his brother. And he had always been drawn to her in the way young children are drawn to a beautiful woman with a quick smile and an easy charm. But there had always been something between them. Perhaps she was too much like his father, a person who was larger than life, engaged in a career that made her the envy of mere mortals. As correct, proper, and amicable as she was to him, Nathan had never been able to feel the sort of warmth from her that all children crave.

Perhaps that was it, Nathan concluded. Feeling. A normal family was not the result of biological functions, legal compacts, or financial arrangements. A normal family was a web of interconnections composed of feelings, feelings that he had seen expressed by the parents of his friends, but ones that he was not sure he could honestly admit to having been part of. Had it always been so? he wondered. Had he once belonged to a real family, the one he had been part of before Jan?

This new line of questioning took Nathan down a new path that he wished he hadn't taken, for his quest to determine what a normal family was brought him to the realization that he could no longer recall much of anything about his real mother. He knew her face, but that was only because of the pictures in albums he and his brother enjoyed flipping through when his father or Jan weren't around. Other than that, he drew a blank. As hard as he tried he could not recall the sound of her voice, the touch of her hand, the scent of her fragrance. These and so many other things about her were a complete mystery to Nathan, something that was as unobtainable to him at the moment as was the meaning of the term "normal family."

COLUMBUS, GEORGIA

The burdens of command Nathan faced day in and day out at Fort Lewis were not easily cast aside and forgotten about when he departed that post. As was the case with so many professional soldiers he was unable to simply walk away, leaving his cares and concerns behind him. Unlike an investment banker who has little to lose other than money if he makes a mistake, a combat arms officer must live with the reality that even when he does everything right, even if his unit accomplishes all of its assigned mission in a timely and efficient manner people are going to die. And while it is always a goal to ensure that all of the dying is left up to the other people, there is no escaping the fact that some of his own will also become casualties. Such an awesome responsibility is one that cannot be casually shelved at the end of the day. The best an officer can hope for is to find a way to lock away such thoughts in a dark corner of his mind when he is with his family or in the company of others who haven't the faintest idea of what it means to lose men in battle. Yet regardless of how good one may become at this sort of thing it is always there, like a restless predator prowling through the tall grass just out of sight, threatening the calm and tranquillity.

There were occasions when Nathan felt having a wife who was also a commissioned officer tempered the trials and tribulations that all company commanders must deal with. One of the principal benefits of this arrangement was Chris's understanding of the Army. Nathan seldom needed to explain things to her the way his friends were obliged to do when their military duties came into conflict with family. Nor did he have to bother weaving a long drawn-out story as to how the operation his unit was about to take part in wasn't at all dangerous and that he'd be back home before she noticed he was gone. Chris understood what was going on in the Philippines without having to wait for Nathan to explain it to her, just as she understood the role her husband and his company was expected to play in sorting things out over there. The fact was she knew all too well, a state of affairs that created an awkward dilemma that neither of them seemed to know how to work through.

More and more Nathan found he was having difficulty with this. He marveled at the manner with which Emmett DeWitt dealt with his wife. He had a way of putting a smiley face on everything he did whenever he was with her. Whether Paula believed him or not didn't seem to matter to either of them. The pretense that was created by DeWitt's ever-positive spin on his official activities allowed the two of them to enjoy what time they managed to have together. Nathan always assumed that trying to do the same with Chris would have been a waste of time. He feared that if he tried something like that with Chris, she'd consider it an insult to her intelligence. So he didn't even make the effort.

Alone, this state of affairs would have been manageable had it not been coupled with the difficulties Nathan was having in his dealings with his commanding officer, a man who seemed to be going out of his way to make an already demanding job damned near impossible. If Delmont was aware of the effect his actions and demeanor were having on the battalion, he didn't let on. In theory a combat arms officer does not need to be popular or liked. He only needs to be technically and tactically proficient as well as efficient when it comes to getting the job done. And if there was one thing that Delmont was, it was efficient, perhaps Nathan thought too damned efficient. He had but one standard he repeatedly claimed, and that was perfection, an illusory notion that he strove to achieve and expected everyone under his command to follow likewise.

Despite all of this Nathan wasn't quite ready to admit all was lost. Sooner or later, he kept telling himself Delmont would tire of his crusade for perfection, allowing some sort of equilibrium to be established. Eventually both sides, Delmont on one and everyone else on the other, would come to terms with the other's idiosyncrasies and habits, establishing a new norm within the battalion that everyone could live with. Unfortunately their pending deployment to the Philippines not only made the likelihood of this occurring any time soon doubtful, it threatened to create additional stress. Though none of the company commanders openly discussed it, all felt that if things didn't change quickly, the morale of the battalion would suffer, a state of affairs that could not but have deadly consequences for all concerned.

The only bright spot Nathan could carry away from Fort Lewis as he made his way east to join Chris in Georgia was the performance of his company in the waning days of its grueling training cycle. Thanks to the small aggressor force that his first sergeant had pulled together and unleashed upon the rest of the company they had managed to end their training on a high note. Known as Carney's "Dirty Half Dozen," the six-man OPFOR team took great delight in springing ambushes, conducting lightning-quick raids, and laying insidious booby traps that never failed to snarl at least one inattentive Ranger. This aggressive opposition gave the bulk of the company something tangible that they could focus all their pent-up frustration on. Overnight excruciatingly mundane exercises that some saw as punishment for some imagined wrong were turned into the sort of challenge the Rangers of Company A enjoyed. Though no one ever lost sight of the fact of the deadly nature of their training, it ignited a spark that left the company confident that when it arrived in the Philippines, it would be ready to take on whatever the Abu Sayyaf could throw their way.

This single happy note helped some, but was not near enough to put Nathan in the frame of mind that would have allowed him to enjoy his leave. Not even Chris's cheery greeting when she picked him up at Columbus's small commercial airfield did anything to alleviate the dark mood that had been stalking him since his unit's POM. Though Chris did her best to ignore her husband's brooding, it cast a pall upon the entire visit. For his part Nathan made no effort to explain anything to his wife, leaving her to guess as to the cause of his cool detachment. Hoping that he would snap out of his grim despondency on his own, Chris chose to ignore it, a course of action that turned out to be a mistake.

For several days they went through the motions of spending time together as if they were just another married couple. Chris took as much time off as she could manage. Even so Nathan was left on his own for the balance of the day, free to dwell on the jumbled kaleidoscope of personal and professional issues that haunted him day and night. All his efforts to lose himself in a good book or redirect his nervous energy by pounding himself into the pavement during long, lonely runs around the field where the cadre of Airborne School went through the paces of training their charges failed miserably, leaving him in an ever increasingly grim mood. By the fourth day Chris had had enough. After a particularly lackluster session of intercourse, she propped herself up on her elbow and stared at Nathan as he lay on his back, staring at the ceiling.

In an effort to soften what she was about to say, Chris gently placed her hand on Nathan's bare chest. "There's more going on in that little head of yours than concern for your company and its pending deployment," she declared in a low voice that was as soft and nonaccusatory as she could manage under the circumstances. "I can't even pretend to imagine how difficult all of this must be for you," she stated despite the fact that they both knew full well that it was a lie since her first assignment had been to lead a chemical warfare platoon into Iraq during Operation Iraqi Freedom.

Taking her hand in his, Nathan tried to speak but was prevented from doing so as Chris pulled her hand away and laid her fingertips on his lips. "You're here but you're not with me."

Once more Nathan took Chris's hand, removing it from his lips and returning it to rest upon his chest. He was tempted to turn on the light on the bed stand, but thought better of it. This conversation, if the halting exchange could be called a conversation, was difficult enough without having to see Chris's pained expression. "Things have been a bit strained lately."

Unsure of the source of this strain, Chris was hesitant as she responded. "Perhaps if I knew what was troubling you I could help."

Without taking Chris's feelings into account, Nathan grunted. "What could you possibly do?"

Not being privy to the problems her husband was having with his commanding officer as well as the disquieting questions he had been struggling with over his past relationship with his own family, Chris leapt to the conclusion that it was their relationship that was at issue. Pulling her hand away, she turned away from Nathan and slipped out of bed. Before he could respond, before he could reach out and arrest her flight to the privacy of her bathroom she was gone. For the briefest of moments Nathan considered pursuing her so he could explain everything to her. Of course he didn't, for the truth of the matter was at the moment he found himself incapable of responding as he should have. As he lay there in the darkness, staring at the ceiling and listening to Chris doing

her best to stifle her sobs Nathan felt as if the world was
collapsing down upon him. Only the thought that things
could not get much worse saved him from total despair.
This of course was also an illusion, one Nathan allowed
himself to indulge in.

MANASSAS, VIRGINIA

Having screwed things up about as badly as a man could
in Georgia, Nathan fabricated an excuse to justify his
early departure, said his farewells to Chris, and fled north
to spend the last few days of his leave with his parents.
His sudden appearance at their doorstep was both welcome and alarming to Scott. While he was glad to see his
son before he shipped out, Scott suspected that there was
something amiss. Despite Nathan's efforts to put up a
brave front, Scott's worse suspicions were confirmed before Nathan's first night with them was out.

In an effort to enjoy this unexpected visit to its fullest
and get to the bottom of the problem that had motivated
it, Scott took a day off from his duties and spent them
with his son. Though his personal staff and Henry Jones
professed to understand his reason for doing so, all who
knew Scott were stunned that he had taken some personal
time, leaving his aide-de-camp to deal with the same sort
of skeptical response everyone threw at him whenever
he explained to a caller that General Dixon was not in
that day.

With the knowledge that Nathan had something he
needed to talk about in private, Scott suggested that they
spend the day at the Manassas National Battlefield Park,
the scene of two great Civil War battles. Ever the history
nut, Scott enjoyed walking the ground with book in hand,
retracing the ebb and flow of famous and not-so-famous
battles. For him a day tromping over hallowed ground
was better than a week's worth of lounging on the beach,
soaking up the rays. Nathan had also grown to enjoy

these quiet forays, though not for the exact same reason that his father did. Being the son of a professional soldier who had precious little family time to start with, these excursions provided Nathan with an opportunity to discuss things with his father that the hustle and bustle of the daily routine at home did not permit, a fact that Scott appreciated and was counting on.

Having no need to wait on a park ranger's tour, father and son stopped by the visitors center, paid the admission fee, and headed straight for Matthews Hill, a rather nondescript piece of terrain where the first serious clash of the War Between the States took place. As was his habit Scott led Nathan along the route taken by one of the major combatants on the long-ago day, in this case the brigade commanded by a Rhode Island brigadier named Burnsides. Whenever they reached a point of interest, Scott would stop to explain an incident that occurred at the spot they were standing on or to point out across the rolling green fields to where the opposing side stood. All the while Nathan listened attentively, making an appropriate comment or asking a question, for the truth was he enjoyed these walks through history almost as much as his father.

This continued on for the better part of an hour as they followed a well-worn trail that slowly meandered its way from where Burnsides's brigade had first emerged onto the battlefield to where the Confederate units of "Shanks" Evans's brigade deployed to meet it. They were about to emerge from the woods on the southeastern side of the hill where the Confederate line had stood against the mounting Union pressure when Nathan slowed his pace, then stopped. Looking up he studied the flickering sunlight as it filtered its way through the leaves and branches as they gently rocked to and fro in rhythm with the breeze. Sensing that the moment had come, Scott paused and waited for his son to speak.

Intuitively Nathan knew what his father was waiting on. They were too much alike and had share too many moments like this before, allowing his father to all but anticipate what he was thinking. It was an eerie gift that was both scary and at the same time quite comforting to the younger Dixon. Casting his eyes down onto the ground, Nathan used the toe of his shoe to stir some dried, dead leaves as he contemplated what he would say.

His first inclination was to bring up the problems he was having with his commanding officer in an effort to seek his father's advice on how best to deal with him. That, Nathan quickly determined, would not have been wise. For one thing any such discussion would have been between two men who were more than a father and son since Scott Dixon was a very senior general who wielded enormous power within the Machiavellian world of back-alley Army politics and Nathan was a professional soldier who was expected to display the same sort of loyalty to his superiors that he expected from his own subordinates. Knowing his father, Nathan could all but anticipate how he would respond, lecturing him in a manner that would have been awkward for both of them. The second reason Nathan shied away from that issue was a very personal one. Nathan suspected, or rather feared, that to have admitted that he was unable to deal with an issue that all soldiers find themselves confronting at one time or another during their careers would have diminished him in the eyes of his father, a state of affairs that even a captain commanding a Ranger company was unwilling to risk. So he turned instead to a subject that was just as troubling, but more suitable to the complex relationship that existed between father and son, general and captain.

"I think I've screwed things up between Chris and me," he stated slowly without looking up at his father. "This long-range relationship doesn't seem to be working."

Scott sighed. He had been expecting this sort of thing ever since the two young Army officers had married.

Over the years he had known more than his fair share of dual military couples, both officer and enlisted. On occasion he had served as father confessor to friends who buckled under the stress and strain that an arrangement of that nature placed upon two young people who were both venturing out into the world on their own for the first time while simultaneously endeavoring to mold a solid career for themselves in a profession that could at times be as inflexible and brutal to its own as it was to its foes. Scott had watched in silence as husbands cheated on their spouses and perfectly competent female officers were reduced to nervous wrecks when they suddenly discovered that they were incapable of achieving the feminist notion of having it all. Sensing that his son needed help articulating the issue at hand, Scott slowly sidled up next to Nathan. "Is there someone else?" he asked in a manner that was almost shocking by the casual manner with which Scott blurted out the words.

Stunned by the question and a bit hurt that his father would even suggest such a thing, Nathan looked up into his father's eyes. "No, of course not." He was about to ask his father how he could imagine such a thing but quickly checked himself. He was, after all, a grown man, susceptible to and more than capable of indulging in all the sorted follies that humans with serious problems tend to engage in. Instead, he looked back down at the ground, shoved his hands in his pockets and continued to kick at the dry leaves at his feet. "No," he repeated in a more mournful and subdued manner. "We still love each other very much. I'm sure of that. I'm positive of that," he repeated as if trying to convince himself of the truth of his own statement. "It's just that, well, things aren't working out the way we thought they would."

This caused Scott to grin. He didn't mean to and did his best to hide it from his son lest he suspect that he wasn't taking Nathan's problems seriously. Reaching out, Scott laid his hand on Nathan's shoulder and gave him a gentle, comforting shake. "Son, I've got flash traffic for you. Marriage is like a military operation. No plan ever survives initial contact."

Once more Nathan looked up at his Father, this time there was a hint of a smile on his face. "Yeah, I suppose that's true."

"Suppose hell," Scott boomed. Leading his son out into the open, the elder Dixon turned to face the north where the Union line had stood during the fight on Matthews Hill and spread his arms out like a preacher about to deliver his sermon. "On the twenty-first of July 1861 two armies blundered into each other on this piece of terrain. Neither side had planned on fighting for this nondescript pile of dirt but here is where they met and here was where they had no choice but to deal with the situation the Fates had seen fit to hand them. Both sides could easily have pulled back to regroup and try to find a way to get back on track but they wouldn't." Dropping his arms, he turned to face his son. "Why didn't they?"

Nathan thought about the question for a moment, understanding as he did what his father was driving at. "Because they were determined to succeed, to press forward regardless of the odds and overcome the opposition."

With the forefinger of his right hand, Scott touched Nathan's nose in an almost playful, childish manner. "Bingo! Spot on, young captain. When life hands you a pile of shit you have a choice. You can either drop down on your fat ass and whine or you can clean it up as best you can using every means you have at your disposal and get on with the rest of your life. Sometimes you can get someone to help. Sometimes you need to do it all on your own. Either way, how you deal with it is your call."

The ease with which his father was able to address an issue that had been plaguing him caused Nathan to smile. Looking up into his father's eyes, the son nodded. "So, your solution is that I ignore the enemy fire and instead fix bayonets, give a yell, and pitch into them."

Scott found himself a bit embarrassed by the analogy he had managed to invoke between his son's marital affairs and Nathan's statement. "Well, in a manner of speaking, yes."

"I don't suppose you have any sage advice on what avenue of approach I should take?"

Throwing his arm over his son's shoulder, Scott pulled Nathan close to him. "As a matter of fact I do. I wholeheartedly recommend that you get your skinny little butt on the first plane out of D.C. and beat feet back to Georgia. In the words of George S. Patton the Third, once you're there, you'll know what to do."

Buoyed by his father's words and embrace, Nathan felt as if a weight had been lifted from his heart. Though all his concerns over his relationship with Delmont still existed, the prospect of leaving the home front secure and tranquil gave him something promising to hang on to as he sallied into the troubled and uncertain future. "You know, Dad, for once I think I'll take your advice."

In a mocking gesture, Scott looked up into the sky and shouted out, "Praise the Lord." Then he drew his son even closer. "But first, before I allow you to flee this hallowed ground, we must make a pilgrimage to that most holy of holy spots, the one where Tom Fool Jackson chose to stand like a damned stonewall."

Though he stood half a head taller than his father and could easily physically overpower him, Nathan allowed Scott to shepherd him along the trail that wound around Matthews Hill and led to the Henry House off in the distance.

FORT BENNING, GEORGIA

The scene that Nathan had imagined during his flight back to Columbus, Georgia, pretty much played out just as he envisioned it, for in his absence Chris had also been afforded an opportunity to redress her feelings with the help of her own confidantes, coming to the same conclusion that Nathan had managed to stumble upon with a little help from his father. Having profusely confessed their stupidity to each other, the remainder of their time together would have been lost in a dreamy fairy tale that promised to consume the balance of Nathan's leave had not the ever-present responsibility of command intervened.

His call to duty came in the form of a phone call made by PFC Eric White from the Clark County Jail where he and the rest of his cohorts were being held held pending charges. The reason Anthony Park told White he needed to make the call to the captain rather than himself or one of the more senior members of the quintet that had been arrested for busting up a lounge was that he, Park, had already used his one phone call to contact the duty NCO back at Fort Lewis in order to get Dixon's leave number. The truth was quite different. Park figured that since White was the newest of the newbies in the company, someone who had yet to stake out a reputation for himself in the same manner that he had managed to, the company commander just might be more sympathetic to their plight. In this Park was pretty much on target, for White's quivering pleas, his down-home Tennessee accent, and a squeaky clean record was all but irresistible to Nathan.

Still, Nathan was less than anxious to derail his marital reconstruction project while it was still in midstride. After hanging up he made a few calls of his own, sorted out the truth of the matter and decided to leave his wayward Rangers where they were for another day. "I'll call the airlines tomorrow and reroute my return trip via Vegas and see what I can do to bail their sorry little butts out of jail. In the meantime, I think I'll let 'em stew in their own juices for a while," he explained to Chris when he was finished dealing with this unexpected interruption. "It'll make those cocky little shits a lot more pliable when the first sergeant and I get our hands on them."

Chris smiled. "Quite frankly, dear sir, at the moment all I'm interested in is finding out what you intend to do once you get your hands on me."

Taking her hand in his, Nathan began to lead her back toward the bedroom. "Come, my dear, and I shall show you, for there are some things that words simply cannot describe."

14

MORO GULF, SOUTHWEST OF MINDANAO, PHILIPPINES

Contrary to Scott's cynical commentary concerning the ephemeral nature of plans exposed to the harsh reality of war, the opening moves of Operation Pacific Shield unfolded flawlessly as if it were a well-rehearsed training exercise. Based on lively and some-times heated consultations between the commander in chief of the Pacific Command or PAC COM and the Philippines military as well as information provided by both nations' intelligence services it was decided that the first incursion would be made at the head of Sibuguey Bay between the towns of Ipil and Naga. Though the site was selected based solely on sound military logic, an assistant ops officer on Joint Task Force Sierra's staff with a twisted sense of humor saw things differently. In describing the area of operations during a routine briefing just prior to the initiation of operations, the sort where half the people usually don't pay attention to what the briefer was saying, he likened the Zamboanga Peninsula to the west of the landing site and a smaller one to the east off of which the island of Olutanga lay to a pair of legs. As some in the audience continued to doodle in the margins of their notebooks and others struggled to stay awake, he pressed on. "That being the case," he stated in a matter-of-fact, business as usual tone while pointing to the spot on the map, "the site we have selected for our first forward operating base, designated as FOB Atlanta by Admiral Turner, is literally the crotch of the Zamboanga region."

This comment generated a few chuckles that disturbed the slumber of some of the staff officers as well as frowns from those who had been shorted when God issued them a sense of humor. Making no effort to hide the impish grin he always sported when about to spring a prank, the ops officer turned to the assembled commanders and staff officers responsible for carrying out Operation Pacific Shield huddled together in the crowded briefing room of the flagship. "Therefore," he announced triumphantly as he collapsed his folding pointer to signify that he was about to conclude his portion of the briefing, "participation in Operation Pacific Shield makes us all proctologists, charged with crawling up the anus of this nasty big island in order to root out a cancer known as the Abu Sayyaf before it spreads to the rest of the Philippines."

The primary nonmedical instrument that would carry out this task was the ground component, a force that had been drawn from every element of the Army's special operations community and commanded by a Marine Colonel with the unlikely name of Tim Lamb. At its heart was the 3rd of the 75th Rangers, the mailed fist that Lamb would thrust deep into the bowels of the provinces of Zamboanga del Norte and Zamboanga del Sur, a region that the Filipino Army had all but surrendered to the Abu Sayyaf. Working side by side with Robert Delmont's Rangers were elements of the 160th Special Operations Aviation Regiment, a Special Forces "B" Detachment with six "A" teams, and a Delta Force squadron. When not providing direct support to the 3rd of the 75th Rangers these highly specialized special ops and counterterrorism forces would be free to carry out missions of their own.

They would not be the only Americans crawling through the brush hunting down a foe that had managed to humble the best the Filipino Army had to offer. In addition to his charter of securing the FOBs JTF Sierra would use, the commander of the Marine amphibious group was given leave to plan and execute offensive operations as he saw fit within a zone that extended fifteen kilometers out from FOB Atlanta's perimeter. Supporting his own Marine infantry were elements of the Marine Force Recon and the Navy SEAL teams that had been attached to his command for this purpose. Above them all would be the Air Force augmented by naval aviators, ready to provide close air support using precision guided munitions, cluster bombs, and if necessary massive doses of dumb iron bombs delivered by squadrons stationed in Guam comprised of an aircraft affectionately known as Buff. Though designed to fight a nuclear war and considerably older than every crewman that flew and maintained them, the venerable B-52 bomber continued to fill a need that no other weapons system in the Air Force's order of battle could.

Employing all the tactics, techniques, and skills at their command each of these highly specialized units was expected to seize the initiative from the Abu Sayyaf and win back the hearts and minds of the local populace for the government in Manila. They would do this by conducting around-the-clock operations designed to find, fix, and destroy the Muslim insurgents that were doing their best to break those bonds of loyalty while peddling their own brand of Islamic fundamentalism and independence to the same constituency. Unlike the government forces, when the arguments of the Abu Sayyaf failed to sway the people they had one weapon in their arsenal that the American forces did not have and the Filipino Army dared not use: terror, both implied and explicit.

This made the task that faced the Americans all the

more daunting, for they would be facing three foes not one. The first was the most obvious, the Abu Sayyaf itself. Under its current reincarnation engineered by Hamdani Summirat the Abu Sayyaf had reemerged from the wreckage of past setbacks into a force to be reckoned with. At its core were the fighters Summirat himself had taken such care to recruit and train. Numbering around six hundred these men were both dedicated and ruthless, totally committed to their cause and, more important, to their commander. They gave Summirat a lightly armed but very hard-hitting strike force that had the ability to range freely throughout the region, wreaking havoc when and where they chose through the employment of a wide range of tactics and techniques.

Below them in the scheme of things were a dozen or so regional commands, company-sized units made up of young men eager to join Summirat's growing movement. Created in the wake of the renewed war against the government in Manila they were organized to operate in a set geographical area with leadership provided by selected individuals detached from the strike force. These commands were not as mobile, were less well trained, and were not nearly as well equipped as the main striking force, leaving them incapable of executing offensive operations of their own. Rather than spreading the rebellion their main task was to defend those areas that the Abu Sayyaf had cleared as well as augment the strike force if it became necessary for that force to carry out operations in the regional command's area of responsibility. These same regional commands also provided Summirat with a ready reserve from which he could draw both reinforcements and replacements for his strike force as needed.

On the bottom rung of the Abu Sayyaf's military ladder were the local militias. In theory every man between the ages of fourteen and forty in those areas that came under the control of the Abu Sayyaf automatically became a member of this motley band of part-time combatants. Armed with old weapons that had been cast off by the strike force, the regional commands, and the army, even Summirat had little confidence in their ability to do anything more useful in battle than make noise and draw the enemy's fire away from more valuable and effective combat units. Standing toe to toe with the Filipino Army or the Americans was not what Summirat had in mind for the militia. Rather than filling their ranks with first-class material that went to the regional commands, Summirat and his lieutenants selected militiamen from that element of the local populace that had grown weary of the succession of corrupt officials that the Manila government sent to rule them, and saw the Abu Sayyaf as a viable alternative but were either unfit for more active operations or had family commitments that prevented them from participating full time. Their purpose in life was to keep the village chiefs and governing councils Summirat established in each village he conquered loyal to the cause. In a pinch the local militia could be called upon to resist a sudden incursion by government forces by force of arms. Otherwise the members of the militia were expected to melt back into the fabric of their community in order to provide Summirat with intelligence on enemy units and their operations.

The other obvious but nonhuman foes that JTF Sierra would have to contend with were as old as warfare itself: the weather and the terrain. In theory these elements were neutral factors in that they affected both sides equally. Had both sides been similarly equipped and conducted their operations in the same manner this would have been true. Since this was not the case, both the weather and the terrain heavily favored the Abu Sayyaf, a force that had practically no logistical tail, little in the way of heavy equipment, and enjoyed widespread popular support throughout that part of Mindanao that American forces would operate in. As the visiting team, one that relied upon helicopters and a flotilla of warships, the Americans were forced to view both weather and terrain as hostile forces. Though each and every element that made

up the ground component of JTF Sierra had trained exten-
sively to fight in the sort of environment Mindanao had to
offer around the clock, rain or shine, they would still be at
a disadvantage when going against a foe who had been
born and raised on that island. Not even the best training
in the world can overcome the sort of home field advantage that the indigenous elements of the Abu Sayyaf enjoyed. No matter how far American technology went in
peeling back the jungle cover under which Summirat
shrouded his operations, it could only do so much. Once
satellites and drones had located the enemy and helicopters had deposited the Rangers on that spot, the terrain
became a factor that would heavily favor the Abu Sayyaf.

Whereas the terrain was a virtual constant, an element
that could be overcome through careful analysis, planning, and rigorous training, the weather in this part of the
world was a true wild card, especially during the rainy
season. In addition to the oppressive heat and humidity
that could drop a man as neatly as a 5.56mm slug and an
annual rainfall that exceeded two hundred inches in the
coastal regions, the Philippines sat astride the typhoon
belt, a fact naval plans officers ignored at their own risk,
especially during the period of July through October. As
a student of history and a man who had spent much of his
life at sea, Admiral Turner was well aware of the devastation that a typhoon could wreak on a fleet. Such a storm
had once saved Japan from a Mongol invasion in 1281
and almost did so again in 1945 when another typhoon
scattered the armada Halsey had been gathering for his
invasion of Japan. Of all the hazards that JTF Sierra would
have to contend with, Turner's greatest concern was over
what Mother Nature could do to his precious ships should
she get her back up.

These were the overt foes, those that could be quantified and planned for using all the analytical tools and
institutional knowledge available to Admiral Turner's operations staff. To this list one could easily have added
two more items that had the potential of adversely affecting

the conduct of operations, concerns quickly glossed over during the course of the marathon briefings that were held at every level by each of the component commands involved.

The first was the attitude of the people. This would not be the first time that the American Army had come to Mindanao to root out Muslim insurgents. Shortly after relieving Spain of the Philippines the United States found itself engaged in a vicious little war with the very people it had come to liberate. To the Filipinos in 1899 the Americans were not liberators but simply the latest flavor in colonial masters. Though Theodore Roosevelt declared an end to the Philippine Insurrection on July 4, 1902 after a vicious guerrilla war, American troops continued to wage a brutal struggle against the Moros on the southern islands of the archipelago well into 1913. Those staff officers on Turner's staff who bothered to concern themselves with civil military affairs were unsure just how the present Muslim population of Mindanao would react to the return of American troops to their shores. Their institutional memory coupled with the anti-American sentiment that had become the cornerstone of modern Islamic fundamentalism promised to make an already difficult task all the more complicated. Even the most optimistic intel analyst gave JTF Sierra less than a fifty-fifty chance of overcoming the sort of historical distrust that still clouded the relationship between the two peoples.

On top of all of these adversaries, both natural and human, the members of the 3rd of the 75th Rangers could count one more: their own battalion commander. The strain that Robert Delmont's style of command engendered within that organization followed the battalion across the Pacific to Guam where Turner gathered all the various components of JTF Sierra prior to their embarkation for the Philippines. There it manifested itself anew as he rode his staff and company commanders day and night as the 3rd of the 75th Rangers, *his* battalion, became the center of attention. Nothing anyone in the battalion did was ever right the first time, be it staff work or an inspection. "Excellence has to be more than a laudable goal to which we strive," became something of a standard response, whether he was throwing a staff paper back at its drafter or passing judgment on a unit after watching it run through a combat drill. In meetings with his commanders and staff he repeatedly made it quite clear that he would accept nothing shy of perfection from them or their people. "We're the linchpin of the operation, the organization that all eyes will be on. Therefore excellence must be SOP, the only acceptable standard within this battalion."

There was no doubt in anyone's mind that Robert Delmont's insistence on excellence was in itself commendable. After all, every Ranger wanted to be the best of the best, the top of his profession. For many this was a primary reason they chose to become a Ranger. It was the man's utter lack of skill in dealing with subordinates and the means by which he chose to achieve this level of performance that wore on the spirit of the very men under his command. In the eyes of Nathan and his peers he had no redeeming qualities, personal or professional. There was nothing of the quirkish sense of humor that some senior officers use to make an unsavory task more palatable. Nor did he possess the sort of mystical qualities some called charm that compelled men to follow a beloved commander to the very gates of hell.

Even had Delmont been little more than an abrasive, humorless prick, most everyone in the battalion could have overlooked his dearth of personality had he been afforded the opportunity to demonstrate to his subordinates that he was a first-rate combat leader, a man who knew his profession cold and went about his duties with the same impersonal manner that a great white shark goes about prowling the deep. In this regard the Fates and the timing of Operation Pacific Shield had been rather unkind to Robert Delmont. In the few months he had been with the battalion after he recovered from his

unfortunate crash on Jolo Island and their deployment to
Guam there had been no major exercises, no operations
of any sort during which he was afforded the opportunity
to demonstrate his professional abilities. The only inter-
action between battalion commander and his subordinates
that took place during this operational lull had been in a
garrison environment where there were routine inspections, staff briefings, and brief forays out into the local
training areas to observe tactical training. Deprived of
the sort of occasions that he needed in order to show his
stuff, the members of the 3rd of the 75th could only formulate an opinion of their commanding officer based on
what they had seen of him to date, none of which was
flattering or encouraging.

Fully aware of the corrosive effect their battalion commander's personality and style of leadership was having
on morale, Nathan continued to act as a buffer between
Delmont and his own people. He rationalized his adherence to this covert behavior by convincing himself that
Delmont's behavior left him no choice. "I have a responsibility to my men," he explained to DeWitt as the two
paced the flight deck of the USS *Nassau,* an amphibious
assault ship that served as Admiral Turner's flagship as
well as the 3rd of the 75th's home when not deployed
ashore. "They expect me to be more than a taskmaster,
just as you and I expect the same from Delmont. Just because he's opted to be an uncompromising prick and beat
everyone into the ground like a tent peg doesn't mean I
have to do the same."

DeWitt knew from firsthand experience just what Nathan was speaking of. Not even the battalion's executive
officer, a major who was the secondmost senior officer in
the unit and had a reputation as a combat leader to die for,
was immune from Delmont's abrasive manner. Still, De-
Witt's seniority, experience as a company commander,
and position within the staff allowed him to play the devil's advocate whenever Nathan or one of the other company commanders turned to him in search of a sympathetic

ear into which they could pour all their woes and sorrows. During their passage from Guam, when the members of the 3rd of the 75th had something that Rangers seldom enjoyed, free time, Nathan spent a great deal of time with DeWitt discussing issues that he dared not bring up with any of the men in his company.

For his part DeWitt listened, offering what advice he could when he could. "You realize of course that you're playing a dangerous game by not carrying out the old man's edicts to the letter," DeWitt warned Nathan when he explained how he felt compelled to modify some of Delmont's policies and outright ignore others. "Your evaluation reports as a company commander are without question the most important ones in your record. Even the slightest hint that your performance during your tenure of command was anything less than stellar can be a kiss of death to an otherwise outstanding career."

Nathan glanced sideways at DeWitt and snickered. "And I imagine Mumbles knows just how to manipulate the verbiage in the rater's narrative on an evaluation report to have the right effect without making it too obvious."

"Yes, he does seem to have the gift." DeWitt sighed, having already had occasion as the adjutant to see just how skilled Delmont was at turning a seemingly innocent comment into a damning phrase when evaluating an officer he had taken a disliking to. "I think that's part of the final exam they give all officers before they're allowed to be leave the Pentagon."

"Cynicism! Now that's a side of you I haven't had the privilege of seeing."

"What do you expect?" DeWitt responded without a hint of mirth as he shoved his hands deeper into his ACU pockets and kicked at an imaginary stone on the flight deck. "Who do you think Mumbles dumps on when he doesn't have a company commander within arm's reach to slap about?"

"Oh, me heart bleeds for you. It truly does. Remind

me to break out my violin when we get back to the cabin so I can play a few sorrowful tunes for you."

Pulling his right hand from his pocket, DeWitt placed his middle finger on his lower eyelid and pulled it down while staring at Nathan. "Nate, look into my eye."

"Cute, real cute. Did they teach you that at adjutant school?"

"No. Something I picked up from a movie."

When they reached the end of the flight deck both officers stopped and stared out at the sea. "You know," Nathan mused, "if it wasn't for the fact that we were going in with Captain Queeg at the helm, this operation could be fun."

In another place where there were nonmilitary types present Nathan would have never dared refer to a military operation as fun. DeWitt however was cut from the same cloth as he was, a professional soldier who saw the military as something more than a vocation, or even an avocation. Rather than recoiling at his friend's comment DeWitt simply nodded in agreement as he turned and looked back down the long flight deck. "I can't think of a better setup than what we've got here. Go ashore, kick some ass, then climb back aboard where we can clean our weapons, enjoy a hot shower and sleep between clean sheets before we do it all over again. Now this is how to fight a war."

"Which brings up an excellent point," Nathan intoned as he also spun about to watch a mortar team from another company practice setting up their weapon, dry-fire a mission, then break it down before scurrying to another spot on the flight deck where they repeated the drill. "Since you sitteth at the left hand of our lord high master, please explain to me why it is that we are establishing FOBs ashore when we could very easily conduct all of our operations from the decks of this very ship. I mean, it seems to me that if everyone is so nervous about how the indigenous population is going to respond to our presence, the last thing I would think we would want to do is set up a FOB."

Cautiously, DeWitt leaned back on the cable railing as

he crossed his arms and shook his head. "You put too much stock in me my friend. I'm just an adjutant, the errant boy on the staff charged with pushing paper and shuffling people. When it comes to tactical ops and the reasoning behind our current plans, I'm as clueless as the base plate of that mortar."

"Yeah, and just as dense."

With a quick swipe of his left hand DeWitt lightly smacked the side of Nathan's head. "I resemble that remark."

"I'm serious, Emmett. I mean stop a moment and look at all the extra effort and personnel that's going to be wasted in establishing FOBs every couple of weeks. Rather than helping us scour the countryside an entire Marine battalion is going to be tethered to the lodgment providing security for all the Fobbits the task force commander intends to cram into it."

Fobbit, a named coined in Iraq for personnel who never left a FOB was one that replaced the Vietnam era RAMF, or rear area mother. "Hey, I don't mind being a Fobbit if it keeps Paula from worrying."

"And the Marines?"

"It's not like they're going to be totally idle," DeWitt reminded Nathan. "They'll be conducting sweeps of their own."

"And what good will a single platoon going out five, maybe ten klicks do? Does anyone really think the leadership of the Abu Sayyaf is going to oblige us by walking up to our perimeter just so the Marines have something to shoot at?"

DeWitt made no effort to reply. Instead, he took a moment to mull over the issue as he continued to watch the mortar team practice their battle drill. Finally, he drew in a deep breath. "Ever read about the French Indochina War, Nate?"

"With a father like mine, what do you think?"

"Then you're familiar with the strategy behind Operation Castor."

Nathan glanced over at his fellow captain. "The Abu Sayyaf aren't the Vietminh. And FOB Atlanta isn't Dien Bien Phu."

"Yes and no. Look, the moment we go ashore we're going to be like the five-hundred-pound gorilla in the room, something the Abu Sayyaf can't ignore if they hope to achieve their political goals. They're going to have to come up with some sort of response to us. They just might make a mistake, one we can pound on."

Unconvinced, Nathan shook his head. "They've not done anything stupid to date," he countered. "Somehow, I can't see them turning away from what they've been doing in order to impale themselves on Marine barbed wire."

"It's not the Marines I was thinking of."

Casting a leery eye toward DeWitt, Nathan was about to say something but didn't. Like DeWitt, he had come to the conclusion that if the Abu Sayyaf was going to mount a major response to their incursion they would do so against a target that was out of range of naval gun fire and was small enough to take out quickly. This target would need to be small, stationary, and vulnerable. Of all the elements in the task force the only command that fit all those categories would be the company sent out to set up patrol bases in the interior, his company.

Turning about, Nathan once more looked out across the churning sea. "Like I said before," he mumbled without a hint of mirth. "This operation could be fun."

MINDANAO, PHILIPPINES

The arrival of American forces in the Philippines was an event that had been much anticipated. For weeks international correspondents had been following every move the various elements of JTF Sierra made as it gathered itself together in Guam before lurching onward to its final destination. Even the dimmest bulb in the vast galaxy of news TV anchors and commentators was capable of guessing with a fair degree of accuracy when that would happen and what would occur when it did. The only question left out there for the armchair strategists and assembled talking heads to speculate on was the "where." When it came to this answer Admiral Turner had a distinct advantage, thanks to the mobility of his fleet and Mindanao's long, meandering coastline. It was a riddle he intended to keep secret for as long as he could.

Word that the Americans had finally come ashore reached Summirat while he was in the midst of a really close soccer game. It was a rather modest affair played on a crude playing field that hardly deserved that title between his team consisting of handpicked players who were part of his handpicked strike force and one drawn from a company belonging to a regional command. Soccer, or more correctly football to those parts of the world where football is played with a round ball, was something of a passion for Summirat. His most cherished childhood dream was of playing for his national team in the World Cup play-offs. For the briefest moment, when he was the captain of his school's team he allowed himself to imagine that he was actually on his way to doing so. Were it not for his duties as a young officer and the realities of a world where dreams were at a premium Summirat was convinced he would have made it.

His decisions as a young man to set aside his athletic ambitions did not mean that he had completely closed his heart to his beloved sport. Somehow, no matter how bad things became for the guerrilla band he was with, someone always seemed to have a soccer ball tucked away in a haversack or backpack, ready to be kicked about when the tactical situation allowed and a clearing big enough to double as a playing field was near at hand. Those who followed Summirat took as much pleasure in these games as he did, for it afforded them an opportunity to set aside their weapons and once more engage in a friendly game where they could show off their individual skills, laugh at each other's mistakes, and hoot and holler like children when a companion scored.

A professional soldier such as Nathan would have viewed this practice as little more than a means of building unit cohesion, a very necessary quality that all combat units must possess if they wish to be successful on a more important field, the battlefield. On those occasions when he was unable to gracefully duck out of it he participated in organized unit sports, affectionately referred to as organized grab-ass by those who saw games played during duty hours as a vile waste of time.

To Summirat there was nothing wasteful about playing soccer at all. On the contrary, the very idea of passing up the opportunity to play a game was unimaginable. On many occasions he gladly skipped a meal or sacrificed an hour's worth of sleep when a chance to kick the ball around presented itself. For him the game was more than a team-building activity or a way of showing his followers that given a chance he was really nothing more than "just one of the guys." It was an escape. It afforded him an opportunity to leave behind the vicious world he lived in, to vent his frustrations, his anger, and his fears by smashing an unfeeling little ball with his boot, the same well-worn boot that was often stained with the blood of his own men as well as that of his foes.

The vintage flatbed truck overburdened with recently harvested produce trundled up to where Summirat was participating in a very heated game that was, at the moment, tied one–one with only minutes left to play. The member of the local militia unit based in Ipil who had been dispatched to carry word to Summirat that the Americans were landing leapt from the cab of the truck before it came to a full halt and broke out into a run, yelling the news as he went. A silence fell as everyone on and off the field stopped what they were doing and turned toward the excited militiaman.

Having anticipated this moment for weeks Summirat was well prepared for its arrival. Ignoring the messenger, he scanned instead the faces of those gathered around him. To a man he could see that they were apprehensive and anxious. This of course was understandable, given that the American forces sent against them were unlike anything most of these men had encountered before. In every measurable area that mattered when it came to war American superiority was overwhelming. Even where physical quantifiers could not be applied, such as morale, esprit, and determination it seemed as if the Abu Sayyaf was at a severe disadvantage. Summirat understood this. In fact, it was what he was counting on.

Putting one hand on his hip, he turned to where the ball had come to rest across the field from where he was standing at the foot of a player who was on his own team. Mustering up as much displeasure as he could manage, he yelled out so that everyone on and off the field could hear. "Hey! Are you going to boot that ball or do I have to come all the way over there and do it for you?"

Dumbfounded, the man looked over at Summirat, down at the ball then back at the messenger who had arrested his mad rush toward Summirat just as he was about to cross onto the playing field.

"The goal isn't over there!" Summirat thundered as he pointed away from where the messenger was standing and down the field instead. "Ignore him. Ignore everything but the goal. Drive the ball! Drive it until we have won."

In the twinkling of an eye every man on the field understood what their leader was saying. Without needing to be goaded any further the man with the ball before him broke out into a broad smile and let out a hoot as he cocked his leg, smashing the ball with all his might as he sent it sailing down the field. One by one players on both teams resumed the game where they had left off, sparing no effort to achieve the victory each side believed was theirs for the taking.

15

Off to the east night was grudgingly giving way to the pale dawn of a new day. From the south a gentle breeze swept in from the ocean, causing the palm branches of the few remaining trees within Atlanta's perimeter to sway lazily to and fro. It was the sort of moment that had the power to steal the breath of a poet, a serene beauty that was lost to the members of JTF Sierra as they prepared to catapult the sophisticated military juggernaut that Admiral Turner had thrown ashore deep into the heartlands of Abu Sayyaf territory.

Everywhere one turned soldiers and Marines went about executing their assigned duties with a quiet, tight focus that tended to heighten the tension that precedes all military operations. Most everyone in Nathan's company did what they could to ignore the mounting strain as best they could, carrying on as if this day would be no different from any other. All subconsciously fell back upon routines in an effort to present to their comrades and leaders with a business-as-usual, "no big deal" nonchalant attitude. Yet every man felt it, all were affected by it. The only thing that differentiated them was how they handled the "IT" that times such as this brought to bear.

Everyone had their own little coping mechanisms that allowed them to carry on when preparing to pitch head-long into an uncertain future. Even Newbies such as Eric White found ways to pretend that the strain wasn't both-ering them though not as well as those who had been though this before. Those who surrounded White would never have noticed his nervous twitching, the way he glanced about every few seconds, a restlessness that caused him to shift about every so often, had their own senses not been raised to a fevered pitch by the same heightened awareness that was animating White. The only differ-ence between them was that those who had gone through this sort of thing more than once had managed over time to perfect their own little techniques for working through their own apprehensions without becoming psychologi-cally unraveled.

Most did so by slavishly adhering to highly ritualized individual precombat preparations that began the mo-ment they got wind that something was up. From that point on everything they did tended to follow a set se-quence, a well-rehearsed pattern that they dared not stray from one wit lest bad luck befall them during the course of the coming operation. Henry Jones, White's squad leader, always rushed through his personal preparations so that he would have the time to jot off a cheery hand-written note to his wife, a sweet Southern girl who en-joyed fresh-cut daffodils and smelled of vanilla. Corporal Rodriguez Sanchez always drew four hand grenades when ammo was being issued. Returning to his cot he would carefully line them up before him as if they were religious icons, then slowly wrap a strip of electrical tape around the spoon so they could be safely stuffed into various pockets on his combat vest. Corporal George Bannon's thing also revolved around the ammunition he drew. Although the rounds for his M249 SAW issued to

him were already packaged and ready for use, he insisted
on slowly pulling every belt out of its container, carefully
inspecting each round as he ran them through his fingers.
Specialist Four Anthony Park spent whatever time he had
after packing his gear and checking his weapon before
sharpening the black stiletto commando knife he always
strapped to his right ankle. Bryan Pulaski slipped each of
the 40mm grenades he was issued for his grenade launcher
into his combat vest while wearing it, doing so by going
from left to right, top row to bottom row. After snapping
each pocket cover closed he paused to tug on it in an effort to satisfy himself that the snap was properly seated.
Like his squad leader, John T. Washington's ritual had
nothing to do with his equipment or ammunition. Instead
he spent what little time he could steal reading a dog-eared
Patrick O'Brien or Clive Cussler novel in an effort to
keep from dwelling on grim chores he would soon be
called upon to carry out. Keith Stone, the medic assigned
to Lieutenant Hal Laski's Third Platoon, sought both escape and solace by seeking out a chaplain and confessing
his worldly sins.

In many ways the officers assigned to the 3rd of the
75th Rangers were fortunate, for they had little free time
with which to dwell on their own personal concerns, fears,
and misgivings. The same troop-leading procedures that
Robert Delmont and his staff had to tackle when they
received an operations order from above had to be addressed by Nathan at company level and his platoon leaders in turn without the aid of a staff. This included the
most sacred of all rituals for Rangers, precombat inspections. Before going out a soldier like White could go
through as many as four of these. First there was his section leader, in this case Corporal Bannon. During this pre-
liminary once-over he checked White to make sure that
he was ready for the squad leader's precombat inspection
as well as to ensure himself that the newbie entrusted to
his care had properly secured the extra ammo he was
carrying for Bannon's SAW. Next came Henry Jones, who

conducted a more thorough inspection by going from man to man after they were fully geared up but before they headed out to the green line. Out there the platoon leader put them through a more formal inspection, carried out with the entire unit in formation. During this round if Hal Laski missed something it was immediately caught by Frederick Smart who followed close on the heels of his lieutenant just as all good platoon sergeants tend to do.

By the time First Sergeant Will Carney called for the company to fall in and stand by for the company commander's precombat inspection the drill was little more than a formality, a gesture, but one that was by no means an empty one. For most of the men in Company A this would be the last time they would see their company commander up close and personal before going into action. Once they broke up into squad-size caulks and clambered aboard the UH-60 Blackhawks that were undergoing their own precombat inspections at the moment, Rangers like White would most probably never lay eyes on Nathan again until they returned to FOB Atlanta. His orders, the orders that would send White forward into an assault against an entrenched foe or pull him back from a deadly firefight, would be transmitted down the chain of command through White's platoon leader via radio or by word of mouth from platoon leader to squad leader, squad leader to section leader, and finally to White, the proverbial tip of the bayonet.

Knowing this, as Nathan stepped before each man he was about to lead into battle he always took a moment to look into that man's eyes in an effort to gauge just how sharp that point was. In doing so he afforded each of them an opportunity to look into his own unflinching stare to see that he, their company commander, was just as physically and psychologically ready as they were to sally forth into harm's way.

In the past this had been the easiest part of Nathan's own precombat ritual. In the course of his short career he had already seen more combat than most officers are exposed to in an entire career. The sights, the sounds, the smells of battle were as familiar to him as the scenery that lines the route many Americans zoomed by as they commuted back and forth to work day after day after day. And while it was true that no two situations were alike, that each one demanded a prompt and immediate solution unique to it, Nathan was confident in his own judgment and tactical skills, confidence that allowed him to approach each new operation with a calmness and poise that was obvious to all who came into contact with him. It was this confidence that Nathan wanted to share with his men as he made his way through the ranks of his company. It was a confidence that for the first time in his life he was having to fake, for in the run-up for this particular operation he had not been able to find a trace of it in the eyes of his own commanding officer.

Slowly, mechanically, Nathan moved from man to man, taking a moment to give him the once-over from head to toe. Every now and then he'd take the preoffered weapon each Ranger presented to Nathan as he stepped in front of him and gave it the same treatment, running his eyes along its entire length, from muzzle to butt before handing it back. All the while Nathan found it difficult to focus on what he was doing. Behind the poker face that he managed to present to his command on this day his mind was churning with doubt, concerns that were shared by the other company commanders in the battalion. None of them were comfortable with the manner in which they were going about their business.

Emmett DeWitt wasn't the only one to question the wisdom of tromping about the Philippines beating a drum. Noel Cameron, the commander of B Company made no effort to conceal his disapproval of his battalion commander's concept of operations. During the briefing in which the battalion ops officer laid out the particulars of the mission they were about to embark upon, Cameron shook his head or wrinkled his nose as Major Perry laid out the details of Delmont's plan. Clarence Overton, who had commanded C Company longer than Cameron had led B, was a bit more circumspect but no less skeptical. At the end of the briefing, when everyone was preparing to leave the battalion ops center, Overton sidled up next to Captain Thomas Valery, Perry's assistant, and asked him what the battalion commander and his staff were up to. "What ever happened to stealth? We're Rangers for Christ's sake, America's terrible swift sword, the bolt out of the blue. This battalion used to take pride in its ability to get up close and personal with the enemy without him knowing what was going on until it was too late for him to do anything about it. Jesus, Tom, if we're going to carry on like this from here on out we might as well publish our battalion op order in the Davao Daily."

Like the rest of the staff all Valery could do was shrug and grunt. "Don't look at me," he meekly mumbled before turning away from his friend. "I just work here."

An answer such as that from an officer as dedicated to his profession as any other was as telling as it was stunning. It betrayed both Valery's dismay with the manner with which his technical and tactical expertise was being ignored when it came to planning battalion ops and the manner with which things were now being done in the battalion, feelings that were shared by Overton, Cameron, DeWitt, and Nathan. Like disgruntled people on a bus in which they were mere passengers, with no say in where it was going or how it was getting there the young captains who stood between the senior leadership of the battalion and the enlisted men could do little more than vent their frustrations among themselves while soldiering on as best they could.

It was this sense of helplessness, one Nathan was not used to, that was most troubling to them all. By the time an officer reaches the rank of captain most view themselves as hardened veterans of the system, masters and commanders of their little piece of the Army. To be treated like a wet-behind-the-ears, dumb-as-a-rock second lieutenant

again did not sit well with them, any of them. In private
they could question the logic behind their commanding
officer's judgment and his leadership skills, or lack thereof.
But in ranks, standing before his men Nathan had to conceal his true feelings, his fears and apprehensions. He had
to do everything he could to keep the misgivings that were
eroding his confidence in what they were about to do from
seeping down into the ranks of his own command. So he
pressed on, following the tried-and-true routine that kept
the company going, grimly determined that regardless of
what Delmont did, Nathan would do whatever it took to
ensure that the men in his company lived up to the reputation that countless Rangers before them had paid for with
blood and sweat.

At the appointed time, Company A's final formation suddenly flew apart into small clusters. Instinctively each of
them went trotting off in single file to where the pilot of
his assigned Blackhawk strained to keep his bird on the
ground as its massive whirling blades bit into the heavy
morning air. Ducking low, the Rangers were shepherded
aboard the fleet of helicopters by waiting crew chiefs.
Once all his charges were in place the crew chief gave his
pilot a thumbs-up. He, in turn, waited for the signal from
his flight leader. These brief seconds are perhaps the
most anxious for all personnel involved, as the heart rates
of Rangers and air crewmen alike are revved up to a fe-
ver pitch as if trying to match the rpms of their copters.
When the signal is finally given, when the fleet of helicopters finally breaks their tenuous bond with the ground
there is a sense of liberation, of release. All the preparations are over. It is time to execute. It is time to venture
forth into harm's way.

When the massive flock of Blackhawks and its escort
of AH-64 Apaches was but a few feet off the ground, it
executed a sharp synchronized turn till they faced out to
sea before gracefully surging forward into the stunning

blue tropical sky. From his perch Nathan Dixon watched as FOB Atlanta disappeared behind them. Slowly, as his helicopter picked up speed he could feel some of his old confidence returning. Though he was still tethered to Delmont by a sophisticated state-of-the-art radio network, once committed to battle he was the commander, expected to use his initiative and judgment when carrying out those tasks that had been enumerated for him by his superior via the battalion operations order. Since Delmont had the actions of two other companies, attached elements and organizations assigned to provide direct support to the battalion as a whole to orchestrate, Nathan felt he didn't need to worry about unexpected visits by him in the field. That and reports from multiple sources that the Abu Sayyaf had access to sophisticated shoulder-launched surface-to-air guided missiles made it highly unlikely that Delmont would try to micromanage Company A's activities on the ground from the confines of a command-and-control helicopter hovering high above Nathan's units as many battalion commanders had done in Vietnam. Besides, of the three line companies assigned to play a role in the current operation, Company A's was anything but sexy.

After charging headlong out over Sibuguey Bay past the ships of Turner's task force riding at anchor the flock of Blackhawks hauling Nathan's Rangers first made a wide sweeping turn to the west. They held this course but for a moment before coming about on a new heading that took them due north, across the entire width of the Zamboanga Peninsula and once more out over water, this time the Sulu Sea. To those Rangers who didn't care much for the idea of flying over the ocean the sight of land as the Blackhawks eventually turned east, making landfall just north of the city of Sindangan, came as a welcomed relief.

As with most of western Mindanao the government in Manila had opted to abandon Sindangan to its fate in order to concentrate the handful of troops that could be relied upon to stand their ground against the resurgent Abu Sayyaf in an effort to defend other cities in the central and eastern part of the island that were more important to the national economy and the government's political prestige. Hamdani Summirat had wasted little time by taking full advantage of this betrayal to the people of Sindangan. Through intermediaries he made it known to the mayor of that city he had but two choices. He could support the Abu Sayyaf or he could watch as the members of his family and those belonging to the city's most prominent citizens were butchered one by one.

The mayor was no fool. He knew the reach of the Abu Sayyaf and fellow international terrorist groups with whom it was aligned made sending his family away little more than a waste of time. Realizing that the tides of war had turned against him, the mayor readily agreed. Besides, the speed with which the government in Manila had abandoned them left a bad taste in his mouth. "How can they expect us to remain loyal," he had explained to his people when he announced his decision to them, "when they flee at the first sign of danger."

Sindangan and other centers of population now under the control of the Abu Sayyaf were important objectives that would need to be reclaimed if the overall campaign to defeat the terrorist group was to succeed. That task, however, belonged to others, namely the Filipino Army. The mission handed down to the 3rd of the 75th was to create an environment that would allow that Filipinos to do so. Loosely translated, this meant that the Abu Sayyaf had to be hunted down and destroyed. This made finding it the first order of business, a mission that Nathan's company had been assigned.

The tactics that Robert Delmont chose to employ to accomplish this were nothing new to the Army. They had been perfected long ago when it had been dispatched to the west of the Missouri to fight those Native American tribes who had opted to defend their lands against the rising tide of American manifest destiny. Then as now small bands of professional soldiers were dispatched deep into contested territory to establish an outpost from which it would dispatch patrols charged with seeking contact with those forces hostile to the United States. Once they had been found and fixed in place, every unit that could be brought to bear piled on until the foe was either defeated in detail or was forced to concede the territory he had been struggling to defend. After a while, when civil authority had taken root in that newly pacified territory and was able to fend for itself the soldiers moved on to establish a new outpost.

Over the years the Army's mode of closing with the enemy and the weapons it employed changed but to a surprising extent not its tactics. In Vietnam, the Dominican Republic, Honduras, Panama, Haiti, Somalia, Bosnia, Macedonia, Afghanistan, Iraq, Djibouti, and numerous other places most Americans never heard of small bands of professional soldiers were plopped down in the midst of a hostile populace and charged with the mission of establishing a secure, safe environment in which the rule of law and western democracy could take root. Robert Delmont meant to do the same here on Mindanao. Using information provided by both American and Filipino intelligence, it was his intent to dispatch Company A to those regions where the main elements of the Abu Sayyaf were known to be. Systematically Nathan's Rangers would scour the area day and night, literally kicking over rocks space-based intelligence platforms could not see under. As in the old days, when contact was made, when the enemy decided that the time to stand their ground against American forces, the other two Ranger companies would pile while air power "softened up" their foolish foe.

All of this was carefully enumerated in the battalion ops plan with its numerous annexes, appendices, and attachments required to ensure that supporting elements knew their role and were prepared to execute their assigned tasks when called upon to do so. Not addressed anywhere in that order was the threat that Nathan and Emmett DeWitt had discussed, the very real danger that the Abu Sayyaf might not cooperate with Delmont's concept of operation by meekly waiting to be found and beaten into the ground by American firepower.

The possibility that the Abu Sayyaf would choose instead to turn on their tormentors if and when they had the drop on them was a possibility that Nathan dared not ignore. Unlike the balance of the battalion that remained within the perimeter of FOB Atlanta until the enemy was found, Company A would be out there on its own. To safeguard his company against this threat Nathan took great care to ensure that every patrol plan his platoon leaders submitted to him included a contingency that dealt with the possibility of a more aggressive enemy response. When issuing his orders to his platoon leaders he never missed an opportunity to drive home the point that the enemy they were about to face was both skilled and opportunistic. "The second we let down our guard, the moment they sense that they have an advantage they will turn on us. When that time comes, and I suspect it will we must be prepared to do more than simply stave off disaster. If we're to succeed out here, we're going to have to turn every opportunity we are presented with to our advantage."

With this thought never far from his mind, Nathan decided to make good use of the element of surprise that he would enjoy on this first day by having each of his platoons dropped on different LZs located several kilometers to the north, southwest, and southeast of the location where the company established its first patrol base. Once on the ground each of the platoons would converge, fanning out as far as they dared while doing so in an effort to sweep as much area as possible while keeping anyone watching them in doubt for as long as possible as to where they would finally stop and dig in at the end of the day. This would make the day a long and exhausting one. But it would be useful, allowing his people to get a feel for the terrain they would be operating over for the next week or so while shaking out any first-day bugs that training back at Lewis or on Guam hadn't been able to sort out.

It would also force anyone wishing to report the location and progress of Company A via cell phones or other electronic means to make frequent calls to Hamdani Summirat's chief of operations, electronic broadcasts that would be picked up and recorded by an Air Force RC-12D Guardrail reconnaissance aircraft specially designed to collect SIGINT, or signal intelligence, and ELINT, electronic intelligence. When passed onto JTF Sierra's joint targeting cell, a decision would be made as to whether to launch an immediate strike against the station transmitting the signal or to tuck the data away for future use by intel analysts who were charged with gathering up analyzing every bit of information concerning how the Abu Sayyaf operated. Once a profile of how the Abu Sayyaf was organized and operated had been completed, it could be exploited by the full weight of JTF Sierra when the time was right.

What was going on outside the confines of the UH-60 Blackhawk he was in was of no interest to Eric White. Despite all the training he had endured everything he saw and heard suddenly seemed foreign and not a little intimidating. All the way up to the point where the company commander gave the order for the platoon leaders to take charge of their platoons and mount up he had been able to convince himself that he was ready for this, that he had nothing to worry about. But somewhere along the line, as he struggled to stay up with the man in front of him as they made for the waiting helicopters, White found he could no longer hide behind such pretenses. This was all real, as real as the live ammunition he carried for both his rifle and Bannon's SAW, the three day's worth of rations he would need to live off of, and the claymore mines and empty sandbags that would protect him and his squad mates once they had reached their base camp. All of this and a hundred other things that he suddenly became aware of were all too real to ignore. By the time he climbed aboard his assigned helicopter and it sped out over the vast blue ocean below, the only thought that kept racing through White's mind was that that this wasn't Georgia or Fort Lewis.

This time they weren't headed out into a barren, unpopulated training area. This helicopter was taking him away from everything he knew, away from the last friendly non-Ranger faces that he would see for a week, perhaps more. In a matter of minutes it would be dropping him smack-dab in the middle of a province where they had been told the best they could hope for from the indigenous population was an attitude of guarded indifference. In short, he was about to go to war. And for all the training that he had survived, all the mental preparation and toughness his instructors had tried to instill, he suddenly realized that he was not ready for what he was about to do.

With practiced ease the Blackhawks carrying Lieutenant Laski's third Platoon arrested their headlong charge into the interior of Mindanao and came to a complete stop. As a pair of AH-64 Apaches circled about like collies protecting a flock, the crew chiefs of the Blackhawks tossed thick nylon "fast" ropes out of each side of their aircraft. When he saw that the end of the ropes were touching ground, he gave the senior Ranger in his caulk the thumbs up and got out of their way. In White's aircraft this was Staff Sergeant Jones, his squad leader. Looking over at the first man seated by the door next to each rope Jones pointed at each of them and bellowed, "Go!"

On the left side, this meant White. In Jones's squad the newbies always went first. When White asked why, Jones didn't mince words as he explained. "If someone's going to screw the pooch by doing something dumb like letting go or falling out of the bird before he has a firm grasp of the rope it's going to be a newbie. So rather than have him go tumbling arse over heels and knock someone I'll need later off the rope, I send them down first. That way if you do screw up the rest of us will have something soft to land on. You."

This cold hard logic did nothing to allay White's fears as he reached over, grabbed the rope, and swung his body out into the swirling downward wash generated by the Blackhawk's massive blades spinning mere inches above his head. Whether the voice that yelled "Go!" once more came from Jones or from inside his own head didn't matter. Without further ado White loosened his grip a bit and allowed gravity and the weight of his own body to do their thing.

Mercifully it was all over before he could give the matter another thought. One second he was hanging there suspended high above the ground, staring into the open door of a Blackhawk at half a dozen anxious faces waiting to follow him out. The next both feet were planted firmly on the ground. He took but a second to make sure that he was in fact on the ground, that he wasn't imagining that. Then, recalling his training he let go of the rope and scurried away from it lest the full weight of the next heavily burdened man come slamming down on top of him.

Instinctively he brought his weapon up to the ready as he made for the first spot on the ground that appeared to be a good place to drop down and take up a position. In their briefing Jones had assigned each member of the squad a position based on the clock system that he would assume once they had hit the ground. White was supposed to slide into the "nine o'clock" slot where Bannon would join him. From there the two of them would cover the entire platoon's left flank with Bannon's SAW and White's M-4 until the helicopters were gone, their platoon leader had gotten his bearings, and he was ready to lead them along their assigned axis of advance.

That was the plan. Unfortunately, in the excitement of

the moment White had managed to forget that he had been facing into the helicopter when he had started his descent. So when he hit the ground and took off in the direction he was facing, instead of rushing over to his assigned spot he went charging off away from it. Were it not for Corporal Sanchez who had made his exit from the right side of the Blackhawk reaching out and grabbing him by the arm as he flew by, White probably would have kept right on charging until he had reached the platoon's right flank.

Confused by Sanchez's action, White turned and looked into the corporal's eyes. "Where the hell you goin', cowboy?" Sanchez yelled above the sound of the Blackhawks hovering overhead. Raising his other hand and using his rifle, Sanchez pointed White back in the direction from which he had just come. "Over there, meathead. Bannon's over there. Go!"

Embarrassed, White spun about and trotted past Jones who was the last man in the squad to hit the ground. Though he watched White scurry past him, the veteran squad leader didn't bother to stop him and ask what he was doing. He didn't need to. All he allowed himself was a hint of a smile as he shook his head before shuffling off to find his assigned slot on the squad's small perimeter, taking but a moment to look about in order to ensure no one else had gone astray.

It takes more time to describe the deployment of a Ranger platoon via the fast-rope technique than it does to actually execute it. One second there is all noise and mayhem, the next dead silence disturbed only by the faint beating of chopper blades in the distance. Still supercharged by the exhilarating rush of events and the excitement of the moment, White could almost hear his own heart pounding as he squirmed about next to Bannon. "Settle down," Bannon commanded dryly without taking his eyes off the patch of woods he was training his weapon on. As he had when corralled by Sanchez, White instantly complied without a murmur.

In the center of the small perimeter created by his platoon it took Hal Laski but a minute to collect his thoughts, orient himself on the ground, and report in to his company commander that they had landed and were about to press on with their mission. Nathan responded to Laski's report with little more than a crisp, "Roger, out," which was radio shorthand for "I understand, end of transmission." With that the young lieutenant stood up and whistled as he pointed to Jones and signaled him to move out.

Jones in turn came to his feet and gave a low, quick whistle in a pitch that was distinctive from his platoon leader's while snapping his fingers. When he had his squad's attention he lifted his hand signaling for them to rise up off the ground before pointing in the direction of travel. In what seemed to White as one swift motion Bannon was up and gone, leaving him to scramble to his feet as quickly as he could, adjusting his gear as he scurried to catch up.

It was early evening when a succession of runners dispatched by the regional commander responsible for the northern portion of Zamboanga del Norte reached Summirat's temporary command post with word that a company of Rangers had landed east of Sindangan. After conferring with Hassan Rum, who served Summirat as his chief of operations, the two men decided that the objective of this American foray was to either secure the area around Mount Dapiak or draw out Abu Sayyaf forces that had been training there in recent weeks. Rum was quite taken aback by this first major incursion into the interior of the island. "I would have expected them to stay closer to their base camp, to remain well within the range of the guns of their ships until they became acclimatized."

Summirat smiled at his deputy. "These are not like the toy soldiers Manila has to send against us. They are true elites, hand-selected veterans who have done this sort of thing before. They have no need to waste time learning about how we operate or acclimate to our culture and climate. The mission of these Rangers is not to win the hearts and minds of our people. That task belongs to others. They are here for one thing and one thing only, to kill us. When dealing with them we must expect the unexpected. We must be prepared for anything and everything. And," he stated as he raised his index finger to emphasize his next point, "they will not leave until they have achieved that goal."

Rum pondered Summirat's statements. "If that is so, how do we defeat them?"

The dark expression that had cast a shadow over their conversation passed. In its place, a hint of a smile lit Summirat's face as he winked. "In the end, they will not be the ones we defeat. Though we will fight them, and fight them we must, our victory will be achieved on another field."

Having grown used to the manner in which Summirat explained his intent without betraying how he planned on doing things until the very last minute, Rum simply nodded. "Then this will be a contest to remember."

"Yes, my friend," Summirat exclaimed, full well knowing that his deputy had no idea of the plans he had for the Americans. "Exactly my point!"

16

ON THE SLOPES OF MOUNT DAPIAK, MINDANAO, PHILIPPINES

By midafternoon the jitters that had unnerved Eric White earlier were for the most part gone, melted away by the sweltering tropical heat and the blistering pace of the platoon's advance. In its place something akin to mind-numbing tedium began to take hold as the Third Platoon picked its way through farm fields, rice patties, coconut groves, patches of jungle, and along dirt roads of a countryside that showed no sign of the vicious conflict that had brought the American Army back to this island. Were it not for the total absence of another living soul outside the tight little knot of Rangers, their excursion through the erstwhile tropical paradise would have been almost bearable.

It was this failure to come across any civilians throughout the day that conveyed a powerful message to those who were able to see it as such. It spoke of the influence the Abu Sayyaf had managed to establish over the people of the region, of its ability to intimidate them to the point that farmers who should have been working their fields were so fearful of the Rangers that they dared not allow the Americans to even lay eyes on them let alone come near lest those among them who were dedicated members of the militia brand them as collaborators.

It was becoming crystal clear to Henry Jones that this operation would be no simple romp in the woods. Though the scenery had changed, he saw another Iraq in the making. During a break he broached the subject with Frederick Smart, asking him what he thought of the reception they had thus far received.

Before answering the veteran platoon sergeant took a moment to look out over the vacant rice patties that bordered the grove of well-tended palm trees in which they were deployed. "Well," he stated dryly as he continued to scan the abandoned fields, "it can be one of three things, none of which I see as being particularly good. If the farmers here and about have been cowered into submission by the local Abu Sayyaf thugs, that means the terrorists have a lot more sway over the locals than we've been led to believe. That would make it a contest of hearts and minds. If, on the other hand they're actually on the side of the Abu Sayyaf and actively supporting 'em, then the sooner the president declares our efforts here a victory and pulls us out the better, 'cause nothing we do will matter 'cause the Filipino Army will never be able to hold the scraps of ground we manage to secure."

Pausing, Smart took a drink. When he was finished he continued his search of the surrounding fields where he had left off, still seeking any trace of local farmers, children, or anyone who could give him some hope that things weren't as bad as he imagined. Jones, who was doing the same but in a different direction, anxious for Smart to finish his thought, solemnly asked his platoon sergeant to continue. "And the third possibility?"

"In my mind that might actually be the worst of all. If they're not for us, and they're not against us, that means the people are trying to play it safe, leery of both sides and unwilling to commit themselves to either."

"How can that be bad?"

Smart looked over at Jones. "Didn't they teach you

anything back at Benning during that NCO advance course boondoggle we sent you to?"

Jones smiled. "Sure, lots of things. Just nothing that was useful."

"In my personal opinion people who are neutral, people who cannot decide which side they're on are worse than useless. They're a hindrance, an obstacle to progress. Folks like that are no better than a flock of sheep waiting for someone to lead them about. Rather than making a stand and helping one side or the other they tend to go with whatever they think is safest for them at any given moment. They're like the Iraqis were or, even worse, the folks back home who claim to be moderate, people who are all for something one moment, then change sides the second their former position becomes unpopular."

"So we can't trust them."

Smart looked over at Jones and winked as he stood up and stretched his aching muscles. "Oh, you can trust them all right. You can trust them to stick it up your third point of contact the moment you turn your back on 'em and the other people show up on their doorstep."

"Thanks, Fred. That's just the sort of pep talk I needed to hear."

"Hey, don't blame me. You asked me what I thought and I told you."

Jones snickered. "So I did. Just in case I ever do again, do me a favor?"

Smart gave Jones a mischievous smile and a wink. "Anything for a buddy."

"If you have any other pearls of wisdom, kindly keep them to yourself."

Smart nodded as he slipped his canteen back into its cover. "Will do, good buddy. Now, get the lads on their feet and saddle 'em up. We still have ten more klicks to go, a village to check out, and a couple hundred rocks to look under before we can call it a day."

As Jones gathered himself up and prepared to rouse his squad he noticed Eric White staring at him with a look of

concern that told Jones he had been listening to his exchange with Smart. Jones scrounged up what passed as a
smile for him as he pushed himself up off the ground with
a grunt. "I wouldn't worry about all that gibbering between Fred and me. It's just idle speculation. All you need
to concern yourself with is keeping Bannon supplied with
ammo for his SAW and watching your assigned sector."

White didn't find much comfort in his squad leader's
words. If this pair of sergeants understood the situation
as well as they appeared to this early on, what could the
officers and the generals who had sent them here be possibly thinking? Perhaps they knew something his squad
leader and platoon sergeant didn't know. At least, that's
the hope he latched on to as Henry Jones called out to his
scattered squad to get on their feet and prepare to move
out.

Some twenty kilometers off to the northeast Nathan
Dixon was having a far more interesting but equally troubling day. Traveling with his Second Platoon they reached
the first site that his company had been ordered to investigate their first day out. The location was one that local
informants, known in the military as human intelligence
sources or HUMINT, had identified as a training area, a
place the Abu Sayyaf cadre used to drill provincial companies and local militiamen as well as perspective recruits for their main strike force. After cautiously closing
in on the target from three sides Lieutenant Jeff Sullivan's platoon quickly swept through the area with one
squad while a second stood ready to support the first by
fire if it made contact while his third covered the most
likely avenues of escape. All of these precautions proved
to be totally unnecessary for the facility turned out to be
abandoned, just as Nathan had expected it to be. Fact was
he would have been rather disappointed if Sullivan's platoon had managed to catch any Abu Sayyaf there.

That didn't mean that exploring the site was a waste of

time. There was much to learn about what sort of training had been conducted there as well as the number of people that it could accommodate and the sort of weapons they had been trained with. Both would require the Rangers to scour the area, searching for evidence that would assist in putting together a more complete picture of the Abu Sayyaf's capabilities as well as potential weaknesses that could be exploited. The capacity of the training camp was of particular interest. If Nathan's men could determine how many people it could hold at any given time then the intel folks either aboard JTF Sierra's command-and-control ship or back in the States could combine that input with the length of time that the camp had been in operation to derive an estimate at the number of people that might have been trained there. This in turn would permit them to base their estimates on the size of the Abu Sayyaf force in the area on something more than rumor and speculation. Since military training tends to scar the land and leave residue that is not always cleaned up afterward or easy to hide after the fact, an inspection of the small-arms ranges where new recruits were taught to fire their weapons and demolition pits where specialists were trained to work with explosives would give the Americans an idea of the capabilities of their foes. Even the huts where meals were prepared and garbage pits would help in this effort.

Gathering all of this evidence would take time, something that Nathan suspected he had plenty of at the moment. Having no need to tell Sullivan's people what they needed to do, he was left with little to do but wander throughout the area with Sullivan. At one point Nathan did feel the need to speak out. He did so after watching a squad leader scurrying about as if trying to make some sort of deadline. "The Abu Sayyaf won't do much of anything for a while," Nathan stated dryly to Sullivan. "For now they'll be content to simply hang back just out of reach, watching our every move, studying how we do things, looking for a vulnerability or an opening. When they find one they'll take their time to study it, determine how best to exploit it, then train their people how to do so."

Sullivan shook his head as he watched his men sorting through a pile of discarded shell casings in an effort to determine their caliber and nation of origin. "The classic approach to guerrilla warfare, straight out of our own manuals."

"And why not," Nathan agreed. "It worked for the Iraqis and Afghans. No doubt our friends here studied their operations, perhaps even participated in them."

Remembering some of the close calls he had while serving in that sad corner of the world, Sullivan's chuckle was quite humorless. "Hell, given the sort of advantages that these people have you can make book on that." Then his expression turned to one of concern. "How much time do you think we have?"

Nathan looked at Sullivan a minute. "You mean before they hit us or before someone farther up our own food chain decides that we're wasting our time here and puts an end to this operation?"

"Both I guess."

Tilting his head back, Nathan stared up at the clear blue sky and gave this question some thought. "The monsoon season is some three months off," he finally concluded, looking back at the Rangers going about their assigned tasks. "While that's not supposed to be a show stopper it will definitely put a crimp in our operations, particularly the effectiveness of some of the units supporting us."

"Sounds like that would be an excellent time to hammer us."

"Or," Nathan countered, "an excellent time for the folks back home to decide that we've bought enough time for the Filipino Army to regroup and take over from us."

"Well, if I were Hamdani Summirat I think I'd sit back and wait for us to pull out before picking up where we left off."

With a smile Nathan shook his head as he looked at his young platoon leader. "Ah, you're being too cautious, thinking on too small a scale, Jeff. You're assuming that we are a hindrance to his plans, that our incursion to this tropical paradise is a disruption to his carefully laid plans."

Before responding, Sullivan took a moment to reflect upon what Nathan was saying. "You think he wants us here? That he planned his whole campaign of terror in order to lure us over here so he could take us on?"

Nathan continued to walk along, waving his arms about as if to embrace the abandoned training camp. "Why not? What better way to prove your military prowess than to twist the tail of the biggest tiger in the jungle? It worked in Vietnam, twice. Once with the French and then us. It worked in Somalia, thanks to a little help from us." Turning, he looked into Sullivan's eyes. "Why not here? Why not against us? What better way is there for the Abu Sayyaf to show the government in Manila that they are a political and military force to be reckoned with than to meet the best combat troops America has to offer and humble them in battle. They don't have to kill us all. Hell, they don't even have to win a single battle. All they just need to demonstrate is that we can't win. Those wonderful folks in Congress and their helpers in the media will do the rest."

Not sure what to say Sullivan lapsed into silence as the two officers proceeded with their inspection of the camp in silence for several minutes, each mulling over what Nathan had just said while watching the Rangers of Second Platoon root through the abandoned training base. Finally Sullivan looked over at his company commander. When he spoke he did so in a most circumspect manner so as not to sound as if he were casting doubts about their own chain of command. "Sir, do you think that this has all been factored in?"

With a concerned expression, Nathan glanced over at this young officer. "I think what you're trying to ask, Lieutenant Sullivan, is do I think we're out here tromping through the bush like a bunch of Hindu beaters trying to get the tiger to leave his lair and strike? The answer is yes. If we're really lucky, or they're having a serious blond moment, we may surprise or corner some auxiliary elements of the Abu Sayyaf and put some serious hurt on them. But we'll never find the Abu Sayyaf main strike force, not unless it wants to be found."

"Or," Sullivan added glumly, "until they're ready to come out and play."

Nathan's face lit up in a broad smile as he threw an arm around the young lieutenant's shoulder, surprising him by this action and his words. "Ah! Now I see said the blind man as he picked up the hammer and sawed."

Not long after all the scattered elements of Company A came together and began to prepare what would become a temporary patrol base Nathan decided that it was as good a time as any to have what his sergeants liked to call one of the old man's "Come to Jesus" speeches. To that end when the work on their scattered defensive positions was well progressed and he could do so without interfering with their completion Nathan gathered as many of his officers and NCOs together at the center of the patrol base as he dared just as the sun was setting in the west. While the rest of the company continued to scratch out fighting positions all about them, Nathan went over much of the same material he and Sullivan had discussed earlier that day. He did so in a manner that avoided betraying any of his personal feelings toward the wisdom of the operation they were engaged in or the concerns he and the other captains in the battalion had about the ability of their own battalion commander to deal with the crisis when it came, as they collectively knew it would. Instead he kept his remarks restricted to what all of this would mean to them, the officers and NCOs of Company A.

"Since embarking on this little junket I've heard some rumblings in the ranks. It seems that there are a few folks in this company who are questioning the wisdom of sending a unit like ours out here to do things that any old light infantry battalion could do. Some of you think that using Rangers to carry out what amounts to a good old-fashioned Vietnam era search-and-destroy mission is a waste of a valuable asset, one that would be better used doing more exciting things. Well, you're not alone. I'm not going to name any names, but I personally know one company commander who has asked himself that very same question."

A ripple of laughter went through the gathering, causing soldiers nearby working on their positions to stop what they were doing, look over, and listen in.

"Since no one with more brass on his collar chose to confide in me as to why we were picked and not a unit of the 101st all I can do is speculate, just like you. But because I'm a highly trained infantry officer with a degree from a fine old southern military institution as well as the Fort Benning school of wayward captains, I tend to think that my blend of speculation is probably a tad closer to the mark than any of the bilge you guys have been farming out."

More chuckles.

"Let no one here have any doubt that the people we are going against are good." Nathan's sudden change of demeanor sent a chill through the air. "While it is true that there are auxiliary elements of the Abu Sayyaf that are little more than armed peasants the core is a well-financed, highly trained, heavily armed and disciplined fighting force comprised of handpicked men who are dedicated to their cause. In the past few months they have taken on everything the Filipino Army could throw at them and chewed it up without breaking a sweat. They're better than good. In fact, I dare say they're the best we've come across yet."

Nathan paused to let his senior leaders think about this. Almost to a man they had all seen action in Southwest Asia fighting in Iraq, Afghanistan, or both.

"The people we're after aren't wild-eyed fanatics in a hurry to meet Allah. They aren't going to oblige us by charging headlong into our guns. They're cunning, they're skilled, and they're very, very patient. They'll strike us only if and when they think we are vulnerable. They'll hit us when we're most exposed and least prepared to deal with them. And they won't do so until they are one hundred and ten percent absolutely, positively sure that they will succeed."

He let this thought linger in the humid evening air like an annoying insect that could not be ignored. Squatting off to one side Peter Quinn looked down at the dirt he was stirring with a stick. Sensing that it was time for him to play straight man to his commanding officer, he spoke up. "So where does that leave us, Captain? I mean, what is it we can do that we're not already doing?"

Nathan could always depend on Quinn and First Sergeant Carney to bring some of his more ethereal ramblings back down to earth. "The short answer is that we do what we're trained to do and carry out our operations as aggressively as we can. As I said before, I expect that we will catch some of their supporting elements on occasion. Fact is, if the leader of the Abu Sayyaf lives up to his reputation he may even arrange for that to happen just to see how we respond, sort of like the Zulu chief in the movie sending some warriors forward to test the strength of the British garrison."

Carney snickered. "I'll bet that plays hell with their reenlistment rates."

A nervous chuckle rippled through the gathering. Even Nathan smiled. "Speaking of that, First Sergeant, I need to get together with you sometime in the next few days. You're due for your reenlistment talk."

Looking up Carney pointed his index finger at his

commanding officer. "Sir, you and me need to talk about your timing when it comes to those kind of things."

After another round of laughter, Nathan gave his gathered leadership a moment to settle down. "Our greatest weakness is habit. Our most lethal foe is routine. The Abu Sayyaf can only make limited use of electronic communications for he knows that our military has the ability to monitor just about every means of communications that emits a signal and either ride that emission back to its source or copy the transmission and use the information gleaned from it against him. So he's reduced to slower, more reliable and secure methods, methods that do not permit him a great deal of tactical flexibility. He can't gin up a plan on the spur of a moment or be sure that he will be able to change an operation in midstride once it has been set in motion. Any offensive actions he takes against us will therefore depend heavily upon our willing cooperation, for it will require a great deal of time for him to plan it, disseminate the orders needed to implement it, and deploy all the elements participating in it to their proper positions. If we do not establish a coherent pattern of operations, if we're always doing things a little different, varying the conduct of our own offensive operations, he won't have the time necessary to plan and execute his own."

Frederick Smart thought about this for a moment before clearing his throat. "That's not going to be easy, Captain. We tend to be creatures of habit, making radio checks at set times, rotating personnel out on listening posts every two hours on the hour, having our noon meal at twelve o'clock and such."

Quinn chuckled. "First Sergeant, make a note third Platoon doesn't want its noon meal at noon."

More chuckles.

"That's just the point," Nathan exclaimed. "This isn't going to be easy. But it has to be done. And we're the ones, the officers and NCOs of this company, who will

have to be on guard to make sure that we don't allow ourselves to settle into a nice, predictable routine in anything
we do. Starting with me and going down to the most junior NCO in the command every one of us must make
sure that we don't slack off."

Sensing that it was time to wrap this up, Nathan looked
around into the faces of his officers and NCOs in an effort to gauge their mood. He liked to end these sessions
on some sort of high note, one that summed up the most
salient points he had been trying to make or pass on an
important message. It was this part of his briefings that
had led to his NCOs calling them his "Come to Jesus"
sessions since Nathan sometimes delivered them in a manner more appropriate for a preacher than a Ranger company commander. "Our people will do what they're told
to do," he stated in a clear, forceful tone. "They're Rangers. They'll respond to our every order, trusting our every
decision. All they ask of us is that we ensure that those
orders and decisions are well thought out and have a purpose. If we do our jobs the way I know we can, our people
will follow us through hell and when we're done, they'll
ask us to take them back for more."

Inevitably, from somewhere in the crowd someone
would sing out "Amen, brother," when Nathan was done.
So rather than dismiss the assembly in a more traditional
military manner, he played along by raising his right
hand and announcing, "Now go forth, my children, and
prosper." It was a silly thing to do, but an effective way of
maintaining the sort of bond that a commanding officer
needs to have with the men he routinely places in harm's
way.

CENTRAL MINDANAO, PHILIPPINES

The man whom Nathan had been speaking to his officers
and NCOs about didn't feel the need for such antics. He
expected those who flocked to his standard to do so

because they were as dedicated to the vision and the cause he was championing with the same conviction, the same fervor, as he was. Anyone who failed to match his ardor, his willingness to do whatever was necessary to achieve victory, had no place in Hamdani Summirat's arm of the Abu Sayyaf.

Such men were not like ordinary men. They were zealots, men who were risking everything for their cause, men who could not be easily restrained. Summirat knew this and used the dedication of his men to do things that they would never have imagined doing on their own. Thus the challenge Summirat faced at the moment was not how best to motivate his men, but rather how to temper their élan without losing the fine edge he had taken such care to hone. Dealing with the American Rangers, soldiers that were unlike anything they had faced up to this time, called for patience, lest everything they had achieved up to this point be wiped away. It required him to reorganize his forces in a manner that would allow them to avoid the awesome firepower that the Americans could rain down upon them from the land, sea, and air. At the same time he knew he had to give his fighters something to do lest they become disenchanted with his failure to rise up and meet the challenge that the Americans had thrown at them and lose their edge through inaction. Summirat intended to achieve this by scattering his strike force in a manner that would allow it to become familiar with how the Americans operated in the field while at the same time gathering the intelligence he would need in order to develop a decisive plan of action.

To this end Summirat ordered his main strike force to disperse. Its six hundred fighters were divided into ten sixty-man "Cofradía," a term meaning brotherhood. Eight of these were dispatched to a region Summirat expected the Americans to operate in over the next few months. Each of these was further subdivided into ten five-man "scout sections" with two "command sections," a primary and an alternate. One of the remaining Cofradía, organized as the others, had the task of operating in the vicinity of the main American forward operations base. Their task was to gather information on how the Americans operated through observation and infiltration. The tenth Cofradía was held back under Summirat's direct control in a central location where it would function as a mobile reserve, a reduced strike force that gave him a well-trained and disciplined body of troops available to take advantage of any sudden opportunity reported back to him by a scout section belonging to one of the other nine Cofradía.

The scattering of his strike force in this manner served many purposes. First and foremost it denied the Americans a nice, fat juicy target, for even in the jungle six hundred men clumped together in one place is difficult to hide. Five men on the other hand are all but invisible. Five men can easily fit into a single vehicle and roam from place to place blending in with local traffic without causing a stir. A villager can easily provide food and lodging for five men for a night. Yet those same five men have the ability to intimidate a hundred times their number if they suspect the people in a village are becoming too friendly with the Americans or feeding them information. They can maintain an around-the-clock surveillance of an American position or track an enemy unit moving through their area with ease. And if a five-man scout section is discovered, compromised, or otherwise falls prey to enemy action it's only five men lost, five men who have no idea where the other 595 men of the main strike force are.

The regional commands, the company-sized units of semitrained volunteers assigned to defend their region, were kept intact but instructed to do nothing unless they received an order from Summirat. If discovered and attacked they were to scatter and hide until it was safe to regroup. That didn't mean they were idle. In addition to supporting the Cofradía in their area, they were tasked with conducting intelligence gathering operations of their own. They also had another on-order mission, one that

Nathan and some of his compatriots were expecting. When Summirat decided that the time was right Summirat intended to use selected regional commands to execute small-scale raids and attacks against American units, both those that were forward deployed as Nathan's company was and those units operating in proximity to and defending the FOB. These attacks would be for no other purpose than to provoke an American response, one that could be observed by scouts belonging to a Cofradía and studied in detail by Summirat and his lieutenants. Everyone understood that those actions would be costly but a necessary step, one of many that would eventually lead to a final climatic confrontation with the Americans that Summirat was always hinting at.

That of course was in the future. Summirat knew it would be some time before they would be ready to initiate offensive operations against the Americans. For now he was content to do little more than watch and wait. His biggest concern at the moment was not what the Americans did, but rather the population of Mindanao. The one thing that he could not be sure of was the loyalty of the people in those areas he now held sway over. While few on the island had any great love for the government in Manila, only a relatively small portion of the population openly supported the goals championed by the Abu Sayyaf. The vast majority was ambivalent to the political machinations of the two opposing forces, readily acquiescing to the dictates of whoever happened to hold sway in their region, village, or town at the moment. To keep the Americans from eroding his influence with the populace during this protracted period of relative inaction, Summirat would have to rely upon the militia forces he had established.

Like the regional commands they shared the mission of supporting the Cofradía and gathering information. Unlike their better armed and trained brethren, the militias were not expected to take action against Americans. That did not mean they would be totally passive.

As members of their community Summirat saw his militia as being the people best suited to keep the local populace in line, using whatever means the local militia commander felt necessary. To this end Summirat issued them one simple order: "Do whatever you must to keep your people from straying from the fold." Unstated yet understood by all was the price any local leader and his family would pay if they failed to do so.

The only weakness in this scheme was Summirat's lack of an efficient means for passing the information gained by all these efforts back and forth between himself and his widely dispersed elements. With the Americans monitoring all commercial and private communications networks throughout the Philippines, the Abu Sayyaf was reduced to using couriers to relay information and orders up and down its chain of command. While this technique was about as secure as one could get and all but foolproof it was painfully slow, making it all but certain that many fleeting opportunities to strike a telling blow against the Americans would be missed. Still, since the alternative meant compromising some if not all of his operations, it was a handicap he knew he had little choice but to live with.

That did not mean that the Abu Sayyaf lacked a sophisticated communications network. On the contrary, at the same time he had been building up his force structure Summirat had taken the time to patiently piece together a sophisticated command and control network that would allow him to coordinate his far-flung units when the time was right. Purchased with the same funds that were being provided to the Abu Sayyaf by their Middle Eastern benefactors, the state-of-the-art secure military-grade communications equipment, small electronic warfare capability, and GPS jammers were surreptitiously acquired through third-party intermediaries from China, Russia, and several Western European nations. Like his main strike force, Summirat intended to husband these precious resources lest they be compromised and destroyed by American operations. Only when the time was right, when Summirat felt his forces were ready to take on the Americans, would he unleash the full power and might of the Abu Sayyaf.

ON THE SLOPES OF MOUNT DAPIAK, MINDANAO, PHILIPPINES

The coming of darkness brought no promise of rest for Eric White. Rather than signaling the end of a long and trying day, it merely served to provide Company A with a different, more Ranger-friendly environment, for Rangers took great pride in the fact that they owned the night. On this, their first night in the field, the first Squad was assigned the mission of establishing an ambush on a nearby trail that wound its way down the mountain to a village some six kilometers away. That village was the only inhabited locality for miles around, one that the Third Platoon had swept through during the day on their way to the company's patrol base.

That experience had been anything but encouraging. Long before the Third Platoon's point element laid eyes on it, the inhabitants of the village had either scurried off to find a safe place to hide in the fields among their crops or took refuge in a dark corner of their huts of wood and thatch. With the Second and Third Squads under the control of Frederick Smart deployed just outside the village to provide covering fire if needed, Hal Laski led the First Squad on through. For men whose nerves were already strained by the threat of enemy action it had been an eerie ordeal to pass through a village knowing that there were people hidden away all around watching them. Every now and then when White caught sight of a window shade of reeds flutter, they all but jumped out of their skins. Only discipline and the lack of a discernible threat kept them from overreacting.

But the temptation to go into some of the huts, to find

out why the people were hiding from them, was there, a desire that was all but overpowering to Henry Jones. When he reached the center of the village Jones paused to ask his platoon leader if he wanted him to check some of the huts out. Like Jones, Laski felt the urge to kick in a few doors and see what lay on the other side. Of course, he suspected that to have done so would have been a waste of time. He already knew the people who were still in their huts either feared them or were outright hostile. Had Laski been a betting man he could have put his money on the fact that they were both. It was simply a matter of which of those motives was the more compelling. Only his orders to avoid confrontations with the indigenous population unless such contact was deemed absolutely unavoidable kept him in check. Dealing with the people of this village and hundreds of others like it was to be left up to the Filipino Army once Company A had swept the area of organized Abu Sayyaf forces. This was about the only part of their mission that made sense to him since civil military affairs wasn't exactly a strong suit for Rangers.

This cursory sweep of the village by the Third Platoon did nothing to ease Nathan's apprehension over its proximity to his initial patrol base. If anything, Hal Laski's report to him only served to reinforce Nathan's assessment of their situation. While he would never have done so himself Nathan could not entirely ignore the fact that the village provided any Abu Sayyaf fighter wishing to reconnoiter his patrol base with a convenient jump-off point to leave from or as a rally point. To guard against those possibilities he assigned Hal Laski the task of establishing an ambush along the trail at a point midway between the village and the company's patrol base as well as conducting a nightly patrol in the vicinity of the village. On this night Laski assigned the duty of setting the ambush to his First Squad while selecting Second Squad for the patrol. This left him the Third Squad to cover his platoon's portion of the patrol base's perimeter.

On succeeding nights those duties would be rotated, giving each squad two nights out and one night in during each three-day cycle.

Having been warned of his squad's assignment for that night well beforehand, Staff Sergeant Henry Jones kept an eye open for a spot where he would be able to set up his ambush while the platoon was making its way to the company patrol base. He decided on a switchback, or hairpin turn along the trail where it began to ascend the mountain, one that lent itself·to an "L" ambush. The concept behind this technique was simple and quite lethal. The bottom portion of the "L," where the trail curved, was where he placed Corporal George Bannon, together with White and Specialist Four Parks. The rest of First Squad, minus a two-man security detachment hidden away a bit farther up the trail to guard against any unexpected surprises, was deployed along the long stem of the "L." If and when an enemy force was foolish enough to use the trail, Bannon and company would be free to sweep the entire length of the trail while those Rangers arrayed along the long stem of the "L" would take out anyone to their immediate front, thus creating a cross fire that covered every inch of the kill zone from two different directions. Done properly this sort of ambush was all but foolproof.

Setting up and laying in wait in an ambush site is deceptively hard work. To start with soldiers assigned this duty simply cannot march up to the selected site, fall out, and plop down into their assigned positions. The best way to occupy an ambush site was to make a wide circuit around behind the selected spot with each man easing into his assigned ambush position by approaching it from the rear. During the process of occupying that position it was crucial that no one disturb the natural vegetation or leave any visible traces that they had even been there lest an alert foe moving along the trail become aware of their presence.

Though no easy feat, this was by far the easiest part of

the operation, for once in place each and every member of the ambush party was required to maintain a high state of vigilance over a protracted period of time while remaining absolutely still and silent. The slightest motion, the tiniest sound, is often more than enough to blow an ambush, wiping away all chances of surprise and permitting the intended prey to either avoid the ambush or turn the table on it. This was a demanding chore for men already worn out by a long, grueling day. The need to stay awake despite overwhelming fatigue requires a toughness and discipline that few are able to master. Even a veteran like Jones, a man who had been doing this sort of thing for years both in training and in war, still found it to be a struggle that demanded a concerted effort on his part. For someone like White it was all but an impossibility. Not even the creepy, tingling sensations that sent shivers through his body as tiny insects crawled all over him was enough to keep him from dozing off. He tried, he honestly did everything he could to keep from falling off to sleep but the nervous tension of the day, the oppressive heat and the long tedious march up the mountain to the patrol base and then back down to the ambush site were too much for him. Within an hour of settling in next to Bannon White was lost to the world.

It was sometime after midnight when Bannon became aware that White had dozed off. Being a relatively new NCO the young corporal had yet to develop the same subtle approach to leadership problems such as the one White now presented him with that an older NCO like Jones or Smart had been able to develop through years of experience. Bannon's solutions were far more direct, less polished. One could almost say pointed. In this case, the need to maintain silence left him few viable options.

Not having any idea just how far gone White was, Bannon opted to employ a technique that he had no doubt would yield the desired results with the least amount of noise and motion on his part. While remaining on his stomach hunched over his M249 SAW, Bannon cocked his right leg until he was able to reach down with his right hand and grasp the handle of the "K" Bar knife he kept strapped to his leg just above his right ankle. Slowly drawing the knife from its sheath he brought it up and around and shifted it over to his left hand before easing that hand down along his side. When he judged that the knife was level with White's thigh, Bannon turned the blade's point toward the slumbering Ranger and eased it over until he felt it make contact with White's leg. Slowly he began to apply pressure, taking care that the tip of the blade dug into White's thigh.

His efforts had the desired results. Within seconds the pain caused by Bannon's knife cut through the mental fog that held a grip on White's exhausted brain, causing the young Ranger to start. With a jolt he lifted his head up off the ground and stared wide-eyed into the kill zone straight ahead. When he saw nothing out there he next turned to see what sort of creature was digging into his right thigh. As he did so his eyes met Bannon's who was looking right at him. In an instant White knew that he had screwed up, that he had fallen asleep, an all but unpardonable sin for a Ranger deployed as part of an ambush.

Seeing that he had White's full attention the young corporal slowly brought the knife he held in his left hand back up and held it between his face and White's, slowly twisting it as he did so in an effort to demonstrate to the new man that he wasn't fooling around when it came to maintaining discipline in this little corner of the ambush site. And should that not be enough of a warning to him, Bannon took the added precaution of planting his knife blade down into the earth at eye level between him and White where he could easily reach it if he needed to use it again.

Understanding Bannon's message White swallowed hard and gave his corporal a sheepish nod before propping himself back up onto his elbows as he turned his full attention back out in the direction of the kill zone. For the remainder of the night, whenever he felt the urge to relax his vigilance, to allow himself to slip back into a peaceful slumber, White took a moment to glance over at the knife that stood between him and a man who he had no doubt would exercise less restraint the next time he found the need to use it.

17

MINDANAO, PHILIPPINES

The nervous vigilance maintained by Eric White along the trail winding its way up Mount Dapiak was for naught. None of the inhabitants of the village ventured far from their homes or approached Company A's patrol base on that first night, the next, or for that matter any subsequent night. They knew better than that. Even the two members of the five-man Cofradía teams charged with shadowing Nathan's company did nothing more than monitor from afar the comings and goings of the Americans as they went about scouring the countryside for the next six days.

It was not that Summirat was unconcerned with what the Rangers on the slopes of Mount Dapiak were doing. On the contrary, he understood perfectly well the sort of damage Nathan's company could have on any Abu Sayyaf unit foolish enough to allow itself to be found and run to ground. He also appreciated that despite the best efforts of his local militia he stood to lose a fair percentage of the area's populace who saw the Americans as saviors. They were wrong of course. In time Summirat knew Company A would move on, to be replaced with less threatening

American civil affairs personnel and units of the Filipino Army. "What little we lose today," he explained to the leader of the Cofradía in whose area Nathan's company was operating, "can easily be won back tomorrow. Besides, the Rangers deployed in the interior are not the good target. They are the tip of the spear," he mused in a calm, steady voice as if speaking to himself. "You do not defeat your foe by impaling yourself on his bayonet. Rather you sidestep each of his thrusts, watching as you do so for an opening. When your foe makes a false move, and they always do, you strike at the heart."

Seated next to Summirat in a small nondescript Toyota pickup truck packed with crates of produce and parked half a kilometer away from a village being searched by a squad of Nathan's Rangers, the Cofradía leader merely nodded as he warily watched the Americans. He assumed his commander intended to mount his main effort against the massive seaside lodgment that had been thrown ashore farther south. In part he was correct, but only in part. FOB Atlanta, or one of its successors, would in time feel the brunt of Summirat's offensive. But even that effort would not touch the mark Summirat was aiming at. The object of his current campaign was one man, a man who would never set foot in the Philippines. This man would remain safely in the United States, exercising his executive authority through a long and sophisticated chain of command that meandered its way from Pennsylvania Avenue, across the Potomac to the Pentagon in Arlington, Virginia, over to CinCPAC in Hawaii, down to Admiral Turner aboard his flagship riding at anchor within sight of FOB Atlanta, ashore to Colonel Lamb who monitored Robert Delmont's day-to-day operations, and finally to the primitive base camp that moved from place to place every other day the Rangers went about searching for a foe that had no intention of being found.

Eager to impress Summirat with his grasp of the situation, the Cofradía leader nodded. "You are right, as always. It is pointless to kill the ants one by one."

Amused by this clumsy effort to frame his designs using such a hapless analogy, Summirat smiled. "Yes, something like that." Then, after taking one more look at the Rangers, he announced that it was time to move on. "We must deliver the produce as we promised the farmer and return his truck lest he become displeased with us and tell the Americans about us."

The Cofradía leader's expression grew tense. "He wouldn't dare. I am sure."

"Well," Summirat chuckled as he started the truck's engine. "If he did, he would only have the opportunity to do so once."

Within the confines of FOB Atlanta and aboard Turner's flagship there were those who were coming to realize that they were on a fool's errand. To a man they had seen a similar pattern before. They knew that the main insurgent force would avoid a direct confrontation with units like Nathan's company at all cost and the aggressive combat patrols the Marine battalion dispatched on a daily basis. Though each and every member of Turner's and Lamb's staff hoped for a fight in which the full weight of American air and firepower could be brought to bear, all appreciated the fact that the likelihood of this occurring was something less than zero. But like the Rangers tasked with beating the bush for an illusive foe, Turner, Lamb, and their staffs were responsible for executing a plan that was not of their design. By the time Nathan's company had completed its second foray into the island's interior only Delmont, the architect of this campaign, remained confident that the Abu Sayyaf would, in time, show its hand.

Appreciating that insurgent forces had the nasty habit of sniffing out weaknesses and doing things that had not been anticipated, Lamb took all steps he deemed necessary and prudent to organize his entire command to respond should the leader of the Abu Sayyaf actually decide to test the seaside lodgment. In this grand game of cat and mouse the Marines charged with securing the FOB prowled its perimeter twenty-four/seven sniffing, listening, looking for any sign of the mouse. Everyone knew the Abu Sayyaf was out there watching, probing for a weakness they could exploit. And like the mouse they were patient, content to wait for just the right opportunity to scurry out of hiding and rain down their own special hellfire and damnation upon the intruders violating their homeland.

This period of uneasy quiet left Lamb with little to do but ponder the overall situation and ruminate with his staff over when, where, and how the mouse would finally poke its head out of its hole and strike. It was his operations officer that put a different spin on this question by asking rhetorically who exactly was the mouse and who was the cat. Intrigued by the ops officer's views on the issue, Lamb encouraged him to expound upon it. With nothing to fear from his commanding officer Lamb's ops officer obliged, expanding his theory a bit further than Lamb found comfortable by asking him quite pointedly if the real purpose of sending the Rangers out as they were was to use them as bait to lure the Abu Sayyaf into the open. Unwilling to put his greatest fears into words, Lamb quickly dropped the subject, a move that was more than enough to confirm to those present that the ops officer was probably not too far off the mark.

The answer to that question was never in doubt in Robert Delmont's mind. Like Lamb and his staff Delmont understood the nature of the war against terrorism. He knew that the leader of the Abu Sayyaf would not show his hand or make a major move until he was absolutely sure his people would succeed or at least come close enough to victory in order to claim it as such. So in Delmont's mind the trick was not in finding their foe, a task that would have required a force many times the size of Task Force Sierra, but rather it was how best to create a set of circumstances that would appear to present the leader of the Abu Sayyaf with a situation that would prove to be too tempting, conditions that would leave no doubt that he could achieve a quick, cheap victory.

Delmont was convinced that eventually the lure of a lone company operating far from the main American FOB would prove to be far too tempting to his foe, that he would risk taking a swipe at the bait that was being jiggled before him, bait that just happened to be Nathan's company. Whether the insurgent leader did so out of a desire to demonstrate the superiority of his forces over the Americans or simply out of frustration didn't much concern Delmont. All that mattered to him was that his counterpart did so, providing him with an opportunity to pin the Abu Sayyaf with the balance of his battalion before pounding the insurgents into oblivion using all the attack helicopters and Naval aviation that Turner had at his disposal. The ensuing victory, even a marginal one, would give the Filipino Army the encouragement it needed to return to central and western Mindanao in force, a move that would in turn allow the government in Manila to claim that it was now able to reassert its authority, thank the American president for his support, and send Task Force Sierra packing. With a major coup such as this to his credit, his promotion to full colonel and return to the Army staff would be assured. Such was Delmont's campaign plan.

Naturally Hamdani Summirat had a different concept of operation, one that he wasted little time implementing once he had finished the restructuring of his forces, had a clear picture of what his people were facing, and a feel for the rhythm of American operations. When he had reached the point where both regional commands and the detachments of his main strike force had gathered as much intelligence as they could using purely passive means, Summirat decided that the time had come to twist the tail of the tiger.

To this end he paid a visit to those regional commanders where American forces were operating and ordered them to initiate aggressive patrolling in an effort to test the alertness and response time of the American forces. Though this phase of their operations would be costly, a fact Summirat made no effort to downplay he emphasized to them that it was crucial if they were to learn just how far they could push and how the Americans would react when they did. Like the Americans who remained hunkered down within the confines of FOB Atlanta or went tromping about the jungles and farm fields under Nathan's watchful eye, the Abu Sayyaf were ready to ratchet things up a notch.

After two trips to Mount Dapiak and fourteen days of round-the-clock patrolling during which Nathan's company had yielded nothing of note, Delmont found himself becoming concerned that perhaps he was using the wrong bait. The locals were just as leery of the Americans during the second time around as they had been the first. The only blood that had been spilled in the course of two weeks belonged to a mouse deer that had wandered into one of Sergeant Jones's ambushes, an event that earned his squad the title "The Deer Slayers." Even the crew of the USS *Wake Island*, the amphibious warfare ship they returned to at the end of their second foray into the interior, joined in on the fun by printing up a large banner that read "Bambie beware, the Deer Slayers are here."

Nathan and the rest of the company shrugged off this good-natured ribbing. So long as the crew of the *Wake* kept providing them with their hot showers, warm meals, and a bunk where they could catch up on lost sleep they didn't much care what the swabbies said. It would take a lot more than a silly banner strung up by men who had never heard a shot fired in anger to piss off the sort of men who wore the black and yellow Ranger tab.

Company A was in the midst of enjoying their second period of R & R aboard the *Wake* riding at anchor within sight of FOB Atlanta when five members of an Abu

Sayyaf regional company became the first real casualties of the campaign. Their mission that night was to find gaps in the defensive perimeter of the FOB that could be used for infiltration at a later date by a team of sappers drawn from Summirat's main force. Their leader, a young man who had been a schoolteacher before joining the Abu Sayyaf, had thought he had found one, a blind spot between two bunkers. Taking far more time than the other men with him thought prudent the young teacher turned insurgent carefully crawled up to the rolls of razor wire that delineated the actual perimeter until he was close enough to touch it. Pausing, he carefully lifted his head as far as he dared looking to his left, then to his right to see if he could be observed by the Americans in either of the bunkers. Only when he was satisfied that the vegetation and lay of the land obscured their line of vision did he ease back to where he had left his four companions. Relieved to see their leader had returned safely without alerting the Americans, the other members of this small patrol turned their backs on Atlanta and began to retrace their steps, taking great care to make sure that they left no trace that they had ever been there, just as the main force fighters had taught them.

All these efforts proved to be in vain, for while it was true that no one standing watch in the sandbag bunkers saw anything, the Marine sniper team that had taken up residency in the presumed blind spot had tracked every move the five Abu Sayyaf fighters had made. The urge to pick off the Muslim insurgents one by one as they made their way toward the perimeter and then away from it was tempered by the steely discipline that made Marine snipers a fearsome weapon. The spotter, the more senior of the pair, knew there was much more to be gained by observing the Abu Sayyaf fighters and vectoring in one of the roving Marine patrols to intercept.

Exercising the same sort of caution that the former schoolteacher and his cohorts were using as they made their way back into the jungle and what they thought was safety, the pair of Marines stalked the retreating insurgents, matching their progress step by step. Along the way the spotter paused when he felt it was safe to do so and updated the Marine ops center with their current location and that of their prey. There an assistant ops officer seated before a computer moved a cursor across a map displayed on his screen to mark the progress of the snipers, the roving patrol that was closing in on that spot and a foe that had no clue that they were being hunted in much the same way the Marine spotter had once pursued deer in the mountains of western Pennsylvania. With a click of a mouse the computer-generated data was instantly thrown up onto a larger screen where everyone in the Marine ops center could see it. Simultaneously the data was transmitted through the ether to the ops center aboard the *Wake Island,* Turner's flagship. He was in the midst of a coordination meeting with Lamb to iron out last-minute issues concerning the establishment of their next FOB, dubbed Baltimore, when Turner was notified of the incursion.

Taking a break from their discussions on the next phase of their operations, Lamb joined Turner in his ops center to watch as the situation developed. As they did so the two senior officers quietly speculated as to whether or not the Marines would come back with any live prisoners. Lamb didn't give the Abu Sayyaf much of a chance. At most he predicted they would be able to net no more than two of the intruders alive, wounded but alive nonetheless and capable of being interrogated. Turner was far more optimistic. Despite the inbred rivalry that all sailors harbor for Marines, he admired their discipline and expected them to bring back at least two alive and unscathed. "Your people may enjoy projecting the image of steely-eyed killers with the IQ of a rock," he mused as he sipped coffee while watching the converging tracks on the big screen, "but they know when to put some serious hurt on the enemy and when they need to exercise restraint."

Lamb was tempted to ask the admiral to put his money where his mouth was and place a bet but thought better. As hardened as he had become during two wars in Iraq, one in Afghanistan, and an assignment to the Pentagon that saw him filling the place of an officer killed on 9/11, the idea of betting on whether or not men would live or die was distasteful to him. Life, even that of a man determined to kill him, was still a precious thing to the Oklahoma Baptist who had already seen enough killing to satisfy even the most gung-ho Marine.

Out in the pitch-black jungle not more than two miles from where the pair of senior officers were exchanging opinions, the Marine sniper team stalking the insurgents and the members of the patrol who were being guided to intercept them didn't have the time to ponder such things. Their entire focus was on maneuvering themselves into positions of advantage from which they could engage the insurgents. When the Marine staff sergeant leading the patrol found a piece of ground that suited him, he rapidly directed his seven men into firing positions that would enable them to cover a small, thinly vegetated patch of ground the approaching insurgents would have to traverse. When his people were set and he had reminded them to hold their fire until he gave the word, the staff sergeant reported his location and status into the Marine ops center.

Monitoring this report the Marine spotter signaled to his shooter to settle in and prepare to go to work. They would wait until the roving patrol initiated the engagement before opening fire on the rear of the column.

They didn't have long to wait. A minute, maybe two, passed before the lead insurgent entered the kill zone covered by the roving patrol. Easing the safety of his rifle, the staff sergeant took aim but hesitated. Instead, while keeping his weapon firmly planted on his shoulder and his eye glued to the night-vision sight mounted on the charging handle he shouted out an order to halt.

The sudden demand in English to halt stunned the five

Abu Sayyaf insurgents. Four of the five instinctively froze
in place, their eyes darting about as they did so in a frantic, vain effort to discover where the voice had come
from. The fifth, their leader, turned to face the spot from
where he suspected the voice had come, swinging his
weapon up to the ready as he did so. The Marine staff
sergeant leading the roving patrol didn't give him the opportunity to bring his weapon to bear. Two rounds of the
three-round burst he let fly found their mark, sending the
former schoolteacher sprawling onto the jungle floor at
the feet of the man behind him and sending the two insurgents bringing up the rear into a panicked flight back
toward FOB Atlanta. Neither of them was able to take
more than a few steps before the one in front was physically knocked back off his feet by the impact of a 7.62mm
round and thrown against his startled companion.

Confused and with their courage draining away
quicker than the urine running down their legs the three
survivors tossed aside their weapons as if they were the
most venomous snakes imaginable before throwing their
hands up. When the Marine staff sergeant's report came
in over the command net Turner let out a sigh of relief,
relief that he hadn't been foolish enough to bet the Admiral.

As the commander of the ground component of Joint
Task Force Sierra Colonel Tim Lamb was responsible for
coordinating the activities of all units involved in executing and supporting the ground campaign. In addition to
the 3rd of the 75th Rangers, charged with conducting offensive operations, and the 1st Battalion, 5th Marines,
who were responsible for the security of the base camps
there was a detachment of AH-64 Apaches and the aircraft
belonging the 160th Aviation Regiment which included
both Blackhawks and OH-58D scouts. These aerial assets
provided both the Rangers and Marines the sort of close
support usually furnished by field artillery.

Supporting all these units when they were ashore was the task of a main support battalion, or MSB. The MSB was a conglomerate of combat service support people who provided the ground component with everything needed to sustain soldiers in combat from bullets to Band-Aids. The technical expertise and mechanical muscle needed to carve an FOB out of the jungle large enough to support all these units and their activities belonged to a detachment from a naval construction battalion, better known as Seabees. These hardworking land-locked sailors leveled helipads, scraped out ramps for the lighters to land on when bringing supplies in from the ships offshore, scoped out bunkers to provide protection for Lamb's staff and the Marines defending the FOB, and took on the jungle itself, clearing away a wide swath that provided the Marines manning the perimeter with a clear field of fire.

To manage and oversee the day-to-day operation and coordination of the units assigned to him, Lamb had assembled a staff that consisted of officers and non-commissioned officers from each of the services. This mini joint staff engendered the sort of inner-service rivalry that plagues all such ventures. Rangers on Lamb's staff consciously exaggerated the swagger that comes when you know you're the best of the best. The Marine staffers countered by doing everything imaginable to live up to the rough-and-ready image that was something of a hallmark in the Corps. Aviators went out of their way to contribute the sort of panache that only those charged with upholding the traditions of the United States Cavalry of old could. Not to be outdone by their ground-pounding coworkers the naval contingent did everything within its power to lend an air of dignity and decorum to what one naval officer described as an ad hoc collection of rogues who behaved more like a college fraternity run amuck than a military staff.

So it should have come to no one's surprise that when the Marines drew the first blood of the campaign their reps on the staff went out of their way to highlight this fact in a manner that no one could ignore. On the morning after the Abu Sayyaf probe was cornered and swallowed up by the Marines, Lamb's operations officer, a Marine major, added a new chart to his portion of the oh-seven-hundred hours commander's briefing that Lamb held every day. The chart was a simple one, designed to resemble a high school scoreboard. Only instead of listing home team and visitor, it had a column headed by "Army," "Marines," "Aviators," and "Others." Under each of these headings were zeroes with the exception of the Marine column, where the ops officer had printed a big, bold "2." When the ops officer threw this chart up toward the end of his briefing everyone immediately understood the joke. Everyone that is, but Robert Delmont.

Not noted for having anything resembling a sense of humor, Delmont saw this as nothing more than a personal affront, a childish joke played at his expense. The relish with which others were enjoying it only served to irritate him further, especially since he had taken every opportunity during the run up to Operation Pacific Shield to ensure that everyone understood that his battalion was to be the hammer that would smash the Abu Sayyaf main force units. To be bested by the Marines, even if the incident was in the greater scheme of things trivial was intolerable to him. When the briefing wrapped up he stormed out of Lamb's command post and made a beeline for his own.

Nathan was well into his second helping of pancakes and sausages in the mess hall of the *Wake Island* when a sailor dispatched from the ship's comm center found him and informed him that he was wanted ashore by his commanding officer ASAP. When asked as to the nature of the summons all the sailor could do was reply with a shrug. "The message just said ASAP, sir."

Pausing, Nathan poked the half-eaten stack of pancakes

with his fork as he considered finishing them first before rushing off. Looking up he eyed Peter Quinn and First Sergeant Carney seated across the table from him in an effort to judge their reaction to Delmont's call. Both men wore the sort of blank poker face that hid their thoughts. Unable to gauge their feelings on the subject, Nathan decided that it would set a bad example in front of his subordinates if he blew off his commanding officer just to finish breakfast. Throwing down his fork with a bit more force than he intended, the young captain stood up. "Well, as my father would say, it's time to sound boots and saddle."

Both Quinn and Carney glanced at each other before Quinn asked if he should alert the company to stand by for a change in mission. Nathan took a moment to survey his company as they sat scattered about the mess deck, enjoying a rare treat for Rangers during a deployment, a hot, hearty meal served in a clean setting. "Let 'em finish up here before you do. This could be nothing."

Carney wanted to ask what the chances of that were but didn't. Though his captain never spoke of the bitterness that existed between him and the battalion commander, Carney was kept well informed of how those officers got along via the NCO grapevine. Try as hard as Nathan might it was impossible to keep the problems he was having with Delmont much of a secret. Carney of course never let on that he knew, just as he advised the other NCOs in the company to do.

The trip from ship to shore gave Nathan plenty of time to steel himself for his meeting with Delmont. He was really beginning to hate spending time with his commanding officer, a state of affairs that could have terrible consequences for him and his company.

Ever faithful and reliable Emmett DeWitt was standing on the small floating dock when the motor launch bringing Nathan ashore tied up. Without having to say a word Nathan realized that his friend had slipped out of the battalion command bunker in order to provide him with a heads-up as to the reason behind his summons. Without preamble DeWitt briefed Nathan on the lay of the land as they made their way to the battalion CP. "Delmont's pissed. It seems he views the fact that the Marines drew first blood as something of an insult to the battalion, which means that it is an insult to him."

Despite the number of times he had been called into Delmont's office for no other purpose than to be harangued for something that was not his fault or was totally out of his control, Nathan was still amazed when it happened. At the moment the best he could muster by way of response was an incredulous "So?"

DeWitt shook his head as they walked side by side, saluting enlisted men they passed without giving that gesture a second's thought. "I know, I know."

"Hell," Nathan responded. "You'd think he'd be glad that the Marines whacked a couple of those assholes."

"That's the point, Nate. It was the Marines who did the whacking and not us."

Nathan looked askew at DeWitt. "You mean not me. That's what this meeting's all about, isn't it?"

DeWitt's head drooped between his slumped shoulders, assuming the posture of a man who had been beaten up for trivial issues far too often. "Yeah, something like that."

Seeing little point in pursuing this topic with his friend any further, Nathan let the subject drop. Instead the two men slowed their pace and did their best to enjoy what few moments of peace they could in each other's company.

The landside command post of the 3rd of the 75th Ranger Battalion was a sprawling sandbag and timber bunker that protruded four feet out of the ground. Upon entering it everyone who could flee did so as soon as they saw Nathan. Those who could not did their best to avoid making eye contact with him as he made his way to the small cubicle that served as Delmont's office and quarters.

Due to the utilitarian layout of the hastily thrown-up bunker there were no doors that could be closed to keep a one-on-one conversation private. Therefore every word Delmont and Nathan exchanged was overheard by the personnel on duty throughout the rest of the bunker.

Seated behind a small wobbly field desk, Delmont leaned back in his folding chair before he returned Nathan's hand salute. Sensing what was coming Nathan braced himself by assuming a taut position of parade rest, choosing to stare straight ahead so as to avoid his battalion commander's eyes. Instead he fixed his gaze upon one of the briefing charts hanging on the wall behind Delmont.

"Captain Dixon, I've gone over your last after-action report once more and find that I am decidedly underwhelmed with the results of your company's efforts to date." Pausing, he waited for Nathan to reply. When he failed to Delmont pressed on. "Admiral Turner notified me this morning that he has decided to forgo your third foray to Mount Dapiak. Instead we're going to close down FOB Atlanta and move on to Baltimore, the next FOB. Turner seems to think it would be a waste of time given the fact that your efforts have yielded absolutely nothing."

This bit of news came as no surprise to Nathan. Having spent the previous night aboard the USS *Wake Island* he had bumped into some of Admiral Turner's staff who were just as anxious to hear what he had to say about how things were going ashore as Nathan was to find out what the next few weeks held in store for his company. Doing his best to present the same sort of deadpan expression his XO and first sergeant had given him not more than an hour before, Nathan waited patiently for Delmont to continue.

Seeing that his pronouncement had failed to illicit a response Delmont pitched into the heart of the matter at hand. "The abysmal performance of your company is beginning to make me wonder if I made a mistake when

I assigned the primary task of finding and fixing the enemy to it. To date all you've managed to unearth is an abandoned training site. Two weeks of operations have not resulted in a single contact with Abu Sayyaf. Can you explain this?"

Taking a moment to clear his throat and gather his thoughts, Nathan sensed that no matter what answer he gave, it would be wrong. He could tell by Delmont's tone and expression that he had already made up his mind that he was going to lay into him for not delivering the sort of results that he had been hoping for. Besides, just about every officer in JTF Sierra had come to the conclusion that the real purpose of sending Nathan's company into the interior on its own was not to find the enemy, but rather to let the enemy find it. Like a boxer responding to repeated blows by instinctively bringing his hands up to cover his face Nathan assumed a purely defensive posture. "The company has been carrying out its mission during each of its forays into the interior in strict accordance with your specific instructions, sir. We have not deviated one iota from the patrol plans and directives laid out in the battalion's operations orders. During the day we conduct aggressive patrolling throughout the assigned area of operations. At night we continue those patrols while establishing ambushes along likely infiltration routes at those points delineated in the op order. That we have not made any contact with the insurgents cannot possibly be attributed to the efforts of my men. I suspect that will change only when the enemy feels he can take us on with a better-than-even chance of coming out on top."

Leaning forward, Delmont clasped his hands together and placed them on the table before him. "I do not accept your premise, Captain. The enemy is out there. The intel folks on the Admiral's staff spend a half an hour every night briefing him on Abu Sayyaf activities, information that is passed on to you through this headquarters, solid intelligence that you seem incapable of using."

The urge to tell his commanding officer just how worthless the outdated information dumped upon him was almost got the better of Nathan. To have given in to his mounting anger and done so would have done little more than play into Delmont's hands. The man was intentionally trying to provoke him into a confrontation, a situation that subordinates never win. So once more Nathan kept his temper in check, doing his best to turn things around instead.

For the first time Nathan looked down in order to make eye-to-eye contact with his battalion commander. "It would be pointless to apologize for not producing the sort of results you expect of us, sir, since we both know the maximum effective range of an apology is zero meters. Instead, finding that I am at something of a loss as to how to achieve the results you desire, all I can do is ask you for advice as well as any suggestions as to how my company can be more effective in carrying out your orders and directives."

This was not the response Delmont was expecting. He truly was seeking to pick a fight with Nathan, looking for an opportunity to vent the anger, rage, and frustration that was beginning to gnaw away at him day and night, anger that his people were not performing as he had promised they would to so many of his superiors during the run up to Operation Pacific Shield and frustration that he had no idea as to how he was going to turn things around. To him Nathan Dixon was more than a natural whipping boy upon whom he could vent his anger. He was one of the "Chosen Ones," an officer who many senior officers said would one day surpass his own father. To Delmont having Nathan Dixon in his command was more than a cruel joke. To share the spotlight with another shining star not only threatened to obscure his own brilliance, it could prove to be disastrous.

Of course, Dixon's presence in his battalion also offered Delmont an opportunity. After all, if the scion of a living legend and an officer being groomed for bigger and better things could not achieve satisfactory results, how could anyone blame him, a battalion commander who was tied down in the rear, forced to squander his valuable time managing all the minutia that battalion commanders assigned to a joint operation must deal with. Admittedly it was a rather flimsy plan since everyone knew that he had been the one who had come up with the concept for Operation Pacific Shield. Still, Delmont appreciated that desperate times call for desperate measures. As distasteful as it might be to give up on Pacific Shield so soon, he saw no alternative than to begin the process of laying the groundwork that would be required to shift the blame for its failure from his shoulders onto someone else in order to protect his precious career. All he needed was Nathan's cooperation.

Unfortunately, at the moment Nathan wasn't playing along. Instead of rearing up on his haunches and defending his unit's performance as he would have, Delmont found Nathan seeking guidance and advice, just the sort of thing one would expect a subordinate to do when confronted with a difficult task. That Nathan knew that Delmont was incapable of providing him with any sort of sound advice on the matter was something both men were keenly aware of. After all, everyone in the battalion's chain of command knew that it was Delmont, and not the battalion operations officer, who was drafting the operational orders that Nathan's company were following. If Delmont had any surefire way of getting results, they would have been incorporated in those lengthy and detailed orders.

Finding himself thrown back onto the defensive once more and unable to provide Nathan with a reasonable response, Delmont lashed out. "I'm not buying your story, mister. If you and your people were really doing their best out there we wouldn't be having this little conversation. It would be the enemy and not you who would be running around in a circle like a rank second lieutenant trying to figure out what to do." Standing up, Delmont planted his fists on his hips and leaned over his table as far as he could, glaring into Nathan's eyes in a manner that reminded the young captain of his own father. For a fleeting second, despite the tenseness of the scene, Nathan found himself having to suppress a chuckle as he wondered to himself if the Army had a special school that taught senior officers how to effect that stare on command.

He was lost in this unrelated thought when he realized that Delmont was waiting for him to respond. Thrown off guard by his own inattention, Nathan did the only thing he could think of. Coming to a rigid position of attention, he snapped a smart salute. "Sir, I understand completely. You have my promise I will redouble my efforts and drive my company till they drop."

Once more Delmont was caught off guard by a response that he was not expecting. Easing off of his combative stance, the only thing he found he could do was return Nathan's salute. "You had better. Now, get back to your company and start getting them ready."

DeWitt was waiting for Nathan outside the main entrance to the bunker. "Well, I heard it all, good buddy. Do pray tell, just how do you intend to achieve the sort of results that Mumbles expects? What can you possibly do any different?"

Surprisingly unruffled by his encounter with Delmont Nathan smiled. "Me? Do differently? Why, my dear sir, I have no intention of doing anything differently. There isn't a bloody thing that I or anyone else in my company can do to speed things along. You know as well as I do that our friends in the Abu Sayyaf aren't going to pop their little heads above ground until they're damned good and ready to. All I can do is make sure that my people are ready to cut them off when they do."

"And until then? How are you going to deal with Delmont?"

As they made their way to the floating dock Nathan shook his head and smiled once more. "Dear Emmett,

I'll be like one of those old reliable watches. I'll take my lickin's and keep on tickin'."

"That's one hell of a strategy."

"If you've got a better one I'm all ears."

Unable to come up with anything better, especially since he was basically surviving Delmont's reign of terror using the same philosophy, DeWitt chuckled. "Well, if it's any consolation to you, despite the heaps of dung the old man is intent on piling upon you I'd gladly swap places with you any day of the week."

Nathan threw his arm around DeWitt. "They couldn't pay me enough to do your job."

"I was afraid of that. By the way, have you had a chance to talk to Chris?"

Glad to be on a new subject, Nathan filled DeWitt in on the news from the home front. "I was able to call her last night using the ship's phone system. It seems they allow the crew to make personal calls every now and then. The officer of the deck let me use one of the nonsecure lines in the wardroom."

"And? Is Chris surviving without you?"

"I woke her. It was four in the morning back there so she wasn't exactly at the top of her game. She was really out of it, so the conversation was a bit one-sided."

"Do you blame her? Not everyone is a gung-ho Ranger who can go twenty-four/seven on nothing but coffee and MREs. I dare say if I woke Paula at that hour I'd be lucky if I got a grunt out of her."

"This is different," Nathan countered. "It wasn't like her. She's the type that's wide awake and perky as hell the second she opens her eyes."

"Well, we all have our off days, don't we?"

"Yeah, sort of like today."

DeWitt grunted. "This whole operation is turning into a real nightmare for the battalion. I thought morale had hit rock bottom back at Lewis but man, it's getting worse by the day."

Nathan paused as his thoughts turned to other, more

sinister concerns. "I'm afraid that things are going to get a lot worse before things turn around."

"It's the turning point that concerns me, Nate. If you're lucky someone farther up the food chain will declare victory and put an end to this fool's errand."

Having reached the dock Nathan stopped and turned to face DeWitt. "You want to know something, old buddy? Just between you and me, I've gotten to the point where I don't give a rat's ass how this thing ultimately goes down. At the moment my only concern is making sure that my company is ready for whatever comes our way, good, bad, or indifferent."

DeWitt was tempted to say that he was beginning to suspect that it would be the "bad," but held his counsel. After all, there really wasn't any point in putting into words a thought both men shared.

18

WASHINGTON, D.C.

A call to a working woman from her spouse in the middle of the afternoon for the purpose of suggesting that they dine out that night is not at all unusual in a city such as the nation's capital. Sometimes those dinners are intended to serve as a prelude to a night of romantic bliss. More often than not these spur-of-the-moment deviations from the routine are little more than an opportunity for two busy people who lead hectic lives to spend some quiet quality time together. Every now and then it's a special occasion meant to celebrate an unexpected spot of good news. Knowing her husband better Jan Dixon suspected Scott's suggestion that they dine out that night didn't fit into any of the usual categories. Scott was a compulsive planner, the sort who didn't leave the house even on a weekend without a definitive list of destinations and a fixed timetable for hitting them. Whenever he broke from the norm in this manner it usually meant that something was up, something Jan suspected she would not care for.

Setting her apprehensions aside, Jan was determined to enjoy this rare treat for as long as she could. When Scott picked her up at her downtown office she made no effort to find out why he left the Pentagon some two hours earlier than normal and drove all the way into the heart of D.C., something he loathed to do even on a Sunday morning. Throughout an enjoyable dinner at the city's top-rated steak house the professional husband-wife couple exchanged small talk that ranged from the current events of the day to long delayed weekend plans including a number of "honey-do" projects Scott had been postponing for months. It was only during coffee and a shared dessert that Scott felt brave enough to inform Jan that he would be headed for the Philippines in the morning.

Doing her best to downplay her apprehensions, Jan casually asked what had brought about this sudden excursion to that particular part of the world.

He didn't answer right off, taking a moment instead to ponder just how much he wanted to tell her. It wasn't her position as the chief of a news bureau that caused him to hesitate. Rather, it was the same reason why most soldiers tend to be close-mouthed about what they actually did on a daily basis when it came to their spouses. He didn't want Jan to worry. Glancing up from his coffee, he could tell by her demeanor that this strategy wasn't going to work this time. Deciding that not telling her would only serve to heighten her concerns he opted to forge ahead with the truth.

"You'll love this one," he began slowly, toying with the spoon in his coffee as he spoke. "It started over on the Navy side of the house. It seems the commander of JTF Sierra sent a back-channel message straight to Admiral Pulaski, the chief of Naval Operations. In it he expressed some reservations concerning how our people are conducting operations." Pausing to take a sip of his coffee, Scott looked about the room before he hesitantly took up where he left off. "Both Pulaski and Turner know what the genesis of Operation Pacific Shield was, so quite naturally Pulaski buttonholed Henry after a meeting of the Joint Chiefs, took him off to one side, and showed him

Turner's message before asking him what he was hearing from the field."

Jan raised an eyebrow. "I take it your boss was blind-sided."

"That's putting it mildly. After reviewing the daily operational summaries that make their way up the chain it dawned upon him that the language in them was more vague and noncommittal than usual. It didn't take him long to figure out that the Ranger battalion is spinning its wheels on Mindanao."

Perplexed by this, Jan's journalistic nature overcame her tendency to avoid delving too far into Scott's affairs. "Correct me if I'm wrong, but in a counterinsurgency operation like the one being conducted in the Philippines, isn't it normal for there to be long stretches when there's little or no contact with the enemy punctuated by sudden flurries of vicious small unit engagements?"

Scott smiled. "You've been sneaking into my library at night and reading up on this, haven't you?"

Jan returned his smile with a seductive flutter of her eyes. "It's osmosis, dear boy. After sleeping with you all these years it's only quite natural that some of that G.I. Joe stuff leach across the pillows, making its way from a more dense to a less dense receptacle."

"I think I've just been insulted."

Reaching across the table, Jan placed her hand on Scott's. "Oh, heavens no, dear. I don't think you can be insulted."

Scott winked. "Yeah, right."

"Be that as it may, why the sudden concern? They've only been on the ground for three weeks now."

"The crux of the problem is that the only contact that the joint task force has had with the Abu Sayyaf has been along the perimeter of the shoreside lodgments and not where the Ranger battalion has been operating."

"And that makes the Navy nervous?"

"It doesn't make them happy, especially since they

were told during the run up to this operation that it would be the Rangers who would bear the brunt of ground combat operations. The only people who seem to be happy about this are the Marines. They're the only ones who've made contact with the insurgents."

This little tidbit of information came as news to Jan who had no idea that there had been any fighting. When he saw her expression, Scott realized that he had let the cat out of the bag. Trusting that she would not betray his confidence in her he explained that there had been several run-ins between the Marines manning the perimeter and small groups of Abu Sayyaf probing it. "Turner's real concern is that these probes are becoming more aggressive. It was two weeks before they tested the security of FOB Atlanta. When JTF Sierra established Baltimore, its next lodgment, it took the insurgents less than two days to begin trying to infiltrate its defenses. Turner seems to think they're not only growing bolder but are beginning to get a feel for how we're operating over there. This fact got him to wondering who really was doing the hunting. Hence, his message to Pulaski."

"And your trip," Jan added.

"Exactly. As a result of some of the things Turner said in his back channel Pulaski is under the impression that there's some in-house Army issues that need to be sorted out. Henry would have loved to have gone himself to escape his gilded squirrel cage but feels that if he goes over there it will only confirm Pulaski's notion that the operation is in trouble."

"So instead he's sending his most trusted minion, the ever indispensable and totally reliable Scott Dixon, savior of the universe."

Scott could not miss the bitterness in Jan's tone. He knew how much she hated it when the quiet, reassuring routine they always strove to maintain despite their respective professional lives was suddenly disrupted by an unexpected call for Scott to pack up his gear and head off to those parts of the globe where sane people would not think of going. Now it was Scott's turn to reach out to his wife. Taking her hand in his, he gave it a reassuring pat. "It'll only be for a few days. Besides, by sending me Henry can always claim that the trip was my idea, that its real purpose was to pay a visit to Nathan."

"Henry knows you better than that. In all the years I've known you you have never once taken advantage of your position on behalf of your family, something I can personally vouch for."

In an effort to make light of the situation, Scott chuckled. "Dear lady, is that an accusation?"

"It's a statement of fact. Why can't Jones find someone else to go? Isn't it bad enough there's already one gung-ho Dixon sitting out there on the firing line?"

"There's no need to get yourself worked up over this, Jan. It's nothing more that a quick fact-finding tour."

Pulling her hand from Scott's, Jan folded her arms in a huff. "I'm sure there are facts that need to be found in Brussels. Why can't you go find them and let someone else root around in the jungle of that pissant little country?"

"Jan, Henry trusts me. He knows that I'll cut through the bull, get to the heart of the problem, and give him a straight-up, unvarnished evaluation of the situation. As much as I'd like to dodge this, if only to escape the appearance that I'm using my rank to pay Nathan a friendly visit, I can't."

Realizing that she was being unreasonable, Jan unfolded her arms and reached back across the table. When their two hands touched she managed to muster up a smile. "Well, who am I to stand in the way of God and country?"

Relieved that Jan's anger dissipated so quickly, Scott smiled. "That's my girl. Now, let's get the check and head home so I can give you my farewell kiss in a more appropriate setting."

"And hopefully," Jan cooed playfully, "a less appropriate spot."

MINDANAO, PHILIPPINES

By any standards the small farmhouse that stood in the center of the neglected fields and overgrown pastures was a modest affair. It had little to differentiate it from the adjoining sheds built to shelter the family's precious livestock. Whether this sad state of affairs had anything to do with the reason why the farmer had left it months before to take up arms against the government in Manila was one of those questions that no one, even the thirty-two-year-old farmer himself, would ever be able to answer with any degree of satisfaction. All that mattered at the moment was that the farmer had done so, throwing his lot in with Hamdani Summirat and becoming a member of his elite strike force. The cost for turning his back on farm and family proved to be rather steep for the peasant. Within a week of his departure his wife, left to fend for herself and her children in a region where the rule of law no longer existed had also given up on the farm, choosing instead to flee to the city of Labason on the north coast of Mindanao. There she hoped to find a job that would provide enough income to feed herself and her three children. Failing that, she'd little choice but to do as so many Filipinos before her had done in order to survive. Leaving her native country she would all but sell herself into domestic servitude to a foreign family or become a wage slave to one of the hundreds of multinational corporations that ringed the Pacific rim.

Deserted by the family that had once tended the surrounding fields, the humble house nestled in their midst became a refuge for other, less domesticated sorts. When rumors of this made its way by word of mouth around the community, through the Filipino intelligence network, and into American channels, the farm was added to a long list of targets of interest maintained by JTF Sierra's intelligence staff. As such, not long after Company A, 3rd of the 75th Rangers, began its operations from FOB Baltimore a junior officer on that staff determined that the time had come to find out exactly who those people were and what they were using the farmhouse for. Whether the nocturnal visitors were Abu Sayyaf or common criminals was something that the Rangers under Nathan's command would not be able to determine until after they had managed to corner and confront them. Though the tasking order issued by Admiral Turner's headquarters stressed bringing back at least one of the farm's new residents alive so that he could be interrogated was highly desirable, it included the caveat that tactical considerations and force protection concerns took priority. When translated into plain English this bit of military phraseology meant Nathan was not to gamble unnecessarily with the lives of his men just to capture insurgents.

Robert Delmont saw things differently. By the time JTF Sierra's tasking to investigate the farm had been repackaged into a battalion operations order the focus of the mission had been radically altered. The primary task handed to Company A by its battalion commander was now to secure live prisoners. Not one or two, but a well-defined three, minimum. No one on the battalion staff who participated in preparing this particular order had to be told why they were deviating from Turner's stated intent. Day after day each and every one of them was present at their posts in the battalion's small command bunker when Delmont stormed in after Colonel Lamb's evening briefing and coordination meeting. They all bore witness to their battalion commander's growing resentment over the fact that JTF Sierra's Marine detachment was caulking up one victory after another as visits by Abu Sayyaf infiltrators became bolder and more frequent while his Rangers did little more than wander about the countryside with nothing to show for their efforts.

Deserving or not, collectively and individually the battalion staff suffered Delmont's wrath as he lashed out at whatever subordinate just happened to afford him a convenient target upon which he could vent his frustration. These daily fits of rage made carrying out their already demanding tasks under primitive conditions all but intolerable. Emmett DeWitt was not joking when he took Nathan aside as he was preparing for his first foray into the interior from FOB Baltimore and asked if there was any way he could smuggle him aboard one of the choppers. "I've got to get out of this madhouse, Nate, if even for a few hours before I lose it and this battalion finds itself short one battalion commander."

In response to his friend's plea Nathan smiled as he removed a hand grenade from his vest and handed it to DeWitt. "For the colonel, with my compliments." Surprisingly DeWitt neither smiled nor chuckled. Instead, he kept the grenade.

Now, as he followed his Third Platoon step by step through the tall grass of an overgrown field toward the abandoned farmhouse, Nathan wished he had kept that grenade. He knew it was now only a matter of time before the leader of the Abu Sayyaf decided to teach them an object lesson in guerrilla warfare. Everyone in his company expected as much. In their travels throughout the countryside they had all seen them, young, lean Filipino men in small groups of three or four watching them from afar, men who scurried away the moment anyone in Company made any effort to approach them. Attempts to lure them into an ambush were thwarted by strict rules of engagement, rules that forbade Nathan's people from taking any aggressive actions against unarmed Filipinos unless they posed an immediate and unequivocal threat. Everyone chaffed at these restrictions, rules that Corporal Rodriguez Sanchez likened to cops blissfully cruising by street gangs, unable to do a damned thing till they broke the law.

This state of affairs forced Nathan to conduct his

operations in the field in a very circumspect manner. Every patrol, every ambush, every sweep he planned incorporated two assumptions. The first was that at some point during its execution his people would be observed by someone belonging to or sympathetic with the local elements of the Abu Sayyaf. The second was that the insurgents were biding their time, holding back waiting for the Rangers to commit a grievous error they could take advantage of or circumstances that were right to set into motion a deliberate plan already drawn up. It didn't matter to Nathan which of these would serve as a trigger for the insurgents. The result would be the same. At some point his people would be hit while they were poking and prodding through the jungles and countryside tracking down some phantom that haunted the imagination of intel folks back at the joint task force headquarters. When the day of reckoning he feared came, and he had little doubt that it would come, Nathan knew the Abu Sayyaf would come at them with everything they had with overwhelming firepower and numbers under conditions that were favorable to them.

It was the specter of this sort of incident that kept Nathan and his people on the edge. In small, measured doses this is a good thing for it heightens a soldier's state of vigilance, allowing him to draw upon all his senses and training at a moment's notice. Without an appropriate release however such unrelenting pressure tends to be corrosive and wearing, like a rubber band wound too tightly for too long. Eventually even the most robust rubber band will snap. Keeping his people's morale high and their growing apprehensions in check under these conditions was fast becoming a far greater challenge for Nathan than planning and overseeing his company's operations in the field. It was a challenge that was never far from his conscious thoughts, even at moments like this when the tactical situation before him should have been the only thing on his mind.

The abandoned farmstead that was the objective of

this day's mission lay at the edge of the field where the Third Platoon was. On either side of the main house were a number of small ramshackle sheds and pens where the family's prized deer still lingered, forgotten and forlorn. Beyond this cluster of single-story wood and straw structures lay a single-lane dirt road that meandered its way through the untended fields until it linked up with a wider, but equally unimproved rural thoroughfare. To cover those roads and perhaps catch anyone occupying the farmstead should they scatter before the Third Platoon reached it was First Lieutenant Jeff Sullivan's Second Platoon. Like the Third Platoon, the Second used the overgrown fields to conceal its approach from prying eyes. In a further effort to keep their ever-present stalkers busy and away from this day's main objective, Nathan had made a show of shaking out his First Platoon from the company's base camp earlier in the day with orders to make a show of conducting patrols in another sector. Whether that endeavor fooled anyone or not was something Nathan could only guess at. The best he could do was hope that it bought him some time, dissipated the insurgent's available trackers, and mislead them if only for a while.

Lost in his own thoughts and concerns Nathan and his RTO followed Laski's Third Platoon. Like all good company commanders he kept himself well behind the platoon's skirmish line, close enough to see what was going on up front without interfering with the platoon's battle drill, while at the same time hanging back far enough to keep from being pinned down by enemy fire if that skirmish line drew enemy fire. The decision as to where a commanding officer should place himself during an operation like this is always a tough call, one that is very much personality driven. Nathan liked being up front, as close to the action as prudence and his responsibility as a company commander permitted. Normally he had to force himself to hold back, to keep from intermingling with the platoon he was with, thus adding to Laski's concerns. Having had company commanders who could not help themselves from doing so, Nathan understood just how unnerving and disruptive it could be to have an anxious commanding officer in your hip pocket, breathing down your neck as he watched his every move.

The plan for this day's operation was to have the Third Platoon move to a point a hundred meters away from the farm compound. There it would hunker down and wait for nightfall. The Second Platoon, covering all known roads and trails leading to it, would do likewise, reporting to Nathan the comings and goings of any civilians that they suspected of being insurgents. Only when he was sure that their quarry was well in hand would Nathan give the order for the Second Platoon to seal off the area and the Third Platoon to saddle up and sweep forward and into the compound. With luck the unwelcomed surprise would cause some of the insurgents to choose flight over fighting, flight that would send them straight into the arms of the Second Platoon. Those who chose otherwise would be dealt with by Laski's lads.

As was the case in most operations of this sort, the most difficult aspect of it revolved around the long, tedious hours of waiting under the broiling tropical sun in a position where the vegetation blocked any hope of a cooling breeze. To succeed in carrying out its assigned tasks this day both the Second and Third Platoons would have to remain concealed in the overgrown fields while maintaining a close watch over the target as well as all the roads and trails leading to it. This sort of work, as PFC Eric White had discovered on his first night out, was much harder than he had ever imagined. Relaxing for someone like White under these conditions was still difficult, for he had yet to develop the sort of sixth sense that allowed Corporal George Bannon, the SAW gunner, to stretch out and doze off with his weapon cradled in his arms. Bryan Pulaski, perhaps the thinnest man in the entire company despite his ravenous appetite, sat a few meters away from White cross-legged with his grenade launcher in his lap wolfing down some of the MREs that he never seemed to run out of. Even his squad leader, Henry Jones, seemed to be unconcerned with their current situation, spending his time reading a well-worn W.E.B. Griffin paperback novel. Yet White knew that each and every one of the men around him was capable of going from zero to flat out in the blink of an eye if and when the moment to do so came. He had seen it during his brief time with them while training up for this operation back at Fort Lewis and during their current deployment. Just how long it would be before he would be able to be as nonchalant about what they were doing as his fellow Rangers seemed to be was as much a mystery to him as the true nature of the farmhouse that lay just beyond the field they were in was to their company commander.

At the moment, that commanding officer was also taking advantage of this lull in operations to rack up a few Zs. Seated back-to-back with Specialist Four Hoyt, his RTO, Nathan was dozing off when his radio call sign penetrated his subconsciousness. Equally annoyed and concerned, he reached up with his right hand over his shoulder to grasp the handmike he knew Hoyt would be offering him without having to be told. With his eyes still shut Nathan placed the receiver up against his ear, keyed the radio, and responded. "Last call station this is Alpha Six. Send your traffic, over."

"Six, this is Five, message from Blue Six, over."

Peter Quinn, the company XO who used the call sign Alpha Five, always remained at the company's patrol base camp monitoring the battalion command net while coordinating the activities there whenever Nathan was out with one of the platoons. It was a practice that Robert Delmont detested, insisting that his company commanders maintain continuous communications with his headquarters. Nathan being Nathan, as well as a company commander who was charged with leading his people into harm's way, chose to ignore this dictate despite the tongue lashings he received every time Delmont caught him doing so. "Why should I be forced to saddle myself with two radios while tromping about in the jungle," he explained to DeWitt in an effort to justify his defiance, "when Quinn can monitor the battalion command net for me when he's not using it to coordinate the company's logistical and airlift. It makes no sense."

No longer able to defend Delmont DeWitt merely shrugged. "Since when does common sense have anything to do with how we do things in this battalion?"

Based on the tone of Quinn's voice alone Nathan could tell he wasn't going to like what he was about to hear. "Five, this is Six. Send it, over."

"Blue Six dispatched a slick to pick you up and return you to the FOB ASAP."

"What, now? What for?"

"Affirmative on the first part, negative knowledge on the second. When he asked to speak to you I had to inform him that you were not at this location. He then asked for your location so he could divert the slick directly to you. I tried to explain your tactical situation and plans but . . ."

Agitated, Nathan looked down at his watch. It would be hours before the sun finally set and they had any hope of luring the nocturnal visitors to the abandoned hut into his company's ambush. "What's the ETA on that bird?"

"Ten minutes."

"What?" Unable to contain himself Nathan startled the members of the Third Platoon who were within earshot of him. Thinking that something had gone terribly wrong with the plan, most of them perked up their ears, flipped the safety off their weapon and began anxiously scanning their assigned sectors of responsibility. It took them several seconds to realize that their commanding officer's loud and animated conversation had nothing to do with them. Easing back some, Corporal Bannon took a moment to look back to where Nathan was gesturing wildly as he spoke on the radio. "Looks like the old man is having another friendly chat with the battalion commander."

Eric White, still shaking from the unexpected alert, glanced over his shoulder. "Those two don't get along, do they?"

Bannon chuckled. "Hell, boy. No one in this battalion gets along with Bobby Delmont, our very own boy wonder from the Pentagon."

As he checked his assigned sector, making sure that everything was in order White continued. "The battalion commander seems to know what he's doing."

This remark drew a chorus of snickers and hoots from everyone who heard it. Bannon shook his head. "That man is a grade A, government inspected asshole. How he ever earned the right to wear a Ranger tab is beyond me."

From out of nowhere Staff Sergeant Jones emerged, sporting an expression that would give a maniac pause. "What the hell is all this chattering about?" he snarled as loudly as he dared.

No one answered. Instead everyone began searching their sectors. Only when he heard his company commander unleash a string of vile oaths did he turn to where Nathan was just in time to see him pitch the radio hand mike he held as far as the coiled cord connecting it to the radio would permit.

19

Sitting in the open door of the UH-60 during the flight back to Baltimore did nothing to cool the raging anger that enflamed Nathan. The whole operation he had taken days to plan and prepare for was fatally compromised the second the helicopter Delmont had sent to pick him up made its appearance on the edge of the abandoned farm fields where his Second and Third Platoons were concealed. If it had been Abu Sayyaf that had been frequenting the place they would never do so again, leaving him and his company no choice but to hope someone on Admiral Turner's intel staff could come up with another lead that would finally allow his company to come to grips with the wily foe they had been pursuing for weeks.

Long before Baltimore came into sight Nathan could see the combat and support vessels of JTF Sierra riding at anchor just off the coast. Shelving his own frustrations a moment Nathan wondered what it must be like for the sailors aboard those ships, lashed to one spot and condemned to a daily routine that he imagined bordered on being nothing less than mind-numbing. As difficult as it was for his people to spend days on end roaming the jungles with nothing to show for their efforts, it had to be even worse for men and women who spent countless hours confined to small overcrowded compartments crammed with electronics, machinery, and all sorts of things needed to keep a massive organization like JTF Sierra going. Well, he thought as his sympathies for his seafaring brethren faded, at least they didn't have to spend the night in jungles with all sorts of four-legged lizards scurrying across your face while you were trying to sleep or discover that some sort of insect decided that your meal time was a good time for it to explore the mysteries hidden deep within the crevice that creased your buttocks.

As the UH-60 drew closer Baltimore came into view. None of the pilots operating out of Baltimore flew directly into the FOB from its landward side. They did this in an effort to discourage some adventurous soul on the wrong side of the wire from taking potshots at their exposed underbelly while making a straight run into or back from the interior of the island. Instead they always approached the FOB from the sea, where they were free to gain or lose altitude without the fear of being shot down. And if the Abu Sayyaf opted to launch one of the many portable surface-to-air missiles they were known to have at the copters a seaward approach gave the pilot a fighting chance to spot the incoming missile and take evasive maneuvers while popping flairs as a countermeasure.

The protracted approach allowed Nathan to study the D-shaped compound below. The white sandy beach formed the straight edge of the D. The bow of the D was a wide, empty strip of bare earth that butted up against the lush green jungle on the landward side. From the air the place looked more like a construction site than a military installation. There were no neat structures, paved avenues, or well-manicured lawns that dominate established stateside military bases. The only things that stood out from the reddish-brown mud were a scattering of bunkers, olive drab tents easily spotted under indifferently erected camouflage nets, piles of stores and supplies that seemed to be dumped wherever a clear spot could be found in a rather haphazard fashion, a few vehicles and roads that were nothing more than parallel ruts that randomly crisscrossed the entire area. All helicopters, both Army and Naval were kept on the amphibious warfare ship until they were needed by the 3rd of the 75th Rangers since it allowed Baltimore to be smaller than it would have needed to be if they were shore-based. Shipboard basing also permitted maintenance crews to work out of the vessel's shops, which were infinitely cleaner and better organized than anything that could have been thrown up ashore. Only along the landward side, where the perimeter defined the forward edge of the FOB did there seem to be any real effort made to follow a prescribed and logical plan. A broad strip of cleared land that served as a kill zone for the Marines defending Baltimore was bordered on one side by the leading edge of the jungle and on the other by well-spaced bunkers fronted by razor wire that twinkled in the midafternoon sun. All in all Baltimore didn't look any different than Atlanta had. No doubt, Nathan thought glumly, Chicago would be no different.

At the moment JTF Sierra's next jump was the farthest thing from his mind. Anxious to get on the ground and be finished with whatever it was that Delmont had found so damned important, Nathan leaned forward in his seat as far as his seat belt would permit and peered off toward the FOB's helipad to see if DeWitt was waiting to give him the lowdown on what Delmont was miffed about now. In the distance he could see someone was indeed waiting just off to one side of the steel mats of the helipad. But long before the face was recognizable Nathan realized that the figure standing wasn't Emmett. The figure's posture left no doubt that it could only be his battalion commander. "Well," Nathan muttered to himself. "At least I won't have to wait to find out what's on his mind."

Over the whine of the helicopter's twin turbine engines the crew chief heard Nathan's mumbling. Turning toward his own mike, the aviator held his hand over the boom mike that hung before his face and leaned over. "What was that, sir?"

Nathan grinned. "I was just commenting on what a wonderful day this is."

Not believing that line for one minute, the crew chief returned a perfunctory smile and got back to watching out for obstructions, obstacles, and other hazards as the helicopter prepared to flare out and landed.

As soon as he felt the wheels kiss the perforated steel mats of the helipad, Nathan unsnapped his safety strap, took up his rifle, and bounded out of the open door. Instinctively he crouched over low to avoid the helicopter blades that were still spinning about over his head. Only when he was sure he was clear of all danger did Nathan straighten up, look Delmont in the eye, and march toward him.

Without waiting for his subordinate to render the obligatory salute that serves as a greeting and mark of respect, Delmont shouted out over the noise of the helicopter. "We need to talk, mister."

Nathan felt like saying "Duh" but checked his tongue. No doubt, he reasoned there would be ample opportunity in the very near future to express his disgust.

Without waiting for a response from his subordinate, Delmont turned and began to walk away from the helipad at a brisk pace to a spot where their conversation would not be overheard. Nathan had no choice but to trot along behind him like a naughty pup that had just been punished by his master. When he was sure that they were well out of earshot from anyone, Delmont pivoted about to face Nathan who was on the verge of catching up. "Just how long have you known that your father was going to pay this command a surprise visit?"

Having anticipated just about every possible reason for this untimely summons but that one, Nathan was quite taken aback by Delmont's question. Genuinely stunned he stood there before his superior staring at him with his mouth agape.

Knowing how things worked at the Pentagon, Delmont had already made up his mind that the son of Scott Dixon was somehow in on the sudden appearance of his father, a senior member of the Army staff who was here representing the Army chief of staff. He was therefore in no mood to play games with one of his own subordinates. Placing his hands on his hips, he leaned forward into Nathan's face. "Save your bullshit 'I know nothing' line for someone else. All I want to hear from you is what sort of crap you've been feeding your old man behind my back."

Setting aside his surprise, Nathan slipped back into his black mood. Mimicking his commanding officer's posture, Nathan closed the gap between them until they were literally standing toe to toe. "Colonel," he stated in a manner that was as insubordinate as he could manage, "I don't know a goddamned thing about a visit by my father. Unlike some people I don't have the Pentagon on speed dial."

Now it was Delmont's turn to be stunned. He hadn't expected the captain standing before him to respond in a manner like this. Though he knew he wasn't the most popular figure in the battalion and his company commanders and staff officers went out of their way to make this fact known in subtle yet unmistakable ways, he had always counted on his position as their commanding officer to restrain them regardless of how he treated them. Thrown completely off guard by Nathan's ferocity he needed a moment to regroup.

Having already crossed the line that separated acceptable dissension and outright insubordination Nathan had no intention of allowing Delmont the opportunity to collect his thoughts and pitch into him again. "Since we've come to this shit hole my complete focus has been what's going on out there," he stated crisply, jabbing his finger toward the jungle that lay just beyond the wire. "Unless something has a direct bearing on my company's mission and the welfare of the men I have under my command I don't bother myself with it. I leave the shit house politics to those who are better suited to play that game."

Regaining his footing, Delmont returned to his previous line of attack. "I don't believe you for one minute, *Captain* Dixon. I know your type. I've seen them before, the sons of famous generals riding up the chain of command on their daddy's coattails. You might be able to buffalo every other officer in the command, but you can't fool me."

Realizing that he was already decisively engaged, that there was no going back, Nathan decided to make the most of this confrontation by letting it all hang out. Straightening, Nathan folded his arms across his chest and smirked. "What's the matter, *Colonel?* Jealous?"

Stunned, Delmont glared at Nathan. Unable to speak he pointed toward the Blackhawk that was still sitting on the helipad and hissed. "Get the hell out of my sight before I do something you'll regret for the rest of your short military career."

Coming to a rigid, parade-ground position of attention, Nathan gave Delmont a crisp salute. "With pleasure, sir." With that, he spun about on his heels as best he could in the mud and marched away.

ABOARD THE USS *WAKE ISLAND*, OFF FORWARD OPERATIONS BASE BALTIMORE, PHILIPPINES

Upon his arrival aboard Admiral Turner's flagship Scott Dixon was treated with all the deference befitting his rank and the warmth one would accord a leper who showed up unexpectedly at your doorstep to join you at dinner. For his part Scott was cordial to his hosts but guarded, stating only that his unannounced visit was nothing more than a routine fact-finding tour. During the initial round of introductions to Turner's staff Scott tried to defuse some of the tension by claiming that his trip was little more than a boondoggle, an excursion that had no real purpose other than to get him out of his office and away from the Pentagon for a few days. "They felt I needed to stretch my legs and get some fresh air," he joked. It was only when Turner invited him to his cabin for coffee while his staff threw together a briefing on the current situation and future operations that Scott leveled with the commanding officer of JTF Sierra.

"There's growing concern that this operation is not panning out as planned," he stated bluntly to Turner who already suspected that this was the real reason for Dixon's visit after the two were alone. "With our special operations forces already spread dangerously thin we cannot afford to keep precious assets chasing their tails in an effort that has little prospect of achieving anything of lasting value in our ongoing war on international terrorism." Pausing to allow this to sink in, Scott took a sip of coffee as he watched Turner to see how he responded to his declaration. Turner said nothing, maintaining his poker face as he waited for Scott to let loose with the other barrel. "There's a growing feeling among the Joint Chiefs," Scott continued, "that this operation is an unnecessary diversion from our efforts in Southwest Asia that we simply can't afford."

If he felt any anger at Scott's likening the efforts of the task force he commanded to a fool's errand Turner didn't show it. Instead he took his cue from Scott, dropping all pretenses as he spoke frankly. "Is that how the wise men back in Washington see this operation?"

With a deadpan expression that he had perfected in his thirty-plus years of service, Scott countered with a question of his own. "How do you see things?"

Turner took a moment to consider his answer as he

stared down into the half-filled cup of coffee he held. Then, without looking up at Scott, Turner grunted. "I'm afraid I'd have to agree with them. We all knew that this would be a tough nut, one that depended heavily upon the hope that the Abu Sayyaf would find little choice but to come out and confront us in an open fight that would allow us to pile on. But . . ." Turner stopped for a moment as he looked up, waving a hand vaguely as he did so.

Then, sitting upright, Turner set his cup on the table that separated the two men. "They haven't made a single mistake that we've been able to capitalize upon," he stated crisply and emphatically as he leaned forward and stared into Scott's eyes. "And you know what? I don't think they're going to anytime soon."

For the longest time the two men sat there looking at each other, neither one daring to state the obvious, that Operation Pacific Shield was morphing its way into a failure. It took a sudden knock on the door to break the tense silence. Clearing his throat, Turner called out, "Enter."

Opening the door just enough to allow him to stick his head into the room, Turner's young aide announced that the staff was ready to brief whenever they were ready. With nothing more than a nod Turner dismissed the aide who quickly withdrew his head and closed the door behind him.

Looking back at Scott, Turner waited for the more senior officer to say something. Having participated in more than his fair share of operations that failed to meet their established goals, Scott knew just how difficult it would be for Turner to accept defeat and sail away without having accomplished a single mission objective of note. Still, like him Turner was a professional warrior, a man who knew that from time to time it was necessary to admit that you were holding a losing hand, cut your losses and fold. Standing, Scott stretched and looked around the admiral's office before turning toward Turner. "So we're agreed."

Turner knew that this was a statement and not a question. Following suit, he stood up and shook his head. "If it were my decision to make I'd declare victory, stick a fork in this turkey, and move on to bigger and better things."

Scott didn't let on that the decision to do that was already being considered, that his only purpose in coming halfway around the world was to consult with the commanding officer in the field to get his take on things. Instead, he managed to whip up a bit of a smile. "Well, let's not keep your staff waiting. Please, lead on."

Turner was relieved that someone else would be saving him from the humiliation of having to go to his commanding officer and admit that his best efforts just weren't good enough, that he had failed to accomplish a task that had been assigned to him. Now that the burden of putting an end to Operation Pacific Shield was no longer his, Turner found he was able to smile for the first time since Scott stepped foot aboard his flagship. "Yes, of course. No, there's no point in putting things off, is there?"

While he understood what was behind the sea change in Turner's mood, Scott found that he could not reciprocate. Rather, he was saddened by the fact that now he was the official bearer of bad news, the man who would have to go back to the Joint Chiefs and tell them that the decision they had made to carry out Operation Pacific Shield had been a bad one. Without a wit of enthusiasm he nodded in agreement. "Quite right, quite right."

COMPANY A'S FORWARD PATROL BASE, MINDANAO, PHILIPPINES

During the entire trip back into the interior Nathan went over his brief but contentious meeting with his battalion commander. Every time he found himself beginning to wonder if he had strayed too far out of line a little voice in the back of his head whispered, "Don't be stupid. You

knew this day was coming." The only thing that he re-
gretted was the issue that had pushed him over the edge.
It was a subject that every son of a general has to deal
with from time to time when he chooses to follow his father's footsteps. In Nathan's case his burden was perhaps
greater than most, for his father was a man who had a
record and reputation that was the envy of most professional officers. The name Dixon stood out in dozens of
history books that addressed recent conflicts. His father's
exploits were held up as an example to aspiring young
officers in classes on leadership at West Point, Fort Benning, and a dozen other Army schools. At the Armor
School he was regarded as something of a demigod, hailed
by the armor community as its last great tank warrior. As
the scion of a legend, Nathan could not help viewing his
father as both a blessing and a curse, a fate he wouldn't
wish on anyone, not even himself.

These troubling thoughts and the contentious meeting
he had just had with his commanding officer were swirling about in his mind when he heard the pilot and copilot
of the Blackhawk begin chattering over the intercom about
a pillar of smoke. Rousing himself out of his gloom, Nathan twisted about in his seat in order to see what it was
that the crew was talking about. Turning his head, the copilot looked at Nathan. "Isn't that the location of your base
camp?"

After taking a moment to check the surrounding terrain features Nathan nodded. "It sure looks like it," he
stated a bit confused. "Do you have my unit's frequency?"
he asked.

Knowing what he wanted, the copilot punched in the
preset that switched the helicopter's FM radio to Company A's frequency. "You've got it, Captain."

Keying his mike, Nathan Began to hail Quinn. "Alpha
Five, this is Alpha Six."

The speedy response cued Nathan to the fact that his
XO had probably heard the beating of the copter's blades
and was expecting his call. "Six, this is Five."

Knowing that other ears might be listening in on his company command net, namely Delmont, Nathan was very careful as he chose his words. "I hope I'm seeing things, 'cause from where I am I can see something that I shouldn't be."

There was a slight pause before Quinn replied. "Roger that, Six."

"What do you mean, roger that?"

Again Quinn hesitated as if he was trying to come up with an explanation as to why there was a pillar of smoke hanging over the center of the company's base camp. Unable to think of something, Quinn decided to delay the inevitable. "Six, this is Five. I'll meet you on the ground."

Though tempted to yell, "You bet you'll meet me," Nathan didn't. Still agitated over his run in with Delmont, Nathan found himself all but unable to restrain himself from jumping up out of his seat and out the door as the Blackhawk made its descent into the small clearing near the company's base camp.

From the open door Nathan could see three figures waiting for him. To his surprise two were in boonie hats. Not waiting for the copter's crew chief to give him the thumbs-up, Nathan released his seat belt and sprung up and out as soon as he felt they were near enough to the ground to allow him to dismount safely.

With all the grace of a charging pitbull Nathan made his way toward his reception party. To Quinn's right was First Sergeant Carney, to the left, Sergeant First Class Smart. All three seemed oblivious to their commanding officer's anger. Instead they saluted, more or less when Nathan was within six paces. "I'm sure there's a good reason for this," Nathan bellowed.

Quinn did his best to keep a straight face but found he couldn't. "Well, it's like this, sir. Not long after you left Second and Third Platoons, a car loaded with members of the local constabulary came thundering down the road. When they reached the farm they all jumped out. Two ran into the farm compound while another pair went running about, beating the brush until they found the Second Platoon."

"Yes, sir, they did. And they found the Third Platoon right off," Carney stated, picking up the story. "Now you and I both know that those folks are either part of the Abu Sayyaf militia or in league with them. Seeing how the ambush was already blown, Lieutenant Grimes decided to move into the farmstead and look about for anything that might be useful to the intel folks."

"When we did," Smart stated as he threw in, "we found some indications that someone had been using it as a staging area, but nothing of any real value."

Folding his arms, Nathan began to realize that there was something else going on and that he was being set up for something. "That's all very interesting," he stated sharply. "But it doesn't explain why you're sending smoke signals up from our patrol base that every asshole toting an AK on this island can see."

"Well, we were getting to that," Quinn hastened to declare.

"Yes, sir," Smart chimed in. "You see, while we were scouring the area around the farmstead some of my people came across this poor, abandoned carabao just standing there, looking forlorn and rather hapless."

Suddenly it dawned upon Nathan where his most trusted subordinates were going with their tortured explanation. "Please tell me you didn't," he moaned.

"We were in the process of liberating the poor creature," Smart continued, "setting it free when Private White told me that the carabao reminded him of beef cattle, just like the ones that he used to butcher back in his father's shop."

Lowering his head, Nathan shook it from side to side as he raised his hand, signaling Smart to stop. "Enough! I've heard enough."

Then, looking up he stared straight at Quinn. "No doubt the explanation as to why you've got your helmet in travel lock is just as entertaining."

"It's like this, sir. We no sooner got the poor recently departed carabao sliced, diced, and roasting when it was decided that it might be better if we sort of put our rank aside for a while."

"That was my idea, Captain," Carney stated proudly. "Rank tends to get in the way of a man's ability to enjoy a good steak dinner and his beer."

"Beer? You've issued the men beer? And where the hell did that come from? Did White find it when he gutted the poor creature?"

"We're only allowing two bottles per man," Quinn explained.

"You can rest assured that I'm making sure that everyone gets his fair share and no more," Carney added quickly.

Now Nathan turned his face skyward as he threw up his arms. "Dear God in heaven, please tell me that I've landed in a bad dream and when I open my eyes this will all be gone." Then, looking back at Quinn he asked the obvious. "And where did the beer come from? Did White find it when he gutted the poor beast?"

"Remember those local constabulary we told you about," Smart stated without hesitation. "Well, they may be Abu Sayyaf but they're also capitalists."

"So you made a deal with them?"

"The men needed a break," Carney proclaimed in a manner that told Nathan he was now being dead serious. "You know as well as I do that our people are becoming frustrated with the way things have been going as of late. Everyone, including you, Captain, needs a break, a chance to kick back and blow off some steam. So when Fred and his platoon brought that carabao back with them I talked Lieutenant Quinn into throwing a party."

"He didn't need to twist my arm, sir," Quinn admitted. "As a matter of fact I was already beginning to think along the same lines when the first sergeant approached me with his idea."

Again folding his arms across his chest, Nathan looked

down at the ground and began to kick some loose dirt about with the toe of his boot. "You all realize that when we're finished here with this unauthorized barbecue of yours we're going to have to pack up and slip away from here under the cover of darkness."

All three of Nathan's loyal subordinates realized that they had managed to pull off their little insurrection when they heard him utter the word "We."

"Not to worry," Carney boasted. "I made it absolutely clear to every swinging Richard in the company that any man that screws up or mutters a single word of complaint will find my boot firmly planted up his . . ."

"I get the picture," Nathan stated.

The trio facing him was all smiles now. Quinn, reaching around behind his back, stuck it into a rucksack he was carrying over one shoulder. After fishing about for a moment he pulled out a bottle of beer that he promptly offered to Nathan.

Understanding the gesture was Quinn's way of pulling him into their little conspiracy, Nathan grinned. "Wait a minute, I'm not in the proper uniform." With that he unsnapped his chin strap, took off his helmet, and spun it about before placing it back on his head. "There, that's better." With that, he took the beer and raised it in the air in a toast. "To Company A."

Everything was going to First Sergeant Carney's satisfaction. The nerve-racking, hair-trigger tension that had gripped the company was for the moment gone as Eric White, the man of the moment, stood before the cook fire in the center of the base camp slicing off large chunks of meat from the roasted carabao. There were smiles all around as the Rangers of Company A filed by, received their share, and scampered off to find a place where they could sit down to enjoy a beer and fresh-cooked meat. Even those men who had volunteered to refrain from drinking in order to man the perimeter were in high spirits as their buddies brought them their share of roasted carabao.

For his part Nathan was content to sit on his haunches off to one side, nursing the beer his XO had given him as he watched his men delight in their first true break from the brutal grind their forays into the interior had become. Every now and then one of them would look over at Nathan and raise his plate up in an effort to thank him for allowing them this most welcomed diversion.

The sun was beginning to dip low in the west when Specialist Four Hoyt, stripped down to his T-shirt, came trotting over to Nathan. In a low voice, he whispered in his commanding officer's ear, "Sir, we have an inbound chopper."

In an instant Nathan's good mood vanished. "How far out is he?"

"Less than five minutes, sir." Then, answering the next question he expected his commanding officer was preparing, Hoyt informed Nathan that the pilot of the inbound Blackhawk refused to say who was on board.

To this Nathan merely grunted. "There's no need to guess about that one. It can be none other than our fearless leader coming to chew on what little ass I've got left," making no effort to hide the bitterness he felt toward Delmont.

Despite the fact that it was common knowledge throughout the battalion that their battalion commander was reviled by every company commander Hoyt had never heard Nathan utter a single word of disrespect. He was quite taken aback by this unexpected outburst. "Should I get the XO and first sergeant?"

Taking a moment to look about he weighed his options. Quickly he concluded that the chances of ditching everything connected to the barbecue and returning the company and his base camp to some semblance of proper military order in less than five minutes were next to nil. Taking a sip of beer, Nathan looked at Hoyt and smiled.

"No need to bother them. I'll handle this one all by myself."

Baffled by his commanding officer's nonchalance in the face of a crisis that could very well bring his military career to an abrupt and most heinous conclusion Hoyt watched as Nathan made his way toward the perimeter. Concluding that his commanding officer was drunk, Hoyt beat feet over to where the first sergeant was supervising the chow line.

Standing alone at the edge of the clearing, Nathan watched the inbound helicopter come into sight. He had no prepared speech all neatly laid out in his mind. Nor had he bothered to conjure up an excuse that would explain why there was a roasted carabao and several cases of beer in his patrol base. Convinced that there was nothing that he could say whether it be fact or fiction that would satisfactorily justify compromising the security of his patrol base, Nathan decided to simply let the chips fall wherever they might. He was tired of Delmont's attitude and the games he was playing with him and his men. He was tired of acting as a buffer, taking it upon himself to absorb Delmont's abuses and tantrums in an effort to shield his people from them. Long before they arrived in the Philippines he had come to the conclusion that his superior was doing little more than biding his time, waiting until he found an excuse to relieve Nathan of his command. This was not simple paranoia. Every company commander and a fair number of captains on the battalion staff shared this view for they knew that they too were in Delmont's sights.

Impatiently Nathan rocked back and forth on his heels, deciding then and there that if Delmont was so hell bent on bringing his career to an end it might as well be over something that was worth it. Having steeled himself psychologically for the ass chewing of his life, Nathan was

astonished when he saw his father hop out of the Blackhawk and make his way over to where he stood.

"I'm waiting," Scott called out as he drew near.

Nathan shook his head in an effort to collect his
thoughts. "Waiting for what?"

Stopping before his son, Scott smiled. "For you to
make up your mind as to whether you are going to salute
me or hug me. Your call."

Running down off the high ground as fast as they could
in an effort to save their company commander from impaling himself both Quinn and Carney were stunned to
see him embracing another man. Pulling up short the two
took a moment to take in the strange scene, not knowing
exactly what to do. At first Carney thought Nathan had
attacked their battalion commander and the two were in
the throes of strangling each other. Then he noticed that
as they parted, each held the other's right hand.

Quinn spoke first. "What do you make of it?"

Carney shook his head. "That isn't Delmont."

"Then who is it?"

Only when the two officers turned and began to make
their way up the beaten path toward them did Carney realize just how similar the two men were in both stature
and build. The way they carried themselves, their gait,
even how they waved their hands about as they talked,
was eerily similar. When they were less than a hundred
meters away he finally realized who the other officer
with Nathan was. "Oh, my God."

Not having made the connection yet Quinn looked at
the first sergeant, then back at the approaching figures.
"What?"

"It's the old man's old man."

Now it was Quinn's turn to stammer. "Sweet Jesus.
What do we do?"

With the directness that is unique to first sergeants,

Carney drew himself into a position of attention as Nathan and Scott drew closer. "Salute 'em, what else?"

They did just that when father and son were within six paces of them. With a casual wave of his hand, Nathan proceeded to introduce everyone. "Dad, this is my XO, Pete Quinn, and my first sergeant, Master Sergeant William Carney."

Carney had known long before Nathan had reported in to take command of the company that his father was "The" Scott Dixon. Yet to be standing there, in the middle of a field in the Philippines, hearing his company commander casually refer to a three star general as "Dad" was a bit unsettling. Stiffly reaching out Carney took Scott's hand and shook it. "Ah, it's quite a pleasure to meet you, sir."

With a grin and a wink, Scott gave the first sergeant's hand a vigorous shake. "Yes, I'm sure your heart is all atwitter."

Sensing that he was going to like this man, Carney lightened up enough to laugh. "I haven't felt this nervous since I met my ex-in-laws for the first time."

"Seeing how you're my son's top sergeant, I guess in a roundabout way we're related," Scott quipped as he turned to Quinn. "I've heard a lot about you, Pete."

Having recovered from his shock by now, Quinn decided to have some fun with the general as they shook hands. "I would appreciate it, General, if you didn't believe a word of it, at least not the really bad stuff."

While he was still gripping Quinn's hands, Scott looked up at the younger officer's helmet. "I don't suppose you'd care to tell me why both you and my son have your head gear in travel lock."

Before responding Carney and Quinn exchanged glances. Not only did the general use the exact same term as his son had, his tone of voice was all but indistinguishable from one Nathan had used earlier in the day. For the first time Carney came to realize that he was serving a captain who would not only be a general officer one day, but would probably make his way all the way to the top, just as his father was poised to do.

Before Quinn could respond Nathan took his father by the arm. "I hope you're hungry, Dad, 'cause you caught us in the middle of dinner. Care to join us?"

Suspecting that there was something going on that no one outside his son's unit was supposed to know about, Scott hesitated. "Am I going to regret this?"

"Probably, but what the hell. It wouldn't be the first time you caught me goofing off."

Scott glanced over at Quinn, then Carney. Like Quinn, Carney was beginning to sense that Scott was anxious for everyone around him to ignore the fact that he was a general officer. Raising his hands in mock resignation, Carney shook his head. "I'm tellin' you, General, no matter how hard you try to keep these headstrong hard-charging officers on the straight and narrow they just won't listen. Sometimes it's worse than herding cats."

"First Sergeant," Scott announced. "You have my sympathies. Now if you would be so kind, lead off."

The shock that swept through the ranks of Company A could not have been any more pronounced had Jesus himself risen yet again and strolled into the center of the patrol base. It took everyone several minutes to realize that the general officer standing shoulder to shoulder with their company commander was his father and that he was here not to bring hellfire and damnation down upon their heads for their gross violation of tactical doctrine but merely to visit his son. Like Carney they all knew about the captain's father. And like the first sergeant seeing that man in the flesh side by side with someone they were used to being around was a bit unnerving. Still, everyone came to realize that they had nothing to worry about when Scott, seeing what was going on, announced in a loud voice to his guide, "Well, First Sergeant, it seems I'm out of uniform," before turning his own hat about as all the other officers had.

In the twinkling of an eye the mood changed dramatically. Now everyone was anxious to meet the general. Some, like White, didn't quite know what to do, never having met a real general before. In his own polished way Scott sought to put the soldier at ease. "I hear you're the man responsible for preparing this highly unauthorized feast. Do you think there's enough for one more?"

Stammering, White managed to reply in the affirmative before running back to the fire pit to slice off some meat for the general. As he was doing that Nathan brought one of his NCOs over to his father. "Dad, I'd like you to meet Staff Sergeant Henry Jones."

Giving his son a double take as he shook the man's hand Scott tried to figure out if his son was playing a joke on him. Reading his father's expression correctly Nathan grinned. "I'm not kidding. His name is Henry Jones."

After giving White's squad leader the once over, he cocked his head. "By any chance, would you be related to . . ."

Having been the butt of many a joke because his name was the same as the Army's chief of staff, Jones chuckled. "Sorry to say, sir, we're not, at least that I know of. No doubt we were back in Wales before our ancestors crossed the Western Sea, but then everyone over there seems to be named Jones."

Quinn, now totally in the swing of things, chimed in. "I guess someone really got around, didn't they?"

Scott spent the next few minutes glad-handing the troops and exchanging the sort of banter that senior officers do when they're visiting the troops in the field. When White reappeared with two plates of food Scott and Nathan accepted them with a hearty thanks before settling to find a spot where they could speak in private as they enjoyed their meal.

Neither man spoke of the tactical situation or of operations currently under way or planned. Instead they restricted their chatter to family matters, the same sort of banter that any father would engage in upon meeting his grown son for the first time in months. It was in the course of this conversation that Scott remembered he had a letter Nathan's wife had managed to get to him before he departed. As he was handing it to Nathan he explained how he had come to be Nathan's personal postman. "I guess your mother told Chris I was coming over here."

Confused, Nathan looked at his father. "I thought you said this was a spur-of-the moment thing, that you left on short notice. How did Chris manage to get the letter to you before you left D.C.?"

Scott winked. "Chris is a good girl and a fine officer. She knows how to work the system. As soon as she heard about my trip she did some checking around and found out that there was a courier leaving Benning for Fort Belvoir that night. She managed to find the courier and talk him into hand-carrying the letter to me."

Now Nathan was worried. Like him, Chris was leery about taking advantage of the fact that she was related to a very senior officer. Anxious to find out what was so important that she would violate this trust Nathan tore into the letter and began to read it in the fading light of day.

As he did so Scott studied the expression on his son's face, watching his eyes madly dart from line to line. When he had finished the one page letter Nathan looked up into his father's eyes with an expression that Scott didn't quite know how to read. He became concerned when his son took a moment to look away, muttering "Oh my God!" over and over as he did so.

Setting aside his plate, Scott was about to reach across and shake his son when Nathan turned to face him once more. When he did he was wearing an entirely new expression as if he were dumbstruck. Now more confused than ever, Scott lost all patience. "For the love of God, what's wrong?"

Slowly a smile began to light Nathan's face. "Not a thing, Dad. Not a single blessed thing."

"Am I out of line if I ask what it was that Chris said?"

Reaching out Nathan grabbed his father's hand and shook it. "Dad, I am pleased to announce you're about to be promoted. You're going to be a grandfather."

With night falling fast and his military transport at the military airfield outside Davao waiting for him, there was no time to celebrate Chris's wonderful news with his son. After giving his son's company a rather perfunctory pep talk, the pair walked down to the clearing where the helicopter sat, both doing their best to reassure the other about the future. "We'll have plenty of time to chat when we finish up here," Nathan reassured his father as he expressed his regrets about having to run. "Fact is, I've got the feeling that I'll be home in ample time to be with Chris for the blessed event."

For a moment father and son regarded each other. Scott had said nothing concerning the purpose of his trip or the results of his meeting with Turner. Yet his son seemed to know that this operation was in its waning days. Whether he was guessing or if he knew something via the rumor mill was something he did not have the time to discern. Instead Scott spent the last few minutes he had with his son assuring him that Chris would be all right. "She'll be fine. Women have been having babies long before the first man marched off to war."

"Yes," Nathan countered. "And from what I've been told, we men have the easier of the two."

Scott chuckled before looking over at the helicopter that was patiently awaiting him. "Well, it's time."

Feeling his eyes welling up, Nathan nodded. "Yes. I've got a company to get ready to move."

"And I have to get back to the Puzzle Palace."

Once more the two men hugged before Nathan took one step back and rendered a smart hand salute.

Scott took a moment to look at his son from head to toe. As he did so he felt the pride he had for Nathan welling up within him. "You take care of yourself, soldier," he finally managed to say as he returned his salute.

With that, Scott pivoted about and marched away. For his part Nathan remained there at the edge of the clearing until the helicopter had lifted off and disappeared into the dark evening sky. Any regrets that he had entertained earlier that day about being the son of Scott Dixon were long forgotten. In their place he now nurtured the hope that the child his wife was carrying would one day be as proud of his grandfather as he was.

There was a spring in the step of each and every man in Company A when it came time for them to slip away from their compromised patrol base and disappear into the jungle. That night there were no complaints or gripes during the arduous trek through the dense undergrowth. Upon arrival at their new patrol base Nathan's Rangers set about digging their positions, setting out claymore mines, and sighting their weapons to cover assigned sectors of responsibility with a real sense of purpose. By oh-two-hundred hours all was set and ready, allowing Nathan to slump down into the bottom of the fighting position that served as the company command post and catch a few minutes of sleep.

As it turned out a few minutes was about all he managed to squeeze in before he felt someone shaking him. Opening one eye Nathan looked up at the black form hovering over him. "Captain Dixon, are you awake?"

It was Hoyt. Sensing that he wasn't going to like what he was about to hear, Nathan sighed. "What's up?"

There was a sheepishness in Hoyt's tone that told Nathan he really wasn't going to like the answer. "It's the battalion commander, sir. He's sending a chopper here to pick you up and . . ."

He didn't allow Hoyt to finish. In an instant he was on his feet, muttering a string of oaths in a voice that could have raised the dead. Startled, the Rangers all around the perimeter who had been dozing off sprang to the lip of their fighting positions and grabbed their weapons, ready to repel any threat that suddenly appeared out of the dark jungle before them. It took everyone a few seconds to realize that the danger was not from out there, but from within.

By the time Quinn and First Sergeant Carney reached him Nathan had managed to moderate his volume but not the hatred he felt at that moment for Robert Delmont. "That stupid son of a bitch," he hissed without regard for who heard him. "Twice he's done this to me. Twice in one day. What in the name of God could be so damned important," he raged, "that he needs to see me face-to-face, right this very minute."

Trying to make sense out of what was happening, Carney turned to Hoyt. "Did the battalion commander say why he wanted to see the captain?"

Nathan didn't let Hoyt respond. "I'll tell you why," he spat. "Because he's the dumbest, most egotistical son of a bitch who ever wore a uniform. THAT'S why!"

Pulling back Carney gave his commanding officer an opportunity to calm down. That effort of course was in vain. Taking only enough time to issue orders to Quinn and Carney to have the entire company stand to and be prepared to move out again if that became necessary Nathan stormed down to the clearing they had selected as a helipad to await the incoming chopper.

The cool night air sweeping through the open doors of the helicopter did nothing to diminish the rage that filled Nathan as they headed south, back to Baltimore for the second time in little more than twelve hours. His anger was such that he wasn't able to piece together any clear plan of action as to what he would do or say when he confronted Delmont. Wasting little time upon landing he burst into the battalion command bunker, ignoring the looks thrown his way by the graveyard shift manning the radios.

Hearing the commotion, Robert Delmont gathered himself up out of his seat, crossed the small patch of dried mud that served as a floor, and drew back the canvas curtain that separated his small office from the main room of the command bunker. When he did so he found himself standing face-to-face with Nathan. The expression on that officer's face spoke volumes.

Motioning to a folding chair, Delmont told Nathan to have a seat as he turned away from him and walked back behind his desk to his own chair. Making no effort to moderate his tone, Nathan refused. "I'd rather stand, *sir.*"

Delmont ignored his subordinate's impertinent tone. Instead he placed his elbows on his desk, clasped his hands together, and looked down at the edge of his desk for a moment as if he were gathering up his strength for battle. When he was ready, he glanced up at Nathan who had assumed a rigid position of parade rest. Heaving a great sigh Delmont hesitated once more. Then, seeing that there was no sense in delaying the inevitable, he spoke. "Captain Dixon, I regret that I am the one who has to inform you of this, but your father's helicopter was shot down by a surface-to-air missile as it was making its final approach into the military airfield at Davao." Delmont paused, in part to allow this news to soak in but mainly to collect his own thoughts as he tried to decide what to say next. "It seems the Abu Sayyaf knew that there would be a flight carrying a VIP coming in. It was a deliberate ambush using three Russian built shoulder-fired missiles launched from three separate positions. The pilots had no chance to evade."

He heard the words and he understood them. Yet no matter how hard he tried Nathan could not accept what they meant to him. Or rather he refused to. Stunned, he found he could only look down into the eyes of a man he hated in the hope that this was nothing more than a mistake, or perhaps a cruel joke being played on him by a heartless bastard.

"I felt it better," Delmont mumbled when he managed to muster up the strength to go on, "if I told you in person rather than doing so over the radio."

Struggling to hold himself together, Nathan managed to choke out one word. "Survivors?"

With a shake of his head Delmont confirmed Nathan's worst fear. "None."

Nathan tilted his head back, blinking his eyes in an effort to hold back tears that could not be stopped. Gone was the dank smell of the battalion command bunker. Blocked out by his mounting grief were the words of his battalion commander. The only thought left swirling around in Nathan's mind was a faint memory, a hazy recollection of a small boy reaching up to his father who was towering over him, imploring the man he loved over and over again to pick him up and hug him. "Daddy, pick me up and hug me." The words rang in his ears as clearly as if he were saying them. And for the briefest of moments, Nathan imagined he could still feel his father's arms around him.

Then, like the morning mist the distant memory disappeared. In its place reality finally hit home.

20

Like ripples in a pond. That's how Scott Dixon had once described to his young son how the loss of a single soldier resonated in the world around him. As with so many of the one-on-one conversations Nathan had with his father this one took place in the den, a place where Scott surrounded himself with his books and all the seemingly insignificant mementos he had collected as he moved from one tour of duty to the next. It was the only room in the house where Nathan could be sure that he would have his father all to himself. He was twelve years old when he put down one of his father's books that he had been reading and asked what effect casualties had on a combat unit. Never sure if such questions were truly inspired by intellectual curiosity or little more than a son's desire for his father's attention, Scott never failed to stop what he was doing and reply in a manner that he felt was befitting Nathan's age and ability to comprehend.

Rather than confuse his son with all sorts of quantifiers such as whether the man was merely wounded or dead, on this occasion Scott kept things as simple as he could. "When you throw a stone in a pond it makes but a small hole, one that quickly disappears as the water around it rushes in and fills the void. In a combat unit that's pretty much what happens when a trooper goes down. Everyone makes adjustments to compensate for the loss. In the Civil War and Revolution this was achieved simply by closing up the ranks, pushing the soldiers to the left or right of the gap together. In modern warfare it entails shifting people about to cover the sector of responsibility belonging to the man who was lost or reassigning his duties to another if he was part of a heavy weapons crew."

Before he could explain any further Nathan hit his father with another question, one that stirred the sort of painful memories that old soldiers seldom share. "Does it bother his friends and the other soldiers in the unit?"

It was a long time before Nathan was old enough to understand that there were certain questions that one did not pose to a person like his father, questions that forced him to relive painful episodes from his own past. His father's ability to set aside his own emotions and provide him with a well thought-out and reasonable answer was something that Nathan came to appreciate only when he had experienced the bitter taste of battle for himself.

On this particular occasion when his son did stray onto sensitive ground Scott managed to wade through the brutality of his own recollections, explaining as best he could how there is a difference between the practical aspects of viewing casualties and the actual impact one feels when a fellow soldier to your left or right goes down. "There is seldom time for one to grieve when a man is killed or severely wounded in battle even when the individual was a friend or someone in your command that you were particularly fond of. The tactical situation demands that his chain of command and comrades keep their feelings in check," he explained in a cold and detached voice. "You have to focus all your attention and efforts on carrying on with the mission at hand, otherwise you risk becoming a casualty yourself."

His father paused at this point, looking up at the ceiling as if searching for the answer. When he looked back at

Nathan the boy of twelve really didn't understand why there was the hint of a tear in his father's eye as she continued. "It's only when the firing stops and you've had time to catch your breath and reflect over what has just happened that the full impact of the casualties your unit has suffered hits home. Those who knew the dead and wounded best are affected the most. Even the most hardcore trooper can be reduced to tears when he has to face the fact that the man he hung out with, shared his most intimate secrets with, and trusted with his life is gone. These soldiers represent the first ripple caused by the hole, a ripple that is always strongest. Though not as devastated the rest of the squad is the next ripple, for they also personally feel effects of the loss. A man they knew is no longer with them. They know they will miss his jokes, his willingness to share their load when they grow weary, the reassurance they felt by his mere presence when they found themselves in a tight situation. As the ripples radiate farther out the shock diminishes but is no less painful. The platoon leader and his platoon sergeant have to make do with fewer people. The company first sergeant has to make arrangements for the evacuation of the casualty, tend to the personal belongings that everyone leaves behind as well as request a replacement. This sets in motion a response that moves farther and farther away from the initiating event with each ripple becoming a little more impersonal, a little less emotional, until an individual casualty becomes nothing more than a line number in someone's summary of personnel actions at brigade or division. Yet even at the highest level one can still detect a ripple in the pond, one that radiates farther and farther out from the center, effecting all who are touched by it."

"And the families?" Nathan asked innocently.

It was questions like this that made Scott even more uncomfortable, for he was never sure just how honest he should be with his son. Like all fathers Scott was always torn between a desire to protect his child from the harsh realities of the world in which he lived and the need to prepare his own son to enter it. "The same more or less applies," Scott finally stated in a guarded tone on that day. "Though none of the loved ones a soldier leaves behind are ever forced to witness the loss up close and personal, the impact is no less devastating. If anything it is more brutal for the families. Men who survive combat have no choice but to move on, to set aside their grief and soldier on. Families back home on the other hand have little else to do but mourn."

Pausing, Scott looked down at his own son sitting on the floor before him, hanging on his every word. Realizing that this conversation was becoming too difficult to carry on he took a moment to blink away the moisture he felt welling up in the corners of his eyes as he patted his son on his head. "For the parents, the wives, the sons and the daughters of soldiers who fall in battle everything changes," he finally concluded. "In the twinkling of an eye a family's entire world is shattered. They lose the dreams that had once been the foundation upon which the family had stood. Around them the community loses a neighbor and the town a citizen as the ripples roll on till every drop of water in the pond is in some way touched by the loss."

Whether his son fully appreciated what he was trying to tell him didn't really matter to Scott. As with all his undertakings he dealt with the situation before him as best he could and hoped for the best. On that day, he seemed to have succeeded in satisfying his young son's curiosity, for Nathan gave his father a faint smile before turning his attention back to his reading. Scott on the other hand could not go back to his own reading as his mind strayed from the book before him and wandered instead through the dark recesses of his memory to the only place where the names and faces of men he had once known and were no longer alive now lingered.

Nathan didn't really feel the full impact of Scott's death until he entered his father's den with boxes in hand on the day following the internment ceremony at Arlington. For him the task of sorting through the books and personal mementos that defined Scott Dixon's life, deciding what items were to be kept and by whom, was an admission that he was really gone, never again to return.

That he was the logical choice for this heart-wrenching chore did nothing to ease the grief that had come to dominate his every waking hour. An effort to enlist his brother Andrew to assist him in the task had been easily parried. "You'll be a much better judge of what is important and what isn't," Andrew pointed out. "You know what will be of use to you in your career and what will mean something to Jan and . . ." He hesitated when he realized that his efforts to keep his tears in check were about to fail. "Well," he continued after managing to regain a temporary degree of composure, "I trust you Nate. I always have. I know you'll do what's right when it comes to sorting through Dad's things."

The thought of dragging his wife in to help him was quickly chucked aside with just as much ease. It didn't surprise Nathan that Chris had taken his father's death almost as hard as he had. Chris had become the daughter Scott had never had, a vibrant young woman he could dote on and spoil. The loss of a man who had become something more than a second father to her, coupled with the realization that she would never be able to give him the grandchild he longed for had left Chris crushed.

Jan, of course, was being Jan, putting up a brave front and carrying on in a manner Scott would have been proud of. Nathan of course knew better, he knew her business-as-usual manner was little more than a façade, that sooner or later it would collapse when she finally accepted the fact that the love of her life would never again walk in the door covered in mud and smelling of diesel fumes. Not wishing to be the one to push her over that edge, Nathan didn't even ask her if she wanted to help him.

So in the end it was left to him to sort through his father's most sacred belongings, a task that would only serve to highlight the cruel, brutal fact that his father was dead.

Stopping in the middle of the room Nathan took a moment to survey the rank upon rank of books on military history that his father had collected over the years. He was quite familiar with many of them for there were books on the shelves that were older than he was. Like Scott these books represented more to Nathan than a simple collection of memoirs and histories that offered him a window on the past. Many of those books spoke to him in that strange and subtle voice that only the written word can, recounting in awful detail great and glorious battles from the past, battles fought by every sort of man imaginable. Some of those men were larger than life, men whose conduct and deeds defined the very meaning of the word hero, natural-born leaders who always found a way to prevail no matter how desperate their situation might be. The books also introduced him to other men, men who found themselves to be little more than spectators to tragic episodes that they were powerless to control, events that overwhelmed them and the unfortunate soldiers they commanded.

Over the years Nathan had found that by studying these men, the good, the bad, and the unlucky he had been able to develop his own set of core beliefs concerning the fine art of leadership, philosophically pitting them against those held by soldiers who had gone before him. In this way he came to settle upon those principles he felt comfortable with long before his first battle, tenets that had endured and still guided how he lived his life and commanded his company. Though Nathan knew that his father's choice of reading material was keyed to his own taste and curiosity and not with an eye toward influencing his son, Nathan could not escape the fact that the man who had plucked these tomes from long lists of competing titles would no longer be there to make those choices or share his thoughts on their content. He would not be there to advise and challenge him, even if only through such an indirect and impersonal manner as books. His father, like so many of the men he had learned to admire through his reading, was now reduced to little more than words scrawled across a page and memories locked away in a troubled and grieving mind.

Finding himself unable to begin his mournful task Nathan let the boxes he had been carrying slip out of his hands. Instead of stuffing his father's possessions into containers that would be carefully stored and eventually forgotten, he slowly made his way to the well-worn chair his father had dragged from posting to posting. Settling down in it, he picked up the book sitting on the small side table beside it, opened the book to the page that was marked with a yellow three-by-five card that his father always used instead of a proper book marker, and took up where his father had left off.

Nathan had not meant there to be any symbolism surrounding his decision to put aside his assigned duties and read awhile. In his conscious mind he rationalized his actions as being nothing more significant than a grieving son doing all he could to put off the need to accept the cold hard realities that the death of his father presented him with, if only for a while longer. Yet in a strange way, Nathan was doing his best to hold on to the father he had lost. To some, trying to commune with his dead father one last time by reading a book is strange. But given the sort of relationship a fledgling boy enjoyed with a father who had been something of a living legend, it was quite fitting.

MINDANAO, PHILIPPINES

Half a world away the architect of that death found it impossible to set aside the realities of his situation with such ease. Upon hearing who his men had slain, Hamdani Summirat knew instinctively that his well-crafted game of cat and mouse he had been playing with the American military would soon be over. Whether they did so out of a sense of righteous vengeance or a simple desire to alter the status quo that he had engineered, Summirat came to the conclusion that time would no longer be an ally of his if he chose to continue playing the game using the same rules. Something would need to be changed. At the moment he had the opportunity to decide what those changes would be, an opportunity that was fleeting.

Still, Summirat did not see this unanticipated need to alter his campaign plan as being all bad. If anything it could be quite fortuitous. Like the Americans some of his people were becoming a bit disenchanted with what they were doing, leading to a drop in morale even among his most trusted lieutenants. Some were even beginning to question his courage. The death of the American general created an opportunity for Summirat to claim that this was what he had been waiting for, that the time to act was at hand. It didn't matter that it was nothing of the kind. All that was important to him was that his men continued to believe in him and follow his orders. The rest, as he was fond of saying, was in the hands of Allah.

With the same calm demeanor with which he conducted all his affairs, Summirat went about setting in motion a new phase of his campaign against the Americans. Refusing to be panicked into using the electronic means of communications he had been so carefully hoarding, Summirat dispatched a steady flow of couriers bearing seemingly harmless messages to his scattered commands throughout southwestern Mindanao. Within each of these messages were words and phrases that meant nothing to anyone else but the subordinate commander to whom it was addressed. It was as effective a means of passing secrets from one distant commander to another as it was ancient.

None of the Abu Sayyaf commanders who received these new orders needed to bother with acknowledging their receipt. Such administrative niceties only provided American and Filipino intelligence with more opportunities to intercept and perhaps through interrogation divine future Abu Sayyaf intentions and plans. The only responsibility each of Summirat's far flung subordinates had was to execute the particular contingency plan they already had in hand. Some of those instructions assigned a unit a predetermined target that was to be hit at a particular time. Others required the subordinate commander to initiate certain activities such as reconnaissance by force or the assassination of a local official who was suspected of cooperating with the Americans within a predetermined number of days once the order had been received. A few were less specific, requiring the insurgents to key their actions to enemy operations should the Americans enter their area of responsibility.

Orders that leave the methodology of accomplishing a mission up to a subordinate are what the United States Army refer to as mission-oriented orders and the Germans as *aufstragtactics,* concise directives that establish a desired result but which allow the commander carrying out the order the freedom to determine how he'll go about getting the job done. This approach to leadership requires a commander who has confidence in both his subordinate's training and his judgment. Since Summirat had handpicked the men who led the scattered elements of his command he felt no qualms about leaving it up to his people to decide just the way they went about skinning the cat they had been handed. This left Summirat free to plan and prepare for his next move, one he expected would determine the outcome of the campaign.

FORWARD OPERATIONS BASE CHICAGO, MINDANAO, PHILIPPINES

Even if he had been afforded the opportunity to select his own company commanders, Robert Delmont would never have been comfortable issuing the sort of orders that Summirat relied upon to achieve his ends. It just wasn't in his nature to trust a subordinate to carry out a plan he had conceived. There was more to this lack of confidence than

the usual fear of being held accountable for the shortcom-
ings of someone else or a zero tolerance for failure that
plagues the modern career-oriented officer corps. Delmont held people who were not his intellectual equals in
disdain. This included just about everyone he knew including some of the same senior officers who were doing
all they could to push him along. Every profession has its
fair share of such men, overachievers who believe they are
the only ones who know exactly what needs to be done
and possess the ability to make things happen.

It was Delmont's great misfortune to be a member of a
profession in which one has no choice but to rely upon a
whole string of others to carry out their orders, a condition that becomes more pronounced as one moves farther
and farther up the chain of command. A squad leader has
the physical ability to keep an eye on one of his riflemen
if he suspects that soldier to be a weak link, taking up the
slack for him in a pinch. A battalion commander of an
infantry unit, especially a Ranger battalion, cannot personally supervise all of his line company commanders.
He may accompany one of those units as it goes about
carrying out an assigned task, but he does so at the risk of
losing his ability to influence the actions of his other
companies, not to mention squandering time that would
better be used planning for the battalion's next mission.
This uncomfortable reality frustrated Delmont, especially
when the officers he relied upon to translate his plans
into action were not only strong-willed and capable, but
soldiers that had more combat experience than he himself possessed despite his seniority.

Herein lay the true dilemma that he faced as his battalion went about executing its role in Pacific Shield. In
order for the operation he had conceived and sold to his
mentor to succeed he needed to rely on his subordinates
he had no hand in selecting or training. Each of them had
their own style of leadership and were proven commodities. Only when the present crop of company commanders finished their tour of duty and moved on to other

assignments would Delmont be afforded the golden opportunity to bend their replacements to his will and style of leadership. Until then, he found he had little choice but to stake his career on the abilities of the officers the previous battalion commander had molded, using the best of that lot to execute the more difficult tasks.

That was how Company A, led by Nathan Dixon, had become Delmont's primary strike force, a choice that was proving to be frustrating to a micromanager like Delmont. Nathan was used to being given a great deal of leeway as to how he accomplished the missions battalion handed him. Initial efforts to restrict this freedom of action by Delmont created friction as Nathan chaffed under, then rebelled against them. Had it not been for the death of General Dixon, the situation would surely have come to a confrontation that Delmont was not at all sure he wanted.

If there was one thing that Delmont did have in common with the man he was hunting it was his appreciation that the Scott Dixon incident handed him an unexpected window of opportunity, one that needed to be acted upon before events and the decisions of others closed it. With Nathan Dixon out of the picture for the moment it made perfect sense to have Company A swap places with Captain Noel Cameron's Company B, which up till then had been the battalion's quick reaction force. When explaining his decision to do so to Colonel Tim Lamb, Delmont took great pains to point out that while he had little doubt that Nathan's executive officer was more than capable of carrying on in his commanding officer's absence, he preferred not to put that officer on the spot when he had a full company that was well rested and led by a captain who was fully qualified. What Delmont did not tell Lamb was that of his three line company commanders Cameron was the most junior, having assumed command of Company B a mere two months before he took over the battalion. In Delmont's mind this made Cameron more pliable, more susceptible to the sort of close supervision than Nathan and Clarence Overton, commander of Company C were. Relying on his subordinate's judgment when it came to such issues Lamb saw no reason to raise any objections for he shared Summirat's view of leadership, not Delmont's.

Thus a series of unfortunate events led Robert Delmont to believe that he had been afforded a chance to start over when JTF Sierra made its next jump to FOB Chicago. From there Cameron's company would launch into the interior in an effort to do what Nathan's people had so far failed to do, which was to find, fix, and destroy the Abu Sayyaf main strike force.

MINDANAO, PHILIPPINES

With the enthusiasm more befitting a young pup that had slipped his leash than the commander of a Ranger company, Noel Cameron all but pushed the file of men clogging the trail before him forward in an effort to quicken their pace. He was anxious to reach the village that was his company's objective. Time, he had been told by his battalion commander, was critical. Throughout the briefing that launched this foray Delmont had repeatedly stressed to Cameron the need to get his company into position before they lost the element of surprise, allowing the insurgents to once more melt away and seek refuge in the jungle or seamlessly merging into the civilian population from which they came. After spending weeks of serving as the battalion's quick-reaction force, waiting for a call to arms that never came the young commanding officer of Company B raised no objections to the admonishment by Delmont that Nathan would have interpreted as unnecessary browbeating and ignored out of hand.

The animosity that existed between Delmont and his senior company command as well as a serious clash of personalities with his commanding officer did not bother Cameron as much as it did his fellow captains. He was the new kid on the block, the most junior of the line company commanders. He had yet to establish a reputation of any sort or accumulate the sort of record of accomplishments that would allow him to openly cross his battalion commander with any hope of surviving. It was an uncomfortable situation he could live with for now.

At the moment all that did matter to him was that he and his company were out in the field, doing the sort of thing that they were trained to do. Even if it turned out that the foe they were supposedly closing in on had already flown the coop and this particular operation turned out to be a wasted effort, there wasn't a man in Cameron's company who would argue that what they were doing wasn't a damned sight better than cooling their heels in the close confines of the JTF's forward operating base, primed and ready with no place to go. Like their captain they too were highly trained professionals, men who only really came alive when they were given free rein to put their training and finely honed skills to use. Just the thought that they were about to be afforded the opportunity to prove just how good they were was more than enough to keep them hustling down the trail that took them from their primitive company patrol base, through the thick jungle, and toward their objective. Thus Cameron found he really didn't need to push very hard to keep his people moving along. If anything, had he taken the time to assess the situation they now faced he might have come to the conclusion that it might not be a bad idea to slow his people down.

From the get-go fortune smiled on Company B. On the second day of their initial foray into the interior they were handed a mission based on intelligence that was determined to be reliable but time-sensitive. As with most information concerning the Abu Sayyaf, the intelligence that led to this tasking came from provincial officials who had been told that a remote hamlet was being used as a sanctuary by insurgents believed to be members of the main force.

Unlike previous leads, the sort that had sent Company A scurrying hither and yon chasing phantoms this particular report was not only quite detailed, it had been collaborated by multiple sources. This latest treasure trove of info was dumped on JTF Sierra's intelligence section by their Filipino liaison officer just as the task force was in the throes of completing its third jump. The detailed information passed on to them was stunning, giving them the exact number of insurgents said to be operating from the newly identified sanctuary, a detailed description of the unit including the names of the insurgent leaders, and the types of weapons the insurgents were armed with. According to the JTF J-2 or senior intel officer it was an opportunity that was simply too good to pass up despite repeated Cassandra-like warnings by one of his analysts that the material they had been handed was so unlike anything they had received before that it made him fear that it was simply too good to be true.

Planning for this operation was done amid the usual confusion and frenzy of activity that always took place every time a new FOB base was being established. This atmosphere only added to the misgivings that the junior intel officer had over the nature of the information being used to launch the raid by Noel Cameron's company. Cameron however had no such qualms as he prepared his company to carry out his battalion commander's orders, for this would be his first time out on a combat mission as a company commander.

The only regret he took with him into the interior was his failure to take up Peter Quinn's offer to send a few of his people out with Company B for a few days during their first foray. Though Company A never did make any meaningful contact with the Abu Sayyaf during their tenure as the lead company they had managed to get a feel for what was normal vis-à-vis the indigenous population and what warranted a closer look. Those tactical instincts that Cameron did possess had been honed while dealing with Afghan insurgents who operated in barren terrain that bore no resemblance to the cacophony of thick jungle and overgrown farmland his company was now treading through. Even his most senior NCOs found they could not shed the lingering dread that one feels the first time you are experiencing the closeness of a jungle inhabited by a skillful foe. The bravado with which Cameron had dismissed Quinn's offer had been as foolish as it had been overplayed. It was a gesture he hoped he would not come to rue.

These and other unrelated misgivings were still rattling about in Cameron's head when the company command net crackled to life with a report from the lieutenant leading his Second Platoon informing all who were listening that they had reached the point where his platoon would peel off from the company column and circle around to the left of the village they were closing in on. Like the Third Platoon behind them the Second Platoon was assigned the task of establishing a perimeter around the village in order to provide a base of fire if needed as well as block all possible avenues of escape should the enemy choose to flee instead of fight. The task of going into the village and sweeping through it was left to the First Platoon, the one Cameron was traveling with.

In an instant all the petty concerns and apprehensions that had been nagging Cameron were forgotten as all his thoughts turned to the situation at hand. Even those Rangers who had not overheard the report from the Second Platoon sensed that their moment had arrived, causing them to clutch their weapons a bit tighter as the mental haze that tended to descend over a person during a long protracted approach disappeared. Suddenly all became more attuned to their surrounds and what was going on around them as their eyes became fixed upon their immediate superior, watching for any hand and arm signal that would send them this way or that. Even their bodies braced for the coming demands that would soon be placed upon them as the heart released more than enough adrenaline to overcome fatigue brought on by tropical heat and the physical exertions required to cut through the dense jungle.

The time it took for the two lead platoons to deploy and establish the perimeter proved to be the most un- nerving part of the entire operation for Cameron and the First Platoon. There was nothing for the young company commander to do as he waited for word that all was set. In these last anxious seconds before he sprang into action his mind was free to conjure up all sorts of nightmares that he might have to deal with if an alert insurgent stand- ing guard became aware of the Rangers closing in on the village or one of his own people prematurely opened fire before the Second and Third Platoons were in place. So it came as something of a relief when the lieutenants lead- ing those platoons reported in that they were set and ready. Turning to the platoon leader of the First who was standing right next to him, Cameron only needed to nod. Whether it was a feeling of relief from the strain that they had been under up to this point or if he really was over- come by a sudden burst of joy at being let loose to launch his platoon into the attack the lieutenant grinned before pushing past Cameron in order to move to the head of the column and lead his platoon into the village.

Pausing only long enough for a quick assessment of the situation and lay of the land ahead, Cameron's First Platoon shook out of the single-file column they had been traveling in and deployed. Leaving one of his squads and his platoon sergeant behind to provide cover, the young platoon leader took his other two squads forward through the untended farm fields that surrounded the silent vil- lage. On either flank the Rangers of the Second and Third Platoons watched from their concealed positions at the edge of the jungle, ready to pour accurate suppressive fire on any insurgent who might be foolish enough to open fire. In the wake of the First Platoon Noel Cameron emerged from the jungle with his small company command group, stopping as soon as they reached the edge of the jungle where the platoon sergeant and the squad with him were deployed. Despite an urge to keep going, Cameron took up a position from which he could observe the advance of the First Platoon.

Now that they were in the open and committed to the assault there could be no stopping, no hesitation. The slow, cautious approach march and the deliberate deployment of the encircling platoons was replaced by a rapid-fire rush of events. As quickly as his company reached and passed one critical point without incident there was another confronting him, one that seemed to be just as daunting as the previous one had been. Cameron found himself comparing this nerve-racking experience to being on a roller-coaster ride, one that did not allow its helpless passengers to catch their breath after taking them through a sharp turn before whipping them about a curve and onto a new and even more frightening stretch of track.

Left behind with nothing better to do but watch the skirmish line advance ever closer to the village he actually found himself hoping that something would happen. A single shot, the explosion of a grenade, a hail of suppressive fire unleashed by either of the encircling platoons, anything was preferable to the unnerving silence that threatened to drive the young company commander mad. There was nothing malevolent about this. He was just being human, responding as any reasonable person would in a situation like this, for once contact was made with the enemy his long, agonizing struggle with his fears, real and imagined would be over. There would be something to do. He would once more be in command, free to exercise control over the situation instead of being a hapless bystander waiting for someone else to do something.

Eventually the two squads of the First Platoon disappeared into the village. Now, Cameron found himself thinking. Now was the perfect time for the enemy to open fire. But nothing happened. Seconds slowly passed like the beads of sweat that trickled across his brow, down the bridge of his nose, and into his eye sockets where they gathered in shallow pools before continuing their journey. When those seconds began to accumulate and turn into still, uneventful minutes, Cameron bowed his head, taking a moment to wipe his face with a sweat-soaked rag before he reluctantly found himself realizing that all their meticulous planning and the extreme care with which they had conducted their approach march had been in vain. Like Company A before them they had hit a dry hole. Balling up the olive drab bandanna between his hand, the young officer swore and muttered. "Well, shit. I guess no one's home."

He was about to order the small party of Rangers that served as his company command group to gather themselves up and follow him across the fields and into the village when the oppressive stillness that had weighed so heavily upon them all was ripped by a shattering explosion. Instinctively Cameron dropped to the ground, managing to bury his head in the moist jungle floor just as the heat of the shock wave washed over his prone figure like an invisible wave. When it had passed and a stunned silence once more descended upon the small gathering around him, Cameron looked up.

The tranquil, crystal clear blue sky was gone, corrupted by a huge, ugly dirty white plum of smoke laced with bright orange tongues of flames welling up from the center of the village. The first thing that came to Cameron's mind was that the insurgents had detonated an IED, or improvised explosive device no different from those used by Iraqi terrorists in Baghdad to such gruesome effect. But that didn't make any sense to the young captain. In all their briefings and all the photos taken of the village by drones prior to the operation there had been no sign of vehicles of any type within the village. That the Abu Sayyaf insurgents would rig an entire structure in the same manner as the Iraqis did with automobiles never dawned upon him or anyone else for that matter. Not that this made any difference at the moment. Only one thought filled Noel Cameron's stunned brain and that was to get forward as quickly as he could and sort out the situation before relaying the grim news back to battalion.

Though he was still dazed by the shock wave that had slammed him like a hammer and the sudden unfavorable turn of events, Cameron wasted no time scrambling to his feet and taking off at a dead run. Behind him his radioman, a medic, and another Ranger who made up the company command group didn't need to be told that they needed to follow. All did so without the slightest hesitation, leaving the squad they had been with on the edge of the jungle at a loss as to whether they should hold in place or go forward to assist their platoon mates as best they could. Taking a moment to assess the situation and be sure that no one, either friend or foe, was firing the platoon sergeant jumped to his feet, turned to the squad with him and waved them on. "Let's go. They'll be needing all the help they can get."

As with Cameron's party there was no hesitation. Coming to their feet, the squad rushed forward. Ahead they could see Cameron disappear between two huts silhouetted by a raging fire that was enveloping the center of the village they were advancing on. With the exception of one of the newbies who had joined the squad back at Fort Lewis each and every one of the Rangers accompanying the platoon sergeant had seen dead and dying friends and fellow Rangers before. They knew what they would find and began to prepare themselves.

What greeted them just before they reached the edge of the village however was even more appalling than anything the most battle-hardened among them could have imagined. As before, the scene before them was transformed by a series of violent explosions that consumed the ring of huts that formed the outer perimeter of the village.

To a man the Rangers who were with the platoon sergeant were physically bowled over backwards by the force of the explosion. Momentarily blinded by its flash and suffering from a concussion the platoon sergeant found it difficult to gather his thoughts and reorient himself. When he finally did manage to gather up enough strength to do so, he propped himself up on elbows, rubbed his eyes, and looked about. The jungle that they had emerged from was still there. But all traces of the village were gone. All that remained was a wall of roaring bonfires before him, each consuming the pathetic remains of a hut, huts that had been the home to humble farm families until a keen and ruthless mind had transformed them into weapons of mass destruction. Now all they were good for was to serve as the pyre for a Ranger platoon and the young captain who had led them here.

21

OVER THE PACIFIC OCEAN, WEST OF HAWAII

There was very little difference in the time Nathan spent en route back to the Philippines than he had when making the same trip in the opposite direction in the company of his father's flag draped coffin. That journey had been a solemn one, a pilgrimage of sorts for Nathan who spent most of his waking hours recalling hundreds of long-forgotten events and memories centered upon his relationship with a man he both loved and feared, admired and on occasion despised in a manner that made him no different from any other son. With his mind thus occupied the eastward trek had passed quicker than anyone watching the solitary figure seated next to the standard issue military coffin could possibly have imagined.

The westbound flight on the other hand seemed to take forever. For the first time in his military career Nathan found himself regretting the need to leave his wife and family in order to rejoin his unit in the field. In part this was given Christina's condition, a state of affairs that he had chosen not to share with the remainder of his family lest his announcement add to the grief they already felt over Scott's untimely death. Nor did Nathan want to detract from the somber tone that military etiquette demanded when bidding farewell to a legend. Throughout his stay stateside he knew without having to be told that there was a prescribed role he was expected to play, a supporting one that would have been compromised had he opted to draw even the slightest bit of focus away from the honors the Army and nation felt obliged to pay to a fallen warrior.

The ambiguous status that his father's death left his stepmother in didn't make departing any easier. For years she had been as much a part of the Army as Scott, a member of a very special community that was unlike any other in the world. That she suddenly found herself exiled from that tight-knit group, physically and psychologically cast off with as much ceremony as a surgeon observes when disposing of an amputated limb, was almost as traumatic to her as had been the news of her husband's death. Though Nathan knew those who counted themselves as true friends of his father would endeavor to stay in contact with Jan and invite her to as many military functions and ceremonies as practical, he also understood that there was no place in the Army family for a widowed spouse whose presence would remind the other wives of the fate that their husband's duty threatened them with. It was an aspect of a soldier's death that Nathan was familiar with but had until now been at liberty to ignore.

If there was one bright spot in the otherwise grim pomp and ceremony that surrounded his father's burial it was Chris. On that day she had surprised him and a number of other people by opting to wear a simple sleeveless black dress and matching black jacket. To the uneducated eye this seemed to be perfectly normal. To Nathan and those who knew his wife Chris's decision to forgo her dress uniform on such an occasion in favor of attire more appropriate to a military wife was her way of announcing that she had made up her mind to pursue a more traditional and far more rewarding career path.

That little encouraging ray of sunshine was quickly eclipsed by other, more worrisome concerns that added to the despair Nathan felt as he returned to the Philippines. While stateside a shocking number of Army, Marine, Navy, and Air Force officers found themselves unable to resist the temptation of hustling Nathan off to one side in order to ask him for his personal and professional views concerning the conduct of JTF Sierra's operations and the situation on the ground. Quite naturally this put the young company commander in a very awkward situation. Having spent time as a staff officer himself he appreciated just how starved for firsthand information concerning an ongoing operation those deskbound Pentagon officers were. As the commanding officer of JTF Sierra's primary ground-based strike force they saw Nathan as something of a godsend, someone who could give them the rarest of all military commodities, an unvarnished view of what was really happening out there, a fresh data that was uncontaminated by the views and opinions of layer upon layer of intervening staffs and the commanders they served.

The quandary Nathan found himself dealing with over and over again was just how much truth did he dare provide. The acrimonious nature that existed between him and his commanding officer didn't help matters for they tended to color Nathan's views on every aspect of the operation, forcing him to exercise extreme care when it came to framing his responses to each and every question thrown at him. His extraordinary effort to keep his personal feelings toward Delmont from tainting those answers proved to be ineffective as more than a few astute listeners such as Henry Jones picked up on the labored manner with which Nathan replied, adding to their concern over the state of affairs in the Philippines. Even when Nathan didn't give them anything of value, his demeanor was more than enough to send them back to their own staffs and order them to seek out the answers to the riddle Nathan had presented them with.

This unorthodox means of gathering military intelligence on friendly forces was not a one-way street. Despite his need to deal with the trauma of his loss, Nathan was able to pick up and piece together little tidbits of information that each of the senior officers who accosted him left behind, allowing him to formulate not only a general idea of how the military establishment in Washington felt about Operation Pacific Shield but what they were considering. Most of the clues were found in innocent, seemingly in-consequential statements. Other answers to what the future held in store for Nathan were quite obvious, such as when the commanding general of the Tenth Mountain Division buttonholed Nathan and asked him point-blank what he needed to do in order to prepare his people for their deployment to the Philippines. As a man known throughout the Army for his directness, the general re-peatedly poked Nathan in the chest as he spoke. "I don't want my people to stumble into the sort of thing that your B Company did," he explained as he did everything he could in an effort to extract something of value from Na-than.

News concerning the disaster that befell Noel Cameron only served to add to the pall Nathan was already laboring under. It added to the misgivings that he perceived were beginning to permeate the Army's senior leadership in re-gards to the wisdom of launching Pacific Shield. It didn't require a great deal of imagination on his part to figure out what had gone down in the Phillipines. Having faced simi-lar tactical situations himself both as a platoon leader in Iraq as well as the current operation on Mindanao, Nathan understood how easy it was to be blindsided by an enemy that was just as determined and just as skillful in the an-cient art of killing as his Rangers were. Nor did he have to guess how Delmont would respond. Long before they had even set foot on the ground in the Philippines Nathan had come to the conclusion that Delmont was the sort of com-manding officer who had but two rules when it came to failure. Number one was that failure in any endeavor to which his name was attached was unacceptable, period. And should failure actually dare rear its ugly head, rule number two demanded that he find someone else to blame. Since he had been on the far side of the world and his company had no part in the calamity that befell Company B, Nathan knew he had nothing to worry about there. Noel Cameron, or more correctly his good name and reputation on the other hand, would be fair game when it came time for Delmont to explain how one of the nation's premier combat units had managed to allow itself to be decimated by a lightly armed foe that was living hand to mouth.

That he could do nothing to alter the strained command environment in which he had to operate was a cold fact Nathan accepted. So long as Delmont managed to avoid making a serious blunder that would force his superiors to intervene into the internal affairs of the 3rd of the 75th Nathan and the other company commanders would have to carry on as best they could, watching their backs while doing their damnedest to carry out a mission that was on the fast track to becoming something of an albatross around the Army's collective neck. Alone in the nylon jump seats of the Air Force transport Nathan knew in the days ahead the only option open to him was to exercise great care when it came to deciding which battles to fight in the ongoing clash of personalities that was becoming more important than the one involving an illusive foe his company had yet to meet in battle.

CENTRAL MINDANAO, PHILIPPINES

Success on the field of battle can create as many problems for the victor as it does the vanquished. Hamdani Summirat knew this, allowing him to be more than ready to deal with his subordinates when he gathered them together to discuss their future operations. As he expected

Hassan Rum was the most outspoken of his lieutenants. It was this character trait, Rum's readiness to stand up and question Summirat's decisions that made him such a valuable deputy. Rum challenged him, forcing him to think everything through and defend his decisions in a manner that left no doubt when he was finished that the course of action he was advocating was both correct and the wisest. That evening's council proved to be no exception.

"You are a trained military man," Hassan Rum exclaimed as he thrust his arm out toward Summirat who sat opposite him. "The failure to exploit a victory, to run your enemy to ground when he is off balance is the greatest mistake a commander can make. Now is the time to hit them hard," Rum shouted as he pounded his clenched fist on the table with a force that knocked over cups of water, scattering streams of water about the tabletop.

Summirat's only response to this unexpected interruption was to lift his forearms up off the table and lean back in his seat, crossing them loosely against his chest. With a bemused smile he watched his key subordinates, men who were all hardcore veterans of many a desperate fight frantically scarf up notebooks, maps, and stray papers to save them from becoming soaked, behaving more like a gaggle of government bureaucrats than the fearsome warriors they were. For a fleeting moment he could almost imagine these same men ten years hence, seated about a highly polished table in a government conference room gathered to discuss trivial issues facing the Islamic republic they were struggling to cobble together from parts of the Philippines and Indonesia.

The reality that faced them and the decision they would have to piece together quickly replaced this ethereal vision. Rather than waste any additional time speculating about the future Summirat used this unexpected interruption to frame his response to Rum's call for immediate and decisive action.

Hamdani Summirat was having difficulty with the choice

of what next was an issue. Though he was the undisputed leader within his faction of the Abu Sayyaf, he could not rule by simple fiat. He had no real means of compelling the unquestioning loyalty of those who followed him. The people surrounding him were there because they believed in their cause and they believed in his ability to make it a reality. By the very nature of their movement they were after all operating outside every known system of laws and governance. Only after they secured a victory by replacing the government of Mindanao with their own would the Abu Sayyaf be free to create the illusion of legitimacy. Until that day they were little more than a band of outlaws, one whose code of conduct was little different from that of a pack of wolves, a code that demanded that the alpha wolf jealously defend his authority. Summirat could not ignore the views and opinions of his most trusted lieutenants. To do so would risk alienating the very men he would soon be depending upon to carry out the most hazardous part of his grand strategy.

When all were once more settled and ready to return their full attention to the matters at hand Summirat picked up where they had left off, taking care to avoid any puddles that remained. "The question of how best to exploit our recent success on the battlefield is an issue that I have been struggling with. As a trained professional soldier my instincts tell me that we need to guard against becoming carried away by the wave of enthusiasm that one victory has created among our followers. Even here," he stated in an even voice as he locked eyes with Rum, "among veteran fighters such as yourselves it is proving difficult to suppress the urge to press home an advantage that is in reality illusory."

Pausing, Summirat scanned the faces around the table as they took in his statement. He could tell that some were surprised to hear him describe the decimation of an American Ranger company an illusion. A few were visibly angered. "But suppress it we must," Summirat stated as he continued with an even tone. "The truth of the matter is that we have done little more than inflict a pinprick upon our foe."

Ricardo Sukandar, a man who had cut his teeth fighting the American military in Afghanistan and was responsible for engineering the ambush of Company B was unable to hold his tongue. "A pinprick? You call what we did a pinprick? That is an insult!"

Rather than being upset, Summirat smiled as he shook his head. "The beast we fight is like the elephant standing before the three blind men. None of them can grasp just how large the creature is. Each believes he understands the nature of the beast, but they don't."

"And you do?" Sukandar shot back.

"We killed and wounded how many Americans? Thirty-six? Forty? How long would it take us to replace that number of our best fighters if we lost them in a single battle? Three months? Six?"

No one answered, for all knew that the six hundred who formed the corps strike force were all but irreplaceable, men like Sukandar and Summirat who had cut their teeth in far-off battlefields like Iraq, Afghanistan, and Chechnya. "The Americans can replace each and every one of those men within a matter of days, even hours if they felt the need to. We do not have that luxury."

Having effectively silenced Sukandar, Summirat picked up where he had left off. "We do not have the ability to strike a killing blow. What we do have is the ability to break the will of their political leadership by simply surviving. They will tire of chasing shadows."

"But can we survive?" Rum countered. "Can we hold our own men together and maintain our hold on what we have won without striking out at our enemies?"

"Dear friends, you misunderstand me. I do not intend to roll over and play dead or hide in the jungle waiting for the day when the Americans go home. We shall continue with our programs of harassment and quick strikes until a favorable opportunity presents itself."

"And I suppose it is up to you to determine what those

conditions are?" Sukandar sneered in what was little more than an open challenge to Summirat's authority.

Narrowing his eyes for a moment, Summirat glared at Sukandar. "Until such time as another takes my place, yes."

FORWARD OPERATIONS BASE DETROIT, MINDANAO, PHILIPPINES

Even before Delmont's operations officer stood up to brief the staff of JTF Sierra's ground component command it was clear that Colonel Tim Lamb was agitated. His own operations officer, a Marine major who had served with Lamb on numerous occasions saw that all the telltale signs of a pending eruption were present. It always started with him fidgeting, either squirming about in his seat or tapping the toe of his right boot while drumming the fingers of his right hand in double quick time on his thigh. Normally staff officers familiar with Lamb would pick up on his departure from the laid-back attitude he normally assumed during briefings of this sort and took care to make sure that they were not the source of Lamb's irritation. In those cases when the hapless briefer pressed on, next came the twisting of the colonel's head during which he all but refused to look at the officer standing before him. This was the briefer's last chance to stop and ask the obvious question, which of course was, "Sir, is there something wrong?"

Unfortunately Major Lawrence Perry, the operations officer for the 3rd of the 75th Rangers, was unschooled in the idiosyncrasies of the man charged with overseeing the ground component of JTF Sierra and had not been afforded an opportunity to observe them firsthand during previous briefings. Blissfully unaware of the indicators that his briefing was not going down well with Lamb, Perry pressed on. Of course even if he had been cognizant of the warning signs Lamb was giving off he would not have been at liberty to alter either the manner with which he was delivering his briefing or the material he was charged with presenting. For Perry had a devil of his own that he dare not ignore, one who posed a far greater danger to Perry's career than a mere colonel in the Marines. Despite being a field-grade officer, a graduate of the Army's Command and General Staff College, and pegged as an up-and-comer himself, Perry did not have the freedom to deviate from the briefing notes he had no hand in preparing. To do so would have incurred the wrath of the man who had written them for him, Robert Delmont himself. Perhaps he would not have been nailed right then and there by his battalion commander, right in front of the combined staff of the ground component, but sooner or later Perry knew Delmont would find out, leading him to rip Perry's head or some other precious part of his anatomy off before handing it back to him. On that fact he could make book.

So Perry droned on and on with all the enthusiasm of a well-rehearsed marionette until Lamb could take it no more. Without uttering a sound he leapt to his feet, glaring at Perry with eyes that glowed like hot burning embers as he snorted like a bull preparing to charge home. In stunned silence the assembled commanders and staffs watched as Lamb stood before a dumbstruck Perry, waiting for the Marine colonel to rip the hapless Army major a new one. Fortunately for the forlorn Ranger, Tim Lamb managed to hold his rage in check. Instead of castigating Perry in a manner that would have made a Paris Island drill sergeant proud, Lamb turned toward Delmont. "Colonel," he whispered in a tone that belied the fury that filled him, "a word with you outside."

Making no effort to camouflage the indignation he felt at being treated in this way, Delmont slowly rose to his feet while keeping his eyes firmly fixed on Lamb's. Without another word the two senior officers stormed out of the forward operations base command post and into the hot, humid tropical night.

When he had gone as far as he cared to and giving no

consideration as to who might be in earshot of them, Lamb came to a dead stop, spun about and ripped into Delmont. "If you don't mind, *colonel,* could you please tell me where in the hell you've been for the past week?"

Barely able to contain his own anger Delmont did not trust himself to respond to Lamb's sarcastic question. Instead he chose to stand his ground, nose to nose with the furious Marine colonel charged with the responsibility of overseeing all ground operations.

When he saw that Delmont was not going to respond to his challenge, Lamb continued. "What part of my latest directive did you and your staff not understand? Don't you appreciate just how much the tactical situation on the ground has changed? We've lost the initiative to our friends out there. The cat and mouse game we've been playing with them just doesn't hack it anymore. We need to come up with something a bit more dynamic than wandering about this shit hole of an island, hoping that we stumble upon their main force units."

When Lamb paused in order to allow Delmont to respond, Delmont took a moment to draw in a deep breath before doing so. "That's not how I see it, sir," he stated in as calm a voice as he could manage. "In my opinion the tactical situation we face today has not fundamentally changed. As regrettable as the incident involving Company B was, the concept of operations with which we began this campaign is still sound. General Palmer, deputy chief of staff for Special Operations at DA concurs with me on that point."

Lamb had long suspected that Delmont had been routinely bypassing the normal chain of command by speaking directly to his people back in the Pentagon. It was a curse of modern communications that allowed maverick subordinates like Delmont to skip over the heads of their immediate superior and appeal to a higher authority, a curse that Lamb could do little to prevent short of sending in a detachment of his Marines with orders to rip every radio and phone out of Delmont's command bunker. Not that he hadn't given that idea more than a passing thought. What Lamb could do, what he was well within his rights to do, was to demand that each and every officer under him complied with his orders regardless of who they knew or how well connected they were to the powers that be.

Stepping even closer Lamb thrust his entire head forward, forcing Delmont to take a step back. "Now you listen up and you listen good, Lieutenant Colonel Delmont. You will march right back to your CP with your staff in tow where you will draft a plan of operations that conforms to the planning guidance I issued to you yesterday. You will not deviate from any of the instructions contained therein. You will not draft any supplemental orders or contingencies that deviate in any way from the orders published by my headquarters. You or any of your subordinates will not undertake any sort of operation outside the perimeter of this FOB without first seeking my personal approval. And you will personally present your revised plan at oh-seven-hundred hours tomorrow morning aboard the *Wake Island* to me, my staff, and Admiral Turner. Is that clear?"

In the darkness it was difficult to see Lamb's eyes even at this range. That however was not necessary. Delmont realized that he had overplayed his hand, that it was time for him to pull in his horns and for the moment become a team player. Taking another step back he came to attention, saluted, and gave a crisp, "Yes, sir," in a manner that left little doubt in Lamb's mind that there wasn't an ounce of respect or deference in either gesture.

Without further ado, Delmont spun about in the mud and began to stalk away until Lamb called out. "I have been informed Captain Dixon will be back in country tomorrow." This caused Delmont to stop short. "Though it is against my grain to dictate how a subordinate employs his assets to accomplish an assigned task," Lamb continued, "in this case I am going to make an exception to policy. In my professional opinion it was a mistake to assign your most junior officer such a critical task, one which we cannot afford to make again. So be sure that any plan you come up with puts Dixon and his company back out on point. Is that clear?"

Enraged at being dictated to like an errant second lieutenant in this manner Delmont dug his fingernails into the palms of his hands. "Very clear, sir."

DAVAO, MINDANAO, PHILIPPINES

The excuse Emmett DeWitt used to fly up to Daao with the covey of helicopters to police up Nathan and replacements for the battalion was flimsy at best. Any one of his NCOs together with the B Company first sergeant were more than capable of handling the simple chore of gathering up the new men and their equipment, breaking them down into ten-man caulks, and loading them into the helicopters. DeWitt however felt the need to fill his friend and fellow officer in on what had transpired in his absence. He also wanted to question Nathan in private as to what the prevailing attitude was concerning JTF Sierra.

For his part Nathan was glad to see his longtime friend and comrade in misery standing at the base of the ramp as he and his fellow passengers tromped out of the dark, cavernous maul of the C-17 transport and into the glaring bright tropical sunlight. For the first time in days Nathan managed to smile as he reached out and grasped DeWitt's waiting hand. "God, I've almost managed to forget just how ugly you were," Nathan shouted loud enough to cause some of the Rangers flowing around the pair of captains to stare at them askew.

While still shaking Nathan's hand DeWitt pulled him closer so he could speak over the noise of the jet transports that surrounded them without yelling. "How's Chris?"

Pulling away, Nathan flashed a broad smile. "Pregnant!"

Taken aback by this announcement, DeWitt shook his

head. "Good God, man. How the hell did you manage that? You've only been gone for twelve days."

"Not even I'm that good. The best we can figure is that her current condition is the result of our farewell romp before we shipped out on this goat rope they call an operation."

"Speaking of that," DeWitt stated in a more somber tone as he let go of Nathan's hand and shepherded him off to one side. In a flash the grin left Nathan's face as he realized that the purpose of DeWitt's presence was more than an effort to escape the stifling atmosphere of battalion headquarters and greet him.

When he judged that they were far enough from everyone else DeWitt stopped and faced Nathan. "Man, if you think that things within the battalion were bad before I'm afraid you're in for something of a shock."

Crossing his arms, Nathan took a moment to study the worried expression that distorted his friend's face. "That bad, huh?"

"Lamb has had it up to here with our colonel. Last night, when Perry was laying out Delmont's latest master plan to him, Lamb stopped the whole thing midstride and marched Delmont out of the bunker for a little one-on-one, me Tarzan you Jane speech."

Knowing Delmont's penchant for taking things out on his staff, Nathan winced. "Ouch. I'll bet you guys felt that one."

"That isn't the half of it, Nate. You know how we captains always debated the wisdom of throwing one of the companies into the wilds of this island to run about chasing shadows, and how some of you thought the real purpose was not to find the insurgents but rather to allow them to find you?"

Believing he knew what was coming but not sure if he wanted to have it confirmed, Nathan braced himself for what he suspected was coming next. "Go on."

"Well, my friend, it's official. Since we've been unable to sniff out anything resembling a base of operations or track down anything resembling a core unit that we can engage, our whole plan of operation now relies on luring them to us."

"Cat and mouse," Nathan mused. "Toss a bit of cheese out on the floor and wait for the mouse to muster up the courage to dart out after it."

"Yeah," DeWitt affirmed glumly. "Something like that."

"And who's been tagged to serve as the cheese to lure our illusive rodents? Overton and C Company?"

"That was the original plan, until Lamb directed Delmont during their little tête-à-tête that the only way he would buy off on this high-risk strategy was if you and your company were the one sent out to tempt our neighborhood jihadist out into the open."

Taking a moment Nathan stared up at the sky a moment. "God, it's hell being popular," he finally sighed. "I wonder what General Dwyer is going to say when it comes time for Colonel Lamb to brief him on this aspect of our operation?"

Confused by Nathan's reference to the commanding general of the Tenth Mountain Division, DeWitt gave his friend and fellow officer a quizzical glance. "What's he got to do with this?"

Lowering his gaze, Nathan smiled. "My man, I've just returned from Olympus where I rubbed shoulders with the gods."

"We're being replaced by the Tenth Mountain?"

"That seems to be the way things are shaking out, provided they don't pull the plug on the whole shebang before that."

"When will that decision be made?"

"Soon, I expect," Nathan stated flatly. "It seems someone finally woke up to the fact that this battalion is far too valuable an asset to waste running around this shit hole."

DeWitt placed his hands on his hips and looked over at the replacements who were busy sorting out their gear.

Shaking his head he lamented. "Too bad it took the loss of Noel and a fair chunk of his company to drive that message home."

"The chief of staff was already beginning to lean in that direction before I left."

"You think?"

A dark shadow clouded Nathan's face as he leaned forward a bit and looked down at the toes of his boots in order to keep DeWitt from seeing his eyes water up. "That's what my dad was doing out here, sniffing about on behalf of the Chief of Staff."

There was a moment of silence as both men pondered this thought. Finally, DeWitt reached out and placed his right hand on Nathan's shoulder. "Hey, Nate. That means your father's death wasn't in vain. He died as a soldier."

Nathan glanced up into his friend's eyes. He wanted to say something or at least acknowledge DeWitt's effort to lessen the sting he felt at the loss of his father. But the wound was still too fresh to be eased with a simple gesture. The best Nathan could manage was a quick nod of his head before turning toward the replacements who were now lined up and ready to board the waiting choppers. "Guess we better get going and claim our spots before all the good seats are taken."

Realizing that his friend didn't care to discuss the matter any further DeWitt gave Nathan a friendly shake. "Yeah. Once more unto the breech, dear friend."

22

The changes Nathan noticed right off were due to more than the relocation of the FOB. The routine, almost lackadaisical manner that had become endemic within the confines of the previous FOBs was gone. In its place was a true sense of urgency, tainted by a hint of nervousness made more acute no doubt by the growing tensions between the senior leadership that DeWitt had warned Nathan of. Soldiers needed to be confident in their leadership. They needed to believe that the people who were issuing the orders that would place them in harm's way had their act together, that the operations they were being sent out on were based on well thought-out plans that would get the job done, but would do so without subjecting them to undue or unnecessary risk.

There was more than just the demeanor of the troops he saw that colored Nathan's thinking as he took in the sights and sounds around him. It was one that Nathan was only vaguely aware of. The death of his father and its aftermath had an impact upon him that he was only now beginning to comprehend. His failure to fully absorb the shock associated with that trauma and effectively sort out his own personal and family issues were keeping him from slipping back into his comfortable and familiar role as a company commander. Rather than picking up where he had left off, Nathan found himself viewing the people and activities around him as if he were little more than a visitor, someone totally disassociated from them and their mission. It was a dangerous state of affairs, particularly since Nathan refused to acknowledge that this was a problem at all.

One thing he was able to focus his attention on was the new tactical reality he was about to face and the role he and his company would play in it. This only served to accentuate the air of unreality with which he was viewing the activities around him and his response to them. As an American officer the idea of using his entire company as little more than a lure to draw out a very capable and determined foe was alien to him. It went against everything he believed in. Placing one's self in harm's way was one thing. Tromping about in hostile country with a "Hit Me" sign pinned to the back of each and every man in his command was quite another. As with most truly important matters with which he had to deal, Nathan chose not to confide in anyone but opted instead to keep his own counsel until he had devised a feasible solution.

Having heard the covey of inbound choppers, the staff of the 3rd of the 75th Rangers was waiting for Nathan when he entered the command bunker. Nathan paused at the entrance. In part he needed to give his eyes a few seconds to adjust to the dark interior. This also gave him an opportunity to survey who was present and assess their demeanor. It came as no surprise that the bunker was sparsely manned. Those who were present, either standing about before the operations and intel maps hung along the entire length of one wall or seated at folding tables cluttered by phones, radios, computer monitors and the ever-present stacks of paper that are the hallmark of an ops center, represented the absolute bare-bones minimum required to keep the place functioning.

The one person he did not see was his battalion commander. Instinctively he glanced over to the corner of the crammed room where the cubbyhole that served as Delmont's office was always located. Without having to be asked Major Castalane, the battalion XO, answered the question that was giving Nathan pause. "The colonel is aboard the *Wake Island* attending a briefing by the admiral's staff concerning our next jump. Major Perry and I will brief you on the current situation and what's expected of your company."

Nathan looked over at Major Perry, the battalion operations officer who gave him a sly wink. So, Nathan thought to himself as he made his way to where the pair of majors were standing, this is the way we're going to play it.

Having no desire to deal with a subordinate he disliked but was saddled with until such time as he could manufacture a suitable reason to have him relieved or reassigned, Delmont had opted to attend a briefing concerning routine logistical matters that was usually handled by the XO, leaving the responsibility of issuing the operations order for the next foray into the interior, something he normally did himself, to Castalane and Perry. For Nathan this was something of a gift from the gods, for at the moment he was in no mood to play mind games with a man he had come to despise. Taking up his spot between the XO and the ops officer, the trio exchanged strained pleasantries while they waited for the battalion intel officer to gather up his notes and join them. When everyone was ready Castalane clapped his hands together as he turned toward the maps on the wall. "Okay, sports fans, today's nightmare looks something like this."

The irreverent tone of Castalane's comments were in stark contrast to the stern, almost stifling manner Delmont demanded of his staff when he was present. It was a change that put Nathan's mind at ease for it demonstrated that the battalion's number-two and -three men had not been beaten down into total submission by their superior's imperious manner, that they were still officers who could be relied upon to run interference for the line company commanders at the battalion command post if the situation required them to.

While the briefing Nathan received was quite informal, it was thorough and very illuminating. It filled in the blanks that had been left by the brief overview of the new concept that DeWitt had given to Nathan at the airfield outside Davao. For the most part Nathan was responsible for carrying on operations as he had before. "We know you've not been able to show any results," Perry stated glumly in the course of his discussion. "And we don't expect that will change anytime soon. What we need you to do however, is to lull the other people into thinking we've not changed anything."

"Of course that won't be true," Castalane added. "The change will be how we go about finding the bastards."

"Noel didn't die in vain," Perry stated solemnly. "It woke folks back at Pacific Command and I imagine DoD that we needed more sophisticated intelligence-gathering assets than they had initially allocated to this operation."

"You may or may not be aware of this," Castalane stated, "but Pacific Shield has been running on a shoestring. CENTCOM pretty much has a monopoly on all the gee-whiz high-tech stuff for their operations in Southwest Asia."

"Until now," Perry chimed in as he took up where the XO left off. "In addition to being allocated a number of Predator and Global Hawk UAVs to cover you while you're out there in the bush, we've been assured that we're going to have access to whatever surveillance platform we feel we need and can effectively employ. Even the Marines are willing to let us use some of those tiny UAVs they've been toying with. The idea is to track the trackers. We know every move you make while your company out there is watched, if not by Abu Sayyaf themselves, then by locals sympathetic to their cause. If we can track their flow of information, link by link, we think we have a decent chance of finding targets that are of value."

"That's going to take time," Nathan stated after giving the matter a moment's thought. "Do you think we'll be able to show any results from this before the Tenth Mountain takes over from us?"

Confused by Nathan's question, Castalane and Perry glanced at each other quizzically before Castalane leaned forward toward Nathan. "The Tenth Mountain is taking over from us?"

Having assumed that they already knew, Nathan had seen no harm in letting that little snippet of information slip out. Backpedaling in an effort to cover his tracks, Nathan mumbled that he had heard rumors that mentioned the Tenth.

Reminded by this comment of where Nathan had just come from and who he had been associating with the pair of majors both huddled close to Nathan in a most conspiratorial manner. "What else did you hear while you were back home?" Castalane asked.

Having no desire to lie to these officers, men whom he would need to depend upon to keep Delmont off his back, Nathan told them everything that he knew, including the fact that there was the very real possibility that the whole operation could very well be terminated. "It's common knowledge that the Army is stretched beyond the breaking point," Nathan explained. "Though no one told me this in so many words General Jones is under a lot of pressure to pull the plug on this operation. I imagine that the reason we're getting the sort of resources you two are talking about is that he's been given an ultimatum by the Sec Def. Show some results or close this sideshow down."

The officers gathered in the tight little knot about the maps all took a moment to consider what it would mean to them if the battalion was withdrawn from the Philippines with nothing to show for their efforts except a stunning defeat at the hands of a group of insurgents who were considered little more than bit players in the national war on terror. Not only would it reflect badly upon the battalion as a whole, a thought that could not be ignored, but the very idea of having to live with a failure like this with the sort of battalion commander they had was appalling. Professionally none of them would survive the ensuing massacre as Delmont took his revenge upon each and every one of them through poor evaluations and an even harsher command environment.

Straightening up, Castalane, Perry, Nathan, and the intel officer looked about the room as each man pondered what, if anything, they could do to prevent such a cataclysmic end to Operation Pacific Shield. After a moment Nathan turned to Castalane. "Can you pry up some of those discretionary funds the JTF staff is hording before my company moves out?"

Castalane gave Nathan a puzzled look. "I'm pretty sure I can. Why? What do you want to use them for?"

"We, the battalion, could be long gone before the UAVs and other platforms to gather up the sort of detailed picture needed to generate a decent target list arrive. Isn't that so?" he asked, turning to the intelligence officer.

Glumly, the young captain nodded. "I'm afraid so. It'll be like putting together a jigsaw puzzle in a dark room."

"I have an idea of how we can kick-start the process," Nathan announced.

Anxious for anything resembling a solution, Castalane and Perry shot each other a glance and in unison announced, "We're all ears."

There wasn't a man in Company A who was not pleased to see their company commander standing before them, ready to conduct his precombat inspection as the ground and air crews of the UH-60s that would be taking them back out for the first time in over two weeks went about performing their preflight preparations. Even Eric White was glad to be off the *Wake Island* and back on shore, geared up and ready to go back out into the bush. He knew he'd miss the meals, the clean bunks, and the daily showers. Only a complete moron or a really twisted fool would deny that. Enjoying simple creature comforts like that are something all combat soldiers dream of. But it is not what White and those gathered about him joined the Army for or endured the rigors of Ranger training to achieve. They were the rarest of combat soldiers, men who became antsy when times were too good and things were too easy.

Besides, they had a score to settle with the Abu Sayyaf. Each man in Nathan's company felt a twinge of guilt about what had happened to their comrades in Company B. Each knew that had things been just a little different, had their company commander stayed with them rather than being pulled out of the field, it would have been they, and not Noel Cameron's people, who would had suffered. This realization created something of a blood feud within the ranks of Company A, a feeling that it was their sacred duty to revenge the deaths of their fellow Rangers. Some of the NCOs like White's squad leader, even used this as he steeled his men for their next trip into the interior. "There will be no slacking off," he growled as he slowly paraded back and forth before his assembled squad while they waited for their commanding officer to make his way to them. "I'll personally cut the nuts off the first swinging Richard that screws up out there." As Staff Sergeant Henry Jones passed before him uttering these words, White looked into his squad leader's eyes. Instinctively he understood that this man was sincere, that his words were more than an expression of the rage he felt, a burning anger that could only be extinguished with blood. It was a chilling thought, one that White was not only beginning to understand, but shared. Nameless and faceless people, people he had no reason to hate before, would need to pay for the deaths of soldiers who were no different from him.

Sanguine sentiments, such as those expressed by Jones and felt by White, while useful when it came time to whip up the enthusiasm before a pending operation, had to be kept in check. Nathan and every officer and sergeant in his company who had served in Iraq and Afghanistan appreciated this. They knew from experience that troops bent on revenge could be dangerous, particularly when engaging a foe who was indistinguishable from the populace they would be moving through. The deaths of civilians in war, euphemistically referred to as collateral damage, are as unfortunate as they are unavoidable. Creating a command environment that fosters those sorts of mistakes is a crime. So Nathan took great pains as he was issuing his operations order to emphasize that no effort was to be spared in enforcing the rules of engagement under which they labored. "We're all anxious to extract our pound of flesh from these bastards," he warned. "No one more than I. But we must make sure that the carcass we butcher belongs to someone who deserves it and not some innocent schlub who just happened to be in the wrong place at the wrong time." Every man who heard those words took them to heart, for they expected that their commanding officer had more justification than every one of them combined to extract a measure of revenge from the people they were hunting.

When all the preliminaries were finished and the appointed time arrived, Company A broke down into small groups and headed for the waiting choppers. As they had so many times before, the Rangers charged headlong into the whirling mass of wind and dust thrown up by the massive blades, scrambling aboard their assigned aircraft. Without having to be told or directed, they found their place and settled in for the ride.

This is always a strange time, a time when a soldier, though he is crammed together with his comrades while they are being carried into harm's way, is free to pass the time however he pleases. Most let their minds wander freely as they look out the open door, allowing it to lie upon any stray thought that just happens to pop into their head as they enjoy the scenery below. Inevitably one or two men in every stick manages to block out the roar of turbine engines and the steady beating of blades and nod off, catching up on sleep that soldiers always seem to be in need of. A few, too fired up with anticipation as well as a healthy dose of adrenaline fidget with their personal gear or their weapon. Even Nathan managed to snatch a few moments of blissful peace as the swarm of Blackhawks shattered the morning calm and announced to all who heard them that the Americans were coming, again.

All of this came too an abrupt end the instant the pilot of the lead chopper turned to Nathan and announced, "Five minutes." Whatever serenity the Rangers of Company A had managed to find during the short flight out disappeared into thin air like the morning mist. All thoughts were now focused on the next few minutes. Muscles tightened as every man prepared to propel himself and the load he carried from the confines of his chopper back onto terra firma. It was a well-honed drill, one that most Rangers could execute while half asleep. No one however could find it within themselves to become complacent at moments like this, for each assault landing was unique, presenting everyone with a situation that had to be assessed and acted upon on the fly.

For White this was a simple task. All he had to do was follow Bannon, the SAW gunner he carried ammo for, and make sure that when Bannon went to ground he found a spot as close to him as possible that provided cover while allowing him the freedom to feed ammo to Bannon. The only drawback to this was that Bannon, being quite human, always did his best to find a dry spot of ground that allowed him to cover his assigned sector of responsibility. With his attention riveted to finding such a spot for himself Bannon seldom had time to do the same for his assistant gunner, White. On occasion this presented something of a problem for the young Ranger, forcing him to decide on whether to seek cover farther away from Bannon than the tactical situation dictated or suck it up down onto a muddy patch of ground. On this day White opted to do the manly thing and plop down in the pile of mud Bannon had taken such care to avoid.

Even before his elbows oozed through what he had

thought was mud and make contact with firmer soil beneath it, White realized that he had made a most dreadful mistake. The stench of the massive pile of dung he was settling into assaulted his nose, causing him to gag as he scrambled to push himself up onto his knees. Not realizing what White's problem was, Staff Sergeant Henry Jones glanced over at White as he was running to find his platoon leader and took a moment to lift his right foot, plant the sole of his boot squarely in White's back, and push him forward, yelling, "Get your sorry ass down, Ranger," as he did so.

Once more White's body hit the dung heap with a resounding squish, causing Bannon to turn toward his assistant gunner and grimace. "Jesus Christ, White. Don't splatter that shit on me!"

Utterly defeated and thoroughly nauseated, it took every ounce of White's willpower to roll over on his side, away from both the dung heap and Bannon. Twisting his head to one side, he let loose with a stream of vomit that shot forth from his mouth like a fountain. This commotion caused both Specialist Anthony Park and Bryan Pulaski to look over to where White was spewing. Pulaski, who was on the other side of Park and away from White, could only see the fountain of vomit. When he finally pushed himself up onto his elbows Pulaski began to howl. "Wow, dude! That's awesome!"

Park's response was quite different. Being closer to White, Park scrambled out of the way, lest he become splattered by Whites gastronomic ejaculate. With his attention focused on the open ground before him, Bannon's first inclination that there was a problem with the one man in the squad he was responsible for was Pulaski's exclamation. When he turned to see what the problem was, all he could see was White's back as White convulsed on the ground beside him. Without hesitation Bannon yelled out for help. "Medic!"

In a flash a dozen sets of eyes turned to the spot where White lay, quickly followed by a scramble as Sergeant

First Class Frederick Smart beat feet to the stricken Ranger, shouting for Keith Stone the medic with his platoon, as he went. Though both men reached White at the same instant it took Stone, intent on finding where White was wounded to realize what had happened. Smart put two and two together in a flash, pulling back in disgust as he did so. "Jesus H. Christ. You stupid bastard. You scared the living hell out of me."

Still reeling from throwing up his breakfast as well as every drop of vile fluid his stomach held White was unable to respond. Together the two men who had rushed to his aid rose to their feet without taking their eyes off of the unfortunate soul before them. Turning to Stone, Smart shook his head. "See if there is anything you can do for the dumb bastard."

Stone shook his head. "Unless someone has got a portable shower in their rucksack there isn't a damned thing I can do for him."

Though sympathetic to the fact that he was ordering Stone to remain with a man covered in shit and help him, Smart didn't relent. Placing his hand on Stone's shoulder, Smart gave the medic a friendly pat. "Humor me." With that, Smart beat a hasty retreat to where the air was untainted by the stench of freshly stirred water buffalo shit.

As it turned out White's misfortune was the only difficulty Company A encountered that day. A ten-minute break near a pond later in the afternoon allowed White the opportunity to clean some of the dung from his uniform and his gear but did nothing to rid him of the horrific stench that hung over him like a cloud. By nightfall every man in the squad was referring to White by the new nickname Bannon had coined, "Duppie."

In accordance with Nathan's orders Company A broke up into three platoon-sized columns upon leaving the landing zone. Each followed a prescribed route as it openly marched through the countryside during the balance of the morning and all afternoon. The plan that had been briefed to the company as a whole was that the platoons would converge after nightfall at a designated spot where it would establish a patrol base, marking this operation as no different from any of the other operations Company A had carried out since arriving in the Philippines. It was only after the sun had set and the Third Platoon was passing through a particularly dense patch of jungle that anyone in First Squad realized that there was to be a difference this time around. Without so much as a word Smart stepped out of the line of march and into the jungle. In quick succession he reached out and tapped each of his men as they filed past him, indicating that they were to follow suit. When he had collected all of his people, Smart signaled for them to settle down as they waited for the Third Squad to pass them by.

Not knowing what was going on but realizing that something was up each of them settled in as best they could as they watched the remainder of the platoon file by and disappear in the jungle. A couple of men, expecting that they would follow or move out to another location, began to rise up. Smart immediately put a stop to this. "Stand fast," he hissed as he eased farther back into the jungle and away from the trail. In an instant the mental fog that had collectively settled over the platoon dispersed as each man came to appreciate that something was up. Slowly, silently, they shifted their weapons from the comfortable carry position up and to the ready, resting their thumbs on the safety while taking care not to wrap their index finger about the trigger.

Impatiently the Rangers of First Squad crouched beside the trail, waiting for Smart's next order. With nothing better to do each man began to speculate on what their next move would be. They didn't have all that long to wait. Park, who had been taking up the rear of the squad column heard the approaching footsteps first. Using hand signals he alerted the rest of the squad. Smart responded by ordering his men to lay low, again using nothing but hand signals. This did not prevent each of his men from training the muzzle of their weapons at the stretch of trail before them, following the trio of dark figures that made their way along it as they came into sight. From where he lay White could clearly see that all three were attired in civilian clothing. Each clutched an AK at the ready. It took a second for each to appreciate that for the first time in his life he was literally in the presence of his enemies. Had he wanted to he could have reached out with his hand and touched each of the shadowy figures. To have done so of course would have been foolish. Besides, White was doing all he could to keep what little content he had left in his stomach from bubbling up and out, again.

On either side of him other members of the squad who had seen action in Iraq immediately understood why Smart had pulled them out of the line of march. He knew they were being followed and had laid an impromptu ambush, one that was about to become their first effective ambush since deploying to the Philippines. It therefore came as something of a shock when Smart failed to give the order to fire but instead, remained silent and motionless as the trio of insurgents disappeared along the trail headed in the same direction the rest of Third Platoon had traveled earlier. Only when he was sure they were long gone did he stir. When he did he moved onto the trail, signaling the rest of the squad to follow suit.

Once more the veterans of the First Squad assumed they knew what they were about to do. And once more Smart befuddled them by doing something they did not expect. Instead of signaling them to pursue the armed strangers who were stalking the rest of the platoon, Smart pointed them in the opposite direction. Without a word he took the lead, moving out at a brisk pace away from everyone.

It was well past midnight before he finally reached a spot where he could call a halt. In whispers he ordered the squad to pair up, form a tight perimeter and settle down. "Every other man awake. Switch off every hour." Turning to Jones, White's squad leader, Smart told him to catch some sleep. "I'll take first watch." With that, the First Squad settled down for a fitful rest. Only Bannon found it difficult to comply, stuck as he was with a buddy who literally smelled like shit.

It was thirty minutes before dawn when Smart roused the squad and ordered them to prepare to move out. As the exhausted Rangers stretched and gathered themselves up for a new day Smart pulled Jones off to one side. After giving him detailed instructions as to what was expected of him Smart divided the squad, sending half with Jones while leading the rest away and in a different direction. They kept going until just after sunrise when they came upon a small patch of woods not far from a well-traveled dirt road. Realizing that it was pointless to speculate as to why they were there or what was going to happen next, the five men with Smart settled down into the positions he assigned to each of them before digging out an MRE and tearing into it. Even White, still smelling like fresh manure, managed to choke down a full MRE before Smart decided it was time to fill them in on what they were about to do.

Gathering Bannon, White, Pulaski, Park, and PFC Washington into a tight cluster about him Smart laid out the plan their company commander had cooked up with the battalion staff. "We're to lay low here until noon. Shortly after that we're to waylay the first fair-sized truck that happens along and commandeer it."

Bannon gave Smart a worried look. "What if the driver isn't cooperative? Do we use force?"

Smart grinned as he reached into his breast pocket and pulled out a roll of money. "No, we use something better."

"Okay, so we have a truck. What do we do with it?"

As he stuffed the money back in his pocket, Smart yawned. "We pull it off the road, park it, and wait."

"For what?" chimed Park.

"For Captain Dixon to show up." Standing, Smart pointed across the farm fields that lay on the other side of the road at a hill in the distance. "The captain should be popping out of the jungle over there sometime around fourteen hundred hours with two platoons. He'll have the folks with him make a show of taking a break, setting up a perimeter, and generally farting around."

"And us? What are we supposed to do?"

Settling back down on his haunches, Smart looked about at the Rangers gathered around him. "We wait for our friends to make an appearance."

It was well past noon before a suitable vehicle came trundling down the road to where White lay in the ditch. Glancing up at the small clump of trees where Smart and the other four sat covering him, White looked for a signal from Smart. When he gave White the high sign White jumped to his feet and scurried into the middle of the road. While he understood that it was his task to stop the vehicle, the young Ranger wasn't all that sure he knew what to do if the driver decided not to cooperate. He hoped that the sight of an American Ranger with his rifle leveled at him and at the ready would be enough to bring the truck to a full stop but wasn't exactly betting on it. Assuming the most menacing stance he could affect, White faced the oncoming truck and nervously waited to see what happened.

To his surprise the driver stopped well before reaching the spot where he stood. For a moment neither party moved as the two men eyed the other in order to determine how best to proceed. This standoff allowed Smart to make his way down from where he had been hiding and yank the driver's side door open before the Filipino realized that he was there. Startled, the Filipino all but toppled out of the cab of the truck and onto the road, thrusting his hands straight up into the air as quickly as he could while muttering something that no one understood. Sensing that he had the advantage Smart lowered his weapon and smiled as he pulled out the wad of money he had been issued. Pointing at the truck with the wad of money, then thumping his chest Smart did his best to communicate his intent to the Filipino. At first the man thought Smart wanted to buy the whole truck forever. Having regained a degree of calm and appreciating that there could be a profit in this for him the Filipino protested. Only through a great deal of gesturing at his watch and other unorthodox gestures was Smart able to convince the Filipino they simply wanted to borrow it for a few hours. Though still leery of the Americans, especially after the one who reeked of dung joined them, the Filipino relented. Putting Specialist Washington in charge of babysitting the Filipino in the crop of trees where they had been hiding, Smart directed White and Bannon to climb in the back of the truck. Since Park was the closest to looking like a Filipino in the squad, he was assigned to drive the truck after stripping down to nothing but his T-shirt. Smart rode in the cab, scrunched up behind the dashboard in such a way that he would be free to peer out the side window or the windshield as necessary without being seen. After carefully backing the truck up and off the road, the four Rangers settled down once more to wait.

Shortly after two P.M. Park tapped Smart, who had been dozing off on the shoulder. "There's the old man," he announced. Peeking over the top of the dashboard Smart looked across the fields to where Nathan had told him he would set up housekeeping.

"Okay, Anthony, keep a sharp eye out for our friends. If they stay true to form they'll come tooling along the road any minute now."

For once they didn't have long to wait. A small car with three men came around the curve of the road, slowly putting along. From his vantage point Smart could see that all three were staring at the hill where Nathan and the platoon he was with were putting on a great show of digging foxholes and preparing them for defense. Lifting the mike of his small squad radio to his mouth, he made a call to Jones. "Bird Dog Two, this is Bird Dog. We're in business. Stand by."

As he watched, Smart saw the driver of the small car turn his gaze in their direction. After saying something, the passenger next to him did likewise.

"You suppose they're on to us?" Park nervously asked as he did his level best to remain calm.

Smart had been wondering the same thing. When he saw that the passenger of the car returned to watching the far hill while the driver continued to creep down the road at a snail's pace, Smart sighed. "They haven't got a clue." When the car disappeared behind the next bend in the road, Smart called out to the pair in the rear. "It's show-time, lads. Lock and load."

After having been confined in an enclosed space with Duppie White, Bannon cheered. "Hallelujah. Salvation is at hand." White said nothing. How could he? He was so foul he couldn't even stand himself.

With a wave of his hand Smart motioned Park to pull out onto the road and follow the car that had just passed by. As he was doing so, Smart radioed Jones. "Bird Dog is on the move. Stand by for action."

Jones responded with a curt, "Roger that."

When they saw the car again it was pulled off to one side of the road. Two of the men, the passenger who had been seated in the front and the one who had been in the back, were standing just off the roadway, several meters away from the car. Only the driver remained with the car. "Slow down, Anthony," Smart whispered. "Wait till you see Jones and his truck coming."

Park was about to tap the brake when he saw a truck

not much different than the one he was driving, appear around another bend farther down the road headed their way. "Is that Sergeant Jones?"

Smart peeked over the dash. "That be him. Now, slowly, bring us up right behind the rear of that car till your bumper is almost touching."

Doing his best to maintain a steady speed so as not to alarm the Filipinos on the ground or the one still with the car, Park maneuvered his truck into position. Just ahead of them Jones was having his driver do likewise. Only at the last minute did the Filipino driver realize what was happening. By then it was too late. He was hopelessly boxed in and both Smart and Jones were giving the order for their men riding in the rear to pile out and deploy.

Both Bannon and White leapt out of the truck, breaking into a sprint as soon as their feet hit the roadway. Bannon broke to the right, lowering his SAW to waist level as he trained it on the pair of Filipinos who had been standing on the side of the road. White took off to the left, circling the truck and heading for the trapped car. He hadn't gone two steps when he saw the driver's door fly open. Coming to a dead stop he dropped down to one knee, brought his rifle up to his shoulder, and trained it on the Filipino driver as he piled out of the car, grasping an AK assault rifle in one hand. Not knowing what else to do, White yelled at the top of his lungs. "Halt!"

White's shouted order only served to warn the Filipino of his presence. In a single reflexive response the Filipino, still hanging halfway out of the car swung the muzzle of his weapon around as he brought it to bear on White. Realizing that he had no other option, White flipped the safety of his weapon to the off position and gave the trigger a steady, even squeeze.

White's first round found its mark, dead on but it didn't seem to have any effect. Again White squeezed the trigger. Again the 5.56mm projectile struck home and again it didn't seem to faze the Filipino driver except to arrest his efforts to train his AK on White. Pausing only long enough to take a deep breath, White elevated his front sight a bit till the Filipino's head filled his field of vision before firing once more.

This time the effect was immediate and dramatic. The Filipino driver collapsed on the road like a rag doll. The man was dead.

Slowly White came to his feet, never once taking his eyes off the man he had just shot. For several long seconds he saw nothing but the corpse sprawled across the road as he slowly advanced toward it. Even stranger White realized that he felt nothing either. He didn't hear Smart as he came running up behind him. He didn't see Hoyt, who had been with Jones come around the front of the car with his rifle tucked into his shoulder, ready to use it if need be.

White ignored them all as he studied the body of the man he had gunned down with a casualness that was both amazing and appalling. About the only thing he did feel was a sense of pride. He had done it. All his efforts, all the long months of putting up with grief from drill sergeants at Basic, Ranger cadre at Benning, and even his own company mates had paid off. He had proven himself to be a Ranger in the only way that really mattered. He had come face to face with an armed foe and bested him. That, in any soldier's book, is the only measure that counts.

23

FORWARD OPERATIONS BASE DETROIT, MINDANAO, PHILIPPINES

Robert Delmont was not the only officer who knew that his future career was tied to the success of Operation Pacific Shield. To make his appointment as the commander of JTF Sierra more palatable Admiral Turner had been informed in a one-on-one chat with the Chief of Naval Operations that it would only be a temporary assignment, something to keep him "occupied" until the command of a carrier battle group became available. That a prize of that magnitude had to be offered as an inducement made it clear to Turner just how risky command of JTF Sierra could prove if whoever accepted it failed. And just to be sure that the message was understood after he accepted command of JTF Sierra Turner was informed in no uncertain terms that in order to win command of his very own carrier battle group he needed to sail away from the Philippines with a victory in his wake.

This presented Turner with something of a problem. Despite the fact that he was the overall commanding officer of a substantial force drawn from all four services, the entire operation depended upon just one unit, the 3rd of the 75th Rangers. Everything hinged upon the ability of that battalion to draw the Abu Sayyaf into a fight in which the Navy, Marine, and Air Force components of JTF Sierra could pile on, inflicting a crippling defeat upon it through the lavish use of firepower. Thus far the commanding officer of that battalion had been unable to deliver as he had promised back when Operation Pacific Shield was little more than a concept being briefed in cool, well-lit conference rooms of the Pentagon. Instead of administering a swift and crippling blow against an obscure but dangerous arm of Islamic terrorism, Pacific Shield was turning into something of a snipe hunt, one that was tying down valuable assets that were desperately needed elsewhere.

It therefore came as no surprise to anyone directly involved in the operation that the capture of two Abu Sayyaf fighters and the death of a third was hailed as something of a victory by the entire chain of command. By any rational measure the incident was nothing more than a minor affair, one that was not even worthy of being called a skirmish. Neither the documents that were in the possession of the insurgents nor the equipment found in the vehicle they were using provided Turner's intel staff with any actionable information. Even the presence of factory-fresh night-vision devices manufactured in China, a satellite cell phone capable of secure conversations, and weapons that were in mint condition added nothing to the overall intelligence picture of the enemy's capabilities. Still, Company A's coup did provided Turner with the first tangible evidence that Delmont's battalion could actually deliver positive results. The only disquieting aspect of this whole affair was the fact that the senior Ranger ashore had had nothing to do with the small but encouraging success, a fact that did not escape either man's attention.

This bit of insight came to Turner via Colonel Tim Lamb. As the ground force commander Lamb made it his business to know what was happening throughout the FOB he was responsible for by using every means available to him. This included monitoring the ever-present enlisted men's grapevine, a source that crossed interservice boundaries and kept him well informed via his sergeant major on the goings-on within the headquarters of the 3rd of the 75th. Equally underwhelmed by the performance of the Rangers and anxious to find a more active role for his Marines, Lamb lost no time in gleefully sharing this information with Turner, a man who had more in common with Robert Delmont than he dared admit. This was how it came to be that Nathan Dixon, an officer who was as close to being at the bottom of the chain of command as one could be and still be part of it, was invited to attend a joint planning session aboard Turner's flagship.

When Delmont was informed Nathan was to accompany him to the Admiral's nineteen hundred hours evening briefing he was livid. He saw this as nothing more than an insult, a slight by his superior, a clear sign that Turner had no confidence in him. Even more troubling was the potential damage Dixon's newly found stature would have upon him. Having bypassed the established chain of command whenever he felt that it was to his benefit to do so, Delmont understood the precarious position Dixon's presence at the joint planning session put him in. If the young captain took full advantage of this golden opportunity by putting forth an idea that actually bore fruit Dixon would be the one who received credit for turning the operation around.

As improbable as it seemed Delmont had no doubt that if things did turn out that way no matter who wrote the final after-action reports, word of what really happened in the Philippines would slowly percolate all the way up the chain of command to his benefactor, a man who had no use for deadwood and fading stars. Palmer wouldn't think twice about withdrawing his patronage from Delmont, leaving him to be bumped off the fast track and back into the teeming mass of faceless lieutenant colonels who commanded nothing more than a desk far removed from the Pentagon. Thus, instead of being a stepping-stone along his path to the stars Operation Pacific Shield threatened to become a headstone for a career that would be all but dead in the water unless he managed to come up with something that once more put him in control of events.

Under different circumstances the summons to the USS *Wake Island* would have sent Nathan's stomach into free fall. Junior line officers didn't mix well with flag officers and their bevy of senior field-grade staff officers. The fact that his superior wasn't exactly held in high regard by just about everyone who would be there should have added to Nathan's concerns.

It was therefore unfortunate from a purely career stand-point that Nathan was in what could best be described as a self-destructive mood. Even now he still found himself struggling to come to terms with the death of his father, especially since he could not keep himself from blaming Operation Pacific Shield, the brainchild of his battalion commander for his father's death. It was an easy conclusion to draw, after all it had been the lackluster results of the joint task force, one that included his own company, that had caused the Chief of Staff of the Army to send his father to the Philippines, a trip that had cost him his life. As Nathan saw it, had the OPLAN that put Operation Pacific Shield never seen the light of day his father would still be alive. Of course he knew that it was both unprofessional and foolish to blame his father's death on that sort of convoluted reasoning. But Nathan was human and humans sometimes find logic has no standing when dealing with matters of the heart, especially when those matters involve the sort of grief Nathan still felt over the loss of his father.

So it should not have been surprising that Nathan approached the coming meeting with a combative attitude. The savaging of Company B at the hands of insurgents that his company had been unable to run to ground only added to the mounting anger and frustration that simmered within him and led him to resolve that if he was asked for his opinion on the manner in which the operation was being conducted he would tell them the truth as he saw it, consequences be damned.

Nathan wasn't going to the *Wake Island* unarmed. In his efforts to find a way to make sure that the loss of his father and the death of Noel Cameron were not in vain Nathan had an epiphany. During the long trip back across the Pacific when he had little more to do than think Nathan had managed to convince himself that his father had been on the verge of proposing a change in policy that would have resolved the pointless morass that JTF Sierra was currently mired in. He had no solid proof to support his supposition, only clues, circumstantial evidence such as his father's unannounced visit to the Philippines as well as the nature of the reading that he had left behind in his den. To Nathan they had to be related for that was how his father tackled the big issues he often found himself dealing with. First he would define the nature of the problem, which was probably why he had been in the Philippines. Then he would research all aspects related to the problem which explained why he had been reading up on past campaigns involving conventional Western forces pitted against insurgent forces. It was as simple an approach as it was effective, one as ingrained in him as it was in his father.

If he was right, and Nathan was sure he was, then he felt he had an obligation not only to his father but to the men he would soon be leading back into harm's way to see to it that what his father had been trying to do succeeded. To achieve this goal, Nathan was prepared to throw himself under the bus, speaking his mind if and when the opportunity to do so was offered to him. The trick would be to take advantage of whatever opportunity afforded to him to put forth his thoughts, or more correctly what Nathan believed had been his father's thoughts.

Nathan was pondering this question as he stood waiting

on the makeshift floating dock where the launch that would take him and his battalion commander out to the *Wake Island* lay idling. When Robert Delmont showed up Nathan rendered the required salute that was answered with little more than a wave of Delmont's hand as he climbed into the launch where he took a seat in the bow of the launch. Nathan followed but remained in the stern as far from Delmont as he could in order to maintain a physical as well as a psychological distance from a man he regarded as the architect of the debacle that had claimed his father's life.

Granted a few moments of peace Delmont turned his back on Nathan, the crew of the launch, and the chaotic and overcrowded mud hole that was characteristic of each of the forward operations bases they had occupied. Instead he faced into the clean, crisp breeze that swept in from the sea as if hoping that it could clear his troubled mind. Things were coming to a head. A crisis was in the offing. Delmont could feel it, just as he felt the fine salty mist of the spray whipped up by the offshore wind.

Just when all hell would break loose was difficult to gauge but Delmont suspected that it would be tonight, sometime during the evening's briefing. He knew it would have to be either the Admiral or Colonel Lamb to alter the course of the operation for they were the only ones with the rank and authority to do so, leaving Delmont unsure of how he would go about defending himself and the operation he had been so instrumental in bringing to fruition from the savaging he suspected it would be subjected to. If it was Lamb he would be able to be more aggressive in stating his case as they were both subordinates to Turner who would more than likely sit back and let them have at it for a while before stepping in to adjudicate their differences. If Turner was the one who loosed the expected salvo Delmont would be forced to present his case with considerably more tact and without any hope of appeal since Turner was the senior man on deck. Complicating his efforts would be the presence of his

most senior company commander. Whoever it was that
was engineering the pending confrontation had a specific
role in mind for Dixon, one that Delmont could not quite
figure out but would need to be ready to counter using
whatever means he could under the circumstances.

Casting a fugitive glance back toward the stern of the
boat Delmont took a moment to study the young officer.
As it so happened, Nathan was staring intently at him
with a blank expression, one that told Delmont that his
greatest threat would not come from what Turner or Lamb
said or did, but from a man who was in theory his subordinate.

Both Delmont and Nathan were escorted to the conference room where an earlier update for the Admiral was
just wrapping up. As with any traditional organization,
whether it be military or part of the corporate world the
proximity of a person in the room to the head of the organization established his relative importance. In the conference room this evening Turner was flanked on his right
by Lamb, his ground force commander, and on his left by
his chief of staff, an Army colonel Nathan had met once
while the task force was still assembling in Guam. Arrayed along the remaining seats in the front row were the
principal staff officers of Turner's staff. Occupying the
next two rows were various secondary and special staff
officers. Behind them standing along the rear wall of the
conference room on either side of the door were the strap-
hangers, people who were on Turner's or Lamb's staff
who managed to find an excuse to elbow their way into
the room. Nathan expected that he would wind up
squeezed in between a pair of field-grade staff toadies
who would spend the next hour or so wondering what on
earth gave a line officer such as Nathan the chutzpah to
think he belonged in a room with them.

It therefore came as something of a shock when a Marine posted at the front of the room motioned to Nathan

to come forward. This caused several heads to turn in his direction. With more than a bit of trepidation Nathan stepped forth from the obscurity of the military equivalent of the peanut gallery to the front of the room where Turner's chief of staff stood up and motioned everyone to his left to shift over one seat. With a sweep of his hand the chief of staff indicated to Nathan that he was to take his former seat. Before doing so, Nathan took a moment to look about the room at the stares being directed at him, especially by his own commanding officer.

When everyone was settled once more and the murmuring that the reshuffling of the deck necessitated by Nathan's entry had subsided, the chief of staff cleared his throat to get everyone's attention. When everyone was once more focused on the front of the room Admiral Turner stood up, thanked his chief, and turned to address the crowded room.

"I'll cut to the chase, people," he stated in a gruff tone that conveyed the frustration he was feeling at how things were going. "We're failing. I know that, my boss knows that, each and every one of you knows that. But even more important, the enemy knows that. He knows that we can't go on like this forever, that eventually we're going to leave. If we do that without doing any serious damage to the Abu Sayyaf, they win."

Turner paused to let that sink in a moment before he continued. When he was ready to proceed he placed his hands on his hips, leaned forward slightly and scanned the faces before him. "I for one do not intend to sail away from this shit hole with nothing to show for our efforts. One way or another there's going to be some fresh hides nailed to the bulkhead of my cabin as trophies. While I would much rather they be Abu Sayyaf hides, rest assured my trophy case will not be empty when it comes time to leave." Once more he took a moment to allow his assembled commanders and staff to mull this threat over before continuing.

"Desperate times call for desperate measures," he mused almost to himself. "So I'm going to do something that goes against almost every tenet and principle under which we operate. I'm not only going to call for you people to think outside the box, I'm going to demand that you throw the damned thing overboard. And I'm going to start that by calling on the most junior man in this chain of command to stand up and give us his opinion on not only how things have been going, but what he thinks we should be doing."

Like a thunderclap Nathan realized what Turner was saying. While he had hoped that he would be asked his opinion at some point during the proceedings, in his wildest dreams he never imagined that Turner would cut him loose like this.

Looking up from Nathan who was at that moment giving him his best "deer in the headlights" impression, Turner turned his attention back to his commanders and staff. "I've no idea what Captain Dixon is going to say. Having had the honor of meeting his father and expecting that this apple hasn't fallen far from the tree I doubt if I'll like some of what he has to say. Neither will you. Be that as it may, when we are finished here tonight," he added as he leaned forward and scowled, "I don't want to hear tell that someone in this room"—he stated staring directly at Delmont—"took offense and sought to extract retribution. Is that clear?"

There was a smattering of affirmative response but not enough to satisfy Turner. "I said, is that clear!"

This time everyone in the room, including Delmont, responded with a crisp, clear, "Yes, sir."

Satisfied, Turner looked down at Nathan who was still scrambling to collect himself. "Captain, you have the helm."

After taking a deep breath, Nathan came to his feet and pivoted about. Taking but a moment to collect his thoughts, he scanned the room. Off in the rear of the room he spotted a yeoman seated before a computer attached to a projector. Raising his hand, he got the yeoman's attention. "Sailor, can you pull up a photo of Hamdani Summirat?"

With a nod the yeoman acknowledged Nathan's request. Taking but a moment to scroll through his library of files he threw up an image of the Abu Sayyaf leader that Nathan's company had been pursuing in vain. "Gentlemen," Nathan stated, sounding more confident and self-assured than he felt, "the man we are dealing with is cut from a different cloth than the insurgent and terrorist leaders we have become accustomed to. He is a school-trained professional soldier, a man who is no doubt familiar with the same military classics that we use at our own military academies and staff colleges."

Doing his best to ignore the expressions of the senior ranking officers before him Nathan scrambled to think on his feet as he pulled his thoughts and ideas together and translated them into words and phrases that made sense. "I expect before he began this campaign he did what we all do when preparing ourselves for an operation like this, he studied past insurgencies and guerrilla wars." Nathan of course knew this was a lie. He doubted if half the officers in the room bothered to pick up a history book and tried to enlighten themselves on what others facing similar situations had done. It just wasn't the way modern American professional officers went about things. Like their fellow Americans, they viewed history as a bore, a subject that had no useful purpose in the modern technologically oriented world in which they lived and operated.

Ignoring that uncharitable thought Nathan continued on. "In 1954 the French and in 1968 the Americans established FOBs very much like ours deep in enemy territory with the expressed purpose of drawing the enemy into an engagement in which the conventional forces, the French and Americans, could use their superior firepower to smash an insurgent force. In '54 Giap, the Vietminh commander managed to trump French firepower and win a military and political victory. In '68 the same man failed militarily but because of a failure of political will-power in the United States he managed to set the stage for eventual victory."

Nathan paused to scan the faces of the officers before him. He could tell by some of their expressions that a few of the officers were quite put out at being lectured by a junior officer like this. Remembering that his father had once told him that at a time like this only one man in the room mattered, Nathan looked down at the admiral in an effort to solicit a response that would provide him with a clue as to whether he was cleared to proceed or if it was time to wave off.

Turner understood what the young officer he had given the floor to was waiting for. When he had called on him Turner had expected the younger Dixon to make some observations from his standpoint as a line company com-mander who had been out there beating the bush, nothing more. He had never expected him to launch into a full-scale pitch that might actually be of some value. Of course Turner immediately reminded himself just how foolish it was for him to judge the captain before him as he would an ordinary officer of similar rank. Few O-3s had fathers who were living legends. Even fewer had one that was, or had been the deputy chief of staff for Operations. Curi-ous as to where Nathan was taking them, Turner gave Nathan a hint of a smile and a nod in an effort to encour-age him to continue. Setting aside his apprehensions, Na-than pressed on.

"That man," he stated crisply while pointing to the pro-jected image of Summirat, "knows his history as well as any man or woman in this room. He knows he has no hope of matching or trumping our firepower as Giap did in fifty-four. And he knows we possess the same, if not better, mobility to take the fight to him as the Marines did in sixty-eight at Khe Shan. That leaves him with only two options. One, he can wait until one of our forays into the interior makes a tactical error which he can exploit as he did against Company B, or two, he can simply wait until we tire of running about in the jungle and quit, sailing away with our tails between our legs and leaving him free to continue his campaign against the government in Manila. He's already demonstrated that he has the capability to inflict terrible damage on us."

Nathan paused here, figuring that he had no need to dwell on the fate of Company B. "He's also proven, to me at least, that he possesses the sort of discipline needed to wait us out. In the end this is what I think he intends to do. It's what I would do if I were in his place. To date he's not done anything that could even be remotely construed as foolish or ill advised. I doubt if he's going to begin anytime soon. So, that means that one day, perhaps very soon, someone in our chain of command is going to say 'enough, we've done our best' and issue the necessary orders that will take us away from this tropical paradise."

This last comment caused more than a few officers about the room to snicker. Unable to suppress a bit of a grin himself Nathan took a moment to catch his breath before he pitched into a proposal that he knew would be greeted with a great deal of skepticism and a fair amount of derision.

The plan that had been germinating in the back of his mind involved the sort of risks that most American officers tended to shy away from. It followed a principle his father was a firm believer in, one not taught at Fort Leavenworth, but was quite familiar to the Las Vegas crowd. It was in a nutshell "Gamble big, win big." Of course, the flip side of that coin was "Gamble big, lose big," an aspect that Nathan was well aware of, but he had no intention of allowing it to keep him from doing what he knew he had to do.

After taking a deep breath Nathan set about explaining to Turner and his covey of staff officers how he would go about bringing the interminable impasse they found themselves in to a quick if brutal end.

If the trip in the motor launch out to the USS *Wake Island* had been chilly, the return run to shore was downright frigid. Delmont could not believe what had happened. He found himself totally unable to comprehend how an operation that he had thought of, pieced together, and struggled to promote had been hijacked by one of his own subordinates. Operation Pacific Shield was supposed to be his ticket to the eagles of an O-6. It was supposed to be a résumé enhancer that would all but assure him a shot at flag rank. Now, if Turner was able to talk his superiors into buying into Nathan's controversial plan, and if it worked, the credit for bringing the operation to a successful conclusion would go to Nathan and not him.

Unfortunately, at the moment there wasn't much that Delmont could do but wait and see how things went. If Turner did manage to sell the CinC PAC on Nathan's plan, Delmont would have to do all he could to place himself back into the picture, to take back what was rightfully his through any means. Just how he would manage to do so was something he had to do. His career, after all, depended on it.

24

FORWARD OPERATIONS BASE
EMPORIA,
MINDANAO, PHILIPPINES

Company A was in the interior, blundering about in the jungle as was their wont when word was passed down to them through battalion that the USS *Wake Island* along with its escorting battle group was being dispatched to assist in humanitarian relief efforts in the wake of an earthquake-initiated tsunami that slammed Java and southern Sumatra in a repeat of the 2004 Christmas event. At a gathering of his officers and senior NCOs late in the afternoon Nathan explained to them that the withdrawal of the naval contingent meant that they would lose the bulk of the helicopters that had been supporting them as well as the five-inch guns of the *Wake Island*'s escorts standing by to provide fire support for the Marines securing the FOB.

To the majority of those listening to Nathan's news it was a bit disheartening. When the first wild rumors spread through the company announcing that the *Wake Island* would be weighing anchor and sailing away to participate in a humanitarian relief effort, almost everyone believed that the 3rd of the 75th would be going with it, that someone at the top of the military food chain would seize upon this unfortunate act of God as an excuse to shut down Operation Pacific Shield and pull them out. That, it seemed, was not to be. Instead, according to their company commander the ground component of JTF Sierra minus a Marine rifle company was going to remain behind and proceed as before.

The calm, almost sangfroid manner in which Nathan explained how they would be conducting incursions into the interior in the absence of the *Wake Island* and its escorts was somewhat unnerving to those who had served under Nathan for any length of time. All the little tells and quirks that they had relied upon to cue them into what their commanding officer was thinking or how he felt about the orders battalion had handed down to him were absent. In fact, since his return from the States they could not but help notice how withdrawn he had become. While he was never one who was into being overfriendly with the troops, he was always the sort of officer they felt comfortable being around. Almost everyone blamed the change on the personal loss their commanding officer had suffered.

Whatever the cause, Peter Quinn and First Sergeant Carney both agreed that neither one of them cared much for the change. The present detached, almost aloof manner of their commanding officer stood in stark contrast to the previous easygoing manner that had made working with him such a pleasure. It wasn't as if either of them entertained any doubts about Nathan's ability or judgment. His performance in the field during the current foray was on par with what they had come to expect of him. It was just that his new attitude created a bit of a strain in the day-to-day operations of the company that hadn't been there before.

As with any close-knit organization in which personality exerts a major influence on the ability of that organization to function a sudden and pronounced change in the behavior of a key player sends reverberations throughout the entire unit. Shortly after moving from the forward patrol base from where they had been operating the previous night into an open field that would serve as a landing zone for the choppers coming in to pick them up, Staff Sergeant Henry Jones stepped back from his squad's portion of the First Platoon's perimeter to where Sergeant First Class Smart was squatting, watching his platoon. After looking about to make sure no one could hear what he was saying, Jones asked Smart what he thought was really behind their commanding officer's sudden trans-formation. Smart took a moment to consider the question as he scanned the horizon beyond the First Platoon's pe-rimeter. "The loss of his father hit him hard," he mused. "They were close, you could see that the way they talked and behaved the day the General came out here to see him. You know what it's like to have someone who's close to you suddenly go the way his father did. It's like a little piece of you dies. Well," Smart stated as he exhaled and came to his feet, "the General was a big piece of our C. O. I imagine it's gonna be awhile before Captain Dixon will be able to adjust to the loss he's . . ."

The sound of a thud, quickly followed by a second off in the distance, stopped Smart midsentence as his ears perked up in an effort to track the direction from which the all-too-familiar sound was emanating. A thud a few sec-onds later allowed him to get a decent fix. Pointing to a spot just inside the tree line not far from where the com-pany had recently emerged, Smart was about to shout an order when the first mortar round impacted in the center of the landing zone the company was deployed around.

Together the two NCOs dropped to the ground. After the third mortar round impacted, Jones lifted his head a bit and faced Smart. "Well, this is new."

Ignoring the casual, almost nonchalant manner with which the squad leader was handling the unexpected bar-rage Smart scrambled to his feet and raced over to the nearest Rangers on the outer rim of the perimeter with Jones on his heels. They plopped down on the ground on either side of Corporal Bannon and Eric White just as another trio of thuds erupted from the spot Smart had tagged as the location of the mortars. Thrusting his arm out he pointed toward it. "Over there. Light up that tree line, Bannon."

With the coolness of a man who had been in tight spots before, Bannon took a second to study the tree line. "What do you make the range to be?"

Closing his eyes, Smart mentally scrolled up the map of the area in his mind's eye and tried to compute the distance. "Five hundred meters, maybe six."

With this Bannon raised the rear sight of his squad automatic weapon and adjusted it for the range. When he was ready, he tucked his weapon's stock into his shoulder tightly, took careful aim, and let fly a fifteen-round burst. When he was satisfied that he was hitting his mark he began to cut loose quick twenty-five-round bursts, sweeping back and forth across the area Smart had pointed out to him. Seeing this, Jones rose up onto one knee and shouted to his left and right to the rest of his squad *"Open Fire! Open Fire."* Using the tracers as a guide the rest of First Squad opened up, chewing up the vegetation and sending splinters and tiny bits of trees and shrubbery flying through the air.

A few seconds after the entire squad began firing Nathan found his way over to where Smart, Jones, Bannon, and White were. On his heels were Peter Quinn and Smart's platoon leader. Taking a moment to look away from the distant jungle, Nathan counted the number of officers and NCOs gathered about him. "Are you people crazy?" he yelled. "Spread out." Reaching out, he grabbed his executive officer's sleeve just as he was preparing to leave. "Peter, get on the radio and wave off the chopper till we sort this out. Notify battalion as well. Go."

Next he turned to Hal Laski. "Go over to the squad on your left. On my order go forward and around the left edge of the tree line over there," Nathan ordered as he pointed to a spot where the far tree line ended. "While this squad provides a base of fire I'll take your other squad on the right and go in there. Now move."

When Laski·was gone Nathan turned to Smart. "Stay here and provide a base of fire. Lift fire when you deem prudent."

Smart nodded just before Nathan took off to the right and yelled to the squad leader of Laski's Second Squad to come to their feet and follow him.

It was simple and elementary. Smart and the First Squad provided a base of fire, suppressing the enemy. Nathan was taking the Second Squad straight ahead while Laski led his Third Squad in a wide flanking maneuver.

While Smart questioned in his own mind Nathan's decision to go straight at the enemy mortar position he didn't question his commanding officer. One simply did not do that while under fire, especially when the officer giving the orders was one with Nathan's proven abilities. Instead, Smart concentrated on keeping track of the Second Squad's forward progress while watching that the fire of Jone's First Squad didn't block Nathan's advance or stray into the ranks of the Second Squad. When he judged that it was becoming too dangerous to maintain the suppressive fire he ordered Jones and his people to cease fire. "Keep your eyes open," he shouted once all firing stopped. "If you see something, make sure you identify your target and take careful aim before firing." Then, raising up on one knee he watched as the Second Squad began to disappear into the jungle.

The stench of freshly burned propellant from the mortar rounds that had been lobbed at his company mingled with the sweet smell of freshly hacked vegetation and tree bark as Nathan carefully made his way forward. Here and there Nathan could see evidence that some of Smart's men had hit their marks as he came across small pools of blood and clear evidence that someone had been hit before being dragged away. From off to his right a voice called out to him. "Over here."

Pushing aside some ferns Nathan came upon two of his Rangers standing before a mortar that had been left in place. One of the pair was about to lean forward for a closer inspection when Nathan yelled out, "Don't touch anything. Back up the way you came." Though confused, the two Rangers complied.

As they were doing so Laski came up behind Nathan. "We missed them. I guess they called it quits when they began taking fire."

"How many mortars did you come across over there?" Nathan asked without looking back at Laski.

"None. But we came across spots where two had been."

One of the Rangers who had discovered the mortar before them pointed over his shoulder. "There was one over there but it's gone too."

Nathan thought a moment. "I heard three mortars fire, not four."

"Maybe this one malfunctioned," Laski offered.

"I don't think so," Nathan mused, shaking his head. "Drag away their dead but leave a mortar behind? That doesn't sound like the sort of people we're dealing with. Even a mortar that's malfunctioning is worth more than a corpse. A broken mortar can be repaired." After giving the problem before him a bit more thought, Nathan glanced over his shoulder at Laski. "Who's got some rope?"

From somewhere behind him a coil of rope was passed forward and handed to Nathan. Taking a moment, he tied a loop in one end. Motioning to everyone around him to step back, Nathan tossed the looped end toward the mortar's muzzle. It took him three tries before he succeeded. "Okay," Nathan announced as he began to take up the slack in the rope. "Everyone find something substantial to hide behind."

After checking to make sure everyone had complied he took his own advice, snuggling up behind a tree that was a few inches wider than him. When he was ready, Nathan pulled in the last of the slack, shouted out, "Fire in the hole," and gave the rope a good tug.

Along the forward edge of the perimeter out in the middle of the field Peter Quinn and Nathan's radioman had made their way back to where Henry Jones and Frederick Smart were waiting and watching. All three cringed when they saw the blast rip through the jungle where Nathan had led the Second Squad. Whatever dark thoughts each man entertained, he kept them to himself as they continued to watch and wait. Finally Quinn broke the silence. "I sure hope the old man meant for that to happen."

From a concealed spot two kilometers away Hamdani Summirat watched intently through his binoculars for any indication that his latest surprise had been effective. When he saw the American Rangers slowly emerge from the jungle in single file moving at a leisurely pace he concluded that they had somehow managed to avoid falling for the booby-trapped mortar a detachment from a regional command had left behind.

The commander of the Abu Sayyaf regional company from which that mortar had come had been quite reluctant to deploy those precious weapons in a position that even he, a part-time warrior with only rudimentary understanding of tactics knew would be exposed to enemy return fire as soon as he gave the order to commence their barrage. He wanted to deploy them farther back in the jungle where the balance of his command had been ordered to deploy. Summirat however would not waiver and the regional company commander knew better than to argue with him. So he dutifully deployed his four Chinese 82 mm mortars and watched as one of Summirat's explosive experts wired the one that he was to leave behind to a homemade bomb consisting of plastic explosives and ball bearings. The fact that the booby-trapped mortar would in all likelihood kill more American Rangers than the other three combined was little consolation to the commander of the regional company.

Lowering his binoculars Summirat sighed. Everything he had seen in the last few minutes indicated that this company of Rangers was not going to be easy to take down. The speed with which they were able to place fire on the mortar position, the manner in which the enemy commander responded to the attack, and his refusal to pursue the fleeing mortar crews deeper into the jungle where the bulk of the regional company had been waiting in ambush told Summirat that this American company was not the mark he was looking for. While he was confident that under the right circumstances his chosen six hundred could take these Americans on and win, the losses they would suffer in such a confrontation even under the best of circumstances would be heavy, crippling his main striking force and leaving him in a poor position from which to carry on the struggle once the Americans were gone.

No, he told himself as he slid his binoculars back into the case, he would have to go with his alternate plan. While he expected that fight would be equally vicious and bloody it had the advantage of being something the Americans would least suspect and most probably be unprepared to deal with. It would also yield results in a far more stunning victory, provided of course he could pull it off.

The greatest enemy Summirat now faced in his mind was time. At most he could count on the American warships being gone for two weeks, no more. By then other vessels from the American Pacific Fleet would have reached the disaster area off Sumatra, freeing the units supporting operations here in the Philippines to return to their assigned stations just offshore from the forward operations base.

Turning his back on Nathan's company Summirat smiled at his companions. "It is time for us to go," he announced. "We've much to do before the cat returns," he stated in a cheery voice. None of the men with him had the slightest idea what he was talking about. They did however have complete confidence in their leader. Without a word they followed him back into the jungle and onto their next task, whatever it might be.

It didn't take long for Delmont to figure out that he could use Nathan's response to the mortar attack to take him down a peg or two. He was so animated by the prospect of doing so he wasn't able to wait for Nathan to report into the battalion command post. Instead, like a starving pit bull sensing his first meal in days, Delmont headed out to wait at the helipad as the choppers bringing Company A back from the interior began to arrive.

Realizing what was going on, Emmett DeWitt walked over to the Ops NCO on duty as soon as Delmont had departed the command bunker and instructed the NCO to switch the radio tuned to the battalion command net over to Nathan's company command frequency. The NCO gave DeWitt a knowing grin and complied, handing him the mike when he was finished. Without fear of being betrayed by anyone present, DeWitt proceeded to call Nathan and give him a heads-up.

Thus forewarned Nathan decided to make a show of taking his time disembarking from the aircraft and making his way over to where Delmont was standing in his typical combative posture. With a nonchalance that was just shy of being insubordinate Nathan saluted his commanding officer and steeled himself for the initial volley he expected. Robert Delmont did not disappoint him or keep him waiting.

"Why in the name of God did you not pursue those people when you had an opportunity to do so, *Captain?*"

His emphasis on the word "captain" was meant to convey the same degree of animus that Delmont felt for Nathan that Nathan's bored expression was intended to impart to his commanding officer. Ignoring this, Delmont continued without waiting for a response that Nathan had no intention of giving.

"Can you explain to me why you let the best opportunity we've had to date to grab hold of those people and run them to ground slip away as you did? Can you give me one good reason why you're standing here, in front of me safe in the rear, instead of out there beating the bush?"

Nathan was about to respond with an answer that was all but guaranteed to cause Delmont to become totally unglued when he noticed a small party of officers making their way toward him. Coming to attention Nathan snapped a crisp salute unlike the one he had greeted Delmont with.

Caught off guard by Nathan's actions Delmont glanced over his shoulder. When he saw Colonel Lamb, accompanied by his operations and his intelligence officers, he pivoted about and joined Nathan in saluting them.

Like Delmont, Lamb did not waste any time with preliminaries, cutting to the chase but in a more measured, professional manner. "Okay, Captain, what have you to report?"

Unable to resist, Nathan took a second to glance over at his own battalion commander out of the corner of his eye before turning his full attention to the Marine colonel. As the balance of his company made their way to their assigned assembly area, giving the gaggle of officers a wide berth, Nathan laid out the situation he had faced at the LZ in the interior less than an hour ago, describing his response to the attack, and explaining his reasoning for breaking off the pursuit. "Sir," he concluded, "in my professional opinion not even a rank amateur would place his mortars where those people did. There was no reason for them to do so unless they wanted us to see them. The people who took my company under fire wanted us to follow them into the jungle."

Placing his hands on his hips, Lamb looked down at the ground, kicking a clod of dirt with the toe of his boot as he thought about what Nathan had said. Finally, he looked up at the young captain and nodded. "I imagine you're right. Of course, we'll never know for sure but," he added, looking over at Delmont for a second, "given what they did to B Company, your actions were both prudent and justified. How about putting that report in writing and running it up to my intel people as soon as you can."

Clearing his throat, Delmont turned to Lamb. "Sir, with all due respect Captain Dixon's report should go through my headquarters first and be folded into a battalion report before being forwarded to your staff."

Giving Delmont a smile that didn't have a wit of warmth in it, Lamb threw his arm about Delmont's shoulder and began to lead him away. "I think it's time you and I had a little chat over how we're going to do things while the admiral's away, don't you think?"

Though he was able to conceal the anger welling up from within him Delmont went along with Lamb, leaving Nathan standing on the FOB's landing area with a self-satisfied smirk on his face. Oh, he knew he'd pay for this somewhere in the future. But at the moment he didn't give a damn. His commanding officer was about to receive the "Me Tarzan, you Jane" sort of speech that he had intended to bludgeon him with. It was a small victory but at the moment it was enough for Nathan.

With post-combat inspections to conduct and a report to write, Nathan turned his back on the BS drama that so occupied the upper rungs of his chain of command and turned his full attention to the simple task of soldiering.

25

The departure of the fleet from the Philippines was delayed twenty-four hours at the request of Turner in order to shift the ground component to a new FOB, one that was located in an area that was as close to the Abu Sayyaf heartland as they could get. It was a bold move that not everyone agreed with, but as Turner reminded his staff and subordinate commanders, if they were going to roll the dice they might as well do what young Dixon had suggested and gamble big.

The time constraints forced the support elements that populated the FOB as well as the Marine units charged with securing it to cut corners when it came time to abandon the old FOB and set up the new one. Fortunately for those responsible for executing this task the cookie cutter approach that they had been using all along simplified things. With the exception of shifting a bunker, an emplacement, or a supply point a few meters this way or that due to the lay of the ground at the new location, Fresno was basically a carbon copy of all those that the joint task force had occupied to date. Once all the necessary personnel, equipment, and enough supplies to maintain the ground component for two weeks was ashore Turner bid Lamb farewell, wished him luck and set sail.

Initially the idea of sailing just over the horizon and cruising about ready to rush back when and if the Abu Sayyaf made a move had been discussed but rejected. There were simply too many ways of physically tracking the naval component of JTF Sierra, from the low tech approach that would require little more than a fishing trawler to shadow the fleet to reliance on the space-based platforms owned and operated by nations sympathetic to the Abu Sayyaf's aim of humbling the United States. Besides, when the USS *Wake Island* and the helicopters it carried didn't show up on the evening news within a couple of days shuttling relief aide ashore in Indonesia the insurgents would know something was amiss.

Thus Colonel Lamb found himself in command of an isolated outpost. In addition to the 3rd of the 75th Rangers which represented his strike force and two Marine rifle companies charged with the security of the FOB he had four UH-60 Blackhawks capable of shuttling back and forth to Davao to pick up whatever supplies the FOB required, four OH-58D Kiowa Warriors that provided Lamb with both reconnaissance capability as well as mobile firepower, and close to six hundred combat support and combat service support personnel. While still far superior in most regards to anything the Abu Sayyaf could throw against it, this force represented what most American commanders who had a say in the matter considered to be the leanest force they were willing to leave behind as bait in what some staff officers were calling behind their commanding officers' backs Operation Mouse Trap. The only questions left were one, would the Abu Sayyaf nibble on the bait and two, if and when they did would the occupants of FOB Fresno have the wherewithal to inflict enough damage on the enemy to justify the risk. The answers to the first would be provided by one man,

Hamdani Summirat while that of the second rested in the hands of God and a few good men.

The temptation to do something bold was definitely on Summirat's agenda. For the moment however he opted to be patient. The last-minute shift of JTF Sierra to a new forward operating base caught him and his lieutenants completely by surprise and in the midst of marshaling their forces for a major campaign against the Americans. He had expected the Americans to remain in place where they were already established and familiar with the surrounding area and population. Their relocation to a region that was a known Abu Sayyaf stronghold gave Summirat pause.

The scramble to dispatch couriers with orders to his scattered commands to shift from the assembly areas they had already occupied to others that would place them within striking distance of the new American base was a hassle and cost Summirat valuable time but was not his greatest concern. What bothered him the most about this unexpected development was why the Americans had chosen to place their unsupported ground forces in an area he dominated. When he had been able to confirm that the American naval units and the carrier battle group supporting the American ground troops were in fact gone Summirat assumed that the Americans would use this event as an excuse to pull all their troops out of the Philippines. When it became clear that they weren't going to, he thought they'd leave those forces slated to be left behind right where they were. Catapulting them into the heart of territory that he dominated surprised him.

That they were up to something was clear. He wondered if the Americans were actually taunting him, throwing down a challenge they knew he could not resist? It certainly seemed that way, especially in the eyes of many of his lieutenants and most of his fighters.

Naturally it didn't make any sense to Summirat. To him putting their ground troops where they did just before withdrawing the two assets he had no hope of matching, naval gunfire and naval aviation, was a decision that had to have been made at the highest level. Not only did this go against the American philosophy of war, which dictated that they pummel their foe to oblivion through the lavish application of firepower, it left their ground units vulnerable to being drawn into fights in which they would sustain casualties, something the American public and its political leaders had come to abhor. It was a puzzle Summirat had no answers for, yet.

The one thing that the American move did give him, though he would have preferred otherwise, was time, time he needed to think his way through this enigma. His initial orders to the scattered elements of his main force units to assemble in the vicinity of the previous American forward operating base had to be rescinded and new orders issued to suit the current situation. Intelligence needed to be gathered on the layout of the new American base by the members of the regional command responsible for the area where it was located, analyzed by Summirat, and incorporated into a revised plan of action that would set the stage for the decisive engagement he had now determined to bring on.

In accomplishing these last two tasks Summirat was fortunate in a decision he had made when he had been preparing to unleash his insurgency against the government in Manila. In order to establish a secure base area Summirat had placed an old comrade in command of the regional forces that would be responsible for protecting that province. Haji Agus Salim was highly skilled, totally reliable, and as dedicated to Summirat's vision as he was himself but due to a leg wound that never properly healed unable to participate in more active operations. Salim took his support role in stride, working to make the part-time fighters under his command almost as good as those belonging to Summirat's main force units. Both he and Summirat were confident that in a confrontation they would more than be able to hold their own against the Americans, something that until now he had never thought he would need to put to the test.

Things of course had changed. As Summirat prepared to make his way to where his old friend was gathering his forces he took the time to give praise to Allah for having blessed him with such men and prayed that in the coming days together they would be able to accomplish what so many before them had failed to achieve, establishing a truly independent Islamic republic from which the word of the prophet could be spread across the length and breath of Southeast Asia.

The Rangers of Company A greeted the change in their routine with silent resignation. No one was willing to be the first to complain about having had to begin their foray into the interior from FOB Fresno by marching twenty kilometers to their first assigned area of operations where they expected they would be conducting four days of patrols that found nothing, set up ambushes that ambushed no one, and participate in sweeps that collected little more than the mud that clung to their boots. The prospect of doing this for two weeks had the old hands in the units longing for the days they spent in Afghanistan running up and down the barren rock-strewn mountains in search of Osama bin Laden.

In an effort to derive some benefit from his company's march out, Nathan had taken it upon himself to coordinate with the Marine officer charged with the security of the FOB to sweep through some of the dominant terrain beyond the FOB's perimeter that posed a danger to the FOB if occupied by the insurgents. Naturally Colonel Lamb applauded the young captain's initiative, thus preventing Delmont from reprimanding Nathan for going outside his normal chain of command without checking with him first. That Delmont would eventually find some way of extracting a pound of flesh from Nathan for all the wrongs he had committed against him, real and imagined, was something that neither Lamb nor Nathan doubted. At the moment however concerns over his career would have to be put on hold. He had a company to lead into territory that was about as hostile as nature and the people who claimed it as their own could make it.

As the shadows grew longer the young Abu Sayyaf section leader began to realize that their hours of patient vigilance had been for naught. Like so many of the previous drills and exercises that Haji Agus Salim, his regional commander, had thrown at him and the twelve men under his command, this one had wasted an entire day, a day none of them could afford to squander, on a pointless training exercise. Most had farms to tend to. One was the only skilled butcher around for miles. All had families. None could afford to waste their precious time squatting in shallow holes in the ground being stung by the vicious insects merrily feasting upon their blood.

Looking at his watch the section leader pondered how much longer he should wait before calling his men in from their scattered positions and releasing them for the day. The only thing that had kept him from doing so until now was his fear of Salim, a fanatical veteran who frightened him more than the Americans. They were many, many kilometers away. Salim on the other hand lived in a village not far from the one the section leader called home. And though Salim had never raised a hand against any of the part-time fighters under his command, his demeanor left no doubt that anyone who dared cross him or disobey an order of his would not be afforded the opportunity to do so again.

It only took the sting of an insect, or more correctly one more sting, to convince the section leader that this foolishness had gone on long enough. He would tell Salim when he saw him again that they had waited until after darkness before abandoning the hilltop that they had been ordered to picket. The diehard Abu Sayyaf commander wouldn't know any different seeing that he was off on another hilltop with another section waiting for foreign intruders that the section leader was convinced would never dare show their face in his province.

Rising up out of the hole he had dug earlier in the day, the section leader took a moment to stretch before calling out to his men to rally on him. With his back to the setting sun he watched as the rest of his section rose from their concealed positions like phantoms.

The exhausting march out to their first patrol base drained Eric White of energy and whatever enthusiasm he still had for being the member of an elite combat unit. At the moment his sole ambition was to get to wherever it was they were going, find a place he could settle down in and catch a few hours of sleep. By volunteering to go with the company executive officer as part of the quartering party, charged with securing and marking out the patrol base that the balance of the company would occupy after the sun had set, assured White that he would not be tagged to go out that night on another pointless patrol or have to participate in another unproductive ambush. The prospect of being left in peace by his squad leader for an entire night was the only thing keeping him going.

Staggering a bit under the weight of his equipment and the oppressive heat White paused a second to look up and see just how much farther they had to go. It was only then that he caught sight of a figure emerging from the dense underbrush that covered the side of the hill. Mesmerized by the apparition that stood before him not more than fifty meters away White watched as the ragged Filipino stretched out his arms and began to look about as if searching for something. What he was seeking didn't matter to White. All that White was concerned about was the AK-47 rifle the figure held in his right hand.

Acting purely on instinct the young Ranger brought his own weapon up to his shoulder, flipping the safety off with his right thumb as he did so. At this range White knew he didn't need to waste much time taking aim. He simply pointed at the center of mass of the unsuspecting figure before him and let fly with a quick three-round burst before going to ground, confident that his initial volley had found its mark.

Peter Quinn, in charge of the six-man quartering party had been content to let his mind slip into autopilot as soon as they had reached the base of the hill his commanding officer had ordered him to secure. Sergeant First Class Peter Prescott, the platoon sergeant for the Second Platoon, could handle things from here on in given how the routine hadn't changed a wit since their first protracted foray into the interior. Quinn liked to use Prescott as the senior noncommissioned officer for these nightly quartering parties. He was the sort of NCO who had no qualms about telling an officer to relax, that he would handle everything leaving Quinn free to enjoy a casual late afternoon hike through the countryside.

The sudden crack of small-arms fire just ahead quickly followed by the sound of Prescott's booming voice rattling off orders jarred Quinn back to the here and now. Startled and a bit befuddled the young officer's first instinct was to seek cover. That however went against his training. He was the senior man present, ostensibly in charge of this small party of Rangers. He needed to press forward, to find out exactly what was going on and report to his commanding officer as soon as he had a handle on the situation. Setting aside whatever fear he had and invigorated by the rush of adrenaline sent cascading through his system by the sound of spreading small-arms fire Peter Quinn charged forward in search of a spot from which he could exercise a modicum of command and control as well as see what in the hell was going on.

When he found Sergeant Prescott he threw himself to

the ground. Prescott for his part ignored Quinn's arrival as he took careful aim at an insurgent that Quinn was unable to see from where he was. After letting Prescott fire off three quick rounds Quinn yelled over to him, "What've we got here?"

Prescott didn't answer at first. The scene before him was typical of a surprise encounter. On the crest of the hill several of the insurgents had turned and fled as soon as they realized that they were under attack by the Americans. Most had dropped back down out of sight. A few foolishly had opted to return fire. "Hard to say for sure," he finally replied as he continued to scan the area to his immediate front. "There's half a dozen of them still alive up there for sure, maybe more. Most of them have gone to ground and don't seem too keen on returning fire."

After taking a moment to assess the situation Quinn finally decided he had enough of a handle on the situation to both report in to his commanding officer as well as make some decisions. After sucking in a deep breath and letting part of it out he began to issue his orders to Prescott. "Hold here with two of the men." Pausing, Quinn looked about to see who was nearby. "That'll be Albright and Kahn. I'll take the rest and cut around to the right."

"Got it," Prescott replied without taking his eyes off the area up ahead. When he saw Quinn begin to back away from the cover he had been behind, Prescott shouted out to him. "Don't forget to let the old man know what's happening."

"Yeah, sure thing," Quinn mumbled as he turned to gather up those who were to go with him.

From where he stood Haji Agus Salim was unable to tell where the sounds of small arms fire was coming from. Unable to resist the urge to do so, for the first time since he had been issued it, Salim keyed his small handheld radio and began to call out the radio call signs of his section leaders. Only after all of them save one responded did he know for sure which of his sections was in contact with the Americans.

Taking a moment he pulled a map from his map case and studied it. When he was satisfied he had a handle on the situation he began to rattle off quick-fire orders to his remaining section leaders. After he was sure that they had understood his instructions he returned the map to its case before looking around at the anxious faces of the men who comprised his small command group. These weren't the sort of people he was used to leading into battle. True, they were dedicated to the cause but they lacked the training and experience needed to stand up to the Americans, especially when it came to an operation such as the one he had just set in motion. He doubted that even Summirat's main force units could draw the Americans into a fight without becoming decisively engaged, a military term that basically meant keeping your people from becoming pinned in place by your enemy. Salim knew he would need to ensure that his scattered command maintained the freedom to break off the action when they had achieved the objectives that Summirat had outlined for him. "I will need your fighters again," Summirat had told his old friend. "Don't lose them all in your first brush with the Americans."

Easier said than done, Salim thought as he gathered himself up, leaned on his walking cane, and prepared to move out to a spot where he could watch the battle as it developed. Easier said than done.

As word of Quinn's contact with the insurgents made its way up JTF Sierra's chain of command, the well-planned response to just such a contingency was put into motion. In the field Nathan deployed the balance of his company, sending the platoons with him on a wide arch to encircle the hill on which his executive officer and the Rangers with him were still engaging the few insurgents that remained. Nathan knew he had scant chance of catching any of them within the pincers he was throwing around behind them but hoped against hope that they would be able to pick up the trail of those who had fled and follow them back to whatever safe house or base camp they had been using.

While Company A engaged the enemy and maneuvered in close proximity to them, Robert Delmont lost little time dispatching his ready reaction force consisting of Captain Clarence Overton's Company C. Using the four stripped-down UH-60 Blackhawks and stuffing as many of his men into them as he could, Overton was charged with the task of going several kilometers beyond where Nathan's company was deploying to establish a blocking position on key terrain that the battalion's operations staff had identified beforehand. Though the dearth of helicopters meant that it would take several lifts to shuttle all of Overton's command out to the field, the short distance involved would allow them to accomplish this well before any insurgents fleeing from Quinn and escaping Nathan's close-in envelopment could reach where Company C was deploying.

While all of this was going on Company B, now under the command of Captain Steve Rivera, struck out overland from FOB Fresno following the trail blazed by Nathan's company earlier in the day. They would move out to a point just short of where Company A was before initiating a wide sweep to the west in a clockwise direction, dropping off small detachments to cover probable escape routes as they went. By then Overton's command would be in place and ready to begin a similar maneuver but to the east, also moving in a clockwise direction and throwing out blocking detachments as they went.

During all this maneuvering on the ground the small detachment of OH-58 Kiowa Warriors would be buzzing about overhead, tracking the enemy movements as best they could, sending reports on what they saw and launching attacks of their own when the opportunity to do so arose.

Few in Company A knew of the grand maneuvers that were going on around them. The attention of the individual Rangers under Nathan's command were totally focused on their assigned sectors of responsibility and what their companions to their left and right were doing, as they moved forward toward the sounds of guns.

Having dispatched his First Platoon to the immediate aid of Peter Quinn and his small quartering party Nathan met with Jeff Sullivan and Hal Laski, platoon leaders for the Second and Third Platoons respectively. After giving them a quick rundown on the tactical situation as he knew it, Nathan ordered Sullivan to take his platoon around to the left of the hill where his executive officer was and Laski to the right, in effect attempting in miniature the same thing his battalion commander was hoping to achieve on a far grander scale. Before sending them on their way Nathan did warn his platoon leaders to take care lest they blunder into an ambush. "Just remember what happened to Company B," was all he needed to say to drive his point home.

With little more to do after issuing his orders and seeing that they were being executed with the speed that the situation demanded, Nathan decided to tag along with the Third Platoon. There was no particular reason why he had chosen this one over the other two. They would all come together on the hill Quinn was on. It was simply one of those spur-of-the-moment decisions.

Ever mindful of how nerve-racking it could be to a platoon leader to have his company commander breathing down his neck during an operation, Nathan took care to hang back. He and his small command group were following in the wake of Henry Jones's squad when one of his men spotted movement off to their right. Giving a quick whistle, Specialist Washington managed to get his squad leader's attention, pointing in the direction of the disturbance. Noting this, Nathan also turned his attention to where Washington was pointing.

The glint of late-afternoon sun on metal allowed Nathan to pinpoint what had caught Washington's attention. Company commanders weren't supposed to become intimately involved in a squad or platoon firefight. Nathan knew this. Still, he could not help but do so in this situation. Without a second thought he bellowed at the top of his lungs, *"Action right! Three o'clock!"*

With practiced ease Hal Laski issued the necessary orders that brought his platoon into line facing the insurgents who were emerging from a tree line less than two hundred meters away oblivious to the presence of the Americans. Even Nathan's shouted warning didn't alert them to the imminent danger they were facing. It was only when Laski gave the order to open fire that the insurgents came to appreciate the mortal danger they faced. For most of them this came too late. Those who did manage to survive the initial volley responded as one would expect of partially trained men to do when under fire for the first time; they ran. When Nathan saw this he made a snap decision. Scooting over to where Laski was crouched, Nathan yelled for him to get his platoon up and pursue the enemy. "Run them to ground," he yelled. "Grab hold of 'em and don't let them go."

Laski didn't need to be told twice. He also realized that they had managed to get the drop on the insurgents and was just as anxious as his company commander to press home their advantage. Coming to his feet he ordered his platoon to its feet.

Remaining in place Nathan radioed Lieutenant Terry Grimes, instructing him to divert the First Platoon to where he was. Next he contacted Jeff Sullivan and ordered him to abandon his flanking maneuver and instead drive directly toward the hill, link up with Peter Quinn, and secure that position. When everyone acknowledged their new orders Nathan took a moment to collect his thoughts before contacting battalion and rendering a detailed update on his situation.

Disgusted by the behavior of his men and realizing that his leg would prevent him from gaining the safety of the jungle, Haji Agus Salim stopped, turned, and prepared to face the Americans. As he checked the action of his assault rifle he gave the man who had been serving as his aide and liaison to the local community his last orders. "Find Summirat and tell him I am sorry that I have failed him. Tell him that he must take care in how he deploys his regional forces. And tell him," Salim stated in a firm and resolute voice as he drew himself erect, "I will be watching his march to victory from heaven. Now go."

The frightened aide didn't need to be told twice. Without bothering to look back he scrambled into the tree line just as an American OH-58D Kiowa came sweeping in from out of nowhere.

The pilot of the Kiowa caught sight of Salim at the last moment, causing him to make a tight turn in order to reverse course and come back for a second look. He expected that the lone figure he had spotted would be long gone but to his surprise the man was still standing there gripping his weapon. After setting into a hover less than a hundred yards from the man on the ground, the pilot turned to his observer. "Do you believe this guy? He must be a total fanatical wacko."

The observer, who had kept his eyes on the lone figure below, cleared his throat. "Don't look now but that wacko is about to make our lives mighty unpleasant if you don't do something soon."

Looking back the pilot was startled to see that not only was the figure still there, he was actually taking careful aim at them. After uttering an expletive the pilot flipped the red safety off with his thumb and hit the trigger, unleashing a hail of .50 caliber rounds. With measured ease he walked the strike of the rounds up to the defiant Abu Sayyaf insurgent until the man disappeared in the fountains of dirt and dust kicked up by the Kiowa's gun.

From his seat on one of the Blackhawks Robert Delmont listened in silence as Nathan delivered his dispassionate update to the battalion ops center back at FOB Fresno, making him regret his decision to accompany the second wave of Company C. At the moment, crammed in together with Rangers belonging to Overton's Second Platoon with little room to lay out his map and get a clear picture of what Nathan was talking about, Delmont knew he wasn't in a good position to influence the situation on the ground. While it was true he could have issued orders, not only would they have been based on a badly flawed grasp of the tactical situation, they would have thrown the entire maneuver his battalion was in the midst of executing into total chaos. As much as it grated on him to do so, at the moment Delmont knew he had no choice but to allow an officer he was really coming to despise to set the pace of operations for his battalion.

Shortly before midnight the last of Haji Agus Salim's section leaders checked in and rendered their reports to the man who had been Salim's deputy. Seated off in a dark corner of the hut Salim had used as his headquarters, office, and sleeping quarters, Summirat listened to each of their stories, taking in every word. As the night wore on he was finally able to satisfy himself that the sacrifice of his long-time companion and trusted lieutenant wasn't in vain. True, it was a rather steep price to pay in order to gain the information that he had, but Summirat was able to accept the loss by reminding himself that having died a martyr's death, his friend was now in paradise.

It would be dawn before the members of his own staff

returned from the scattered locations where he had positioned them in order to observe the American response to the fight Salim's command had participated in. They would give him the information he desired, the information that would allow him to make a final decision as to which plan he would go with. Some of what the section leaders of the regional force had to say was of interest but on the whole their accounts could not be relied upon. Having never seen a battle they didn't possess the ability to psychologically step back from the chaos and sort out what was important and what was of little value to their commander. Still, they had played an important role, one which Summirat needed to find a way of rewarding.

Gathering himself up off the floor of the hut Summirat walked over to the table where Salim's deputy was seated. Placing a hand on his shoulder he gave the nervous man a wry smile. "Tell your people they did well," Summirat stated with an even tone. "Tomorrow we will mourn the deaths of their brothers and give thanks to Allah."

"And after that?" the deputy commander asked, unable to hide his anxiety.

"After that?" Summirat stated as he looked away as if gazing at a far-off vision neither the deputy nor anyone but he could see. "After that we take what we have learned today and deliver to our people the victory they so richly deserve."

Though he had no earthly idea what Summirat was talking about the deputy accepted the hyperbole and uttered a silent prayer to himself as Summirat walked away, thanking Allah that he wasn't being held accountable for what he assumed had been a total failure.

It was almost dawn before Delmont realized that there was little point in continuing the operation. From the small command post on top of the hill where Quinn had first made contact with the insurgents Delmont issued orders for them to close up into platoon-size defensive perimeters and stand by for further orders. He already knew what those orders would be. He was simply unwilling to issue them until he had absolutely no choice but to put an end to the sweeps by companies B and C and send them back to FOB Fresno with nothing more than a few discarded weapons to show for all their efforts. What damage had been inflicted upon the insurgents had all occurred during in the first twenty minutes of the encounter by Nathan's quartering party, his Third Platoon, and a single Kiowa.

Unable to contain the disgust he felt at seeing his efforts come to naught, Delmont passed word for all company commanders to meet him at his present location. He'd issue them their new orders before heading back to FOB Fresno to brief Lamb, an occasion he was dreading. No doubt the Marine colonel would take this opportunity to once more praise the achievements of Young Dixon as he had come to refer to Nathan.

Without realizing it the campaign to crush Hamdani Summirat and his followers no longer mattered to Delmont. His real enemy, the man he feared would do the greatest damage to his reputation and career was not an Islamic fundamentalist but one of his own company commanders. How he would deal with this most delicate situation was fast becoming the focus of all his attention. The insurgency in the Philippines, Delmont had finally come to accept, would continue long after he had turned his back on this godforsaken place. The same, he feared, could not be said of his career unless he did something drastic.

Whatever hope Eric White had of finally catching up on his sleep was dashed as more officers made their way past his fighting position to where the battalion commander had established a command post. At the moment White wasn't sure who he hated the most, the insurgent commander who had picked this hilltop to defend or his own commanding officer who thought this would be a good place from which to run things. In the end he decided the nameless insurgent was the real culprit. Had he cooperated and simply melted away unseen into the jungle as they had done so in the past, White would have been left in peace.

Looking about, the young Ranger stood up and stretched before settling down on the edge of his fighting position and rummaging about in his ruck in search of an MRE. The fact that he had killed another man earlier that evening didn't bother him in the least. If anything he was glad he had. After all, the bastard had cost him a decent night's sleep.

26

Having briefed Colonel Lamb enough to understand his nonverbal cues the Army major presenting the current intel update stopped in midstride. Planting his feet shoulder width apart and clasping his hands behind his back he stared at Lamb as he and the rest of the staff waited for their commanding officer to vent.

Standing up, Lamb took a step toward the major, mumbled something that no one else heard, and stood there while the major tucked his head in and took his seat as quickly as he could. With his back toward his staff, Lamb took a moment to collect his thoughts before pivoting about and gazing at the expectant faces. Still he said nothing as he mulled over how best to go about informing them of his own conclusions concerning the current situation they faced and the decision he had come to in regards to what they would do next. When he found himself unable to do so, he chose instead to dismiss them. "Thank you, everyone," he muttered in a low voice before making his way to the entrance of the bunker that served as his operations center and command post. Ignoring the buzz of the gathered staff, Lamb's chief of staff, Lieutenant Colonel Gerald Flynn, took off after his commanding officer.

Flynn caught up to Lamb just outside the bunker's main entrance where the colonel was standing stock-still, gazing off into the distance. Having worked with Lamb before, Flynn knew his commanding officer was deeply troubled by a decision that he had to make. Easing up next to him, Flynn made his presence known but said nothing, knowing that when he was ready his superior would share his thoughts and concerns with him. Dropping his chin, Lamb looked down at the ground before him and took a moment to kick a clump of mud with the toe of his boot before heaving a great sigh and glancing over at the one man on the island he could share his darkest thoughts with and confide in. "Do you have any idea how much I loathe doing what I am about to do?"

Knowing it was a rhetorical question Flynn didn't respond. "Before I slit my throat, what do you make of the last three days?" Lamb asked gazing back at the dense jungle that surrounded the FOB.

Doing likewise Flynn took a moment to frame his response. "Ever see that movie about the British and the Zulus at Rorke's Drift?" Flynn asked.

Lamb chuckled. "Who hasn't?"

"Remember the part where the Zulus launched attacks just to see how the British defenders would respond and what the old Afrikaner said when the British officers asked why the Zulus were behaving as they were?"

Lamb shot a quick glance over at Flynn. "You thinking the same thing I am?"

"He's playing us," Flynn answered as he nodded his head. "I don't know if Summirat ever saw that movie but I've no doubt he staged that fight the other day just to see what we were capable of doing and how quickly we could respond."

"I agree. He served us up a handful of his more expendable troops as bait. And like fools we obliged him by snapping it up." Lamb paused as he took a moment to scan the horizon as if searching for something. "We were lucky I suppose. Next time I don't expect we will be."

Flynn was about to ask his commanding officer if he thought that there would be a next time but knew better than to ask such a foolish question. Their foe was too good, too well disciplined, and too well schooled in the art of war to do what he did unless it served a greater purpose. Instead, he just mused as if thinking out loud. "What next?"

His answer was delayed as a pair of staff officers emerged from the bunker entrance Flynn and Lamb were standing next to. Still leery of their commanding officer the pair snapped a crisp salute to which Lamb responded with one of his own that was something less than regulation.

After they had passed Lamb continued where he had left off. "I'm not sure I'm willing to wait to see what's next. Like you said, he's playing us." Then, drawing himself up he turned and faced Flynn, planting his curled fists on his hips. "I'm not about to stick around here with my thumb up my rump waiting for our friend out there to spring whatever sort of surprise he's preparing for us."

"So this is it? We're pulling the plug."

Lamb nodded. "Someone's got to put their head on the block and say enough is enough. This snipe hunt has gone on long enough. We need to put an end to it before things get out of hand."

"Are you sure it's that bad, sir?"

Before answering Lamb glanced over his shoulder, his eyes moving from one familiar sight to the next within the confines of the base camp. "Have you noticed how the number of incidents along the perimeters of the FOB has declined with each and every move we've made?" Looking back at Flynn Lamb continued before his chief of staff could respond. "Do you know why that is?"

Flynn knew what he would have liked to say but realized that answer was too easy, too self-serving. Instead, he did as his commanding officer had done and took a moment to look around, coming to the same conclusion that Lamb had. "He doesn't need to anymore," Flynn finally muttered flatly.

Another member of the staff popped out of the bunker, hesitating a moment when he saw the pair of colonels standing there. Taking a moment, Lamb motioned with his head for the man to pass but not before they exchanged salutes. When he was gone Lamb nodded as he brought his hands up, covered his face with them, and rubbed his eyes with his fingertips. Finished, he gazed up in the sky. "I got to thinking some more about what Young Dixon had said last week. He was spot-on in his analysis of what the Abu Sayyaf wants to do. I'm afraid we on the other hand were a bit off."

Suddenly it all clicked. Now it was Flynn's turn to cast a leery glance about, his eyes darting from one familiar landmark within the perimeter of the FOB to the next, facilities, positions, storage points that he could find in the dark while blindfolded. "He's looking to take us down," Flynn stated in a low, almost astonished voice. Then, looking back at Lamb, he repeated his revelation. "Summirat is planning on taking us on here, not out there. What he did the other day was a trial run, a test to see just how much of our force we were going to throw out there and what was left behind."

"Think of it," Lamb said as he folded his arms tightly across his chest. "What better way to show you're the man than to take down a heavily fortified, well-defended American base of operations."

Flynn responded with a cynical chuckle. "Only we're not a heavily fortified, well-defended base."

Leaning forward, Lamb stared into Flynn's eyes. "You know that. I know that. And I expect he knows that. But his followers, the Filipinos and the world out there, don't. All they'll see is videos he'll make of his men planting their flag on top of my command bunker after they overrun it, just like the Vietminh did to the French at Dien

Bien Phu. And regardless of what we do after that, no matter how many of the bastards we slaughter, they win."

Folding his arms across his chest as well, Flynn looked into his commanding officer's eyes. "So I guess you've made up your mind, we're pulling the plug."

Lamb nodded wearily. "That's what I'm going to recommend."

"You realize what this is going to cost you. Not only are they going to make you the fall guy back home, when you return the Commandant will have someone, probably a former superior or a close friend recommend to you that you start thinking about a graceful retirement."

Unable to look his chief of staff in the eye, Lamb slowly turned his back on him, taking a moment to salute a pair of Marines who just happened to be passing by. "Better that," he finally sighed, betraying the exhaustion he suddenly felt, "then presiding over a military disaster."

"When?" Flynn asked.

Instead of receiving an answer, Flynn suddenly found himself being knocked over as his commanding officer's body pitched backward against his own. Unable to maintain his balance and stay on his feet he tumbled down into the entrance of the bunker where a mad scramble ensued as members of Lamb's staff rushed to his side. After pulling him to his feet Flynn took a moment to collect himself before looking down at the lifeless body of his commanding officer. He didn't need to ask anyone what had happened. The neat red hole in Colonel Timothy Lamb's forehead told him all he needed to know.

In 1954 the Vietminh had 105mm American-built howitzers captured by the Chinese in Korea and given to the Vietnamese Communists with which to pound the besieged French garrison at Dien Bien Phu. In 1968 the North Vietnamese Army used Russian-supplied Katyushas against the American Marines defending Khe Shan. Hamdani Summirat had neither. What he did have were highly trained and well-motivated snipers. In some ways they were superior to large-caliber artillery or rockets in that the Abu Sayyaf snipers were insidious, capable of striking without warning and with an accuracy that was unnerving not only to the poor sod felled by the sniper's bullet but also to those who witnessed their handiwork. It was the fear they would create among those within the perimeter of FOB Fresno that Summirat was counting on to do the real damage. Allowed to go unchecked a pitifully small handful of well-trained and disciplined men could bring an organization to its knees. One only needs to recall the impact that a man and a boy had on the Washington, D.C., metropolitan area in the fall of 2002 to appreciate the power of a sniper.

Unlike the random and senseless murder of innocent American civilians in 2002, the campaign of terror the Abu Sayyaf snipers opened against the soldiers, sailors, Marines, and airmen within the confines of FOB Fresno were part of a larger plan. In time those personnel and their commanding officers would be able to counter the snipers by adapting effective countermeasures, time that Summirat had no intention of giving them.

Aware that time was not on his side either the man who assumed command of FOB Fresno in the wake of Lamb's death moved quickly to take advantage of the opportunity fate had provided him. Unmoved by the case laid out by the dead Marine colonel's chief of staff regarding what he and his former commanding officer had concluded, Robert Delmont wasted none of that valuable commodity staffing his revised plan of action for the conduct of ground operations. After ensuring that Flynn understood that he was the senior officer present by virtue of succession of command as well as date of rank,

Delmont issued new marching orders for the entire command.

In the wake of Company A's last encounter with the Abu Sayyaf and the inability of the rest of his battalion to respond quickly enough, Delmont concluded he stood a better chance of drawing the enemy into a fight if he had two companies operating in the interior as opposed to the one that they had been going with under Lamb's tenure. The unit he selected to join Nathan's company in the field was Company C. In addition to covering more territory Delmont pointed out to Clarence Overton that the real value of using two companies in the field would be their ability to coordinate their sweeps and patrols. When the enemy was encountered, one company would serve as the anvil leaving the other to act as the hammer, smashing the enemy forces between them. Overton's concern that the insurgents might use an attack on one of the companies to draw the other into an ambush was brushed aside by his commanding officer. "Even if that were to happen," he replied, "I am confident in the ability of your company to turn the tactical situation to your advantage. You are after all Rangers. And even if things do go badly at first," he added, "I've got B Company in reserve, ready to sally forth and bail you out."

To solve the sniper problem Delmont ordered Lieutenant Colonel Edward Pinero, the commander of the understrength Marine battalion charged with securing the FOBs, to increase the number of Marine patrols being sent out beyond the perimeter. While this was a common sense solution that few could find fault with, it did have the effect of adding to the wear and tear on the two Marine rifle companies charged with manning a perimeter that was already precariously thin. Pinero's suggestion that Delmont use his Company B for these additional patrols or at least assign them a portion of the perimeter were rejected out of hand by Delmont. They were still offensively oriented he reminded Pinero. In order to exploit any opportunities the Abu Sayyaf presented them or were created by Companies A and C he needed to have something he could throw out into the field. That, he contended, could only be Company B. Again, his decision was eminently logical and tactically sound, provided of course the Abu Sayyaf cooperated.

The one element of JTF Sierra that was pretty much unaffected by Delmont's reshuffling of the deck was Nathan's company. His orders and the tasks his company were responsible for remained unchanged. The only real change concerned the amount of time they spent in the interior. Rather than bringing them in for a few days of rest as had been discussed before Delmont assumed command of JTF Sierra's ground component, it was decided that it would be best if they stayed in the field, a decision that Nathan had no problem with given that the snipers harassing the FOB made rest within the perimeter all but impossible. If anything they would be much safer out where they were, in the jungle moving around, than back in the FOB where they would be little more than stationary targets. "Best to keep the enemy guessing as to what we're going to do next," he told Peter Quinn and First Sergeant Carney, "than afford them the opportunity to study us and decide how best to mess with us." Exactly which enemy his company commander was referring to when he made that comment was a point Quinn debated with Carney when Nathan was not around.

The only changes that Nathan took it upon himself to make was in the manner in which he had been running things concerned with the pace of his company's operations and how they meshed with Clarence Overton's command. Suspecting that the encounter his company had had with the regional forces and the sudden unleashing of snipers on the FOB were but a prelude to something bigger, Nathan reduced the operational tempo of his own command. Something was in the offing he told his officers and senior NCOs as he explained his reasons for doing so, something that would blindside them all and demand a rapid and decisive response. To be prepared for that, he reduced the number of ambushes and patrols he would be sending out each night as well as the size of those patrols. Instead he ordered his subordinates to ensure that every man under them take advantage of whatever opportunity they had to catch up on their sleep. "When the fecal matter hits the fan we need to be ready to move out with a purpose." No one, least of all soldiers like Eric White, objected to this new winkle.

The second step Nathan took was to arrange a coordination meeting with Clarence Overton once his company was in the field. In the military there is nothing at all unusual about the commanding officers of two separate commands meeting to exchange information in regards to their own plans, share information, and coordinate their activities. In fact, this is expected. Being the sort of soldier he was and uneasy about the overall situation, Nathan took things a little farther at his first meeting with his fellow company commander.

As the two captains sat just out of earshot of their respective squads that had tagged along with them to provide security, Nathan put forth his views on the situation. "We're being set up," he explained to Overton. "In my humble opinion everything the insurgents are doing points to that."

While gnawing on a stale cracker Overton nodded in agreement. "That's the general consensus back at the FOB. Major Perry agrees with the colonel for once, thinking that the insurgents are going to try to take one of our companies down, do a Custer on us. Major Castalane and Emmett seem to think the bastards are going to go for the gold, that they're going to try to overrun the FOB."

This caused Nathan to chuckle. He and Emmett DeWitt always did seem to think along the same lines when it came to tactics, a happy coincidence that made taking over Company A from DeWitt so easy for Nathan. He hadn't needed to do a great deal of retraining in order to get DeWitt's old subordinates in sync with his way of thinking.

"We've got to be able and ready to respond to either situation," Nathan continued as he reached over and took a cracker from the open pouch Overton was holding. Spewing tiny crumbs as he spoke while chewing on the cracker Nathan put forth several suggestions as to how they could best achieve this. For the most part Overton listened, interrupting every now and then when he had a suggestion of his own to add to the mix. When they were satisfied that they had covered every contingency imaginable and had a solid plan of how best to respond to each the two officers prepared to part. Before doing so they agreed to meet again in another two days to exchange whatever new information their respective companies had stumbled upon in the interim, review the overall situation, and discuss further the plans they had agreed upon. Until then, they would stay in touch using both the authorized battalion command net as well as a bootleg frequency on which they could chat without any fear of being overheard by any back at battalion. Both knew that this was a serious violation of the chain of command, that it smacked of disloyalty. Yet both understood without having to say so that given the current command climate in the battalion, it was the smart thing to do.

Coming to his feet, Overton stretched as he surveyed the lush countryside that surrounded them. "God, it's great to be out here and away from him."

Having grown wary of tromping through the countryside searching for an illusive foe that was determined not to be found except when it was to his advantage to be, Nathan chuckled. "I hope you feel that way two days from now when we meet again."

Overton gave Nathan a broad grin and a wave as he moved off to join his men who were coming to their feet. "You take care, good buddy."

Nathan just smiled and shook his head. "You too. See ya in two days."

"It's a date."

It was a date that neither man would keep.

27

FORWARD OPERATIONS BASE FRESNO, MINDANAO, PHILIPPINES

The men who planned Operation Pacific Shield had never envisioned turning the forward operations bases into strongpoints capable of withstanding a determined assault or protracted siege. The razor wire and sandbagged emplacements that dotted its outer perimeter were meant to ward off the odd intruder and small bands of infiltrators, nothing more. If the insurgents were stupid enough to seriously test the FOB's defenses, Admiral Turner and his staff were more than confident that the five-inch guns of the task force's escorts, each capable of firing sixteen projectiles per minute, each of which was packed with seventy pounds of high explosives out to a range of thirteen plus miles would suffice to put an end to such foolishness.

Those escorts were gone however, anchored off the coast of Indonesia together with the USS *Wake Island* and one Marine rifle company providing humanitarian support to a Muslim population who viewed Osama bin Laden and Sheikh Sayyed Hassan Nasrallah as folk heroes. This left Lieutenant Colonel Edward Pinero with two Marine rifle companies instead of the three required to protect the sprawling collection of command posts, supply points, helipads, and other support facilities that made up FOB Fresno. His efforts to talk Delmont into dedicating a portion of his Company B or at least planning for their use as part of the overall defensive plan fell on deaf ears. Not only was Delmont convinced that success could only be achieved through offensive operations, the very idea that the Abu Sayyaf might actually attempt to overrun the FOB was dismissed as being nothing more than fanciful. He even went so far as to tell Pinero that he would welcome such an effort, a claim that was eerily familiar to one made by the commanding officer at Dien Bien Phu just prior to the first major Vietminh attack.

Pinero could not be as cavalier as his new commanding officer when it came to securing the FOB. It was after all his sole responsibility, one he took seriously. To this end he did everything within his power to ensure that if Robert Delmont did get his wish, his Marines would be as ready as they could be.

And so Pinero did what Nathan and Overton had. When the direct approach failed, he made an end run. Having failed to convince Delmont to incorporate Company B into the FOB's defense, Pinero did the next best thing. Under the guise of coordinating his efforts with the tenant units within the perimeter, Pinero met with Delmont's operations officer to discuss where units belonging to 3rd of the 75th Rangers, specifically Company B were located and how they were deployed when inside the perimeter. Delmont could not object to this as this was the sort of thing that one expected of an officer in Pinero's position to do.

Quite naturally both Pinero and Major Perry went beyond simply exchanging information. Knowing full well that a determined attack by a sizable force would almost certainly blow through his thin outer defenses, Pinero was able to convince Perry to spread Company B's three platoons out to cover some of the FOB's more sensitive facilities. These included the helipad where the four Blackhawks and four Kiowas were, the FOB's command bunker, and the FOB's aid station. In the event of a failure to hold an attack along the outer perimeter, these dispositions would give Pinero three strongpoints to which his surviving forces on the perimeter could withdraw to or use to channel the direction of an enemy's attack. Together with the one platoon of his own that he held back as a reserve, Pinero was as prepared as circumstances permitted.

Three days after opening his sniper campaign against the American FOB Hamdani Summirat suddenly announced to his subordinates that their time had come. All responded without hesitation that they and their men were ready to strike. Even those belonging to the regional commands that had recently been routed by Nathan's Rangers claimed that they were ready and willing. Summirat knew his people would respond in this manner whether it was true or not. Like them he was anxious to get on with it, to pitch into the Americans not so much because he was confident of victory. On the contrary, like all good military leaders, Summirat understood the fickle nature of war, how in battle even the best-laid plans could be undone by a chance occurrence or a turn of bad luck.

It was more than his belief in their cause or a confidence that victory was theirs for the taking that finally convinced Summirat that he needed this battle. What drove him to adopt a more aggressive strategy was simple human nature. In part his new plan suited a visceral, almost inbred combativeness that created within him a yearning to meet his enemy in open battle, to pit his skills as a warrior and courage as a man against those he viewed as intruders and infidels. Almost from birth he had been taught that only through combat would he prove himself to be a worthy servant of God, one chosen to carry out His will. Not even a man educated in a traditional Western manner could escape the cultural heritage and religious indoctrination that had been such a major element of Summirat's life. In the end it was his heart, not the cold hard logic found in the pages of military history or books on tactical doctrine that tipped the scales in favor of pitching into the Americans.

There was of course one more factor that Summirat fell prey to, another very human trait that tends to plague powerful men who find themselves cast into leadership roles. Having become aware of the discontent within the ranks of his lieutenants Summirat knew that if he didn't do something bold, something that demonstrated that he was truly the chosen one, his position as the leader of the modern Abu Sayyaf movement would be openly questioned by those who saw themselves as even more devote and dedicated than he. A victory in the field against the Americans, something few of his fellow Muslims had been able to achieve, would propel him to a position of strength and power that would rival that achieved by Osama bin Laden. To Summirat that in itself was worth the risks.

In accordance with the informal agreement he had made with Nathan Dixon, as the afternoon waned Clarence Overton gathered his company together. After giving his people a half hour to rest, eat an MRE, and generally relax he ordered his men to their feet and began moving them toward the FOB which at the time was almost due south of where they had been operating. Several kilometers to the east Company A was doing likewise. If nothing transpired between the time the two companies resumed their march toward FOB Fresno and a half hour after sunset each would stop wherever they were, coil up into a tight defensive perimeter, and sit the night out, ready to carry on the following morning with the missions passed down to them from battalion or respond to whatever came their way during the night. In theory both companies were supposed to be sending out a large number of patrols and setting up ambushes all over the place during the night but neither did so. Nathan and Overton dispatched only those patrols and ambushes they felt necessary to ensure local security of their respective companies. They knew that when the hammer fell, and neither man was under any delusion that it wasn't going to, their men would need every ounce of energy they could muster.

It was during this movement that the curtain rose on the first act of Summirat's well-orchestrated attack. At first the encounter between Clarence Overton's Second Platoon and a group of insurgents appeared to be a chance occurrence, little more than a meeting engagement between two opposing forces that simply bumped into each other by accident. That it wasn't quickly became clear as his First Platoon, dispatched to the right of the Second in an effort to outflank the enemy, exchanging fire with the Second ran into a hail of fire from another enemy unit that took them under fire. When an effort to throw his Third Platoon around the other flank met a similar fate, Clarence Overton realized that his company was involved in its first major engagement on grounds of his enemy's choosing. After ordering all of his platoons to hold their current positions and informing the battalion of his situation he contacted Nathan.

Even before his fellow company commander requested that he execute a previously agreed upon contingency plan the two had discussed during their impromptu meeting in the field, Nathan was already issuing orders to his platoons based on what Overton passed back to Delmont over the battalion command net. Back at FOB Fresno Delmont's response was predictable, something both Nathan and Overton expected. Without waiting for either of his commanders in the field to develop the situation any further, Robert Delmont began to launch Company B, just as he had done before. The only difference in the battalion plan this time was that Company C was now to be the focal point around which Nathan's company, operating to the east of Company C, would execute a wide sweeping maneuver to the south and southwest while Company B, coming from FOB Fresno, would assemble to the west of Company C before making a wide sweep to the north and northeast. That the insurgents engaging Overton's company were deployed between that company and FOB Fresno, thus cutting them off from the FOB, wasn't considered to be of any importance at battalion.

The maneuver Nathan was in the process of executing didn't exactly conform to his commanding officer's concept. Rather than make a wide sweep around the insurgents facing Company C, Nathan intended to move his company south a couple of kilometers before forming his company into an extended line facing west and advancing toward Company C. He figured he had a better chance of catching some of the insurgents by making a shallow envelopment than trying to cast a wider net that the enemy could easily slip through.

That plan however quickly went to hell when Nathan's lead platoon, the ever-hapless Third ran into a hail of small arms fire. In one regard fortune smiled on them. The insurgents they ran into were part of the same regional force that they had encountered previously. Wanting to keep the American Rangers at a safe distance, the insurgents initiated their ambush far too soon, unleashing a hail of small arms fire that sounded far more impressive than it proved to be.

This was, of course, cold comfort to Eric White, caught in the middle of the maelstrom. The zing of near misses smacking into tree trunks and sending bits of shredded leaves from overhead vegetation showering down on him and George Bannon was unnerving. Only Bannon's demands that he keep feeding him ammunition for his squad automatic rifle and a steady stream of orders from Sergeant Jones directing them as to where to place their fire kept White from totally losing it. He had heard stories of how grown men went to pieces at times like this, curling up into a ball and crying like babies, leaving him to wonder what it took to reduce a person to such a state. Now he knew.

The heavy volume of fire being directed at his lead platoon as well as the determination of the insurgents to hold their ground in the face of effective return fire was enough to convince Nathan, who had been following the Third Platoon, that there was something more afoot here than anyone suspected. This newest encounter now put the number of Abu Sayyaf detachments his company and Overton's were in contact with at least at four and, judging from the amount of fire that was probably more, making this the largest encounter the 3rd of the 75th had been involved in. Taking a minute to do the math Nathan calculated that between his company and Overton's they were facing a force equal to an entire Abu Sayyaf regional company. Even more disconcerting than this was the fact that there was no indication that the insurgents facing Overton's company or his were giving way and melting back into the jungle despite the punishment they had to be taking. Unable to figure out what possible advantage the insurgents hoped to gain by standing their ground against the combined weight of two Ranger companies Nathan decided to contact battalion and see if Major Perry had any ideas on the subject.

In the meantime he ordered his other platoons to close up but did not commit them to the ongoing firefight that the Third was involved in. Judging from the reports he was getting back from Hal Laski and what he could tell by listening to the exchange the Third was more than holding its own. By keeping the bulk of his company out of it Nathan retained a degree of freedom of action as well as a viable force to deal with any new surprises that the insurgents might decide to send their way.

When word began to circulate back at FOB Fresno that the Rangers in the field were involved in a major firefight with the insurgents Lieutenant Colonel Pinero decided he needed to bring his people up to full alert. After recalling the platoon that had been outside the wire thrashing through the bush in a futile hunt for snipers he instructed the platoon leader of his reserve platoon to stand by for orders. With little information to go on at the moment and having done everything he could there was little left for Pinero to do but personally make a tour of the perimeter to ensure that his Marines were ready to deal with whatever came their way. "Command presence," he shouted out to his sergeant major in order to be heard over the sound of the four Blackhawks as they prepared to take off with the first contingent of Company B. The two Marines were standing at the entrance of the bunker that served as their command post, watching the Rangers sort themselves out into caulks, the term given to a grouping of personnel who could fit into one helicopter. "I can't expect those young Marines out there to put their asses on the line if their commanding officer is cowering in the corner of his CP, now can I?" Pinero shouted into the ear of his sergeant major.

An outspoken veteran of more campaigns than he cared to remember the sergeant major, feet planted shoulder width apart and with his hands on his hips, pulled his head back and glowered at his commanding officer. "With all due respect, Colonel," he grumbled in a gruff manner that was something of a requirement for a Marine in his position, "getting yourself shot isn't the sort of example you want to set. That sort of thing tends to upset the lads."

A smirk lit Pinero's face as he folded his arms over his chest. "Is that so?" he quibbled. "Well, let me tell you . . ."

The whine of the Blackhawk's turbine engines and the deep *whoop, whoop, whoop* sound their massive blades made as they sliced through the thick jungle air drowned out the thud of mortars being fired off in the distance. The first inclination Pinero or anyone else had that FOB Fresno was under attack was the detonation of Chinese-made 82 mm mortar rounds as they smashed the woefully inadequate overhead cover of the Marine CP, burying the staff of the Marine security battalion and decapitating its commanding officer.

The sudden deluge of high explosives caught Robert Delmont just short of the helipad. Ignoring the mayhem erupting about him he rushed to a spot precariously close to the front of the lead Blackhawk. Waving his arms and shouting though he knew he could not be heard over the roar of the aircraft's engines, Delmont frantically motioned to the commander of the small detachment of helicopters to take off. When the copilot caught sight of Delmont he turned to his pilot. "Where the hell does he want us to go?"

The pilot didn't need any prompting from Delmont to know what to do. Ignoring the Ranger colonel in front of his bird he made a quick check to his left and right to see if all personnel on the ground were clear. "Anywhere but here, you fool," he snapped in response to his copilot's witless question as he executed a steep climb followed by a hard bank to the right. Behind him the other three birds under his command also followed suit with two of them making it.

With the same determination with which he forced himself to ignore the incoming mortar rounds, Delmont turned his back on the spectacle of a stricken Blackhawk madly spinning out of control for several brief seconds before pitching nose down and plowing into the ground, finishing the destruction of the helipad that the Abu Sayyaf mortars had started. As others around him dove for whatever cover they could find, Delmont made his way back to the FOB command post. His journey was cut short when he saw what had been the neatly laid out complex from which the FOB's day-to-day operations were carried out being torn apart by a deluge of mortar rounds. Hesitating, Delmont wavered as he looked about trying to figure out where to turn to next. The sight of his old command bunker, undisturbed thus far, provided him with an answer.

The situation that Summirat faced when planning for his attack on FOB Fresno was the flip side of what Edward Pinero had dealt with when trying to decide how best to defend it. Both men had limited assets with which to accomplish their tasks. In Pinero's case it had been too few troops to defend too much perimeter. For Summirat it was making very difficult choices when it came to selecting what targets needed to be hit and in what order to hit them. With seven 82 mm mortars divided into a four-tube section and a three-tube section as well as four 120 mm mortars operating as a separate entity he was limited to three choices during his opening barrage.

Destruction of the FOB's command bunker as well as the one used by the Marine security detachment was a given. Disruption of those elements responsible for coordinating the defense of the FOB would create confusion and slow the response of the defenders to his assault on the outer perimeter. For this purpose he allocated the three-tube section of 82 mm mortars manned by fighters drawn from the local regional force company to hit the Marine command post and the 120 mm mortars to neutralize the main FOB headquarters. How best to employ the second section of 82 mm mortars crewed by members of his main strike force had been the real dilemma to which there was no one right answer. Destroying the third American command post within the perimeter of the FOB, the one belonging to the Ranger battalion, was tempting but would not result in making the ground assault by his main force units any easier. Hitting the helipad just as a Ranger platoon was in the process of boarding on the other hand would quite literally kill two birds with one stone. Without the Blackhawk transport helicopters the Americans would be unable to fly those units already in the field back to reinforce the defenders of the FOB. They would be forced to fight their way through the regional forces which they were engaging before marching overland. In addition to denying the Americans their precious mobility, if he timed it just right his opening barrage would catch a platoon of Rangers in the open as they were preparing to board the helicopters responding to the diversion his regional units were engaged in.

It was a good plan but like all plans in combat this one didn't make it much past initial contact, helped in no small measure by an enemy that failed to cooperate with it. The timing of the mortar barrage directed against the helipad had been good. The reaction of both the Blackhawk pilots as well as the platoon leader of Company B's second platoon was even better. A veteran of Iraq with a platoon full of NCOs who were all veterans of both Iraq and Afghanistan, the young lieutenant didn't need to draw his people a picture as to what they needed to do when the first mortar rounds slammed into the Marine command post little more than fifty meters from where they sat waiting to board the choppers. By the time the helipad was hit the Rangers were gone, scurrying back to the fighting positions Lieutenant Colonel Pinero had directed them to dig. Company B's Third Platoon, which had yet to leave their positions sited around the 3rd of the 75th's command post simply hunkered down while the company executive officer who had stayed behind cautiously peeked over the rim of his position in an effort to get a handle on the situation as the last of the late afternoon light began to fade.

Within the 3rd of the 75th Ranger's command bunker Major Castalane, who had assumed command of the battalion when Delmont took over as the FOB's overall commanding officer, realized with both the Marine and FOB CPs gone they were next. Turning to Major Perry he ordered his operations staff to grab as many portable radios as they could and clear out of the bunker. "Head over to the helipad," he shouted over the scramble to secure radios and personal gear. "Odds are they won't be targeting that spot again."

Next he turned to Emmett DeWitt. "Find the XO of B Company or the platoon leader of the Third Platoon. Get them to move that platoon over to the helipad and set up a defensive perimeter together with the platoon that's already there. Tell him to be prepared to counterattack and plug any holes in the outer perimeter if there's a break in."

After acknowledging Castalane's orders, DeWitt hesitated. "Where will you be?"

Not having thought that far ahead, Castalane hesitated before responding. "I'm heading over to see what's left of the Marine CP and staff. When I'm done there I'll join you at the helipad." With that Castalane, Perry, and DeWitt followed by the rest of the battalion staff piled out of the narrow entrance of the bunker and into the gathering confusion beyond.

It took several minutes for Nathan to realize that something serious was wrong. The confused and harried chatter on the battalion command net followed by silence caused him to order a halt in the maneuver his company had been in the midst of executing until such time as he was able to sort out what exactly was going on back at battalion. His efforts to do so were hampered by Major Castalane's decision to vacate the battalion CP bunker. For several critical minutes the only information Nathan received concerning what was going on back at the FOB came to him via the commander of the four Kiowa Warriors that were preparing to support Company C. They in turn had to rely on reports relayed to them from the Blackhawks that were circling the FOB just outside of small-arms range.

Having already concluded that the forces they were facing were regional fighters both Nathan and Clarence Overton were able to put two and two together. And while neither had a clear picture of the overall tactical situation, both agreed that the Abu Sayyaf's main effort was targeted against the FOB, not them. Sorting out how best to respond wasn't very difficult either. Rather than doing what the insurgent commander expected them to do, the two company commanders as well as Neil Reed, the new commanding officer of Company B who was located four kilometers west of Overton's position with the one platoon that had been moved before the attack began, came up with their own scheme of maneuver.

Judging by the volume of fire coming from the south Nathan assumed the insurgents expected the Rangers to attempt to blow through the regional forces deployed to their immediate south and head straight to the relief of the FOB. Because it was the most obvious thing to do he suggested they take a more indirect approach. With a map spread out in his lap and his XO and first sergeant looking over his shoulder, Nathan shared his thoughts with his two fellow company commanders via radio, ignoring proper radio call signs as he did so in order to ensure that everyone understood exactly what he was saying. "Clarence, you maintain your positions where you are with two of your platoons and one of mine doing your best to create the impression that we're all still here. I'll take my other two platoons and strike out due east until I'm clear of the firefight before turning south and heading for the extreme northeastern portion of the FOB's perimeter. At the same time send one of your platoons due west to marry up with Neil and the platoon he's got with him. Neil, when that link up has been affected you head toward the extreme northwestern portion of the FOB's perimeter. Once my company and Neil's group get within a kilometer or so of the FOB we'll both turn to face each other and press the enemy between us. Clarence, when that happens blow through the people in front of you and head due south as quickly as possible. If we move quickly enough we can box those people in."

Overton readily agreed. Neil Reed, however, could not

but help to state the obvious. "You do realize that the odds are the insurgents will outnumber us?"

Having already concluded that this was most likely the case Nathan brushed aside Reed's concerns in typical Ranger fashion. "The more the merrier."

When he was finished conferring with his fellow company commanders Nathan turned to his XO and first sergeant. "Pete, I want you to stay with the Second Platoon and help Captain Overton. First Sergeant, you're to take up the rear. I'm going to be moving at the double quick and expect we'll drop a few people along the way. Police the stragglers, keep them together, and keep them moving. Any questions?"

Both Quinn and Carney glanced over at each other a moment before nodding. Both men had a thousand and one questions flooding through their minds but neither said a word. Each knew that this was neither the time nor the place for long-winded discussions or debates. "Okay, we have a long way to go and not a whole lot of time to do it in, so let's get moving."

Having managed to organize something resembling a defensive perimeter centered on the pockmarked helipad Major Perry was able to turn his attention back to running the battalion, catching part of the discussion between his company commanders. Unable to reach either Major Castalane or Delmont and with nothing better in mind, he quickly concurred with the scheme Nathan, Overton, and Reed had hatched, promising to assist them as best he could by keeping them posted on the situation within the FOB's perimeter. He also promised that when Reed and Nathan were closer he would support their maneuver with whatever forces he had on hand. In the meantime he turned his attention to establishing contact with the two Marine companies defending the FOB's perimeter and finding a way to employ the Kiowa Warriors that were circling just north of the FOB looking for targets.

Getting a handle on the situation was also foremost in Robert Delmont's mind. With the FOB's main command post out of action and the Marine CP gone he had little choice but to make his way back as best he could to the bunker belonging to the 3rd of the 75th. His journey was not an easy one. With the last of the fading light gone and the familiar landscape of the FOB ripped apart by the initial mortar barrage it took Delmont longer than he expected to reach his old CP. Along the way he was continuously accosted by officers and NCOs belonging to support elements who recognized him and stopped him, asking the same thing, what to do and where to go. At first Delmont felt compelled to give each and every one of them some sort of reasonable response. He was after all not only an officer but at the moment their commander. Eventually it dawned upon him that he was achieving very little by wasting his time dealing with individuals while the overall situation continued to spin out of control. By way of compromise he settled on telling those who sought guidance from him simply to follow him. What exactly he'd do with the gaggle of people he quickly gathered about him once he reached the 3rd of the 75th CP was something he didn't have an answer for.

In his relief at having finally reached his old command bunker Delmont didn't notice that there was no one manning the security checkpoint at the entrance. Only after pushing aside the blackout curtain that covered the doorway and stepping into the center of the small room that served as the battalion's ops center did he realize that no one was there. Confused, he took a moment to survey the overturned chairs and tables littered with scraps of paper that spoke of a hasty evacuation. Frustrated, enraged, and feeling betrayed by his own staff, Delmont spun about and began to make his way back out into the darkness, hell-bent on finding out where they had gone and what idiot had given the order to abandon the command post.

He never made it clear of the entrance as a hail of 120 mm mortar rounds plunged the bunker into complete darkness and brought the ceiling of plywood-covered timbers and sandbags crashing down on top of him.

Having hit both their primary and secondary targets the gunners of Summirat's 82 mm and 120 mm mortars deftly adjusted the traverse and elevation knobs of their weapons to the settings required to hit the next set of targets before aligning the mortars' sights on the candy striped aiming stakes set out before each of the tubes. When they were ready an assistant gunner stepped forward and "hung" a mortar round over the muzzle of each of the mortars, waiting patiently as he had been trained for the order to fire. Having knocked out all the primary command and control headquarters as well as the helipad and an ammo dump it was now time to turn their weapons on selected points along the outer perimeter. Once they had been dealt with and a breach had been made in the outer perimeter by Summirat's specially trained assault teams, it would be an easy matter for the following waves drawn from his main force units to make their way forward into the FOB and systematically eliminate the remaining pockets of resistance.

With the American forces within the perimeter of the FOB eliminated, Summirat would be free to turn his full attention on those Ranger companies that were deployed ten kilometers to the north. Having little confidence in the ability of his regional forces to hold them for very long, Summirat had deployed a third of his main force units, a force amounting to a little over two hundred veteran fighters, along trails the Americans would have to use if they hoped to quickly reach the FOB. Having managed to break free of the regional forces pinning them in place, the Ranger companies would then find themselves forced to fight their way through a series of deadly ambushes. Not only would there be no one left within the FOB for the Rangers to rescue even if they did manage to reach it, Summirat calculated that the American Ranger companies would be so depleted in numbers and low on ammunition that it would take little effort on his part to finish them off.

While it was true that his plan was about as daring as one could dream of, a victory of that magnitude against the best troops the Americans could throw against him was all it would take to convince the government in Manila that it could never hope to defeat him militarily. They would be forced to negotiate with him on his terms, turning Mindanao as well as the islands to the south over to him. Fortune, Summirat reminded his lieutenants, favored the bold.

Eric White found the mad dash through the jungle exhausting, painful, and terrifying. The fading sound of small arms from the firefight they were leaving was soon replaced by the rumble of explosions in the distance ahead that grew louder with each step he took. The thought of rushing headlong into mortar fire scared the hell out of him. In his mind the prospect of being torn apart by high explosives was more terrifying than being shot. A bullet wound was a clean wound, or so he had been told. Shrapnel from a bomb or a mortar shell, however could be ugly, capable of gouging out huge chunks of flesh and severing limbs. About the only thing that kept him going forward at the moment was an even greater fear, that of getting lost in the jungle.

In the pitch blackness it was all but impossible to see the man before him even though he was but a few feet away. Only the sound of vegetation being crushed underfoot, branches being shoved aside and snapping back, and the labored breathing of the man in front allowed him to keep track of the direction they were moving. He would have loved to have taken out his night-vision goggles and snapped them onto the bracket attached to the front of his helmet, but they were all under orders to keep them safely stowed away till they really needed them lest a stray branch snag the goggles as they ran headlong through the jungle and rip the valuable and quite vulnerable piece of equipment off.

So White found himself reduced to playing follow the leader as Nathan led two platoons of Company A in a mad rush from the frying pan and into the fire Hamdani Summirat was unleashing on FOB Fresno.

Having hammered the remaining command bunker the mortars turned their attention to the defensive positions on the outer perimeter of the FOB. Summirat's mortar crews were able to do this with little difficulty and stunning accuracy based on a careful study of previous American bases. They knew that each of the Marine rifle companies charged with the security of the base kept two of their three rifle platoons deployed along the outer perimeter with each of their three squads responsible for manning two mutually supporting fighting positions.

The ground attack would be conducted against two separate points along the outer perimeter. This attack would be preceded by a barrage laid down by the 82 mm mortar sections with each section hitting two adjacent positions. Once those positions were neutralized, an assault force of 150 fighters drawn from Summirat's main force would go through the breach created by the barrage. Even if those assault forces did take casualties from a few diehard Marines, Summirat was convinced that the force ratio he was throwing against the Marines would be sufficient to overwhelm them at the selected points and break into the interior of the American base where the assault forces would find nothing but lightly armed and disorganized support troops. Should they run into pockets of serious resistance after the break-in, Summirat had a reserve of a hundred men under his personal control which would follow up the assault force and move from point to point, mopping up any holdouts.

It was a good plan, one which the men chosen to execute it had rehearsed using the remains of an abandoned FOB. Everyone involved in it knew what was expected of them. Everyone knew what they were supposed to do once they had breached the outer perimeter. Everyone that is but the Americans who were not privy to Summirat's plan or the role they were expected to play.

The first glitch came in the form of the four Kiowa Warriors that had been dispatched north to assist Overton's company before the mortar barrage had opened. When the leader of the flight figured out they were on a fool's errand he turned his tiny command about and headed back south to see what he could do to aid in the defense of the FOB. In the gathering darkness it was difficult to pinpoint any targets of value below. Only an oversight by one of the regional force 82 mm mortar crews gave the Kiowas what they were looking for, a target. It was a stupid mistake, one that an experienced mortar crew or a veteran fighter would not have made. But the regional fighters were neither. Though no less dedicated than any of the men who made up the ranks of Summirat's main strike force, the regional fighters simply couldn't match either their experience or discipline.

The three-tube mortar section had been assigned a series of targets that needed to be hit in sequence. The first had been the Marine command bunker, a task accomplished with great precision and speed. The second had been the FOB's main ammo dump, a large target that Summirat was sure not even the regional fighters could miss. He was right. The series of secondary explosions that lit up the early night sky was all the proof the insurgent mortar crews needed to prove that they had hit their mark. The third target in the fire plan, perhaps the most important, was to support the assault by elements of the main strike force against the eastern portion of the American perimeter. Two bunkers were selected for destruction. With them out of action the 150 veteran fighters ordered to hit that portion of the perimeter would be free to break into the American base where they would begin the methodical process of eliminating it from within.

To accomplish all of its assigned tasks the crews of the regional mortar section carefully prepared the rounds they would need beforehand, removing the rounds from their shipping containers and stacking the number of rounds required for each fire mission next to each tube. It was the packing material from those rounds, carelessly discarded, that betrayed their position.

With deadly precision the four little birds lined up and launched their attacks, shredding the mortar crews with a hail of 2.75-inch rockets. What the American rockets did not achieve the piles of uncased mortar rounds piled high next to each tube did as a string of sympathetic denotations devastated the crewmen of the regional mortar section who had managed to fire but a few rounds at the Marine fighting positions along the outer perimeter.

Farther to the south Hassan Rum, the man chosen to lead the assault on the eastern portion of the perimeter, watched as the first mortar rounds hit a little wide of their mark, missing the two Marine emplacements that had been selected as targets. Dutifully he radioed his observation back to the commander of the regional mortar section supporting his attack. That he didn't receive a response didn't bother Rum as they were all under orders to restrict their use of the radio in order to deny the Americans the ability to locate, jam, or gather information on their activities from their transmissions.

In the silence that followed their first volley Rum waited for the mortars to adjust their aim and continue the bombardment. When that pause began to drag out, turning into minutes, he realized something was wrong. Ignoring his orders he attempted to contact the commander of the mortar section. When he received no response he hesitated, wondering if he should send a runner back to find out what the problem was or press forward with the attack.

A call from Summirat on the radio asking him what his situation was goaded Rum into action. After having prodded Summirat for months to take a more aggressive stance against the Americans, Rum found it impossible to tell him that he was hesitating. Finding himself unable to do so Rum responded by assuring Summirat that his fighters were at that very moment going forward, knowing full well that Summirat had no way of knowing that this was in fact a lie.

It did however satisfy Summirat, leaving Rum to do what he knew he must. Turning to the men selected to cut the perimeter wire and open lanes for the main assault force he ordered them forward. No one questioned the order. Not only did they trust the man they had been following for years, they were confident that whatever happened they would soon be basking in glory, either here on earth or in paradise.

Dutifully the breaching team went forward, covered only by darkness. On the other side of the wire the Marines manning positions unscathed by the half dozen errant mortar rounds that had been lobbed at them nervously stroked the triggers of their weapons as they watched this advance through their night-vision goggles, waiting with growing anticipation for the order to fire. There was no fear among these Marines, no apprehension. If truth be known they were excited, almost overjoyed for there before them, after enduring jungle heat, countless insect bites, and hours of sheer boredom, was the enemy, fully exposed and ripe for the picking. All they needed was permission to open fire and they would finally be free to do what they were trained to do, kill.

When he judged that the insurgents were about as exposed as they were going to get, the platoon leader responsible for the section of perimeter that Rum was charged with breaching gave that order. The initial eruption of fire was all it took to sweep away the six insurgents who had been tasked to cut the wire. It was over so quickly that the Marine lieutenant hardly had time to catch his breath after ordering his men to fire before he had to order them to cease fire.

Though stunned by the speed with which his men had been struck down, Rum, now galvanized into action, ordered the men selected to back up the primary breaching party forward. They too were swept away in a hail of small-arms fire. Enraged, both by the failure of his men and the terrible position he now found himself in Rum stood up, waved his hand over his head, and ordered his entire assault force forward. They would trample the razor wire underfoot and rush the Marine fighting positions, overwhelming them with sheer numbers and a determination he was sure not even American firepower could match.

He was wrong.

Once more the Marine lieutenant watched and waited. He had heard stories from the veterans of the 2003 invasion of Iraq of how Arab Fedayeen had defied all logic and charged into the teeth of American firepower. This however was the first time he had ever seen anything like it. From left to right there was a wall of humanity, armed to the teeth and screaming like demons, coming straight at him. It was a sight that was both terrifying and fascinating. Once more the young Marines under his command waited for his orders. This time, before unleashing them all, he instructed those selected to do so to set off their claymore mines, an antipersonnel device packed with one and a half pounds of C-4 and seven hundred 10.5--grain steel pellets. The effect on the front rank of Rum's assault force was devastating. One second they were there, the next they were gone.

The psychological impact on those behind them was

almost as brutal. In an effort to overcome the collective body blow that his assault column had suffered Rum ran forward and into the wire, shouting at the top of his lungs as he madly waved his arms over his head, doing everything that he could to keep from losing the momentum of his attack.

The Marine lieutenant didn't give Rum much of an opportunity to rally his men or for them to recover from their shock. In an almost causal, businesslike voice he gave the order for his entire platoon to fire. The one-two punch of the mines followed in quick succession by a hail of small-arms fire was all it took to break the assault on the eastern side of the perimeter. Stunned, befuddled, and feeling betrayed, the survivors of Rum's assault group melted back into the jungle from which they had emerged, leaving their leader hanging in the wire where he used his dying breath to praise his God.

28

Though concerned that he had heard nothing from Hassan Rum for some time, Summirat paid little mind to this discrepancy as he closely followed the progress being made by the western assault group under the command of Ricardo Sukandar. At his chosen point of attack all had gone like clockwork for Sukandar as the mortars supporting him smothered the Marine defensive positions selected for destruction followed quickly by the breaching party and finally the assault force itself. And while each of these elements took casualties from scattered and desultory small-arms fire from within the perimeter, the speed and weight of the attack swept all before it. Within minutes Sukandar and his men were through the perimeter and beginning to break down into smaller groups, each assigned to attack a specific target within the American base.

Not far from the point where the perimeter was in the process of being breached, Ben Castalane finally reached the helipad. In addition to Major Perry, Emmett DeWitt, and the operations staff of the 3rd of the 75th he found the Rangers of Company B's Second and Third Platoons feverishly digging defensive positions. Perry, never one to miss the significance of a moment, gave Castalane a wary smile. "Now I know how Benteen felt when Reno joined him at the Little Bighorn."

As keen on his history as was his operations officer, Castalane nodded. "Let's just hope we're as lucky as they were. Now, what's the situation?"

In short order Perry filled Castalane in on what the companies in the field were doing and what he knew of the situation around the perimeter. They were in the midst of this when word reached them that the Marine company defending the western portion of the perimeter was giving way. Having managed to get both Marine company commanders onto the 3rd of the 75th's command frequency and knowing the layout of the FOB, Castalane didn't require much time to decide what needed to be done. In this he was greatly assisted by the Marine captain commanding the company under attack who had already thrown his reserve platoon into a line with its left flank linked to where the perimeter still held in toward the center of the FOB, anchoring its right flank on his own company CP.

"We'll form a pocket," Castalane explained to Perry and DeWitt speaking as fast as he could and still be understood. "Emmett, I want you to take B Company's Third Platoon and put it in a line extending from where the western Marine company's CP is to here facing north. Larry, have the Third Platoon swing into line facing northwest. I'll have the eastern Marine company bring their reserve platoon over and form a line facing west extending from the Third Platoon's right till it makes contact with the perimeter. If we move fast enough we can create a pocket and contain the breakthrough before those people get loose. Now move."

Without waiting for either man to reply Castalane got on the radio and relayed his plan to the Marine company commanders. Both acknowledged and immediately turned to their own company command nets to issue orders to their subordinates.

Having done all he could in regard to the immediate crisis within the FOB, Castalane next turned his attention to the groups of Rangers in the field. After getting a fix on their progress he decided that they couldn't wait for Reed and Dixon to be in place before getting Overton moving. Though he suspected that the insurgents had some sort of force deployed between Overton's composite company and the FOB, Castalane was willing to gamble that the threat of being squeezed between two forces would cause the insurgent commander to either break off his attack or disrupt his timetable and do something stupid. It was a long shot but at the moment Castalane was grasping for straws. If the pocket he was trying to form within the FOB didn't hold, their only hope of salvation would rest with the Ranger companies north of the wire.

All the bad news hit Summirat at once. A runner sent over to find out why Hassan Rum was not responding to repeated calls over the radio returned with the news that Rum was dead, his attack had failed, and the survivors of that attack were milling about in the jungle trying to sort themselves out. On the heels of this disturbing news were the first indications that Sukandar's breakthrough was running into unexpected resistance. While disappointed that Rum's efforts had failed, Summirat had expected that at least one of his attacks would fail. As to the difficulties Sukandar was encountering, that was easily remedied. After all, that's why Summirat had a reserve made up of his best fighters. Without hesitation he ordered those hundred men to move off to the west and link up with Sukandar's force. Assuming that the Americans had stripped their perimeter in the east of Marines in order to contain the penetration his forces had made in the west, Summirat decided to shift the 200 fighters he had deployed in the north to keep the American Rangers contained to the eastern portion of the perimeter where Rum's attack had failed and renew the attack there. Even if they didn't break through, this renewed attack would keep the Marines in the east pinned there. With the regional forces farther north more than holding their own against the American Rangers, Summirat saw little point in tying down some of his best troops. He knew the issue would be decided in the south and to that end, he was willing to throw everything he had into that fight that he could.

Ignoring the pleas from Castalane to expedite his advance Clarence Overton took his time briefing the platoon leaders under his command and making sure their platoons were in place and ready to go before initiating his attack. His efforts and patience were not wasted. With shocking ease they shattered the exhausted regional fighters and sent them scurrying through the jungle. Stunned and without any hope of being able to rally or regroup, most of those who survived the initial onslaught fled into the night with one thought in mind, escape. What few pockets did remain behind were either ignored or quickly brushed aside.

. The collapse of the regional forces was so rapid and so complete that their commanding officer never had the opportunity to contact Summirat and inform him of the calamity.

Shaken by the punishment that they had suffered at the hands of the Marines and the death of their leader the survivors of the attack in the east prepared themselves to renew their attack once they were reinforced by their fellow fighters who were on their way to join them. The sound of men moving quickly through the jungle toward them from the north brought Rum's exhausted men to their feet as they gathered about their section leaders and patiently awaited the order to go forward once more. It therefore came as something of a shock when the new-comers opened fire on them. At first they thought that it was a mistake, that their brethren had mistaken them for Americans. When they realized that the men coming up behind them were American Rangers, all semblance of discipline evaporated as each man sought salvation through flight or surrender.

Nathan's lead platoon was as shocked by their sudden encounter with the Abu Sayyaf fighters as they were to find themselves being overrun by American Rangers. In the ensuing confusion the Rangers of Terry Grimes's First Platoon had no time to sort out which of the Abu Sayyaf fighters before them were fleeing, which ones were surrendering, and which ones were preparing to re-sist. To a man they simply gunned down anyone that didn't look like a Ranger.

The first inkling that Summirat had that something was going terribly wrong with his revised plan was when he heard the sound of small arms fire to his northeast. No one was supposed to be there, least of all Americans. His first thought was that the fighters he had pulled away from the north to reinforce Rum's shattered command had accidentally bumped into the very troops they were headed off to reinforce. Only when men he had come to depend upon, men he had thought to be unflappable, be-gan to run past him in sheer abject horror did he realize that he no longer had the initiative, that somehow some of the American Rangers he had assumed were still well to his north had managed to slip around his flanks.

As if to confirm this a desperate plea from Sukandar for assistance blared from the earpiece of Summirat's ra-dio. In a voice that betrayed his panic the leader of his western assault force reported that he was now being fired on from the rear, that his entire force, both those he had begun with as well as the hundred men Summirat had sent him, was surrounded. In a tone Summirat found distasteful and unmanly Sukandar pleaded with Summirat to come to his aide.

As the two hundred main force fighters he had withdrawn from the north began to gather around his small command group, Summirat made the only decision he could. Ignoring Sukandar's cries for assistance he told those section leaders with him to prepare to breakout to the east. This battle was lost. The best he could hope for now was to salvage what he could and withdraw into the hills where he would, God willing, be left in peace to rebuild a force to replace the one he had just gambled away.

Taking advantage of the lull Nathan made his way up and down the line his company was now deployed in, doing all he could to encourage his exhausted troops and make sure that they were in the best possible fighting positions the terrain and time allowed. When he came across First Sergeant Carney he asked him how he was holding up. Though he was winded and nearing the end of his rope Carney managed to give his company commander a faint smile. "I'm good for one more round."

"Good. Here's what we've got." Nathan quickly explained how the company was deployed. "We're facing west which is where I think the bulk of the enemy forces still are. First Platoon is on the left with Third on the right. I'm expecting C Company to come up on our right and link up with Third Platoon. But there's also the chance that the enemy may figure out what's going on and try to slip away before that happens. I want you to position yourself on the extreme right of the line. Let me know when you make contact with C Company. If on the other hand those other people start flooding past you, I want you to bend the line back. Whatever happens don't let them wrap around behind us."

Carney nodded. "Got it."

"Good luck, First Sergeant."

With that taken care of, Nathan made his way south, once more trooping along the length of his line. When he ran into Hal Laski he informed him of the instructions he had given Carney and ordered him to place himself in the center of his platoon's portion of the line. "If Carney does need to wheel the line back you'll be the pivot point. Don't let the line break. Understand?"

With the same grim determination Carney had shown, Hal Laski acknowledged his commanding officer's orders and headed off to find a good place from which he could carry them out.

Nathan's next stop was at the extreme right of the line where he found Terry Grimes. He told Grimes that he wanted him to stay there in the extreme right. If possible he was to make contact with the Marines still holding along the FOB's perimeter. Grimes reported that he had already done so. "Those guys are nervous as hell but they managed to keep their trigger fingers in check. No one's going to get around the right. No one."

Satisfied that he had done all he could, Nathan returned to the center of the line where the right of his First Platoon met the left flank of his Third. When he noticed that there was a small clearing in front of the spot he had chosen to make his stand Nathan once more made his way along his line until he found what he was after. Looking down at the SAW gunner he motioned for the man to get up. "You, come with me."

Corporal George Bannon rose to his feet, hoisting his squad automatic weapon up and onto his shoulder. He was about to step off following his company commander when he paused and looked back to where Eric White was still lying on the ground. "What the hell are you waiting for?" Bannon demanded.

Calling upon his last reserve of strength, White managed to gather himself up off the ground and follow as well. When they reached the clearing Nathan showed

Bannon where he wanted him to set up. White plopped back down on the ground next to Bannon, took a moment to survey the sector his company commander had assigned him, and settled in to wait. He didn't know exactly what he was waiting for but suspected that he wouldn't have long to wait and definitely wouldn't like whatever it was when it came his way.

As he had feared, the sound of small-arms fire to his front told Summirat that the Americans had indeed encircled him. Realizing there was no time left for sophisticated maneuvers and no need to explain things to the men with him Summirat gave the only order he could. Attack!

Without hesitation every man who heard Summirat's battle cry rushed forward, firing their assault rifles as they went. Within the span of a minute, maybe two, the opposing lines of combatants collided.

Having given the order to open fire Nathan had little more that he could do but join in the mayhem, firing his own weapon as quickly as he could bring it to bear on a new target. To his right the SAW gunner he had placed to cover the open field hammered away at the dark figures and shadows that came hurling toward them. When those who managed to make it across the clearing reached his position, the young corporal rose to his feet, drew his knife from a sheath strapped to his boot, and hurled himself against the first figure that came within his reach.

Eric White, terrified yet fully alert, managed to parry a blow directed at him by an insurgent who was swinging his rifle about like a club. Not knowing what else to do White bowed his head and lurched forward, hitting the menacing figure before him in the stomach with his helmet and knocking him to the ground.

All along the way the neat, orderly formations that

both Nathan and Summirat had taken such care to organize disappeared as dozens of vicious little battles between individual combatants broke out. In the confusion no one asked for quarter as each and every man on both sides knew that none would be granted.

From his open-air command post in the middle of the torn-up helipad where he had been directing the battle Ben Castalane took a moment to stand up and look toward the northeast, helpless to do anything more to help Nathan but utter a silent prayer for him and the men under his command.

With the coming of dawn Emmett DeWitt knew it was time to tally the cost. As the battalion's adjutant it would fall upon his shoulders to make sure that the names of those who did not answer the roll call that morning were properly recorded and reported. But before he turned his attention to this grim task he had a more personal matter that he needed to look after.

Making his way through the lanes cleared in the outer perimeter DeWitt headed off to where Company A had made its last stand. As he went a steady stream of stretcher bearers and walking wounded passed him headed in the opposite direction. Whenever he recognized the face of a man who he had once commanded, DeWitt made an effort to say something. Few returned his greeting. Those that did were able to muster up little more than a single muttered word or a nod.

It wasn't difficult to find where Company A had fought. The bodies of the insurgents were still where they had fallen. Mixed in among them were some of the Rangers who had died but a few short hours before. It was, DeWitt thought, a scene straight from Stephen King's worst nightmare.

He found his friend Nathan sitting in the middle of this carnage, bare headed and staring down at the ground between his feet as a Navy corpsman tended to a gash on his right arm. Squatting down before him DeWitt managed to find a smile. "Hey, good buddy. How's it going?"

With monumental effort Nathan managed to lift his head and gaze into DeWitt's eyes. The dull, vacant stare he returned sent a chill down DeWitt's spine. Reaching out DeWitt placed a hand on Nathan's good shoulder. "You did good last night. Your whole company did good."

By way of answering DeWitt Nathan turned his gaze to one side where a pair of combat boots protruded out from under a poncho. Hesitating, DeWitt wondered if he knew the man, if the motionless figure stretched out on the ground before him had once been one of his when he had commanded A Company.

Eventually it dawned upon Nathan that this was what was going through his friend's mind. Clearing his throat Nathan did what he could to put his friend's mind at rest. "He was a new man," he croaked. "I think his name was White. Never had a chance to get to know him."

DeWitt heaved a sigh. "You knew him, Nate. He was a Ranger."

Looking up at the clear morning sky, Nathan blinked his eyes in an effort to hold himself together. "Yeah, I guess I did know him. He was a good man. They all were." All of them Nathan thought as an image of his father flashed before his mind's eye. "God," Nathan muttered, "make this man's life count for something."

Not knowing what to say in response DeWitt stood up and waited patiently while the corpsman finished binding Nathan's wound. When he was done DeWitt took Nathan by the arm, helped his friend to his feet, and led him away. They had done all that they could here. It was time for others to make sense of the night's slaughter and perhaps give some meaning to it.

Epilogue

Unable to wait, Admiral Turner hopped from island to island as he made his way north by helicopter, refueling as he went. Arriving an hour after dawn he was greeted by Major Castalane, Major Perry, and Captain Andrew Boinavich, the senior Marine officer still on his feet. As they made their way around the shattered FOB, Castalane briefed Turner on how the battle had unfolded. He was interrupted by Turner when the admiral spied a familiar figure lying on a stretcher next to the FOB aide station. Feeling the need to apologize in person he made his way over to the wounded Ranger.

Dropping to one knee, Turner smiled. "I had my doubts about you, Delmont," Turner beamed. "I didn't think you could pull it off, but by God, you did."

From where they stood behind the admiral Castalane, Perry and Boinavich exchanged glances. No one had bothered to mention to Turner that Delmont had only recently been dug out from under the debris of his command post, that the man he was giving all the credit to for having beaten off the Abu Sayyaf attack and inflicting a mortal blow to it in the process had done nothing during the battle except become a casualty. If Delmont came clean and decided to set the story straight, informing the admiral who really deserved the credit, that was his business.

Of course both Castalane and Perry knew better than to expect that. The best they could hope for was that Delmont would realize that he had nothing more to gain by staying with the 3rd of the 75th and would choose instead to use all his connections to have himself reassigned back to the Pentagon where he belonged. They understood that their silence on this matter would be more than a great disservice to those who actually fought and won the battle. But if it got Delmont out of their hair, then a little injustice would be worth swallowing. This was after all the Army and there were some things that would never change.

MINDANAO, PHILIPPINES

Only when he was sure that they weren't being pursued did Hamdani Summirat allow the handful of men with him to rest. Sitting away from the others Summirat took a moment to recount his errors. Yes, he had made many. He had expected too much from his own men and had thought too little of the Americans. The one error he refused to admit to was his decision to attack. If his enemy held true to form they would use this day's victory over him as a means of ending Operation Pacific Shield. After keeping a few troops on the ground for a month or so the Americans would make a big deal of turning the final task of running the last of his fighters to ground over to the government in Manila, a task he was confident they would never be able to complete.

Looking about him Summirat realized that he had little

to work with. Of course, he quickly reminded himself he had been in worse situations before. Time, he told himself, was on his side. Time and of course his God, all praise be to Allah.

Turn the page for a preview of

Harold Coyle's Strategic Solutions, Inc.

VULCAN'S FIRE

HAROLD COYLE

Available now from Forge Books

A FORGE HARDCOVER

ISBN-13: 978-0-7653-1373-7   ISBN-10: 0-7653-1373-1

1

SOUTH GOVERNATE, LEBANON

The stalkers awaited the signal.

It came in the dappled gray light of 5:00 A.M. because delay was as much an enemy as the dedicated men inside the remote building.

Outside the five-room house, the assault leader gave a quick *click-click* of his tactical headset. The eleven members of his team recognized it as the preparatory signal. Receiving no response, he proceeded with his countdown.

"Ready . . . ready . . ."

A long three-second wait allowed anyone to delay the inevitable. No one did. The four men on perimeter guard saw nothing to interfere with the operation. Meanwhile, the two assault teams and the command element were tensed, leg muscles coiled to propel them from the shadows.

The team leader licked his lips. He had extensive experience but it was always like this: an eager dread. He glanced around. Only his radio operator returned his gaze; everyone else was focused on the objective. It looked good: they had probably achieved surprise, but surprise without violence was useless.

"Ready . . . go!"

Two explosions shattered the Mediterranean air, two seconds apart. The first was a Chinese-made RPG whose high-explosive warhead blew a hole in the brick-and-mortar wall facing the sunrise. The second was another RPG near the opposite corner that smashed through a window and detonated on the interior wall.

Assaulting together, each section was preceded by Rheinmetall flash-bang grenades to compensate for any defenders who escaped the RPG blasts.

A quick two-count, and both teams entered through the holes. It was doctrine: avoid the usual entrances, which could be mined.

The attackers' mission was simple: kill or capture everyone present. Take no unnecessary chances.

There were no novices on either side of the door.

The raiders held the advantage, exploiting the stunning effects of the grenades and flash-bangs. Moving with fluid rapidity, they "ran the walls," closing the distance on the defenders, firing short, disciplined bursts. The Egoz reconnaissance unit allowed its members a great deal of latitude: most chose 7.62 Galils but a few carried AK-47s. Both were lethally effective.

Three defenders were shot down in the front room; only one got off a round and it went high. A fragmentation grenade arced through the entrance to the next room. Before it exploded, the men inside opened fire with their AKs. The 150-grain rounds shredded the blanket separating the two rooms, and some were deliberately aimed low. One raider dropped with a Kalashnikov's bullet through the left thigh.

The grenade fizzled. Too long in storage—the result of clandestine acquisition policies—it exploded in a low-order detonation that inflicted minor wounds. Inside the small room, a close-range firefight erupted. It was fought at near muzzle contact.

One raider was killed, taking a round above the ballistic plate of his tactical vest. Another was clipped in the right bicep.

The defenders were shot down in an ephemeral moment

of loud noise, bright muzzle flashes, and icy terror. Each body received one or two rounds to the head before the last brass clattered on the wood floor.

One man escaped the house, fleeing through the back door. The designated marksman with a scoped Galil shot him from sixty meters.

Order, if not quiet, returned to the shattered structure.

"Clear!"

"Clear!"

Without awaiting instructions, the raiders moved through the house according to their individual priorities. Two guarded the bodies on the floor while two others secured the victims' hands with flex cuffs. The fact that they were dead was irrelevant; some of the raiders had seen dead men kill the living.

The number two man turned to his superior. "No useful prisoners, Chief. Sorry."

The team leader shrugged philosophically. "I know. It couldn't be helped." As papers were gathered, the radioman began taking photos with his digital camera.

Hearing the all-clear, the team medic entered through the door—the only one to do so. He had one immediate case and two lesser. He was experienced and calm; combat triage was nothing new to him.

"Arterial bleeding here," said one man, leaning over the first casualty. The medic went to work, knowing that his friends would treat other casualties for the moment. He glanced at a green-clad form, not moving. One of the raiders merely shook his head. The decedent's family would be told that he died in a training accident, body unrecoverable. Knowing it was a lie, the parents would accept the fabrication.

The other killers began tearing the place apart. They searched thoroughly, quickly, indelicately. They opened every cabinet and drawer, spilling the contents, and pulled mattresses off beds. They searched for loose boards and pried at the ceiling. Finally one of them returned to the living room.

"Nothing here, Avri."

"It has to be here. Look again. Everywhere."

Abraham pulled the kaffiyeh off his head and allowed it to drape over his tactical vest. "We've already looked everywhere. Twice. I'm telling you, it's not here."

Avri looked around the house. "God damn it!" For the grandson of a rabbi, he was famously profane.

He grabbed the radioman. "Get me Capri Six. Priority."

The RTO handed over the instrument. "Scramble mode selected."

"Capri, this is Purchase. Pass." The commander released the transmit button, allowing the scrambler to do its work. In an instant the carrier wave was back.

"Purchase, I read you. Pass."

"The well is dry. Repeat, the well is dry. End."

The response was decidedly nonregulation, but the transmission from the south drew no comment. After all, this time the offending voice belonged to an agnostic.

SSI OFFICES, ARLINGTON, VIRGINIA

"Ladies and gentlemen, we're in trouble."

Rear Admiral Michael Derringer had been retired for longer than he cared to remember but he had lost little of his command presence. As founder and CEO of Strategic Solutions, Incorporated, he had conned the company through its early years, building success upon success as the military contractor market expanded. Working around the world, performing often clandestine tasks for the U.S. Government, SSI had become the go-to firm when DoD or State needed something done without official recognition.

But that was then; this was now.

"Still no new contracts?" George Ferraro, SSI vice president and chief financial officer, had no problem guessing the admiral's intent.

"Correct." Derringer's balding head bobbed in assent. "SecDef canceled our electronic warfare project in Arabia and State vetoed us for another African job. Oh, we're still getting business but it's paper-clip money: security work, training assignments, small-scale jobs. About the only advantage is that they keep some of our regulars on the payroll. But they don't reduce the red ink, and we can't operate on our stock portfolio indefinitely."

Among the nine people sitting around the polished table was Lieutenant General Thomas Varlowe, U.S. Army (Retired), the gray presence who never quite shed the three stars he once wore. As chairman of SSI's advisory board, he had little financial stake in the firm but remained interested in the fascinating projects that came down the Beltway. Though he seldom spoke up in board meetings, the situation called for an exception.

"Ahem." Heads turned toward the former West Point track star. "I wanted to talk to Admiral Derringer before the meeting but I didn't get the chance. In case there's any doubt about the company's lack of work, I can elaborate."

Derringer barely managed to suppress a tight smile. The two retirees were "Admiral" and "General" to one another in SSI meetings but friendly rivals named Mike and Tom the rest of the time—especially in November for the Army-Navy game.

"Go ahead, General." The Navy man knew what was coming.

Varlowe shoved back from the table. "It's that job with the Israelis. Damned poor situation to get into . . ." He came within an inch of adding, *As I tried to tell all of you*. Instead, he pushed ahead. "I've snooped around and found that new business dried up almost before that ship sank . . . what was it? Three or four months ago? Sure, our people prevented the uranium ore from reaching Iran, but that hardly matters."

"I've been traveling in Europe, General. What *does* matter?" Beverly Ann Shumard, with a PhD in international relations, was one of two women on the board of directors, and among the most outspoken of all.

Derringer interjected. "Dr. Shumard, the mission summary is still being prepared owing to, ah, security concerns. But the short version is, our training team in Chad got involved in a double play set up by the Israelis, presumably against the Iranians. Colonel Leopole can provide some operational details, but basically our tasking changed from instruction to interdiction, preventing a load of yellow cake from being shipped to Iran."

Shumard shook her head. "I'm sorry, Admiral. As I said, I've been away and didn't know the particulars. But why would Iran want ore from Chad? I mean, Iran has its own mines."

Derringer nodded to the chief of operations.

Lieutenant Colonel Frank Leopole looked, talked, and acted as Central Casting would expect of a Marine Corps officer. He was tall, lean, and hard with a high and tight haircut that screamed "jarhead" to the Army and Navy men in the office. His tenure with SSI had been marked by some notable successes and few failures.

"Deniability, ma'am. At least that's what our intel said. Presumably Tehran wanted foreign yellow cake to use in a weapon and avoid the nuclear fingerprints of its own ore. So our team went chasing off across Chad and Libya, then through the Med and down the west coast of Africa to overhaul the shipment. All the time we were working with the Israelis, who provided most of the information and logistics. We caught the ship, which was scuttled with its cargo, so presumably everybody was happy."

"But I take it nobody really is happy."

"Nobody but the Israelis," Varlowe added. It was an uncharacteristic interjection from the normally taciturn soldier. "As I was going to say, our team—this firm—was stiffed by Mossad. The Israelis concocted the plot in the first place to distract us—the U.S.—from their genuine concern. They had their own operation going against Iran's nuclear program but were afraid we would learn about it and bring pressure to bear. Apparently their real plan failed but what matters is, they tossed us a straw man: something credible that we could pursue and leave them alone." He gave an eloquent shrug. "It worked."

George Ferraro spoke up. "See, that's what I don't understand. We did what the government and the administration wanted done. So why are we the heavies now?"

"There are several major players," Derringer replied. "Not least of which is the CIA. The agency accepted the Israelis' ploy, apparently almost at face value. Our own sources—mainly David Dare—sniffed out the facts but too late to affect the operation."

Shumard accepted that explanation without reservation. Though not involved in intelligence or operations, she and everyone connected with the firm knew the eye-watering reputation of the former NSA spook. It was said that if you wanted to know what Japanese porn film Kim Jong Il watched last night, ask Dave Dare.

"So Langley's embarrassed that SSI figured out what was going on, and wants to cover its hindquarters."

Derringer spoke again. "It's bigger than that, Doctor. We've taken hits before from various agencies, and I admit that a few were justified. But usually when some agency tries to stiff us, it's as you say: embarrassment or jealousy or some sort of perceived rivalry. In this case, we're criticized by State and Langley and to an extent by DoD." He grimaced, then adjusted his glasses. "In a way I can understand it. Considering the high stakes involved in any Israeli-Iranian conflict, nobody this side of the pond wants to be blamed if something goes wrong."

Marshall Wilmont spoke up for the first time. As SSI president and chief operating officer, he had a finger in most of the company pies. "So much for the reason for our drought. What I want to know is, what can we do about it?"

The question hung suspended above the polished table, lurking in brooding silence.

SOUTH GOVERNATE, LEBANON

The dream returned again.

"Afrad mosallah!"

At the command, the executioners assumed their positions: squatting or kneeling with their rifles aimed at the condemned men's chests.

The sequence usually resembled a grainy black and white newsreel, for the sleeper was one of those who seldom dreamed in color. When awake, in the rare moments when he had nothing else in mind, Ahmad Esmaili sometimes pondered the odd situation. As a participant in the event that stalked his nights, he expected to relive the glorious, dreadful moments from behind the sights of a Heckler & Koch rifle. But more often his perspective was that of an observer, seeing himself and his colleagues from several meters away.

In 1979, at eighteen, Esmaili's first full-time job had been on a revolutionary firing squad. The first day had been dreadful, and if anything the second day was worse. But by the end of the week it was tolerable. After a while, to display his revolutionary fervor, he notched the wood stock of his G3 for each of the Shah's vermin he shot. However, as the imams noted, hell was reserved for infidels—those who rejected Islam. Presumably even Muslims who oppressed others of The Faith had a chance to achieve Paradise.

Apart from former government officials and Savak policemen, Esmaili also had dispatched evildoers such as drug addicts, perverts, and Kurds.

Esmaili had to admit that most of the dictator's men had died reasonably well, some with the Koran in hand. Resigned to their fate, they had stood their ground, eyes bound but hands free, and accepted the ayatollah's justice delivered almost from powder-burn distance. But the former revolutionary guard seldom alluded to that aspect of the process. A few early attempts from twenty meters or more had resulted in some messy episodes, and eventually the range was diminished almost to muzzle contact.

"Atesh!"

Esmaili felt the heavy trigger pull, then somebody was shaking him awake. It was two hours before dawn.

Forcing his consciousness to swim upward through the haze of REM sleep, he surfaced to think: *No good news arrives in darkness.*

He was right.

Esmaili sat upright on his cot, rubbing his eyes and stifling a yawn. He merely said, "Tell me."

"It is Malik's team." The tone of the messenger's voice told Ahmad Esmaili as much as the words. "They are all with God."

The Iranian was fully awake now. He focused on the face of his colleague, a young man from Tyre who called himself Hazim: Resolute. He was more enthusiastic than capable but occasionally he showed promise. Esmaili had decided to cultivate him.

"All of them?"

Hazim nodded gravely.

Esmaili swung his bare feet onto the floor of the small house. His toes found his sandals and slid into them, rising in the process. Otherwise he was already dressed. "When?"

"Early this morning. We only got word a little while ago."

The senior man shook his head. "They could not have been more than forty kilometers from here. Why the delay?"

Hazim defaulted to his passive setting. "I do not know, Teacher. I only pass the message from the courier."

"Then I need to speak with him, not an errand boy." The

words were selected to cut, to hurt. To teach. He stalked
from the house, making for the larger building that served
as headquarters for a few days.

Hazim trailed in his master's wake, biting down the
pain. Belatedly he realized that he should have informed
himself of more details before awaking the Iranian. *Or I
could have brought the messenger with me.*

He was learning.

In the main building Esmaili found the courier drinking thick tea and devouring some biscuits. Showing deference to the Iranian, the Lebanese fighter stood and
inclined his head. "Teacher . . ."

Esmaili waved a placating hand. "Please sit, brother.
You are a guest here."

The two men were within three years of one another's
age, both in their mid-forties, both dedicated and competent. But few Hezbollah operatives possessed Ahmad Esmaili's depth of experience. From the revolution onward,
through the nightmare of the Iraq war of the 1980s and
what the Zionist lackeys called the present "terror" war,
the Iranian liaison officer had been constantly engaged.
His masters in Tehran knew his worth—and so did his
acolytes in The Lebanon.

The messenger was called Fida, and while he surely
had sacrificed much of his earthly life to the service of
God, it had been a willing sacrifice. This night, he knew
what the Teacher wanted to know without being asked.

"We were to meet Malik and his team this morning for
a joint reconnaissance. When they did not appear, we
searched for them." Fida sipped more tea but did not taste
it. "We probably arrived two or three hours after . . . after the Jews."

Esmaili's obsidian eyes locked on to the courier's face.
"You are certain it was Israelis?"

Fida reached into his vest pocket and produced a metal
object. From across the table, Esmaili recognized an IDF
identification disk. Neither man read Hebrew but both
recognized the characters.

The Iranian's mind churned through various options. "This might be a ruse to mislead us. The killers could be local militia trying to drive us from the area." He thought for an additional moment. "Was there expended brass?"

"Yes. It was unmarked—no head stamps."

So it was the Jews.

"In any case, Malik and his men are dead," Fida continued. "We buried them properly and came here. I thought it best to avoid the radio. We are almost certain that the Jews have learned our frequencies again. We will have to change . . ."

"You did well, my friend. Now rest here. I have much to do this night."

SSI OFFICES

The intercom buzzed on Derringer's desk. "Admiral, there's a message for you at the front desk."

Derringer turned from his copy of *Naval History*. There wasn't much else to occupy him that morning, and besides, as an admiral himself, he often sympathized with Takeo Kurita's dilemma at Leyte Gulf. "What is it?"

Mrs. Singer's contralto voice crackled over the line. "Cheryl said it's just a calling card in an envelope addressed to you. She can bring it up."

"No, I should stretch my legs. Tell her I'll be right down."

In the lobby fronting on Courthouse Road, Derringer greeted the receptionist. "Hello, Miss Dungan. I understand there's a message for me."

"Here it is, Admiral." With her Peach Street drawl, Cheryl Dungan pronounced it "hee-yer." She handed over the envelope and beamed a heartbreaking smile. Office gossip said that she had been engaged twice but was having too much fun to change her marital status after just twenty-six years.

Suppressing his sixty-something male hormones, Derringer forced himself to concentrate on the message. It was a plain white envelope with the recipient's name and "PERSONAL" typed on the front. The CEO opened the envelope to find a business card.

Mordecai Baram, Minister for Agriculture and Scientific Affairs, Embassy of Israel, 3514 International Drive Northwest.

There was also a handwritten note that Derringer read in a glance. He turned to the receptionist again. "Who delivered this?"

"Oh, a man who spoke with an accent. Maybe thirty, thirty-two. Kinda cute." She said "kee-yute."

Minutes later Derringer walked into Wilmont's office and closed the door. "Marsh, take a look at this."

Wilmont looked up with a furrowed brow. "Agriculture and science? That's got to be some kind of cover."

"Concur. If I'm not interested, I'm to leave a phone message. Otherwise the note says to meet him at Natural History, 1100 tomorrow. At the evolution exhibit."

The SSI president slid the card across his desk. "What do you plan to do?"

"I see no reason to pass this up. I admit that I'm curious."

Wilmont's paunch bulged beneath his vest as he leaned back. "Obviously that's what Mr. Baram intended. But I wonder why he didn't just call or send an e-mail." He thought for a moment. "Have you ever met him? I've never heard the name."

Derringer shook his head. "Me neither. But that's probably the way he wants things."

"So you're going to keep the appointment?"

"Affirm. But I'm not going alone."